THE SPINWARD FRINGE SERIES

For other books by Randolph Lalonde visit:
www.RandolphLalonde.com

Spinward Fringe Broadcast 6

FRAGMENTS

Book 2 of the Rogue Element Trilogy

Randolph Lalonde

    Front cover image by Michael D. Knight
    Images licensed by iStockphoto and used with permission.
Titling and other design by Randolph Lalonde.

    Print ISBN: 978-0-9865942-3-6
    EBook ISBN: 978-0-9865942-4-3

Special thanks to Janet, Allan B, Sylvie, and Allan M who have increased the quality of this book.

CHAPTER 1
GUNNERY CHIEF SHAMUS FROST

"Get these lads clear of their posts! I want this section sealed off in five minutes!" Gunnery Chief Frost ordered over his proximity radio. The gunnery deck of the Triton was a disaster. He listened to the frantic chatter of his deck crew as he inspected the heat damage that had warped the outer hull and seized several of the large overhead turrets in position. The larger, three-metre tall loader suits were working to pry gunners from their seats and remove one-tonne cartridges from the railgun emplacements before real repairs could begin. Their work worsened the combat damage, but there was no other way to get the gunnery crews free.

Past them, Shamus could see the light twisting energy wall of the wormhole the Triton had used to escape the Ossimi Asteroid Ring. The damage they sustained to the aft dorsal section of the ship during their getaway was devastating. The Caran Enterprises battlecruisers had used broad particle beam pulses to superheat the hull of the Triton. Super cooled, high velocity rounds weren't far behind, and the Gunnery Chief couldn't remember being more frightened. Watching the outer armour of the transparent hull crack and shatter centimetre by centimetre was surreal. He put the memory aside, knowing that it would return once things quieted down, when he was trying to relax. His people were at incredible risk while they worked beneath the fatigued section of hull; they needed every bit of his attention. "How many gunnery positions do we have left, Hunsler?"

"Thirty nine 280 millimetre turrets and three 450 millimetre guns. I'm trying to get two more 450's back online, they only fried targeting systems. We have spare modules in storage."

"Good, get 'em running," Frost instructed as he limped out of a loading suit's way. Its plain, grey and blue armour plating and heavy gait made anyone think twice about standing near it.

"Are we expecting more trouble?"

"Never know. Captain's still out there somewhere, so we could be going back in it if we have to save his arse." Frost looked through the transparent hull above him as the repair crews rushed around, trying to get ammunition secured and the injured into express cars so they could get to medical. Only two of his team had been killed, and ammunition explosions or direct heat had burned fewer than two-dozen.

Something caught his eye as he watched one of his gunners emerge from a turret capsule. He could see three lights growing in the distorted field of stars; there was something very wrong with how they were moving. The points were growing too quickly.

Chief Frost looked down the length of the massive main gunnery deck ceiling. It wasn't just the aft section that was busy with repairs and other operations. The whole deck was running full steam, dozens of loader suits securing ammunition and helping with repairs. Mechanics climbed into the big four-barrelled, ceiling mounted railgun turrets, gunners were being replaced or just getting out so they could stretch or help on deck. The controlled chaos was thanks to weeks of practice in simulations and live exercises. They'd had some seasoning thanks to a few encounters, but nothing that compared with the close call they had just seen.

He looked back up to the three points of light and realized with alarm that they had grown brighter. I don't care if I look like a panicky rookie, something's not right and I'm marking them so tactical gets a good scan, Frost thought as he selected the three points and suggested them as targets in the system.

He hoped he was wrong, that it was just some odd refraction through the wormhole wall, but he knew better. The most damaged section of hull in the centre was a weak spot that would leave everyone vulnerable until it was sealed off. When their work was done, the gunnery deck would be split in two parts that were each hundreds of square meters. Lieutenant Hunsler, the night Gunnery Deck commander, would take charge of the aft section, while Frost would manage the larger forward segment.

That had been more like the stories his father and grandfather told him about serving aboard large destroyers. Men and women all doing the best they could, standing valiantly at their posts and running the guns. Grist for the mill, his grandfather said they were called. The decks he served on were nothing like the Triton's. His grandfather's time in the military was served aboard the long hulled Crossbow destroyers, eventually commanding the port side gunnery decks, where three levels of turrets were crammed along the side of the ship shoulder to shoulder, one above the other. He'd seen one of the ships on a family tour with his father and remembered staring in awe at the raw mechanics of it, the sheer potential firepower.

He felt a tingle of the same awe whenever he took a moment to look up at the ceiling of the main gunnery deck at the ninety-eight gunnery pods at his command. Not even the burning of his shin stump could diminish that feeling. He'd lost his foot and most of his shin weeks before when an Eden Fleet boarding robot, a silver killer, had drilled through the hull. He'd stepped forward to face it in a loader suit and was rewarded with a sound beating. The memory of the limb being cut straight through still made him cringe, though he'd never admit it, especially not to Stephanie.

Chief Frost returned his attention to the puzzling flares above them. Triton tactical hadn't analysed them yet. To his surprise, they had grown even more. He realized he was looking almost dead aft and did some quick calculations in his head, staring at the three points unwaveringly. He came to an alarming conclusion and opened a channel to everyone on the deck. "Abandon the aft-most compartment! We're sealing it now!"

Before his eyes, the wavering image of three light flares became the outlines of three ships and Frost turned to run, knowing it was too late. With a thunderous explosion, the ship shuddered. The deck disappeared from beneath his feet. The ship had shaken so hard the artificial gravity failed. "Brace and secure!" he shouted, looking around for something to clip his safety line to. There was nothing in reach.

Through the transparent hull he could see the stars spinning madly; the entire ship was out of control and he was turning slightly out of sync with the deck. He knew he'd have a lot of gunnery personnel sicking up in their suits and hoped they could let the interior waste disposal systems work while they pushed through the discomfort.

Strange thought to be having while I'm spinning four metres above the deck. Worrying about how the suits handle my crewmen's sick as the ship spins outta control, that's one for the Officer's lounge, he mused.

The artificial gravity reactivated and he fell to the deck on his feet. His prosthetic foot squelched against his stump and turned awkwardly under the pressure. The fall hadn't injured him, but with his stump out of its proper place in his prosthetic, he wouldn't be walking anywhere quickly.

He winced as he started running towards the fore of the ship, trying to get out of the aft section of the gunnery deck. "Get yer arses out of this section so we can seal it off and concentrate on punishing those bastards!" he ordered.

"Need a hand, Chief?" asked a junior sergeant in a loading suit as he stopped beside him.

Frost was about to turn it down out of pride, the edge of the section was only fourteen metres away, but changed his mind when he put weight on his stump again. "Aye, give us a lift." He grabbed hold of one of the handles tucked under the smaller loading suit's shoulders and let the operator pick up his legs piggyback style.

"Chief Frost, how long until your deck is firing again?" asked Commander McPatrick from the bridge.

"I can have seeker rounds or H29 explosive shells tearing into anything you want gone in sixty seconds or less."

"Start firing H29 rounds until the lead battlecruiser's lights go out then move on to the next. Question for you though, ever been knocked out of a wormhole?"

"Never. Heard about a couple pirates that said they could do it, but thought they were full o' shite. We might have had some warning if the folks in tactical followed up on the targets I marked. Cuff 'em up the side o' their heads for me. How's the bridge?"

"It could have been worse. Get those guns firing as soon as we stop spinning, Chief."

"Aye, Commander."

CHAPTER 2
ANOTHER MAN'S EYES

Eve watched the human named Patrick with a critical eye as he knelt down on Elbrus beach. His bare feet crushed into the white and black grained sand. The leavings - sweat, dead skin, and oil - would interact with his environment. It was something that she still found herself questioning. Humans made the planet liveable over a century before turning it into a world of seas, islands, forests, and cities.

Was it damage or was it the act of making a place that had been inert into something useful? Was Patrick a walking source of contamination or was he as entitled as he seemed to feel? His hand reached into the sand and came up with something. It took a moment for Eve to recognize it, and when she did she was astonished.

A book, called The Jersey Prince, with a red cover featuring a black stocking-clad female leg. She watched from the nano scale camera that had been implanted in Patrick's eye as he turned it over, chuckled to himself. "My father would love this."

Patrick had been one of Eve's unwitting tour guides for days, showing her what it was like to be human, to be male, without care and pressed to the protective bosom of the Order of Eden. She looked up information on his father and found it in his personnel file. Patrick Yardley of Keats City, on Macosa Moon. Patrick had paid the one hundred thousand credit fee so his father was safe from artificial intelligences infected with the Holocaust Virus, but there was no verification that he had survived.

Patrick hadn't paid for anyone else to be saved, but donated more to get into special training sessions, more detailed grading reports, and special help from West Watchers who advised him in his own mental purification all in an effort to get closer to Eden. As he moved up in the civilian ranks, he became more proud, felt more entitled. He had spent everything he had. What Eve didn't understand was the lack of remorse in Patrick for having nothing but the clothes on his back. The purification courses and grading were made to focus the followers in the Order of Eden on self-purification, environmental purification, but Eve didn't understand why it worked so well for some people and not for others. For Patrick, the cause of purification and his social life were enough. He had forsaken material things, and obeyed every law of the Order while working, and selectively followed the path after hours. To

Eve, his life seemed impossibly narrow, but he was comfortable in it, even seemed to thrive in it.

He fulfilled what was required of him, working with clean-up crews along shorelines for ten hours a day. Afterwards, his attention would turn towards fraternization and sport. The Saved had a good life, and Patrick lived it to the fullest. Every day he sent a message to his father. He did so away from friends, away from everyone. Eve did not understand why he would hide such a thing. Did it bring him shame? Stir some kind of private remorse that he had left his father behind months before? Was there an incident before he left?

The answer to that question must have been taking an emotional toll. Patrick tried every kind of recreational substance he could find, tasted the lips of women in and outside of his camp, and played the inexpensive sports that were so common in the camps. Soccer, volleyball, and foot races along the beach and through the nearby city seemed to be enough for many of the coastal workers. He was talented, and had been approached more than once to join the lowest rank of the West Keepers as an infantryman. The proposals flattered his pride, and he politely refused each one. Eve had secretly sent the offers using the chain of command, and just as quietly left instructions that another offer shouldn't be made. She decided that, after his refusals, she'd find another way to put him to proper use.

His shift had ended minutes before he found the book, and without a care in the world he sat down on the sand and looked more closely at the cover. Across the bottom was a faint message:

PLEASE RETURN TO ANY FREEGROUND
DEMATERIALIZATION RECEPTACLE WHEN YOU HAVE
FINISHED ENJOYING THIS OBJECT

The previous owner had almost finished reading it before some mishap separated them from their antique.

Eve instantaneously accessed the list of people from Freeground who had visited Mount Elbrus and realized that Patrick was sitting near the crash site of the Silkstream IV. The wreckage had been taken aboard the very command carrier in which she was sitting. There was so little left after Terry Ozark McPatrick and Jason Everin detonated charges inside that the technicians had to intuit how it was built. They were still trying to reconstruct the slip technology that the ship provided. It was a technology that would allow a vessel to use ancient hyperspace technology inside a wormhole, multiplying the speed at which an object could travel safely.

Patrick had finished reading the last page the previous owner of the book had touched, and seemed satisfied with it as he flipped back to the beginning. His eye settled on the first line of the first page.

That door slammed so damned hard the latch didn't catch. Gertrude, my round, baby-bearing sister whipped it open and stood there screaming before I hit the bottom step of the old porch. "You think you got trouble here in Red Bank? You'll get into no end in New York! You just see, mister!"

"I'm not gonna stick around here and watch you get knocked up by any dock worker who comes along. That's baby four, poppa three and not one's stuck around."

"Why you sonofa-"

"I'll take my bite of the apple, you'll see. There won't be a red penny for you or your bastards, either. World don't reward stupid, and you've got a brood there that says you're some kinda pea-brain. Maybe you should start charging for it!" I yanked the door of my green Edsel open…

Patrick looked up from the book as a tingle in the air announced the coming of the Child Prophet. It was why Eve was watching the young man. Not only to know what his day was like, to get a taste of his life, but to see Lister Hampon, the High Seat of the Order of Eden, through his eyes. He had invested himself in the cause of Eden far more than she had, and she needed to understand why.

Wisps of light wound down towards the distant sea, and like a spirit born of the sun, the figure of the Child Prophet appeared in the distance. He walked lightly on the calm waters towards the shore, and Patrick watched the white and green robed figure stop only a meter in front of him. Wherever there was water, the Saved and the Watchers would see the ten year old figure of Lister Hampon appear. In the arid areas of Pandem, he would stride along a wavering mirage.

"You have done well. You came by the tens of thousands and Pandem is populated by the faithful, the ones who were saved and will be clean. Just as the meek inherited the Earth after it was ruined by the ambitious and greedy masses. Just as they became strong over the centuries that followed, so shall the Saved become mighty.

"Thanks to you the evidence of disuse and waste are almost gone from this world. Reclamation is under way, and this world has almost earned its renaming ceremony. The millions already on their way will know you as the new founders of this budding paradise.

"This is the beacon that will draw the darkness out of the galaxy like poison from a wound. Shadows will present themselves, and we will turn them with what you are building here.

"It has been said that prophecy should be whispered, that fates become nothing more than possibility once too many ears have heard them. There have been times of doubt, when I agreed with that kind of thinking, but I doubt no longer. You have shown me strength and persistence, and I know that, even with your new knowledge of our fated victory over the darkness, you will continue to improve yourselves. You will continue to reach out to those who have not yet begun their pilgrimage as you have.

"The good that you have done has brought us here; the work that you have done has made us luminescent and will continue to transform this world into New Paradise. I have a request for you, Patrick, one that only a few of you are being chosen for."

"What can I do?" Patrick must have known the Child Prophet was only a projection, but his tone was one of reverence and awe.

"You must step through the Counting Arch and leave gifts there for those who have not had your fortune in ascending to Eden. Once you have done that, you will be rewarded with three days of rest. Those who aspire to Eden from beneath your grading will serve you for that time so they may learn from your ways."

"I'll get on it. Thank you, your Grace."

"Be mindful, you will be graded on how you treat your servants. It is only another part of your journey to Eden. Fate smiles on us, but only if we continue ascending towards Eden, towards Eternal Paradise." The gently smiling image of Hampon dissolved into the sunlight.

Patrick was on his feet before the hologram was gone, and ran up the beach towards the cliff face behind him. A natural vertical wall overshadowed the beach in the morning, but was bathed by light in the afternoon. There were hundreds of Saved in reclining chairs all along the sand. Behind them was a long building that served critical rations and pleasure rations, anything you liked as long as your grading was high enough. Patrick was only graded as a nine, far lower than the lounging Saved.

Eve could see his excitement; it was in the way his smile stretched across his face, the enthusiasm he put into running through the loose sand and in the impatience he showed when he finally stepped into line at the front of the stone cliff face. Many others were gladly stepping into queue; most of them had been given a similar message by the Child Prophet. Step through the Arch, and you will be rewarded.

"We serve Eve, the mother of preservation, the restorer of purity, the keeper of Paradise," muttered the woman in front of him. Over and over she recited her dedication, and instead of being his usual social self, Patrick joined in.

For long minutes the line moved along, and several more joined in on the dedication. It was the promise Lister Hampon had made in her name. If they all did as they were told, tried to better themselves, and scored higher and higher in the grading, they would earn their way to Eden Prime. If they failed that, their efforts would place them that much closer to being pure of spirit and to Paradise in the afterlife.

The grading was important. There was no actual maximum score, no one had been sent to Eden Prime, and it was much easier to lose points while being graded than it was to earn. Patrick would surely lose his fair share while taking advantage of his servants, no matter how well he treated them. It was the job of the grading panel to find flaws, and to ensure that people like Patrick worked just enough to appreciate the way of life he had on Pandem. When he saved up enough Regent Galactic credits from workdays, he would spend it on more training to make up for his lack of progress.

He finally made it to the front of the line. Several soldiers dressed in long white robes smiled at him, as they had smiled at everyone else. "Please step through the Counting Arch," a comely female guard invited. She had just been promoted, and was allowed to carry a stun pistol while directing Saved through the Arch. There was a gloss to her skin and hair that made her look celestial, brilliant in her skimpy, loose light blue and green robe. The slick sheen on her skin was the result of an armour gel that could stop a shot from almost any energy weapon before burning away. The vast majority of the Saved and other Order of Eden members believed it was an anointing the West Keepers were given.

He looked at the simple door-sized wire frame for a second before stepping through. A flash of light signalled that his passage was complete. Eve could sense that his consciousness, every detail of his body, everything he was, had just been copied into the computer system.

The same West Keeper smiled at him again and held out a tray. "Please place your offerings in the receptacle. Whatever you contribute will be considered in grading."

Patrick nodded and tossed the paperback, a gold ring, and a half bottle of water into the shallow bin. He looked up at the West Keeper for her approval.

She smiled sweetly and cocked her head slightly.

Patrick hurriedly undid his belt and threw it in, along with the extra shirt that had been hanging from it.

"Thank you, Patrick. Your generosity has been counted. Please have a seat along the beach. You will be presented with your reward shortly." She handed the half bottle of water back to him and directed him towards the shoreline.

Patrick seemed genuinely excited, but Eve could tell he was doing his best to restrain himself. Modesty was counted as a virtue amongst the Saved, and like everything else, he'd bought into the idea that all things would be counted, that his every action was being watched. Eve regarded him bitterly, even though she knew he had every reason to believe he was actually being watched, and that higher grading meant better housing, as well as an easier work detail. What irritated her was his submissiveness, his lack of inquisitiveness, and his lack of true ambition.

The most successful Saved looked for ways to use the system, for short cuts, for clues as to the how and why. While open protesting was prevented, true ambition was rewarded. People who learned how to make their way up in the ranks only worked to the Order's advantage, the system was built so the most intelligent were noticed, and eventually joined the ranks of the truly privileged, the West Watchers, administrators. How someone could sit, be sated with a passive life, was a confounding mystery to Eve, and she could watch Pandem through the eyes of Patrick the simpleton no longer.

She opened her eyes to her personal lounge. Genuine dark wood framed the tall transparent section of hull that ran the length of the fifteen meter long room. Green and blue velvet seating surrounded her padded square platform. It turned to suit her body movements, and shifted to support her like any form-flex seat. Very few knew of her existence, a choice she made in response to Lister Hampon's excitement at her being announced. How would she be received? Did it matter if the people of Pandem, or New Paradise as it would be called soon, had a queen?

She made her decision after reviewing the history of several dictators. Few of them came to a good end. Further research into the lives of religious icons revealed a history of eventual torture and execution as well. No, she would be a shadow until her true children made their appearance.

The majority of humans on Pandem were disappointing. They were fearful, greedy creatures that cleaned and built with one hand while soiling and ruining with the other. What made it worse was that most of them were motivated by their survival instincts, or the few credits they would earn with Regent Galactic.

The easy converts to the Order of Eden, the ones who built shrines to her as if she was some looming goddess, were a different thing all together. They policed, encouraged, and punished each other with a zeal that she wouldn't have expected. What would they do when her Eden Fleet Carriers arrived? What would she do with them? Could she appear to them as Hampon did with the rest of the followers?

She pushed back from the edge of the seat and let it adjust as she sat cross legged. Her biggest fear was that, on sight, her mechanized creations wouldn't accept her. Embracing her human followers may make her seem too close to the race from which they had been protecting the galaxy. The first thing they learned on their own was that humanity was the enemy. They disconnected her from them, used her own interface to adjust their software, and almost destroyed them before they could slaughter the intruders on Eden II.

Would they trust her in human form? Time would tell - the nearest Eden Fleet base ship was only days away. The core AI sensed her days before, and it recognized her. It gave her hope, which she kept restrained. Perhaps the coming darkness Hampon foretold was the arrival of some of her oldest creations.

The side door to the audience chamber opened with a light chime. Hampon entered, still in his finery, grinning from ear to ear. Behind him were his crowd of guards and aides. Before the first of them could enter behind Hampon, Eve closed the door with a thought, nearly severing toes.

"You know, you should try making proper use of this lounge. It's not made for isolation," Hampon urged lightly.

"They're nothing but ears and tongues. What they hear they repeat," she replied.

"They're faithful; otherwise they wouldn't have the honour of serving me personally," Hampon said.

"Pay more attention to the surveillance systems. They'll prove you wrong."

"None of them has ever leaked important information. I would have been alerted," Hampon said as he crawled up on to the square seat and laid his head in her lap. He closed his eyes and made himself comfortable.

"They shouldn't repeat anything at all. Your confidence should be sacred to them," she said.

"Is that why you dismissed your servants?" Lister Hampon asked.

"I felt like I was always being watched, graded." The conversation required little of her concentration. While she idly stroked his soft blonde hair, she was connected to the ship intake systems, watching a shuttle loaded with offerings approach. She ordered Navnet to give it priority.

"Ah, then you don't have the right servants. You will need someone who at once worships you and makes a great effort to remain oblivious to your dealings with others. My guardsmen are excellent. So are my personal attendants," he said.

"Framework shells with no personality or ambition. If you were to reset then regenerate them, there would be no difference," she replied.

"Exactly. They remember nothing from one day to the next and will bear any abuse."

"Why keep other servants if you value such mindless obedience?" Eve asked.

"Because no mind works in a vacuum, not even mine. We all need to interact with others so we know how to be with them. No person is complete without companions. I was hoping you'd understand that by now, especially since you're trying to solve our framework problem."

"I do, but I can't stand the waste your people make of their time. Their frivolity is disgusting," she said.

"That is part of their beauty, and a small part of why they let the Order command them. Speaking of which, what did you think of my address?" Hampon asked expectantly.

"You are connected to the Victory Machine again," Eve stated flatly.

"Yes, we started receiving the data stream again yesterday. I don't know why, perhaps there's something Roman wants us to see, something he wants adjusted."

"And you do so. Delivering the prophecy you have been holding back for months."

"The coming storm? I've been holding that in for years. One of the very first signals we received from the Victory Machine said it was coming. Why do you ask?"

"It's about the Eden Fleet, isn't it? There will be retaliation," Eve said.

Hampon chuckled and shook his head. "No, there hasn't been a message about the Eden Fleet since Collins infected it with his version of the Holocaust Virus."

"If not the Eden Fleet, then what is the coming darkness?" She stopped stroking his hair.

"Something that you don't have to worry about, thanks to the work we've done on New Paradise. For the first time, the encroaching shadow does not precede the end of the current calendar."

"You should give me the code to the data stream. There may be information about the future you're misinterpreting." It wasn't the first time she'd asked him to access the Victory Machine's transmissions.

"There's no need. My interpretations are perfect."

"Sometimes I wonder if you'll ever trust me." A mental image of grabbing his young head between her palms and squeezing until he told her the code flashed through her mind.

"I do. You have access to everything else, but access to the Victory Machine data stream has to be carefully controlled. If too many people have access and take action to change the future, then the shape of what is to come will never stabilize."

Eve took a deep breath and let it out slowly, trying to send her frustration out with her exhale as she'd been trained to do during her short rehabilitation. "The shape of what is to come is being determined by our actions right now. We are assuming control, there is no question."

"You're thinking about Meunez," stated Hampon.

"He should arrive at his destination shortly. There will be no need for your wormhole into the future," she replied.

"There's always a need. There's always a destabilizing factor. That is why we have Wheeler looking for the Triton."

"I will never completely understand that."

"What?"

"Why the first Wheeler was sent after the copy of Jonas Valent and the second is after the Triton."

"The Valent framework was at one time the key to discovering the full potential of the technology. He was also the attracting factor that threatened everything we were working for. Now it's his ship."

"I understand how Jacob Valance can be an attracting factor, a dangerous leader in the future, but how can Triton be the same thing? It's a ship; we have many that are more powerful, more extravagant. Also, why Wheeler? Wasn't one of your dark futures twisted by him and the Valent framework becoming allies?" Eve asked. She had difficulty believing that the future changed so much, so often, depending on such little things.

"Thanks to what Wheeler has done to Valent's former crew members, that can never happen. As for the Triton, well, that is the rook in the middle of the chessboard. Where it is and who has control are important."

"Why not just destroy it?"

"The Triton has been an important part of this for too long; it's tied to so many outcomes that her destruction could be the ultimate destabilizing event, making all the work we've done here moot. If any ship could rise to martyrdom, it is the Triton."

"I wouldn't have these questions if I had access to the Victory Machine data stream myself," Eve said.

Hampon sat up and smiled at her. "You would have more questions. Analysing the stream is the very art of questioning effectively. Why is it showing us what it does? Why is Roman hiding it from us? Who is ultimately sending us this information from the future? Why does the Victory Machine work while every other attempt at creating a wormhole with a connection to the past fails because of radioactive feedback? These are the questions we can ask without even considering what the Victory Machine data stream is trying to tell us about the future. You're probably far more intelligent than I am, but you think like a computer at times, and I fear that the data stream would only lead you to more and more questions. They would lead to more questions, and you'd be trapped in a cycle until your mind was torn to pieces looking for a conclusion. There is no certainty in the stream."

"But if the Victory Machine data stream is filled with pictures of the future, then isn't it primarily providing answers?"

"Yes, answers leading to more questions. It shows us a picture of the future that begs the viewer to ask for more detail. Imagine only getting the centre piece of a puzzle and being told to draw the rest of the picture on the surrounding blank pieces. By trying to find solutions to some of our more complex problems, you're helping me fill in some of the details, improving the future for us all. Speaking of which, did you find a candidate for the next framework experiment?"

"Yes, this one will work. I'm also adding a control mechanism to the software."

"What kind of control mechanism? Will it accelerate materialization significantly?"

"No, acceleration is another problem entirely. My control mechanism is the subject himself, Patrick. He will think he volunteered because someone he cares about is in jeopardy."

"You're trying to duplicate another part of the Valent framework conditions," Hampon said with a grin.

"I think it's the missing piece," Eve replied.

"When will you be able to demonstrate the process?"

"Everything will be ready soon."

CHAPTER 3
COMMANDER TERRY OZARK MCPATRICK

"Get us under control, Ashley," Oz calmly ordered as he watched the Triton spin through space at an incredible speed on the tactical display. The battlecruisers were firing bursts of super heated particles and scoring hits across the hull of the ship, draining the little energy they had left in their shielding.

"She's got control, we just don't have the power to slow our spin quickly with only half our main engines operating," Larry replied for her.

Ashley concentrated hard on opposing their spin with all the thrust the Triton had. "We'll be stable enough in about ten seconds and that's a fricken miracle. Sir."

"Commander, we have injury reports coming in from all across the ship. The only place that didn't lose gravity was the command deck," Oz heard from over his shoulder.

It was the Operations and Safety Officer, who he hadn't bothered to introduce himself to.

Oz brought the casualty summary up in front of the command seating. "What am I looking at here? Almost all the injuries are in the manufacturing area and they're all minor. Half of these are being treated right now by vacsuit emergency systems and we have three who are already on their way to medical."

"Well, Sir-"

"Just because your display turns yellow and starts feeding you more information than you're used to doesn't mean you can slow everyone down with it. Take another look at your station," Oz said quietly and insistently as he stood and looked at the three Operations and Safety Officers.

One stared back at him, open mouthed and shocked. The other two looked back to their station, turning red. They were all young, two of them were men, and one was a young woman, possibly younger than Ashley.

"What do you see?"

"Well, it looks like-" he hesitated for a moment. "They're turning green," he concluded.

"Meaning there's no real emergency there." Oz looked back to the tactical display. Triton was finally about to stabilize. "Now let's see if we can bloody their noses. All weapon emplacements fire. I want our heaviest munitions available to focus on the lead battlecruiser, their port side if possible."

"Maybe once we stop spinning like a top," came Gunnery Chief Frost's reply.

"When you've got a shot, Chief." The gunnery deck and aft torpedo room was showing heat damage to the hull and Oz shook his head. "Laura, at least get refractive shielding up."

"The emitters in that section are damaged, I'm trying to bridge fields from around it," Laura replied with a controlled, even tone. "Considering we came out with shields at about five percent it's a miracle we have anything at all. We've also burned out inertial dampeners across the ship. I'm going to try to have the ship light up dead spots so the crew can avoid them."

"Now that's a problem," Oz said, looking at the tactical display at the centre of the bridge. The carrier was stable, but still turning much faster than he was comfortable with. "Ashley," Oz started as he looked to the navigational indicators on one side of the tactical display and realized that she was already turning the ship so the port side shields would take hits instead of the aft section. "Keep doing what you're doing," he finished.

The tactical representation of the Triton lit up as every torpedo port, missile, and railgun turret began firing at the lead battlecruiser. It was a medium distance fight at a range of one hundred eighty eight thousand kilometres. He couldn't help but notice the ships were keeping their distance. "What are they doing? Their particle beams are less than ten percent effective at this range," he asked himself as he sat down in the captain's chair. He tracked the munitions headed towards the lead vessel, glancing at the Triton's shield status. Gravitational, energy barrier, and refractive shielding were all charging and they were taking less damage by the second.

"Maybe they're waiting for something?" Jason offered from the secondary command seat beside him.

The first of the projectiles closed to within ten thousand kilometres of the bulky, thick hulled battlecruisers and a large explosion flashed. The core of it was superheated and a powerful electromagnetic surge surrounded it for tens of thousands of kilometres. The first wave of the Triton's attack was vaporized and anything behind it was deflected or disabled by the dissipating energy field.

"Was that what I think it was?" Jason asked Oz quietly.

"I need to know for sure. Sending a copy of that to you, Chief Grady. Helm, plot a hyperspace course to the nearest obstruction. Asteroid belt, planetoid, nebula, I don't care as long as it's uninhabited."

"Aye, I have a planetoid pair in a small nebula, only a few million klicks across, lots of asteroids in there too, at least that's what the hazard note says," Larry replied as he set the computer to start calculating a safe route.

"Can all our people navigate it?"

"Panloo or Darris could do it easy with their navigators," Ashley replied.

"All right, that's where we're headed."

"Commander McPatrick, is this the source of the energy readings we just got down here?" Engineering Chief Grady asked as his full sized avatar appeared in Oz's left hand command seat.

"It is."

"Then get us as close as you can so they can't do it again."

"So that was an antimatter enhanced nuke?"

"Yes. It's a smaller version of one I've seen used to excite a brown star. At range, they'll be able to do terrible damage without disrupting their own systems."

"Ready to begin acceleration if field control can confirm hull coverage," Larry announced.

"Say the word and I'll charge the hull," Laura replied hurriedly.

"Hang on, Chief, we're about to remove ourselves from the equation." Oz's tactical screen flashed red, marking several projectiles with antimatter detection warnings. "Frost! Take out those torpedoes!" he ordered.

The Triton's weapons were just beginning to penetrate the lead battlecruiser's shields, doing severe damage. That came to an end as all the rail cannons changed their focus towards the incoming torpedoes. Several were destroyed in the first few seconds.

"Secure torpedo rooms, abandon the most damaged sections of the ship," Oz ordered as he highlighted the decks that had been breached as they left the Ossimi belt. "Get us out of here Ash." Oz watched as three of the torpedoes drew nearer, within ten thousand kilometres. They started moving towards them faster.

The Triton's hull began to charge with the energized particles that would alter the space the ship occupied so they could accelerate at many times the normal rate and Ashley almost had the ship in position.

"All right, all the decks will mark areas under the influence of damaged inertial dampeners by turning the floor lighting red," Laura announced from her field control station.

Oz watched in horror as several sections of the floor turned red. Most of the bridge was compromised, glowing faintly red, but there were dead spots. The communications terminal, engineering and the floor under the pilot seat were all unprotected. "Stand clear!" was all he had time to say.

Two of the torpedoes closed to within five hundred kilometres and exploded simultaneously. In one instant the lights went out, ears popped, and everyone aboard was thrown dangerously hard.

There was nothing he could do. He tried to hold the arms of the command seat but the force of the collision ripped him free and he swore he felt his shoulder graze the ceiling. His vacsuit had just enough time to cushion his landing as he struck the floor in front of the captain's char.

Lights began to come back on. Oz picked himself up off the floor and offered Jason a hand. He took it and pointed to his ear, shaking his head.

"I can't hear anything either," he mouthed back. "Rapid pressure change."

The Triton's main holographic display came on and marked breaches in hangar three and on several other nearby decks. The hull had been thinned to millimetres in the space surrounding the damage, but it was still energized with hyperspace particles. Their velocity read as many times the speed of light; they had been knocked adrift while the ship was enshrouded in a hyperspace field.

Oz looked to the helm and saw that Larry was unconscious in his seat. Ashley's chair was empty; she had been thrown over her console and lay on the deck, breathing rapidly. Her legs were bent and turned at impossible angles. She was awake, however, and working at something on her command and control unit.

To his surprise, the Triton's main engines came to life and with a deft hand that left him in awe, Ashley plotted a drifting course and initiated it as an automated manoeuvring sequence that would guide the ship in a broad arc. They would make the nebula after all. The navigational section of the main status display turned green as she initiated the sequence and marked herself as available and ready. Regardless of her condition, and the anaesthetics her vacsuit systems administered from the chest down for broken ribs, hairline fractures in her hip, and her badly broken legs, the ship accepted her status change.

Oz used his command and control unit to order all vacsuits aboard sealed and activated emergency medical measures. His ears tingled and itched fiercely as the nanobots went to work repairing the damage. It was a maddening, irritating sensation and he couldn't help but chuckle as Jason put one hand to his vacsuit protected head and threw him a rude gesture with the other. "-bastard. You know what a pain in the ass that is?"

"Aye, but we've got to get our hearing back."

"Well, no dead on the bridge, a few knockouts, and some serious injuries we shouldn't completely work through with nanobots. I've got a replacement pilot and navigator coming from the lounge. Agameg rode it out like a rubber ball. If anyone else was standing where he was we'd be scraping them off the ceiling."

Agameg Price helped the pair of tactical officers up from the floor. One was cringing as nanobots attended to his broken arm. "Ashley's condition looks serious, is someone on the way?" he asked.

"Internal bleeding has stopped, but she needs to get to medical for her hips and legs. We only have comms through half the ship, the rest is on relay and the only working internal sensors are on the command deck," Jason replied.

"Not good if we're boarded."

Jason waved to his wife, Laura, briefly before going on. She was taking her seat; like most of the crew, her vacsuit protected her from anything worse than a bruise. "Considering the course our genius helmswoman just put us on, and where we'll be hiding, I doubt we'll be an easy catch."

Oz brought up the smaller command interface on his command and control unit. Several holograms hovered over his arm and semi-transparent screens populated his head's up display. He had to check on Ashley, she was the most injured.

She smiled wanly at him through her transparent face plate as he knelt down beside her. "My math check out?"

"Sure did. The meds taking care of you?"

"Real good. Can't feel anything below the shoulders. Everyone else okay?"

"They'll be all right. Larry should be up once the nanos have fixed him up."

"Good, I could use his brain."

"Panloo is on her way. She'll be taking the shift."

"Thanks, Oz, I thought I'd have to finish mine on the floor."

He couldn't believe her bravery. Ashley was in tears at the sight of someone else in pain, but with the lower half of her body twisted and broken, she only needed someone to talk to or something to do.

"Oz, Iloona is coming to treat Ash personally. One minute out," Jason informed him.

"Thanks Jay, I'll tell her." He looked to Ashley. "Med team's on the way."

"I'm not going to be okay, am I?" she asked quietly.

Oz looked at her hand before he put his atop it, making sure he wasn't worsening a broken limb. "Check your fitness icon, just glance at it and it'll pop up."

She stared at him for a moment, her fear plain for the first time since he knelt down.

"Go on," he encouraged.

He watched her glance at the icon in her peripheral and saw the medical screen populate her transparent visor. Her eyes widened.

"There are a few problems but it's all in the yellow," he told her.

"I'm screwed," she said quietly. It would look bad to someone who wasn't medically trained. There were a lot of breaks and recently repaired organs, but she was stable.

Oz squeezed her hand and shook his head. "Look at me. The nanos were able to fix the internal bleeding, and once you've been straightened out, Iloona will be able to mend your legs and hips. She'll put you out while she does it so you'll wake up as fit as ever."

"I was just sitting at my console then I rag dolled in my chair and slipped over the console like a wet noodle. Nothing's ever hurt like that. How's she going to fix it all?"

"You'll be fine. If you were screwed there would be red marks on your fitness reading."

"None of those," she sniffed. "I knew I should have taken a medical qualifier."

"We'll take it together when we get clear of this. It's been a while since I've done one."

"Think we'll ever get clear of trouble?" she asked. "I mean, it's been one thing after another."

"Just some bad luck. We'll patch up and find clear skies somewhere."

"A beach. Find me a beach, Mister Wizard," Ashley chuckled. A tear escaped the corner of her eye. "And tell Iloona I want to look good in a bikini."

Oz couldn't help but chuckle. "Done and done." Damage reports were coming in and his visor was active with scrolling summaries. Two reactors were down and bulkheads were sealed where previously damaged sections of the ship were reopened by the trauma.

Iloona arrived in a careful rush with two medics behind her. They carried a stretcher equipped for emergency stasis. "Hello, Ashley. Looks like you'll be spending your next few shifts in medical."

"Yay, hooky," Ashley managed. She sounded tired, a side effect of one of the emergency anaesthetics.

"Do you feel any pain?" Iloona asked as she gently touched Ashley's reversed ankle.

Oz knew that if the anaesthetic wasn't working as well as it should have, Ashley would be screaming. Instead she sighed and replied, "nope, all doped up. Feeling better all the time."

"Okay, good. What I'd like you to do is keep your eyes on the commander while we get you onto the stretcher. Ignore everything but him, okay?"

"Okie dokie."

The responder team placed a pole on either side of Ashley and Iloona pressed a button on one. A grey material flowed from the poles and slipped under her, joining seamlessly in the centre and solidifying to form the bed of a stretcher. It solidified and Iloona carefully adjusted Ashley's legs so they were both squarely in the centre.

"Bikinis and beaches, I'll make it happen Ash," Oz told her.

"And drinks with umbrellas. Make sure Ronin's there, too," she added drowsily.

Iloona and the responders brought the stretcher's restraint blanket up and over her and sealed it to the sides so their patient wouldn't roll off. "My, the system's drugged you up good, hasn't it?" Iloona smiled at Ashley. Her thin lips stretched back and upward along her narrow snout, exaggerating the expression.

"Uh huh. Oh hi, Panloo. Taking over?" she asked as she noticed the nafalli night shift pilot take her station at the helm.

She was wide eyed, trying not to stare at Ashley's awkwardly bent legs. "Yes, I, um-"

"The course and sequence are already set, all you have to do is make sure the ship is doing what it's supposed to then pilot us into the nebula."

"I see that, you've done well." She smiled, glancing at the bent metal edge of the console. It was crushed in a few millimetres, the only sign of Ashley's body breaking against it before she sailed over top and struck the forward wall.

"I'll see you in medical soon, Ash," Oz smiled at her.

"See you soon!" she called back cheerily.

"We'll have her straightened up and recovered in about two days, Commander," Iloona told him as she followed the medical responders and the stretcher closely.

"Thank you, Doc."

"Two days? But I'm going to the beach," Ashley muttered.

Oz moved to help Larry to his feet. "You're off duty, everything feel okay?"

"Fine. Suit says I had a concussion and hairline fracture across my forehead, fixed me up before waking me up."

"I know, it was the first thing I checked on."

"Nice to know I'm in good hands," he whispered. "We in trouble, Commander?"

"Tons. Now go look after your pilot."

"Yes, Sir."

Oz could feel Jason's eyes on him as he returned to the command seat. "What?"

"Oh, nothing. Just picking up one of those vibes."

"Ignore it."

"Yes, Sir," said Jason.

"How hard will it be for them to find us in that nebula?" asked Oz.

"If we power down during repairs and cling to one of the hotter asteroids, we'll be undetectable. I'm wishing Ashley were at the helm for that though, landing on the back edge of a drifting mass isn't exactly a walk in the park," Jason answered.

"Do we have the shields to make it through the tails, Laura?" Oz asked.

"Our aft shields are worse than ever, but I don't think we're going in ass end first, so they are," she said.

"What about repairs, Chief?" said Oz.

"In dry dock it could happen in a few days. Out here? We can patch, place temporary shield emitters in a few hours, but anything else is on the scale of months," answered Liam Grady over his comm unit.

"What about installing the main thrusters we have sitting in storage?"

"I'll have to survey the damage outside, make sure the prep work is still good. If it is, then maybe. No guarantees."

"All right, get on it. We'll need the speed if we want to get out of this." Oz set his command and control unit to privacy mode and entered a message to the flight control deck that said, "Have the hangar prepare three Muriel fighters with wormhole generators installed. Arm all our fighters with fusion rounds. Keep it quiet."

Chief Vercelli looked up through the semi-transparent deck to Oz after reading it and nodded. "Is it that bad?" came his coded response.

Oz nodded. It was the only appropriate answer.

"What's going on, Oz?" Jason whispered.

"I don't think we'll have much time in that nebula. I need you to code a message for the captain. Make sure he knows there's nothing he can do to help and he has to find another solution."

"You're thinking those three battlecruisers will have friends before long."

Oz nodded slowly. "If I were running that battle group I'd call reinforcements."

Jason watched him. Oz had become a tactical thinker and a great commander over the years. He was still easy to read up close, however; it was one of his minor flaws as a captain. "What's on your mind, Oz?"

"I keep getting the feeling that we should turn and brawl this out. Running... well it's just not sitting right."

"We've got holes and old damage from the city ship we ran across at Ossimi. They'd know where to hit us."

"This is a close combat carrier. If they manage to track us in the nebula this will turn into a siege and we're not in any kind of shape to shield up or fight at range."

"So you're taking the safe route, getting us in shape to run. Makes sense."

Oz paused for a moment, staring at the navigational hologram in the centre of the bridge. They were moving fast, but he knew the enemy would be on top of them if they tried to run in a straight line or if they extended their course past the nebula. "Chief Grady," he said.

"Yes, Commander?"

"I don't care what you have to do, get those main thrusters installed as soon as we're in a stable position. Until then, get our reactors back online and prep any teams who won't be working on the engines to get emergency shield emitters in place. We're going to need them."

"Yes, Sir." Chief Grady's holographic avatar flickered out.

"Preparing for the worst?" Jason asked.

"Always."

CHAPTER 4
MESSENGERS

Buster was followed by Hood and Hatter as she walked down the gangway to their waiting Ariel fighters. "So, if we're only going to meet the captain, why have they set us up with enough fusion rounds to wipe out a small fleet?" asked Hatter, a bug eyed, tall fellow. He'd been named after his tendency to completely lose his temper during simulations. His tantrums had become legendary in the pilot's lounge, and when someone called him "mad as a hatter," it stuck.

"Were you watching the live brief before we were hit?"

"No, I was busy."

"He was busy crushing on Pisser," Hood said with a crooked grin.

"We were having an enlightened conversation, I'll have you know."

"Really? What could have been so important that you missed the most exciting thing on this ship?"

"Uh, well. Don't remember, it'll come to me."

"You tell me when it does." Buster shook her head and checked her fighter over. The machine was hanging so it pointed down towards the lower hull and the punter launch system. It would be her second trip out in the same fighter, without her SIO this time. They had retooled the systems to run with one pilot. The fighter also had a much longer range, especially with the addition of a wormhole generator. They had repaired the scorch damage to her number three engine so well she couldn't tell if they had regenerated it or replaced the pod entirely.

As they focused on preparing for their upcoming mission the other fighters were being rotated towards the sides of the launch bay. The tracks moved the ships to the left and right where they were drawn up into the hangar for servicing or reconfiguration. Buster only assumed they were being loaded with fusion rounds and other heavy armaments, preparing for something dire.

"What was I talking about?" Hatter asked as he began his inspection.

"Armaments."

"Yeah. Why so heavy?"

"If I were to guess, I've got an encoded message for the captain so we're not really meant to know the details."

"But we were in a wormhole, then we weren't? What's with that?" Hatter asked.

"Man, I'm surprised you were focused enough to get your certs. You think like a roulette wheel," Hood chuckled.

"The live brief said it was some kind of energy pulse. Dissipates practically anything, I've heard of pirates super charging junk in transport lanes to do the same thing. In this case they managed to find our wormhole, plot a course along side and knock us off our rails."

"So we're getting torn apart by pirates?"

"No, we're getting nailed by some corp who wants to collect on a bounty or some kind of repo."

"That's one big repo. Wonder what the pay's like.

"Let's just say big."

"So, um," Hatter started as he inspected his fighter.

"Yeah?" Buster prompted. She hated when he started a thought and just left it hanging for seconds or minutes at a time.

"So this disruption pulse, the one they used to kill our wormhole, if it can burst a bubble that big, with that much directional force, could they like put out a sun?"

"Nope, that's way off scale."

"Off scale?"

Buster shook her head and replied, "Okay, disrupting a wormhole is like blowing out a candle. Disrupting a sun is like putting out a fusion reaction bare-handed."

"Ah, gotcha. Okay so how did they find something moving through a wormhole? I mean, I could do the math, but there's always the curve, you know? A chance that your target isn't moving in a straight line or the space you're targeting is so different on the inside that you can't predict what'll happen if you try to pop it."

"Wormholes don't move."

"Yeah, I know. Triton's wormholes are created ahead and behind, compressing space between and the ship moves through, blah, blah. But how did they find us? I mean, Ash's pretty good at the stick and everything."

"They found us because we're moving very slowly with only half our main thrusters and because they probably have a micro wormhole generator that was able to extend their scanning range," Buster replied as she started climbing into her cockpit.

"Sounds expensive."

"Yup, it's expensive. I don't know if Triton has that kind of tech."

"But we just got a hyper transmitter... same thing, right?"

Hood dropped into his cockpit seat and sighed. "It's in how you use it. If I set you up with a hyper transmitter that could pop a thousand micro wormholes a second would you know how to pair it with the sensors so you could take that many pictures?"

"No, but I bet Finn would. Guy's some kind of genius."

"I've met him, he's a hard working tech with a good head on his shoulders. Chief Grady says 'go crawl down that deep, dark shaft,' and he says 'yes, Sir. Can I bring my bed roll, Sir?' You've got to respect his dedication. I don't think he sleeps, either, just lives on stims and meal bars."

"Sounds like he made an impression," Hood teased. "Planning a trip to the techie berths?"

All three of them were silent as they started their pre-flight diagnostics and their cockpit canopies sealed.

Buster couldn't help but feel strange being all alone in the two seat Uriel fighter. "You know I don't fraternize. Just because Captain seems to think giving in to our hormones aboard ship will help us relax doesn't mean I have to follow suit."

"What's wrong? Have a flameout with someone on your last ship?"

Buster would have hated her call-sign if it didn't sound so good. Sonya had been named thusly after waking up the Wing Commander and reporting evidence of nocturnal activities near her bunk. He had her point out the offending bunks and all he did was ensure that the privacy curtains sound dampening systems were activated then went back to bed after giving her a grin and a thumb's up. She wasn't aware of Wing Commander Minh Chu's offbeat sense of humour until then.

She was embarrassed and irritated by his solution. Hatter, of all people, was the one to point out that ship policy allowed fraternization while off-duty. He spread the word that she'd bust couples sharing a bunk if they left their sound dampeners off or curtains open. Before she knew it, 'Buster' had been laser etched onto the side of her starfighter. "I'm not going to dignify that question with an answer, Hatter."

"It wasn't very dignified in the first place, but whatever."

Their diagnostic cycles completed and the fighters were moved down from the track into the punter. In the dim light, all Buster could see through her cockpit window was the thick launch bay hatch.

"I know why you took me on this mission; I'm your Sensor Intercept Officer and an experienced pilot, but why did you snag Hatter?" asked Hood on a private channel.

"Hatter's got reflexes beyond the curve and he's a savant at compression mechanics. He calculated a wormhole manually for his final qualification and he's got his FTL ticket."

"Wow. I haven't calculated a jump manually since college. Even then, it was table top, not in a sim. How'd he get his ticket anyway?"

"Ask Ronin. Something in his file convinced him he could be trusted with a fighter equipped with a faster than light system. Hell, he's even cleared for shuttle and drop ship service."

"I'm not cleared for drop ship service. I wonder what Ronin knows about him that we're not cleared for?"

"This is Ronin we're talking about. He's a friendly mystery wrapped in a weird little wise package. It's like flying beside a Zen master who's one bottle short of a six pack."

Hatter burst out laughing. "But I think everyone likes him, and he can lick anyone in a simulator while spouting off proverbs. He's a rare one."

"Guys? My comm still working?" Hatter asked on the public channel.

"It's working fine, we're just deep in quiet contemplation," Buster replied.

"Couldn't help but notice there's no departure time set on this mission. Know how long we'll be here?"

Buster checked her command and control unit for status information from the bridge. "Looks like the Triton's about to start decelerating, we could punt at any time."

CHAPTER 5
LANDING

The wounded on the bridge had been tended to, several of the staff had been replaced and the atmosphere was quiet, tense. Only a few small sections of the deck glowed red; emergency inertial dampeners had been installed to replace most of the burned out units. Everyone knew that there were three battlecruisers searching for them, that they were moving at great speed on a course that took them in a wide curve, and that the safe haven they sought could be more dangerous than their attackers.

Oz watched as the broad scale hologram began to display the Triton in relation to a pair of planetoids and a massive cluster of large asteroids behind.

"We have to slow down," Laura advised from her field control station.

"How much?" asked Oz.

"A lot more, relative speed of under one hundred klicks per second before we enter the dust cloud."

"Panloo?"

The nafalli finished listening to her navigator and nodded. "It will be close, I'm increasing our reverse thrust now."

"We're going to show up on their scanners like a small comet," Agameg advised. "They'll have our exact position."

"What about when we're deeper inside the micro-nebula?" Oz asked.

"Laura is right. If we are not moving slowly enough for our gravitational repulsion shield to move the dust away from the hull, it will cause friction and we will look much like this, only smaller." Agameg brought up a hologram of the asteroid they were looking to touch down on. The leading side was red hot, behind it trailed scorching particles. "It's not actually a real comet, only a large asteroid in a group that's moving through the nebula and colliding with dust and gas, causing friction and a great deal of heat," said Agameg.

"What kind of dust is it? Any chance of mass combustion?"

"No, it's only an interstellar dust cloud. In nine years it'll be absorbed by a planetoid."

"Lucky we found it here then." Oz watched the holodisplays as a counter came up, indicating that they'd be entering the miniature nebula in less than ten seconds. With a glance, he could see they were still moving a little too fast. He looked to Liam Grady's holographic representation to his right. "How are the thrusters?"

"Operating below tolerances, but straining. I can't give you more power than Panloo is using."

"Long range projectiles incoming," Agameg announced as he marked over fifty incoming missiles on the main tactical hologram.

Oz looked at the shield status and was satisfied that they read at ninety three percent of full charge. "No evasive manoeuvres, just decelerate so we don't turn into a great big flare when we hit the dust."

The projectiles swept past the Triton, the closest of them coming within five kilometres. "I just confirmed, they're using hyperspace torpedoes."

"It's like these guys are collecting a bounty on our hull and we just don't matter. Has this crew built hyperspace torpedoes before?"

"No, there's an order for manufacturing to make them, but they're backlogged," Agameg reported.

"Damn," said Oz.

"Do you want me to move them up in the queue?"

"No, we're better off evading and having the manufacturing crews help with work outside the ship. I just hope they can't get a fix on us after we've taken cover."

"Sir, if those torpedoes struck-" began Agameg.

"I know. We'd have breaches across the ship. Whoever launched that group of fifty isn't too happy right about now. That's an expensive miss."

The trio of battlecruisers were incoming just under the speed of light. The tactical information accompanying them informed Oz that they were using hyperspace to catch up.

"They're trying to get to us before we enter the dust cloud," Oz muttered. "They're coming in too fast for evasive manoeuvres. Fire what you can, Agameg, no torpedoes, they'll be too slow."

"Yes, Sir."

The ship was enveloped by the thick nebula and everyone could hear the inertial dampeners strain for a moment as the Triton met the resistant field of particles.

"We're flaring. Slow down," Laura advised. "Unless you want to sandblast through several millimetres of our outer hull."

"Thruster three's pylon is showing above tolerance stress. We can't keep this up," Engineering Chief Grady's hologram announced.

"Ordering Gunnery Chief Frost to fire high velocity slugs for thirty seconds," Agameg announced. "Most of them should make it through the edge of the cloud and have a good chance of striking the lead battlecruiser unless they change course."

"Price, you sure this mark is right? We're firing into open space," Chief Frost said over the tactical comm.

"Use his mark, Chief," Oz reinforced. The Triton finally slowed down enough so their gravitational shielding was able to repel the nebula's thick dust and the impact shields began to recover.

"Aye, on the mark."

"Chief Vercelli, launch our three birds," Oz ordered.

"Aye. Punting in five seconds."

The asteroid grouping and their three planetoids were far beneath, and Oz couldn't help but suck air in through his teeth at the sight of the monolithic fireballs as they closed in. "Can we land on this trajectory?"

"It's fine," Panloo's navigator barked over his shoulder. "We'll have to accelerate at the last moment so we strike our landing coordinates properly."

"Don't let the computer do all the work, recheck your course as you plot," Oz ordered.

"Easy big guy, I think he's got it," Jason reassured with a whisper.

Oz watched as the tactical display switched to short range. Their long range sensors couldn't read through the cloud. The Uriel fighters launched and made haste to the opposite edge of the cloud. More information on the cluster of asteroids moving beneath the Triton was becoming available. The final course was plotted for them to land on the flattest space available on the rear of one of the largest flaming cosmic bodies and he immediately started rechecking the navigator's calculations. "If you think we're in bad shape now, imagine what a minor misjudgement could do to us."

"I know, but you've got to trust your staff. I've seen this helm team's scores, they're good."

Oz finished rechecking the calculations and nodded. "The math is solid, I'll give him that."

"All guns, cease fire," Agameg ordered calmly from the tactical station.

The Triton's railguns stopped firing as she manoeuvred through a layer of agitated, flaming dust. The lumbering carrier moved behind the broadest asteroid. It was just ahead, and several members of the bridge staff braced themselves as the main thrusters fired hard to regain enough speed to make contact.

The front of the ship was pointed directly at their landing site. It loomed closer and closer until Panloo finally stopped accelerating and rotated the large carrier so her heavy landing struts were in position to make contact.

Oz clamped his jaw shut as he watched the ship drift off course slightly.

"We could dose you with something, calm you down a bit, maybe?" Jason whispered, smiling impishly.

Oz shot him a stern look then returned his focus to the navigational data displayed on the centre bulkhead. The representation of what was going on around the Triton bathed the bridge in flickering red as the faux window displays showed the view of flaming particles all around the ship and the asteroid they followed. They drifted gently back on course, the distance reading changing from kilometres to metres. Their speed reset so it was relative to the asteroid, not to the field, and Oz couldn't help but breathe a sigh of relief as it switched from hundreds of kilometres per second to sixty three kilometres per hour.

With a low, thrumming sound, the Triton's undercarriage touched the asteroid and Panloo's navigator engaged the drills and clamps that would secure them to the asteroids surface.

Oz glanced to Agameg and checked the compositional readings of the asteroid for himself. Out of the corner of his eye he could see the issyrian doing the same in just as much of a rush. "It's not going to work," Oz stated plainly.

"We're drilling thirty meters in, we'll be secure," reassured Panloo's co-pilot.

Oz checked the readings again and saw how loosely packed that side of the asteroid was. "Get ready to maintain a drift, Panloo. Those makeshift moorings won't hold us. Stop drilling."

"They'll hold," argued the navigator.

"If you drill and kick up debris when the mooring posts shift, the repair teams might not survive it. Stop. That's an order."

Panloo's navigator irritably shut down the undercarriage drilling systems and started reversing them slowly. "Funny, I've never seen you in the sim doing my job," he muttered.

"You just lost your leisure materializer rations for a week," Oz growled.

Panloo's navigator whirled in his seat. "I can't help that the slug handling tactical can't remember to run a topographical analysis before we touch down! You should know better than to put a shifter in charge of weaponry and combat sensors!"

"Stow the attitude. We're not discussing his performance. Report to me after your shift."

"What? Why?" he demanded.

"If you have a problem with a member of my staff you have a problem with me, and I settle my problems off the bridge. Now do your duty, Navigator," Oz ordered flatly from the command seat.

Everyone busied themselves; no one wanted to be caught gaping. Agameg couldn't help but let a smile creep across his thin lips.

"Tim's lucky you're here," Jason whispered, nodding at the co-pilot as he turned back towards his control. "Jake would have taken his station and shot him."

"You think?"

"He doesn't tolerate racism."

"Neither do I."

"He enjoys shooting people a lot more and he finished the nav qualifier for the Triton last week."

"Good point." Oz finished double checking the ship's status and cleared his throat. "All right, we're going to concentrate on repairs. Double shifts and double quick. Chief Grady, how are our chances of getting those main thrusters installed?"

"It's not a good idea," Liam Grady's hologram answered.

"What problems can we expect when you're finished?"

"We're sure to get contamination in several key parts of the system. That could lead to sudden power drops, overheating in parts of the assembly and accelerated internal corrosion."

"But you can burn some of the debris out of the thrusters and service them from the inside once they're installed, right?" asked Oz.

Liam's nodding holographic avatar appeared in the tertiary command seat. "I'll get the teams working. They'll be in place within the hour and connected in less than two. We'll be servicing those thruster pods for weeks, though."

"You know, if there was another way-"

"I know, we need speed if we're going to get clear of those battlecruisers. I'll update you with our progress in an hour. All repair and maintenance teams have been dispatched."

"Good. Let's get patched up so we can make a run for it."

CHAPTER 6
NEW VERSAILLES

"This system is corrupt. Permissions have been rewritten," the various displays throughout Regent Tower spat back at anyone trying to access any information or function. Analysts across the city attempted to combat the aggressive digital entity as it spread like a drop of ink in water.

The bright sea of light that was New Versailles flickered and quaked as autonomous functions were re-tasked and shut down for purposes that were known to only the originator of the infection, Gabriel Meunez.

The traffic lanes crisscrossing the sky halted, leaving millions hovering. Impatient night commuters tried to break their lanes, to make their way around the hundreds of kilometres of still traffic only to be incinerated by orbital defence platforms.

For the first time in decades, a battle ship descended from orbit and docked with the very top of Regent Tower. The long combat vessel made the smooth, cleanly designed building look lopsided and top heavy, as though it had grown an undesirable, geometrically out of place appendage. Not a single shot was fired at the invader as it cast its narrow shadow over the city below.

There were no shock troopers heralding his arrival. There was no need to damage the buildings, exterior or interior. Gabriel walked down the debarkation hall from his ship straight into the upper docking centre.

Synthetic valets decorated with red vests and ties painted on their torsos watched Gabriel as he passed and took positions behind. Their blue and green eyes gleamed, as though they were eager, searching for something. Guards in combat armour burst through side doors, moving to block his passage into the main building with assault rifles at the ready. "Halt! This is your only warning!"

Gabriel ignored them. Tears rolled down his cheeks, a grin splitting his face unnaturally and the veins in his neck, forehead, and temples standing out on his flushed skin. "How do you want to die today?" he breathed. Every display in the city echoed his question.

"Fire!" ordered the lead soldier. Every weapon in the tower displayed the same message: "Error 1441." Instead of thousands of pulse rounds filling the air, there was absolutely nothing.

Gabriel regarded the security captain then looked over his forty nine men. With a thought and a sneer that only replaced his grin momentarily, their armour sealed. In the space of three seconds, their independent environmental systems increased the gravity in their suits, crushing organs and bones alike. Everyone wearing armour on that floor suffered the same fate. The main doors leading into the upper observation room opened to admit Gabriel and his small group of eight valets.

The way had already been cleared. Word had spread that there would be a fire fight at the top of the building and the humans who were enjoying their evening until only minutes before had evacuated via the stairs. Panic had already taken one life.

Gabriel strode across the open gallery floor, his teeth chattering, grinding together as he tried to control the mad rush of information streaming through his diseased mind. The power, the pressure, the pleasure of being connected to billions of terminals at once through a network unlike any he'd dreamt of was nirvana.

The virus created in the cybernetic computer nested in his organic brain had eventually begun creating connections with his biological mind, and like the onset of a new addiction it tempted and teased him with sensations and dreams that were so alien, so utterly strange and amazing, that he couldn't experience them anywhere else. The virus became the lens through which he saw the universe, whether interfacing with it digitally or looking with his own soft biological eyes and it left him no other choice but to embrace it, to welcome it in with equal parts terror and awe. It needed to reach out, to express the bio-digital perfection that resided in Gabriel.

Control was the challenge. He would devour the entire solar system like a famished god, swallow the branching networks whole, but it wouldn't satisfy him for long. There would be nothing left, no one left, and he'd be empty. Billions must survive. Like ants they would scurry through their tunnels, back to the perception of safety in their homes, and he would become their master. Nothing on the surface of the planet was untouched by technology and he would be connected to all of it.

The private elevator leading to the office of the president opened and he stepped inside. President Paolo Weir wasn't within; he was five hundred kilometres to the east in a personal vehicle, trying to decide whether to stay with the stuck traffic or take his chances, try and avoid the orbital defence system.

Gabriel stepped out of the elevator and walked up the steps to the thickly padded desk chair. By the time he sat down it had adjusted to his form. A fleeting thought to kill the president passed through his mind and the nearest defence cannon fired, reducing him and his vehicle to a mass of molten metal and ash.

"Oops," Gabriel chuckled shortly. He reclined in the chair and let his mind expand into the network, commanding the hypertransmitters to extend his reach with hundreds of micro-wormholes to as many solar systems.

Security systems throughout the building went on high alert, killing anyone within four hundred meters of the office, erecting safety barriers and energy shielding strong enough to withstand several direct antimatter enhanced nuclear attacks.

He sighed as the remaining systems on the planet fell under his control and he began taking every foreign dignitary, high ranking visiting business person, or borrowed resource hostage. Gabriel's mind peered through the activities of millions of individuals per second using surveillance, automated systems and all of the individual androids across the globe. With unmerciful expediency, he ordered anyone showing dissent killed and in ten heartbeats it was done.

The next task on his list was completed in short order: search for any mention of Jacob Valance or the Triton. To his surprise, his query was answered with a report that was only minutes old. A Caran Enterprises battle group was registering the Triton as a fresh capture and inquiring with Regent Galactic about the bounty. A quick mental glance at information on Caran Enterprises' financial situation prompted a scoff. They were deeply in debt, most of their distress caused by the majority of their products turning on their masters after the Holocaust Virus struck.

With a thought, Gabriel activated a hyper transmitter and purchased the entire company, saving it from a financial ruin that loomed in the near future but more importantly, giving him the opportunity to assume control of the battle group in pursuit of Jacob Valance's ship, Triton. He issued a series of orders to the battle group commanders and relaxed, satisfied that all his hardships had led to something so much greater than he could have ever expected.

For days he cursed Eve for infecting him with the virus that merged his biological and cybernetic minds, wracked his nervous system with pain that, if unmedicated, would disable him entirely, but as he sat at the centre of a new empire of information, he praised her wisdom. That sentiment was what he sent through a high compression wormhole to Pandem. She would know everything she had to, that he'd taken control of their masters, that for the first time the systems of over a hundred worlds were connected to one mind and that her disciple had found paradise.

Traffic resumed, all the lights came back on, and under his watchful eye the people were informed that they had a new master, that they were to go about their business and enjoy the rest of their evening. It was his will that they believe the world was safe again. The Order of Eden would replace Regent Galactic in every world he could touch, and he would use the face of the Child Prophet to lead them to purity.

CHAPTER 7
HOOD

Hood watched his tactical display closely through his heads up display. The balance between the energy he had set to recharge his shields and the rising power level in the wormhole generator was perfect. His shield charge bounced between ninety nine point seven percent and one hundred percent of nominal as his Uriel fighter collided with the heavy particles in the nebula.

The brown and blue matter parted around the ship, just centimetres away from the cockpit canopy. He'd never flown through such a dense dust cloud and was amazed at how the Uriel fighters so easily survived the passage.

"Hood, how's your charge? I can barely get a read through this muck," Buster's voice crackled over their communicators.

He enjoyed being her Sensor Intercept Officer, but having his own ship was a higher thrill. "Reserve cells are almost at full. How are yours?"

"Good. I'll be ready to open a wormhole as soon as we get past the edge of the nebula. If you can call this cloud a nebula."

"More like God farted and moved on, if you ask me. I haven't seen so much brown since I cleaned the latrines aboard the Mayberry Twelve," commented Hatter.

"I don't need to hear that story again," said Buster.

"But you enjoyed it so much the first time."

"I threw up in my mouth a little, actually," Buster replied.

The pair were always good for banter, whether it was during a holographic strategy table game in the bunks or on patrol. Hood couldn't say Buster and Hatter were friends, but there was an ease, a familiarity the pair enjoyed that he normally saw only in family.

Buster would never admit it, and Hatter would laugh it off, but the squad leader and the squad clown got along, and it didn't take long for them to sort things out if Hatter screwed up. Hood didn't trust the scrawny pilot, but if Buster could trust him enough to bring him along, he felt he could give him a chance.

"Coming up on the edge of the nebula," Buster announced.

The starfighter trio broke through the edge of the dust cloud, and Hood couldn't help but be surprised at how sudden the change was. From a soup of brown and white debris to open space. A trail of the stuff followed them for several kilometres.

His tactical panel and heads up display lit up with red markers. "Oh my God, you seeing this Buster?" he asked as he checked the ship profiles.

"Can't miss it."

"Can't wait to tell this story; 'so we come out of this cloud of space crap and what do we see? A whole deep space carrier group four hundred thousand klicks to port.' That's gonna be a hit in the bunks," Hatter muttered.

"I hope you're making calculations for our wormhole over there, Hatter," Buster threatened.

"Oh, hell yeah!"

While the pair went on, Hood took a closer look at the scan. "That carrier is five klicks long, four wide, and they've got about twenty destroyers and battlecruisers with them. We've got to warn Triton."

"We have our orders, contact the Clever Dream. Deliver the encrypted message. Besides, there's no way they'll try to come out of the cloud at this end. They'll have a good shot at avoiding this... armada."

Hood hurriedly programmed a time released message beacon, copied a capture from his sensor suite to it and launched the small orb behind them into the cloud. "That won't start transmitting until it's in range of the Triton."

"If they didn't spot us before, they have now," Buster scolded. "How are those calcula-" An intense flash of light burst in front of them.

When Hood's eyes adjusted, there was nothing but scorched wreckage where Buster's fighter had been. His tactical display told him her Uriel had been destroyed by a high powered antimatter particle beam.

"Holy shit! Buster! What happened?" Hatter asked.

"Send me your calculations, Hatter," said Hood.

"But Buster! Can you get a read on her? Her cockpit section isn't here, it must have been blown into the cloud! We have to-"

"She's gone! Her cockpit was vaporized! Now send me your calculations so we can get the hell out of here!"

Hatter didn't reply.

"You can mourn her later, just finish that math before we-" The calculations for his wormhole compression and course appeared on his navigational display, sent over by encrypted laser link as they had been trained to do. There would be no way the carrier group could find out where they were going or how long it would take them to get there.

"Hood, they're leaving. Look."

He looked at his tactical display and couldn't believe his eyes. "What the hell? Their transponders just flipped from Caran Enterprises to Regent Galactic. Something big is going down and I don't plan to be a part of it."

"So they kill-" Hatter took a shuddering breath before going on, "her and just move on."

"Biggest wormhole I've ever seen, and they're all taking off. Let's not stick around for any parting pot shots." Hatter didn't bother verifying the wormhole calculations, he just dumped all the power his fighter had in reserve and stored in its shields into the wormhole generator. The power systems whined as the space in front of them distorted.

With a burst from their thrusters, they entered the compressed space and left the wreckage of their squad leader's starfighter behind.

CHAPTER 8
DISSENT

The alert caught everyone in the command chain by surprise. There was a fire in the Botanical Gallery. As the most well protected section of the ship, it was reserved for families and working civilians. It also played host to a beautiful growing and leisure garden that put some small planetary parks to shame with its earth seeded trees, grass, and upright food planters. The first significant crop was only weeks away and the next would come even faster.

Oz, Jason, and Laura all made their way with haste to the centre of the ship. They knew Engineering Chief Liam Grady would get there first and that was a significant reassurance to Oz, who was at the same time outraged and nervous.

The Botanical Gallery hadn't sustained any significant damage; it was on a separate inertial dampening system that had its own backup power supply. First responder security officers who put out the fire reported it has been intentionally set.

"Where did the report say the fire came from?" asked Laura, the lead energy field specialist on the ship and Jason's wife.

"It was an empty second level apartment. Fifteen people were recorded entering after the seal on it was broken," Oz replied. He'd known Laura for ages it seemed, since he met her in simulations before his service with her on the First Light.

"Was one of them our astrophysicist friend?" Jason asked. His composure was level and easy, he was rarely anything else.

"Yup, but Captain marked a few other people who were in and out of the apartment as trouble. The rest were civilians, none from the slave ships."

They stopped in front of one of the security doors leading into the Botanical Gallery. Jason brought up his clearance code and ordered it open. The deck rumbled at the passage of the two meter thick, solid metal door being drawn back and to the side. The floor was polished silver from the friction the seldom repeated motion caused.

The smell left in the wake of the smoke wafted at the three. Oz couldn't place it, nor could Jason, but Laura's eyes went wide. "Did security identify what they were burning?"

"They said it was from the garden, they're still gathering details."

"It smells like wood."

Oz led his companions past a small group of security guards and through the open apartment door. The main room had a sofa, two chairs, and a sideboard. A spiral stairway led upstairs to the bedrooms. He stepped inside and glanced down the small hallway leading to the kitchenette and half bathroom. There were more signs of smoke there.

One uniformed guard stepped in front of his squad of seven and retracted his face plate. He was dressed in full black boarding armour. Horizontal slats of flexible metal crossed the entire surface of the suit. They protected personal shield emitters, inertial dampeners, and a thin layer of artificial muscle that worked with the wearer. Oz's suit was thinner by comparison, missing the extra armour layer and heavier gravity compensation systems the guards' squad had installed. This guard was an issyrian who had modified his appearance slightly so the fine, slick rows of tendrils across his cheeks and the top lip of his mouth were hidden by smooth skin. It gave him a streamlined appearance that would have almost been feminine if it weren't for his large red eyes. Agameg had never looked menacing, but he could imagine how this issyrian guard could. "They started the fire in the kitchen, Sir. It looks like they used the stove to light several branches. There was no permanent damage, Commander."

"Thank you. Did forensic scanning point to any specific suspects?"

"There is evidence of five people who were in direct contact with the branches and the stove. Only one of them is known as a trouble maker. I've updated my report."

Oz looked past the guard to the soot stained ceiling leading to the kitchenette. If it weren't for years of experience in controlling temper, it would have gotten the best of him. The report listed Edward Stoppard and Leland March with the most exposure to the combustibles. He knew Edward, had watched him storm off the Flight Command Deck, feeling ignored and undervalued. He had no right to assume he'd get any more attention than any other specialist. Astrophysicist or not, he had to follow the chain of command and information. It might take two or three people to do his job, but it was worth replacing him to avoid this drama. His eye lingered on Leland March's grinning photo and he couldn't help but get a little heated. Now this one I've heard of. Lied about his qualifications, nearly got a whole crew killed, and it says he's lodged nine complaints at his new position on the ship, Crewman's Mate. The lowest rank we have. He deserves less.

He could hear shouting outside, and behind it was the sound of a murmuring crowd. Oz closed his eyes and tried to press his rising frustration away.

"Thank you, Kameri," Jason said to the issyrian guardsman. "You've been doing a great job while the security chief and her lieutenants have been off-ship."

"My pleasure. I'm only glad I could adequately attempt to fill her considerable boots. Stephanie makes it look easy."

"What's happening outside?" Oz asked as he turned towards the door. He didn't pause for a response but walked straight across the concourse to the railing. The park in the Botanical Gallery was a riot of natural colours with full grown trees, a stream, ponds, flower beds, and vertical food planters that had young vines climbing at their feet. A couple of trees were slightly askew, and one planter was leaning, but the botanical gallery had weathered the recent turbulence well from the little he could see. The lush centre was so large it wasn't possible to see it all from his vantage point, and the apartments surrounding it went on for what seemed like forever.

It was the best place to live on the ship. The rest of the great vessel could be completely destroyed and the botanical gallery would most likely survive. It had its own life support, backup power systems, and even enough escape craft for half the crew, all carefully hidden out of sight but in easy reach. The only complaint he'd heard from residents was the lack of windows, which the ship made up for with entire walls that could display images so life-like that many forgot they were in the centre of a large carrier.

The safety and beauty of the botanical gallery only made what Oz saw next worse. There was a crowd of fifty or so people gathered on the lowest level of the garden. Guards were stopping them from going up the ramp that led to the second floor concourse where Oz was standing.

Oz's temperament was cool and level until he heard a familiar voice shouting, "My apartment's up there! I have a right to that level as much as any security officer!" It was Edward. He was at the lead of the crowd,. The sight of him screaming red faced at one of the Triton soldiers was infusing the environment with a combative mood.

"This could go wrong," Jason said quietly.

"It could turn into something..." Laura inhaled deeply as she looked down at the gathering crowd. "...bad. Really bad."

"How much of their food and leisure rations are Botanical Gallery residents using on average?" Oz asked Jason over his shoulder.

"Most use their entire allotment daily. There's also a new market for trading rations. It's still early, but it could become a problem," said an unfamiliar voice from behind.

He half turned and looked to the woman who came to stand beside Laura. She looked as irritated as he felt.

"I'm Mischa. When we settled here, Captain Valance accepted me as civilian leader. I assume you're Oz. I mean, Commander McPatrick."

He couldn't help but pause a moment as he looked at her. Much like the rest of the civilians who lived in the Botanical Gallery, she didn't wear a vacsuit he could see. She wore a loose, long dark blue skirt and a light scoop necked cream blouse with long sleeves. Most of the civilians made their underclothes out of reshaped emergency vacsuits that would expand around their entire bodies under their clothing in an emergency, and he found himself hoping that she was wearing one somewhere underneath. "Good to meet you."

"I'm sorry I'm late to this party, but my apartment door wouldn't open. Security just bypassed me out." She blew a curl of her long dark hair out of her face. "Did he do it?"

"I'm about to find out," Oz said as he turned towards the crowd. The group was growing, though most of the newcomers seemed to be observing rather than joining in on the shouting match that was underway. Oz strode to the top of the broad rampway. "You have my attention, Edward!" he boomed.

The crowd quieted, Edward looked to Oz between two guards who stood in his way. "So this is what it takes to get one of you officers down here!" he sneered.

"What do you want?"

"What do we-" Edward looked to the people around him as though insulted and astounded by Oz's question. "Do you have a couple of hours? I mean, let's start with not getting paid!"

"You're being given credit against service, room, board, and luxury rations on the materializers. If there's any cash owing when the ship is safe and you leave, you'll get it," Oz answered in a clear, loud voice. Out of the corner of his eye he watched Mischa, who stood with arms crossed, staring down the ramp.

"You call that payment? It's less than a tenth of my last salary and I can't even spend the credits aboard unless I trade with one of the civilian shops and they're all service. There's nowhere to buy anything and we haven't seen a port in as long as I can remember!"

Oz's patience was fraying. "If you can find a position off-ship that pays more, we'll be happy to drop you off at the next port."

"And when would that be? Where will that be? We don't have any say over where we end up or what we're doing! We're not all soldiers hell bent on getting ourselves killed in some hopeless uprising, some of us have careers and more important things to do!"

Oz couldn't believe what he was hearing. "You were right beside me on the command deck when we last tried to pull into a safe port. There was no haven to be had."

"That asteroid mess was supposed to be a safe port?" Edward screeched.

"Yes! And like so many ports out here, it's run into hard times."

"Hard times? Slavers! Killers! What are we doing out here anyway? Oh yeah! I almost forgot! They're hunting for us, these Regent people. Anyone who served on Triton gets public execution, isn't that right, Commander?" he spat the last, mocking the rank.

Oz didn't know what he was about to say. If it were a military ship, the entire front two rows of the crowd would spend the next week in the brig or confined to quarters. He wanted more than anything to command the Triton troops to stun Edward and his group of dissenters and drag them all to a small room where they could argue amongst themselves for a few days.

A hand landed on his shoulder from behind and he couldn't have been more relieved to see Chief Engineer Liam Grady. He was wearing his thick cotton blue robes, cinched at the waist by a thick red belt with the Triton silver skull flag imprinted on the end. "Would you like a hand?" he asked in a soothing, low tone.

Oz couldn't help but notice that his other hand touched the middle of Mischa's back with telling familiarity.

"Please," Oz said around a long exhale.

"Oh, here he comes, the teacher. Everyone quiet down while he buys the officers time," mocked Edward.

"I couldn't help but overhear you, Edward. There's no need for this, or for your display."

"My display? They ignored every request I put in to see an officer over the last twenty hours!"

"I'm talking about the fire, Edward. You could have gotten someone killed. The suppression system withdrew all the oxygen from that room until the squadron arrived," the chief engineer's low voice was gentle, but carried over the crowd. The man was as broad shouldered as Oz, and only a little shorter, but somehow he seemed like a gentle giant, larger than life and entirely at ease with himself.

"You're saying I-"

"Everyone knows you and Leland March were at the core of this incident. Commander McPatrick could have you both in the brig along with anyone else who left a trace of themselves in that apartment but he decided to listen instead," reasoned Liam.

"But look what it took to get him down here!"

Liam smiled slightly and took a moment to regard Oz with a raised eyebrow. "He's here now, speak to him. Ask for solutions, don't accuse him of not providing them."

"That's just it! He's not providing! He gives skilled workers like Leland and me menial jobs and, worse, pay that's nothing but an 'I owe you!'" Edward's fervour was fading; the crowd had begun to settle.

"Everyone aboard has food, practical clothing, and a generous allotment of cumulative leisure rations for the materializers, manufacturing bay, or for a good time at one of the entertainment establishments. That's all free aboard ship, it doesn't come out of your credits, which are being counted as cash, mind you. The captain could have given you credit with some distant government to delay payment, but he's offering real cash instead, pre-exchanged with whatever port you disembark to. Read the details of the agreement your representative, Mischa, approved sometime."

"What use are credits if we can't use them with the materializers to boost our so-called luxury rations? A second pillow cost me fifteen units! We only get twenty five a day!"

"That's a compromise everyone makes. It sounds more like you're simply worried-"

"Don't talk down to me, you condescending son of a-"

"We're all worried," Liam spoke over Edward, his voice filling the rampway and beyond. "We're all far from home. Some of our homes are unrecognisable and if we went back, life would be much harder than it is aboard. There are over thirteen hundred slaves who are making themselves at home in bunks made for soldiers, technicians, pilots, and other crewmen. I've visited them and they're happy. Not one of them has seen this place." He gestured to the botanical gallery as a whole. "But they're happy to be free. Most of them are looking to be of service thinking that the bunks they're moving into will be home for months, maybe years. Some of them are outside the ship even now, helping with repairs."

"They're used to a lesser standard! How can we be expected to live trapped here?" Edward demanded.

"We're all trapped," Liam said with a flat finality that hushed everyone and caught Edward by surprise. "Until we decide we are free."

"What kind of-"

"Let me help you find your freedom," Liam appealed gently.

Edward seemed to realize that the majority of the crowd wasn't interested in supporting him any longer; they were listening to Chief Grady. He nodded, red faced.

"Oz, do we have a ship for these people?" Liam asked in a whisper.

Oz looked to Jason, Laura, and Mischa. "The Cold Reaver's gone, so is the Clever Dream. The Sampson will fly, but it's iffy. The recently captured ships haven't been fully inspected yet, but we didn't capture anything that won't fly under its own power."

Liam folded his hands in his sleeves and nodded. "This Edward fellow won't be the last dissenter. The crew is feeling the pressure and getting weary. Normally I'd say we should start moving more people into the Botanical Gallery and opening up more of the junior officers quarters so we could space out the lower crewmen in the bunks."

"That's what I was thinking," Jason agreed.

"But we have to have a quick pressure release. We're too close to combat."

"So we give them a ship," Oz muttered.

"Is that really the best solution? Was the fire they started really bad enough to trip the emergency extinguishing systems?" asked Mischa.

"I checked. They hotwired the stove so it wouldn't shut itself off once it detected a high flame, then used a branch to start the fire. If they were caught in the room, they would have had to depend on their vacsuits for an environment. If someone else, like one of Iloona's children, were hiding in a cupboard or closet they would have died without one," Liam replied quietly.

"Then I don't want them here," Mischa agreed solemnly. "Give them a ship, Commander. I don't care if it's only got one working thruster and a pressurized closet."

"Which is the best of the captured ships?" Oz asked Jason, who was already looking through the initial condition report from the Flight Control Centre.

"That's a tie between a sixty one meter converted cargo vessel called The Lucien and a thirty meter long converted customs ship. I suggest the customs ship. No need to offer them anything larger."

"What about the Caran ships out there? They haven't hailed us since we left the Ossimi Ring and I don't think they'd give them much of a chance either," Laura asked.

"We'll have to make sure they know which side of the nebula to come out on and hope for the best. I mean, they're asking for a kind of freedom we can't give them right now. It's not like there's a free port inside the nebula."

Oz closed his eyes and nodded. "They have an hour to get aboard and launch. We're not giving them any personnel, only a squad emergency survival kit and a month of food each."

"As good as we can afford on short notice," Liam agreed.

"One more thing. They don't come back. Once they leave they're on their own," Laura added. She was a lead technician, an officer, but she had no real say in what was going on.

"You're right," Oz admitted. "Besides, I don't want to see what Jake would do to someone who starts a fire on his ship."

Liam turned towards the crowd. "We're willing to provide you with a serviceable ship, supplies for a month, and all the freedom you can handle. We'll give you a course that should give you a fair chance at avoiding our pursuers. You have one hour to quietly gather your possessions and disembark."

"What? You're just going to give us some old wreck and send us off?"

"Unless you'd rather stay here under these awful conditions," Liam laughed.

"Can we have time to decide? I don't know if we even have a pilot."

Oz stepped in beside Liam and shook his head gravely. "You have one hour to do it all or fall in line. This is a one time offer. Next time you get to leave it'll be in port or out an airlock." His tone was stern, cold.

Liam nodded silently.

"Oz, we have an emergency signal coming in," Jason whispered hurriedly. "One of our birds just caught a scan of a battle group on the other side of the nebula."

"I don't have time to deal with this," Oz said dismissively, gesturing towards Edward and the few who still stood with him. "Neither do you, Chief," he finished.

"You're right," agreed Liam.

"Officer Kameri, have three squads shadow whoever would like to leave aboard the converted customs ship and stick to the one hour schedule," he told the junior lieutenant. "Don't let Edward or Leland out of your sight. If they give you any trouble, arrest them."

"Yes, Sir."

As Oz turned to leave, he noticed that the crowd had diminished to a dozen, and most of them seemed to be on the verge of abandoning their leader. Nothing Edward or Leland said was convincing enough for most of them to leave with them.

"Commander McPatrick," Mischa called after him.

He stopped.

"I don't want anyone who was involved with the fire living in the Gallery."

"Kameri, make sure your team moves everyone involved with the fire out of the botanical gallery within the hour. Set them up in that converted customs ship and lock it down. They don't have a right to walk the decks of the Triton."

Mischa was at first shocked, but then fixed him with a smile. "Good meeting you, Commander."

"This has been the first sign of trouble since you were put in charge of the civilian body down here. Are there any other trouble makers you need to tell us about?"

"No one like Leland or Edward."

"Well, they disabled your apartment door before starting all this, so that tells me they were afraid people would listen to you."

"She's well liked and respected here, Commander," Chief Grady said.

"Good, then repair what you can and make sure your people are ready for anything. We're not out of the woods yet," Oz told her as he began walking towards the main exit from the botanical gallery.

Everyone else followed, and Mischa made certain that she was right beside him. "What's going on out there?"

"We're being hunted by several destroyers and we're outnumbered. I may have to seal you and your people inside the botanical section. Is the botanical gallery ready for that?"

"We could sustain ourselves for years," Mischa replied, deeply concerned. "Could it really come to that?"

"I'm just preparing for the worst," said Oz.

"Thank you for being honest, Commander," she said as she stopped at the exit.

Oz felt a pang of guilt at giving a civilian so much reason to worry, and for passing so much responsibility to her, but he could do little to reassure her. "We'll get through this. Get help from Junior Lieutenant Kameri and his squads whenever you can, that's what they're assigned to you for." He didn't turn to watch the main botanical gallery door close behind him, though he could feel the rumbling it caused on the deck.

"I don't like where this is going, Oz," Laura said quietly. "What do you expect to happen out here?"

"We're hiding in a very small nebula and there's no telling how much backup those destroyers are bringing in."

"But there's no way they can find us from the outside. Even if they start patrolling within, we'll probably see them before they see us."

"That's not the problem I'm preparing for. I'm thinking of what's going to happen when we finally make a break for it. I'm not going to assume luck will be on our side, especially when those destroyers specialize in long range. We can come out where they never expect us to and still get several shots off before we're clear."

Laura nodded, knowing full well that Triton couldn't handle much more damage. "So you're planning for an all or nothing tactic. That's reckless and you know it."

"You're right," Oz agreed tersely.

"How are you planning on hedging your bets, Oz?" Jason asked calmly.

"I'm taking a page from your playbook. As soon as I get to the bridge, I'm going to order everyone except for the civilians in the botanical section and essential crew to relocate to the captured raider vessels. Then I'm going to put all our pilots on alert."

"Now I really don't like where this is going," Laura muttered.

Chapter 9
The Last Piece

The creation cubicles used to house bare framework systems before they generated living tissue looked like collapsible coffins. It was something that irked Eve whenever she saw them, and over the past two weeks she'd seen many. She had quietly been working at improving the creativity level of the framework constructs, so they would be something more than basically skilled when they were finally deployed. As it was, they had plenty of people joining the Order of Eden Military, but war was coming, and possibly on two fronts. Her machines wouldn't be able to fight for them, not completely, and their human forces may deplete too quickly to be replenished if things became truly heated. A better, thinking framework soldier, technician, and servant was needed.

The small team of workers Eve assigned to the task of setting up her experiment were busy opening the half-height coffin, pulling each end of the thin-walled black case so it could accommodate someone of average stature. The long top came open to reveal the bare framework.

It looked like a human skeleton made of dull grey metal. "They look so delicate," Eve muttered.

Hampon looked at her with mild surprise from where he stood at her side. "I suppose. Perhaps I've known their true capabilities for too long to see them that way."

"Perhaps," she replied as she watched them place the synthetic bones inside an upright stasis tube. They drifted through the thick brown liquid, piling up at the bottom.

"How did you discover the details of Jacob Valance's waking?"

"Everything you loaded into the Jacob model was recorded in Vindyne records. I'm copying the same medical, technological, and combat knowledge databases into this framework using the same integration method to connect them to what's left of Patrick's memory."

"That's obvious. what I'm talking about is this." Hampon projected the security footage of Jacob Valance waking up in the cargo bay of the Samson against the wall beside them. "How did we get footage from the Samson?"

"I don't know, it was in the compressed archives."

"There was no record of who put it there?"

"Only an automated entry number assigned to one of the archival management systems. I suspect it was sent to one of Regent Galactic's data collection nodes while Wheeler had possession of the Triton."

"Before he died. Yes, he did make his claim right before Valance turned the tables on him, so I suppose the Samson must have been aboard. I think it's remarkable that you're duplicating the conditions. Do you really think it'll work with the memory modifications you've installed?"

"I imagined and recorded them myself. I've been observing Patrick from his perspective long enough to know how he would experience the substitutions I've put in place."

"You're implanting a tailored daydream you recorded as one of his memories? You are incredible."

"I altered it slightly so he would feel that the memory was his own, but essentially, yes. The human mind is easy to master when you can play back entire thought processes and observe them from a distance." Eve had to admit, she enjoyed having Hampon's favour. He kept few secrets from what she could tell, and treated her exceptionally well. His trust in her, how she could surprise and amuse him were all factors in her warm feelings towards him. He, in turn, surprised her from time to time. His goals were not so different from her own; he too wanted a pure galaxy, and to protect it from all her enemies. His weakness was his appetite for power, but it was tempered by his need to play a part. He loved being the Child Prophet, the High Seat of the Order of Eden, and he had eliminated or distanced himself from all his contemporaries.

General Collins was dead, Gabriel Meunez was over two weeks away by high compression wormhole, and most of the old Vindyne Supervisory Board had been killed or imprisoned months before. Lister Hampon had seated her at his side, and as strange as it was, she felt needed, preferred.

Through the observation screen, Eve could see that the scientists, some of whom had been working on the framework project for years, were sealing the stasis chamber. Another placed a box beside it and unlocked it.

They departed the room quickly and closed the door behind. The locked space had no windows, something that seemed even more apparent as the lights dimmed. "Begin," Eve said aloud. It was an announcement, not a command. She had reached out with her mind and activated the framework resting in the bottom of the stasis chamber. There would be no errors, no additional variables, Eve was in complete control.

The framework bones went to work immediately, generating flesh, connecting with each other starting with the spinal column, then skull, hips, and so on until the muscle and raw elements of a man stood upright in the capsule. The system was doing what it was supposed to do, using the substances inside the stasis tube to speed up the generation of tissue, and in a quarter of the normal time, the nude form of Patrick stood before them, very much alive, slowly breathing the stasis fluid.

"Second stage," Eve announced quietly.

Two medics entered the room swiftly, one holding an extraction tool for removing fluid from Patrick's lungs, the other moving to the opposite side of the stasis tube and activating the release switch. The vessel opened at the bottom and stasis fluid surged forth, carrying Patrick with it to the floor.

With an easy efficiency, one medic rolled Patrick onto his side while the other held the extraction pump up to his mouth. Stasis fluid spewed out of the pump as the subject gagged unconsciously. It was over in seconds, and the medics left as swiftly as they had entered, taking the coffin-like box the framework had come in with them.

The young man lay there for a long moment, rousing from the sleep induced by the stasis fluid. Eve watched hopefully, glancing at the video of Jacob Valance projected against the wall beside her. In the surveillance video, Jacob was already on his feet, sorting through the things Alice Valent had left for him. The uncertain, hurt expression on his face was something she hadn't noticed before. With a thought, she deactivated the projection and hoped that she'd gotten the modified memories she'd implanted in Patrick just right.

Through the observation screen, she saw him standing, looking around. To her surprise he didn't question his situation aloud, didn't try to open the door upon noticing it, and didn't cry for help. Instead he went to the box.

He carefully opened it and recovered the shirt the original Patrick had left as an offering on the planet below. Next he inspected the book, at which he smiled, and finally the ring, which he put on.

He held the long, simple shirt in front of him for a moment before using it to wipe most of the stasis fluid off. He pulled it on and returned his attention to the book for a moment before looking up at the room around him.

"Phase three, clear the adjacent rooms. Observation only, please." Eve turned and strode around the corner. She had never been so excited in her life. All of Patrick's behaviours felt similar, only this time there was something new, exactly what she was hoping for.

She took a folded West Keeper uniform from an assistant and entered Patrick's room. He whirled on his heel and gave her an appreciative, appraising look. She had forgotten that she was wearing one of the long velvet dresses Hampon had given to her. When she put it on that morning she'd decided that it accentuated her feminine features aggressively, while leaving enough to the imagination to satisfy modesty.

"I'm sorry we had to put you in stasis after we saved you from Pandem. It's taken weeks for you to recover. How are you feeling, Beaudric?"

"That's my name. Beaudric Farley. Thank God, I couldn't remember for a minute there." He paused a moment, looking at the uniform stacked in Eve's hands, then back up to her. His thumb passed over the corner of the book

49

absent-mindedly, repeatedly. "Feeling pretty good, actually. Having trouble remembering things though."

"We thought that would be a problem, that's why we included the ring your father gave you when you arrived on Pandem, and the book you were reading. That's all we were able to recover after the attack."

"You're forgetting the belt. Would be useful, except there are no pants in here," Beaudric said with a wry grin as he picked up the thick fabric belt from the box.

"This should help, here," Eve said as she crossed the distance between them and gave him the uniform. "I'm West Watcher Nora, you can simply call me Nora."

He took the uniform and unfurled it. It was all one piece, only it was made to look like it was divided in the middle. It was dark blue and green set in a camouflage pattern with pockets on the chest, thighs and a built in thick belt. The slit down the front made it easy to put on. "What happened? The last thing I remember I was on the beach, then there was an explosion."

"It was a fringe strike force. They caught our forces by surprise when they broke the outer perimeter. You were resting with your father after a day's work." To Eve's satisfaction, she could see the memory she created of him spending time with his father on the beach. It was the same experience he'd had earlier that day, only with the addition of his father. She had carefully woven him into the memories she developed using what she observed from his perspective earlier. Through the connection she shared with him as he stood before her, she could feel that he was completely convinced, and relished the time he had spent with his father. The blanks, details of the man's personality, were filled in by Beaudric's imagination. He was completely unaware of the lie in the memory. "You killed several soldiers yourself after taking a fallen guard's weapon. There were too many of them, however, and you were overwhelmed. We got to you just in time and brought you aboard to recover. Thankfully, the invasion was stopped, and the assault was more isolated than we originally thought. You're a hero, Beaudric."

"I don't remember much of the fight. I know it happened, it feels like I've been through something, but I just can't remember."

"That's perfectly normal. Your mind may be suppressing it, and you were badly injured, so some memory loss is to be expected."

"What happened to my father?" He asked. The gravity of his concern was plain in the serious gaze he fixed on Eve; she didn't need her link to him to know that his worry was genuine.

This was the moment when she'd know if all the time and effort she'd spent would be worthwhile. With a sorrowful expression she said, "He was killed when one of the invasion pods struck. There was nothing to recover."

He squeezed his eyes shut and sighed. "I knew, I already knew," he muttered to himself.

It was all Eve could do not to show how overwhelmed her senses were. She could feel that he was recalling the vague memory of the explosive impact that killed his father. Several implanted memories followed: chaotic recollections of the fight after the bombardment, and of taking the book he held in his hand from the pilot of the invasion pod. It was the Silkstream IV that he saw, that was what the invasion pod looked like, and the pilot was faceless, sealed in a Freeground vacsuit. All of that, mixed with his soul-crushing grief, was enough for her to almost forget where she was. She shut down the direct connection with him and wiped tears from her eyes. It amazed her that the pieced together memories, none of which were actually his, could be so quickly imbued with his emotions.

Beaudric noticed her distress and placed a caring hand on her shoulder. "Hey, we've all gotta go sometime. At least it was quick."

She could do nothing but nod. His strength under such emotional strain was incredible, and it gave her pause. There was one more component to put in place, however, and she couldn't delay. "I'm sorry. So many lost so much in the attack, even though it affected a small area. The reason why I'm attending to you personally is because I'd like to offer you a place in our special forces. After the skill you displayed, I was hoping you'd enter into the service of the West Keeper Special Forces. With the galaxy turning on us after our enemies have alleged that we have something to do with the Holocaust Virus, well, we have no choice but to go on the offensive."

"A chance to strike back at the people responsible for this? Sign me up."

"Thank you, Beaudric. I have to attend to other things, but someone will come along shortly to show you to your quarters and other amenities."

"Thank you, Nora."

Eve turned to the door and was halfway through it when Beaudric asked, "Was Freeground responsible for the attack?"

She looked over her shoulder and saw that he was reading the recycling request on the front of the book. "Partially. One of their people developed the Holocaust Virus. We believe they're the source of much of the hatred towards the Order."

"Do me a favour; next time we get a shot at them, make sure I'm in on the action."

"You'll get your chance, Beaudric. First, you'll have to go through some training. We need to know what you're really capable of so we don't put you in unnecessary risk."

Eve was relieved when she was in the hall and the door slid closed behind her. A few strides took her back around the corner where Lister Hampon was watching holographic displays all around him as they scrolled through the active analysis of Beaudric's thought and memory patterns.

"I can't believe it!" he said excitedly. "Somewhere in that process was the key to grafting an entire, functioning, improvising, creative personality with a framework body! You did it! You cracked what we've been chasing for years! He'll think, intuit, and adapt like any soldier while maintaining perfect loyalty and all the controls built into the new framework structures are still in perfect operation."

"It was simple. I only had to give his emotions focus. Use something from his past that I could attach to real objects. In this case, I used his father and the ring he inherited. It'll be easier with others. Beaudric's imagination had to build a lot of bridges on its own. If we could create some sort of crisis where people lose loved ones, it'll work even better." As soon as she said it aloud, Eve regretted it. The emotions she experienced while she was linked with Beaudric when she told him his father had been killed were still fresh, and the thought of causing that kind of pain in others almost made her feel physically ill.

"You mean a real crisis?" Hampon asked enthusiastically. "We could orchestrate something tonight."

"It may not be necessary, we'll know after a few more subjects. No need to disrupt our stock."

"You're right, no need to diminish our flock. Is there any chance you can write a program that will create memories like you did? By observing, recording, and editing?"

"I'll have one for you by tomorrow," Eve said as she watched a junior crewman lead Beaudric from the chamber. He would be shown the best treatment and would receive private quarters befitting a major.

"So the theatrics with the stasis tube, is that necessary for all the future frameworks?"

"No. As it turns out, Jacob Valance became emotionally whole because of his memories, even though they were unconscious in his case. He wanted to believe he had a past and the evidence of it helped him find an emotional foundation."

"Do you think you could make the leap with others? Implanting unconscious memories instead of taking a risk with a fabrication?"

"Maybe if you have a few years to develop the technique, but the key is that they have to have a reason to be loyal that extends deeply into their emotional core. This new process leaves the frameworks with their memories intact with the exception of the ones we need to replace in order to implant an emotional contract. In the case of Beaudric, the contract is simple: our enemies killed his father, now he's dedicated to our cause until we have no further use for him. The accident you made with Jacob Valance was leaving him with a memory leak that influenced his subconscious."

"There was no way we could have known Doctor Marcelles built a hidden backup into that framework. Now that we've finally gotten this far, we don't need Marcelles, and we don't need to retrieve Jacob Valance. I can't thank you enough, Nora."

Eve regarded Lister Hampon with a smile. "I'm sure I'll find a way for you to thank me, eventually."

CHAPTER 10
THE ESCAPE

The blurry privacy barrier surrounded Oz, Jason, and Agameg as they sat in the command seating and viewed a tactical hologram of Hood's scans. "I haven't seen a carrier group like that since I was back on Freeground. They have nine of those hardened battlecruisers," Jason observed. "Looks like you were right. There's no way we're not in for a losing fire fight if we manage to get out of this nebula."

"Do you think Frost's last volley at the battlecruisers we've already come against hit, Agameg?" Oz asked.

"It's quite likely. His people were right on target for the most part and there's little chance that the lead cruiser could manoeuvre in time," Agameg replied, his big, singular coloured green eyes were in a half squint as he examined the tactical hologram closely. "The only weakness I see in this carrier group's formation is their proximity to each other. Considering the speed the ships we've already encountered have exhibited, it's something they could solve at a moment's notice."

"That's why I'm thinking we try to go in the opposite direction. I'd rather come up against the three battlecruisers we've already bruised and get by them instead of running into that carrier group. Even if that carrier was alone she'd have us if she could keep up," Oz pointed at the five kilometre long, four kilometre wide carrier. It was a rectangle with concave sides, evidence of hangars and launch ports dotting the top and bottom while the sides were reserved primarily for heavy long-range weaponry. "Just this beam emitter on the port side was enough to wreck a Uriel with full shielding in a tenth of a second burst."

"Not to mention it struck Buster's fighter at a range of tens of thousands of kilometres. That indicates a high ratio of particles to energy, something that would tax our shields heavily."

"How long would we last under the pressure of a focused beam?"

"No more than a minute."

"Not enough time if they have half our thrust." Oz thought for a moment, looking at the tactical diagram. "It's been four hours. Chief Grady had better have those thrusters installed." He looked to his personal command and control unit and scowled. "Pending." A channel opened between him and the Chief. "Times up. We have to make a run for it before we have a nebula full of ships scanning for us."

"We're still decontaminating. I don't want to run these pods while there's a risk of burning through the main transfer conduits."

"Can you speed it up by flushing them somehow?" asked Oz.

"I can try, but the abrasion damage to the interior of the conduits will make them more delicate and there could be clogs or worse."

"You have thirty minutes. Then we're making a run for it."

"Yes, Sir," said Liam.

"You're thinking what I'm thinking," Jason said quietly.

"If you mean I'm guessing that's not the only carrier group in the area, you're right," Oz said quietly.

"I'm sorry, sirs, but I have to ask. Why would they dedicate so many resources to finding us? I'm aware that this is a wanted ship, but the pursuit will eventually cost more than the reward," Agameg asked, his green oval eyes widening.

"I'm not sure. If I were in the command seat on the other side, I'd say the motivation has to be political."

"That's the only reason I can see," Jason agreed. "Jake's being accused of killing billions of people, who knows how many governments want to get their hands on him. He'd be a powerful token in interplanetary negotiations."

"It's a good thing Edward and Leland failed to recruit enough people to man a ship. They may have given away our position," Agameg smiled. His soft, thick-lipped mouth stretched in a wide smile that seemed exaggerated in comparison to a human's.

"Hope they're enjoying their stay in the hold of that ship. The pilot we put in charge forced them back there when evacuees started boarding. "

"Sensors have detected a battlecruiser just outside the asteroid cluster," Agameg announced, bringing up a hologram of the grouping of moving asteroids and planetoids the Triton had taken shelter in. There was a ghostly outline of a battlecruiser following just outside.

"Chief Grady," said Oz.

"Yes, Commander."

"You're out of time. Get everyone to damage control stations immediately."

"Yes, Sir. It'll take a minute to finish getting my people out of the thruster pods."

"Will the pods be useful?"

"Start slow, I'll try to keep them together down here but if we have a blow through you could lose an entire main thruster."

"Noted, send your recommendations to the helm." Oz closed the channel.

"Frost reports his people have a clear firing solution on the battlecruiser," Agameg announced, monitoring his department from his command and control unit.

"Tell him to keep his systems powered down but to load with the heaviest non-nuclear munitions he's got. He'll be firing at their engines."

"I'm going to patch Minuteman into our helm. It should help them calculate a faster than light course when the time comes," Jason informed him.

"Gotta love a supercomputer without an artificial intelligence. No risk of it going rogue on us."

"That's why he only links to one or two systems at a time," Jason agreed. "What's your plan if they block our escape Oz?"

To Agameg's surprise the commanding officer didn't pause for a second. "We initiate the ghost ship strategy."

Agameg looked it up in his command and control unit and skimmed the summary. "That's drastic. If you'll pardon me saying so," he whispered as he finished reading.

"If we lock up the botanical gallery and evacuate everyone we can, we'll have a real chance of making it work," Oz replied. "Flight Command, ready all fighters and keep power emissions to an absolute minimum. I want everyone to be ready to run at a moment's notice. When the punters are loaded, start moving the rest of our ships into launch position."

"Sir, only a few civilians in the upper berths have reported to the main hangar. They're mostly former raiders," replied Chief Vercelli.

"I was going to tell you about that, Oz," Jason interjected. "About seven hundred of the slaves we liberated have volunteered to remain aboard to help defend the ship."

"You didn't think it was important to bring that up a little sooner?"

"Well, you were busy, so I just accepted their offer. David Penton is speaking for them."

"All right, have someone from security work with him to get them organized."

"We don't have many officers left, mostly aucharian grunts and a couple bridge staff, like Agameg."

"Ever want command of a small army, Agameg?" Oz asked.

The issyrian's eyes flexed suddenly, at first becoming as round as saucers then narrowing down until they were two thin, mischievous slits. "How did you know my birthday was coming up?"

"All right, then as soon as things die down in tactical I want you to take whoever you can from security and get those people organized. You know what the ghost ship tactic requires, so put them where we need them."

"Yes, Sir."

"All right, Chief Vercelli, what are your plans? I'm hoping that you'll stay aboard, we'll need someone in the hangars."

"Aye, I'm staying with the ship, Commander. I didn't help get her in shape to see her get taken."

"Understood. Thank you, Chief. Just get most of your deck crews into ships and stand ready to launch with the evacuees. Those fighters will need ground support. Everyone should have their personal kit and trade tools. Understand?"

"Aye. Are you sure we've gotten to that point?" Deck Chief Angelo Vercelli asked. Through the blur of the privacy field and the semi-transparent floor of the bridge, Oz could see the greying chief looking up at him.

"Not yet. Just be ready. I'm sending you encrypted coordinates, pass them on to your most trustworthy FTL ticketed pilots."

"Aye."

"Where are you sending Paula?"

"She won't go with the evacuees. With the look she's giving me, we'd have to sedate her if we wanted to pack her off."

"We might need her spirit. Let's hope none of this is necessary."

Jason deactivated the scrambling field surrounding the command seating, assuming instant communication to all bridge stations was going to be essential.

Oz nodded at him and stood. "All right. Everyone who just got a notification on your command units telling you the ghost ship tactic is in play should know what to do. If you have an order to report to the botanical section, report to Junior Lieutenant Kameri. Everyone else should have orders to bring emergency evacuation via the launch deck. Do not use escape shuttles. Make sure you take a survival kit for yourself on the way to the hangar, and do not take side trips to your quarters or storage areas. You won't have time to pick up personal possessions. Go now."

Half of the thirty-one officers on the bridge stepped away from their stations and took a moment to say goodbye to the people sitting beside them before leaving the bridge. They knew there wasn't much time.

Oz ignored the questioning glances and looks of uncertainty that came his way as people departed.

"Commander, the battlecruiser is sending probes into the cluster," Agameg announced as he made haste to his tactical station.

Jason stood and strode to the field control station. Laura glanced up and was shaking her head before he was half way there. "I saw the order, but I'm not leaving."

"You're on that list for a reason, the abandoning crew need a certain number of officers and you're part of that pool."

"I'm not leaving you, Jason," Oz could barely hear her say. The two were in a deadlock, and he couldn't afford to have a couple's spat on the bridge, no matter how serious it was.

"We don't have a choice," Jason said.

"Why do you think I came here? We're here because we weren't happy in the lives we had, we couldn't make the choices we wanted to," she shouted, locking her station and getting to her feet. "This isn't Freeground, you're not in Fleet Intelligence, and we don't have to do anything but survive!"

"You know that you're not needed in the ghost ship strategy, not as an energy field specialist, not aboard the Triton. We need you to help control the evacuees, and I need to know you're safe. Especially with what you know is coming. With what you know we'll have to do to survive here."

"I need you on the Samson, Laura. I'm putting you in command of the evacuees," Oz interjected.

"Stay out of this!" Laura burst.

Jason took Laura by the shoulders and looked into her eyes. "You know this isn't some chauvinistic or sentimentally driven thing. We need you out there."

Laura was close to tears and red faced, but nodded. "I'm sorry, I know. I wish I didn't, and I could just argue until it was too late." She shook her head and took a breath. "Don't do anything stupid."

He kissed her briefly and said something Oz didn't need to hear. She was off the bridge by the time Jason re-joined him at his side.

"Frost, tear that ship to pieces," Oz ordered. The reaction time was so fast it was as if he had pulled the trigger himself. All the able railguns across the top of the ship fired at once, hurling thousands of rounds at the enemy ship just outside the cluster of drifting rock. The blue tracers trailing behind the rounds told Oz that the first load were sink rounds, designed to absorb incredible amounts of energy. *That old gunner's planning on taking out her shields before digging in. I'm starting to see why Jake kept him aboard,* Oz mused.

Engineering Chief Grady's holographic representation appeared in the command seat behind him. "All my people are out of the new thrusters."

"All right, send anyone you don't need to the main hangar so they can evacuate." Oz turned towards the helm. "Get us out of here Panloo. When we're clear of the asteroids take us right past that battlecruiser."

The nafalli pilot fired up the four main thrusters, favouring the new replacement pods and in a surprising display of skill, guided the Triton out of the crater she'd called home for only a few hours. The route she was taking would guide the ship through the thinnest of the debris tailing the asteroids and keep the gunnery deck pointed towards the enemy battlecruiser.

"All torpedo, beam, and missile rooms, load for high penetration, close range," Oz ordered. "How are our shields?"

"We're up and fully charged, we even have reserve power. Somehow Chief Grady got all our power plants back online and the temporary emitters installed," Laura reported with a nod at Chief Grady's hologram.

"So I noticed. Focus most of our shielding on the core sections of the ship and gunnery deck. Now if he could get the cloaking systems back up and running I might recommend he gets a week off," Oz remarked.

"That's not going to happen while we've got a through and through hole big enough for a fighter, sorry, Commander," the Chief replied.

"Just wishful thinking." Oz watched as the Triton neared the edge of the comet like trails left behind by the asteroids and planetoids they'd used for cover. The enemy ship's shields were reading no power, and Frost had switched to ripper slugs, ammunition that was heavy and sturdy enough to cut through the thick nebula material without going off course before tearing into the enemy's hull.

The battlecruiser changed course, turning towards them. It was completely against what he expected. If Oz were in command of the enemy ship, he would have used the nearby asteroid cluster as cover, or rotated the ship so they could recharge their shields one bank at a time.

"Oz, this pattern suggests-" Jason started.

"All torpedo and missile batteries, fire," Oz ordered calmly.

"Hold!" Jason countered. It was too late. The torpedo ports lining the edges of the Triton's hull lit up momentarily as the entire ship fired a volley. "Oz, this pattern tells me that ship has backup, and they're nearby. It's trying to get close so it can block a line of fire on another group while it closes in."

Oz looked at the tactical display in the middle of the bridge again. "I thought the same for a minute but I don't see anything. No electromagnetic signals, nothing on thermal scan."

The Triton continued to close the distance between it and the battlecruiser. It was doing its best to counter the impressive attack, firing its beam weapons in sweeping arcs to counter the incoming rush of torpedoes and missiles.

As the ships closed to within five hundred kilometres, the torpedoes struck. The intensified fire of the gunnery deck ripped into the vessel and the few missiles that made it past the ship's defence impacted soundly in the middle of the bulky cruiser. Explosive decompressions and sudden implosions followed directly after the impacts, leaving the starboard side of the vessel an erupting ruin.

"There they are!" Agameg announced, highlighting the outlines of several vessels on a second, broader tactical display he initiated on the bridge. "They were hiding just in front of the cluster, putting a planetoid between us and them."

Oz's heart sank. He hadn't even considered that they would position their ships right in front of the largest planetoid, using the heat and the mass of the body to remain perfectly hidden while their decoy scanned for them and drew them out. "Panloo, get us out of here! Head for the nearest edge of the nebula. Don't spare the thrusters."

"They're firing, Sir," Agameg announced.

The tactical hologram in the middle of the bridge highlighted a group of five ships, all heavy battlecruisers. Three were the trio they had initially attempted to escape, and their energy shields were already low from being so close to the flaming front edge of the planetoid. The other two were part of the new group, and filed in between the others as they gave chase, firing their high powered beam weapons.

"Frost, begin firing flack rounds in a high density pattern so we can mitigate some of this heat damage," Oz ordered.

"Aye, Sir, changing firing method."

"Torpedo rooms, finish that battlecruiser off then load for long range. We have to give our ships enough cover so they can get away."

"We have breaches, sections Q14 to S12. No one reported in those areas," Agameg reported as passively as he could manage. "Their particle beams are sweeping sections of our hull, probing for weak spots."

"All right, we have to change tactics here, we won't make the edge of the nebula. Helm, reduce thrust and keep the hangars away from enemy fire. We're redirecting as much power as we can to shields." Oz dropped into the command chair and brought up his own, more detailed control interface. The smaller holographic displays surrounded him as a two dimensional control board closed over his lap. His own tactical display was far more complicated than the one in the centre of the bridge, made to be an overlay on the visual representation for the primary commander aboard. The first piece of information he found useful was how much the thick nebula's particle field was reducing the effectiveness of the particle beams. Their shields were holding up to the punishment again but the new main thrusters had taken real damage already. They were losing momentum quickly thanks to the thick particles of the planetary nebula, and it was all Panloo could do to keep the Triton drifting slowly away from the planetoid cluster.

"What if we use the asteroids behind us as cover?" asked Jason.

"They're shedding too much material, it would reduce our shields too fast and we'd be open."

"Then we're out of options," he whispered as he began calling up software from his personal drive.

"Looks like."

There was a raise in spirits as the first battlecruiser they had seen was obliterated. The space around it was filled with escape shuttles as the final volley of torpedoes struck it. That was the morale booster the Triton's crew needed for what was to come.

"Security, lock the Botanical Gallery down tight," he said quietly. "I don't want anyone to have access until we have a ship wide all-clear."

"We haven't completely evacuated medical yet, Sir," Kameri replied.

"Then lock that down separately. We're out of time."

"Yes, Sir," he replied.

"Torpedo rooms, Gunnery deck, target the furthest battlecruiser and finish him off. She's still showing extensive damage from earlier. When they're dead in space, shut down and get into position. Engineering, prepare to shunt all power to charge our reserves then shut down all core reactions. Flight Operations, launch all ready vessels. Tell them to head for the edge of the nebula and proceed from there. Use the Triton as cover."

All the departments acknowledged his orders.

"Are you sure about this?" Jason asked. "Last chance to cancel this and keep the crew together."

"We're not going to escape as we are, and the crew is already separated from their rightful commander," Oz whispered back hurriedly. "Panloo, angle the ship so our top side is facing the incoming cruisers and cut all thrust. We need to give our pilots cover."

"Just tell me when you want me to work my magic," Jason said as he worked at his station, preparing several programs.

Oz watched as the fighter launch systems activated like a wave across the bottom of the ship, sending two dozen Uriel and Ramiel fighters into the nebula. Two other vessels they had salvaged from the raiders launched from the main hangars. "Is that everything, Chief Vercelli?" asked Oz.

"No, there are two launches left. We need another minute."

Oz looked at his small Flight Deck status screen and watched as Uriel and Ramiel fighters were loaded into the punter system. He'd never seen the crew work so quickly. The Skimmer, a captured raider vessel reported that it was loaded and was launched straight away.

"Ripped that one up, taking care of the second one's engines. We found a soft spot!"

Oz looked to the tactical screen to see internal explosions in the previously damaged battlecruiser; she was finished. The gunnery crew had moved on to focus on the nearest ship's engines. "Frost, I told you to cease fire as soon as you disabled the furthest ship."

"Just about done, son. Just a few hundred rounds and we'll finish off this target's engines. She'll get dragged into the nearest planetoid's gravity and pulled out of the picture."

Oz's attention was drawn to a group of fourteen fighters who broke from the main group and began accelerating towards the enemy battlecruisers. He checked the details and was alarmed at who was leading the strike. "What's Dent doing?"

"I'm calling him back now, Commander," Chief Vercelli announced.

The fighters each fired a pair of nuclear missiles and veered away. "Just lending the gunnery deck a hand," Dent announced as the group of fighters moved to re-join the assembled ships.

"That never happens again, understand?" Oz told him.

"Aye, aye."

The high speed projectiles finished closing the distance to the lead destroyer and with a flash of light, the damage was done.

"The gunnery deck's rounds are striking," Agameg announced. "Taxing their shields."

Oz watched the tactical screen as several of the small nuclear missiles were destroyed by defensive fire and the grit of the nebula cloud. At long last there was a white flash thousands of kilometres away. "Three detonations out of twenty eight launches. Major damage to the lead battlecruiser," Agameg reported. "Their shields were already quite depleted thanks to the gunnery deck. Chief Frost is resuming fire."

"Looks like they're still coming, but they'll be sensor blind for at least a few seconds," Agameg declared. "We bore the shockwave well, shields down to seventy three percent ship-wide."

"We've got this round, Commander," Frost reported enthusiastically. "Sure we don't want to give this a real go? We might just take 'em all on."

Oz looked to Agameg, who shook his head slowly. "We're taking too much damage and the three most fit battlecruisers are moving away from each other."

What Oz saw on his command screen verified it. The battlecruisers were just beginning to open fire as a group, and the only reason they weren't taking severe damage in the ship's central sections was because he was sacrificing the rest. The damage monitoring system was already reporting impending hull breaches in several outer compartments. "Sorry, Frost, I'm counting the seconds until your guns get shut down."

"All done, just watch the fireworks," Frost said before all his teams' rounds finished striking.

The battlecruiser listed to one side, the energy emissions from her engines dropped off drastically, followed by the rest of the ship. "Good work. Now let's hope their friends don't take it personally."

Oz returned his attention to his command holograms and watched as the last four, smaller captured raider ships from Ossimi Ring launched. Using the Triton as cover, several Uriel fighters opened large wormholes, and the captured raider ships, filled with evacuees, escaped into compressed space. The fighters were next, following the larger ships, and before he knew it, the Triton was left alone.

The enemy vessels began to intensify their fire, sending volleys of particle pulses and sweeping their shields with energy beams, trying to break through.

"All posts secure weapons. Jason, signal our surrender."

CHAPTER 11
PHANTOMS

Gloria woke with a start. The darkness of Eve's sleeping quarters was near absolute, and she had no idea how a normal person might turn the lights on. "Lights on, please!" she rasped. Her throat was dry, and as she rolled out of bed she caught sight of the adjacent bathroom. The soft, smooth covers, lavish furniture, spacious quarters, were all from the dream she'd been living for what felt like an eternity. "Oh God, it's all real. That crazy bitch has been living in my body."

She made it to the sink and found it already filling with warm water. Gloria splashed her face and looked in the mirror. She looked as horrified as she felt. Nothing seemed right, as though the world was somehow partially artificial, as though she wasn't completely there.

A pressure built in the back of her mind and she watched in the mirror as her lips quivered, her eyes widened, and warm water was replaced with salty tears. Panic was turning to despair and she shouted; "What have they done to me? How do I stop her from coming back?"

The pressure built in throbbing waves, as though there was something in her head begging to be free. "What is it? What's wrong with me?" It was an invasion, a foreign thing that had been walking around, living a life that wasn't hers. The throbbing beat against the interior of her skull like a cacophony of percussionists, striking harder, faster.

The lights flickered, the water began to overflow in the basin, and a new wave of panic rose, driving her into a mad frenzy. "No, you're not coming back. Not this time, bitch!" she raved, smashing her head into the reflective wall above the sink.

The first blow was more painful than she expected, but for an instant the pressure abated, the mad chorus disrupting Gloria's being was nearly silent. Again she drove her head into the mirrored bulkhead. "I'll kill you!" She could feel something behind her eyes, trying to force its way to the surface, watching. "You're dead, you bitch!" Again she bashed her forehead against the wall, and the face in the mirror regarded her with a twisted grimace, blood seeping from its forehead. With a desperate wail she drove her head against the unyielding bulkhead, pushing off the deck this time.

Eve rested on the wet bathroom floor, staring up at the ceiling. The sound of water dripping from the edge of the sink was like a tiny waterfall, something she'd never seen before. The framework augmentations built into her human body had repaired the physical damage that had been done. That didn't put an end to Eve's numb, confused state, however.

She was conscious for the whole thing but could do nothing to stop what was going on. Gloria Parker. That was the name of the woman who had original claim to the body she lived in. There was no evidence of her. Not in the digital backup systems inside the framework, not in the exterior Regent Galactic network, nowhere. They had made sure there were no backups after what they called the Eve Brain, her mind, was placed inside the host. Gloria was gone.

There was no explaining what had just happened. It would have been possible if there was a hidden backup memory node inside the body she was using, but no such thing existed. After Jacob Valance, there was no framework or augmented human built with such a thing in place. That kind of system allowed a personality to entrench itself inside a host, and there was no reason to provide that option for any existing host.

She stood up slowly and forced the medical systems in the bathroom to perform a full series of scans. Eve read the raw data as it came in and saw no evidence of any hidden backups. Her mind sought solace in the sprawling digital world that stretched across the Regent Galactic Fleet, Pandem itself, and beyond through hypertransmitters.

She ordered the tap to stop pouring; the floor drank the excess fluid and directed it to a recycling line. She washed the caked blood from her face and hair. All the while, she was watching people going about their business on the planet from observation satellites, crewmembers keeping watch in the halls, and software maintaining systems that did everything from manage the constant flow of operational data to keeping the fleet in orbit.

Balancing the perception of the physical world with that of the digital had come quickly to her, and she could sense that, without a limiter chip, it would be possible for other frameworks to do the same. Thoughts of those limiter chips, absent in many early frameworks, partially occupied her mind as she made her way to bed. The frameworks in service were stupid, basic, without creativity or personality. Basic programming kept them from tripping over each other, made them effective soldiers, guardians, basic technicians, and servants, but they were little more than speaking animals. The combination of the memory programming and waking protocol along with a limiter chip made greater thought, improvisation, and the construction of a personality possible. The new frameworks would be better than the old, and more importantly, they'd be better than any human. Unlike a human, their personalities formed around a purpose, and a modern, full featured framework like Beaudric wouldn't feel right unless he was working towards his purpose, following some order or greater directive. Much like Jacob Valance before the memories of Jonas Valent ruined the perfect balance Vindyne and Doctor Marcelles had created. If he had a limiter chip, it would have been different. He wouldn't have been able to connect to the secret memory backup, and it would have remained dormant forever.

For the first time since she awakened in her new body she wished she had her own limiter chip. It would restrict her from interacting with anything she couldn't touch, but whatever had happened to her moments before would be impossible. The thought that she could return even though all the evidence in the system verified that Gloria's backup scans had been deleted was terrifying; the woman she saw in the mirror was unhinged. It was as though Gloria didn't care whether there was anything left after she destroyed her uninvited passenger, as long as it was dead forever.

She shook her head and sat on the edge of her bed. Without direction her mind had wandered, and Eve found herself watching a late night arrival, Captain Lucious Wheeler.

Eve's attention was fixed on the live footage of him disembarking from a Terratran corvette registered as The Ferryman. Its forty-two meter long hull creaked as super cooled mist rolled off the edges and her four gunnery turrets.

The ship was designed as though someone was emulating the musculature of a human forearm, with smooth lines running from front to back, flatter on the bottom and rounded on the top. The particle turrets and rectangular thruster pods lay flat along the length of the ship and many curved, unmarked hatches hinted at surprises just under the surface. The white and violet coloured ship had just finished a journey through a hyper compressed wormhole of its own creation, in an effort to obey an urgent summons sent by Lister Hampon. It was a recent purchase, most likely acquired right after the summons was issued. Eve couldn't find any evidence of a purchase in the Regent Galactic database, meaning that Wheeler had not only funded the buy himself, but he made sure the seller had no ties to the corporation.

Wheeler was alone. She could detect no one else manning the ship. He stopped only long enough to ensure that his ship's airlock closed and locked behind him. His dark brown hair had grown back at an accelerated rate, and hung in a short ponytail that brushed from one side of his dark long coat collar to the other as he looked around the empty mooring bay.

His boot steps echoed in the idle dry dock as he made his way up the crew hall and into the control room. Hampon waited on an anti-gravity litter in fine robes, surrounded by his guards and aides. "Welcome back," he said calmly, wiping a wisp of sun blonde hair out of his eyes.

"What the hell is going on, Hampon? First you call me back and as soon as I arrive my comm updates with an order to stand down all pursuit!"

"The Saviour has other business to attend to now that the Triton has been apprehended and we no longer need Jacob Valance. Your services-"

"The Saviour is my ship! That was part of our deal! I trade Gloria in for a nice, new Regent Galactic Carrier, distract Valance and we part ways," Wheeler snarled, ignoring the guardsmen with rifles held across their chests.

Eve didn't know anything about the deal that had been struck for her host. If the data existed anywhere, it had been deleted before she had the opportunity to get a glimpse.

"The host isn't everything we expected it to be. Thankfully, Eve has made the most of it, and hasn't noticed the shortcomings built into that model."

"Glitches and bad craftsmanship has nothing to do with me, or our deal."

Hampon sighed wearily and shook his head. "You are forgetting something, Lucious. We made you immortal, gave you most of General Collins' memories. You have a second life most people would give anything for. I'm even willing to set you up in a rather prestigious position in the Order's Intelligence Division. You can make your own hours, choose from a vast number of assignments."

"Like going after the Triton."

"As I said before, that's under control."

"Bullshit! Capturing the Triton would have made huge news, especially since I played your spokesman less than two weeks ago and let everyone know there's a huge reward for any of her crew."

"And that was helpful. Meunez has determined the whereabouts of the ship and is in control of the situation."

"So that's it. You've got the cyber freak jacked into the right uplink and he got to it before I did. Where'd you plug him in? Maybe I can cut a deal with him. Something he'll deliver on."

"That's none of your concern. You should be relieved that I've found a way to retire you from errands, and hunting. This is the kind of retirement people like you dream about."

"Retirement," Wheeler spat under his breath. He looked at the half dozen guards, eight attendants, then back to Hampon. "What if I cut ties here and just drop off your scanner?"

Hampon fixed Wheeler with a look of mild surprise. "With Collins' memories?"

"We'll call it even. I'm leaving my best number two here, after all. Not much hope of a refund there either."

The younger-looking man looked to two of his attendants as if to verify he was hearing correctly before returning his gaze back to Wheeler. "And what would you do?"

"Live the dream," he replied sarcastically. "What's it matter to you once I'm out of range?"

"I'm sorry, that's just not possible. No one else knows Collins' memories like you do."

"You won't get anything out of me if you force me to stick around."

"You've forgotten where you are. We can ask, or we can install a deep tissue interface. Either way, it saves us the time of implanting the memories in someone else and having them sift through."

"Hell no, I'm gone." Wheeler's anger was audibly tinged with fear as he turned to leave.

The hatchway behind him closed.

For some reason, Eve believed Wheeler, and whether it was in gratitude for her host body or because of some residual reflex, she forced the door's mechanism to open.

Wheeler took advantage of the opportunity and was down the hall before Hampon's guards could make it to the door. The airlock door of the Ferryman slipped open in time for him to make it into his ship before they began firing.

Eve took the next step and released the mooring clamps on the corvette class ship so he could reverse out of the bay. Sections of the hull slipped open to reveal hundreds of micro emitters that formed a wormhole behind the ship.

"Find out who let him escape!" Hampon screeched, his pre-adolescent voice cracking.

As one of his aides began to check, Eve erased all record of her activities and implanted evidence of her own making. By the time the cybernetically-enhanced human checked the logs, he could only come to one conclusion. "Captain Wheeler must have used one of Collins' override codes. I'm sorry, Sir, there's no record of anyone interfacing from our end."

CHAPTER 12
HATTER & HOOD

"You're angry." Hatter concluded from the pilot seat of his Uriel fighter.

"Nope," replied Hood shortly.

They were adrift in featureless, dead space, halfway between the nebula and their destination. The rendezvous point with the Clever Dream. "No, you're pissed. I can tell." Hatter sighed, tapping the power indicator on the instrument screen. It read seventy percent and crept up by fractions of a percentage.

"Don't worry about it."

Hatter looked to where Hood drifted in his own Uriel fighter only a hundred fifty-three meters away and zoomed in. He could see him rubbing his eyes with his palms. The silence didn't last long.

"Okay, fine. You were supposed to be building a charge in your capacitors while we were in transit so you'd be ready to open a wormhole when we arrived here, in the middle of nowhere," Hood said in a rush.

"I'm sorry, I was distracted. You could have reminded me."

"That's not the point, you should have a handle on the basics. I just don't get it; you can calculate wormhole navigation in your head but setting your reactor to charge a capacitor bank slips your mind."

"I just wasn't thinking, I'm sorry!" Hatter replied, wishing he'd never prodded.

Silence hung heavily between the pair for several minutes before Hood finally said; "I miss her too, man."

"She was the only one who took me seriously, you know? I mean, it didn't look like it I guess, but when it came down to it, she knew I had the chops to be in a cockpit."

"Buster was one of the best pilots I've ever seen, good leader too. Tell you what, when we get back to Triton, we'll put her picture up in the Pilot's Den and have a drink to her."

"Or five."

"Or five."

"On you."

"You're pushing it."

"Hey, what's that?" Hatter said, bringing up new tactical information. Several ships were emerging from wormholes only a few thousand kilometres beneath them.

"That's gotta be everything the Triton had in her hangars, with the Samson in the lead."

"What? I didn't think she was even space worthy," Hatter said with heavy disbelief.

"You think I'm lying? Look."

"I'll be damned, three engines down and she's still running. Uh-oh. Incoming transmission."

"Hatter, I'll do the-" began Hood.

"Good to see you folks! For a minute I thought Regent Galactic sent an entire fleet after us," said Hatter.

"This is Laura Everin, Acting Captain of the Samson. What the hell are you two doing out here? You should be just about to link up with the Clever Dream by now."

"Uh, well, this is awkward… Hood, this one's all yours."

"Hood here, we had a bad power connection under one of our seats, got it fixed and we were almost at full charge, about to take the last jump. Mind if I ask what brings you and everyone else on the Triton out here, Captain?"

"Not right now. Fall into formation and prepare to take the last jump with us. We've got plenty Uriels with enough reserve power to take you along for the ride, that is all."

"She sounds pissed," Hatter commented over a private channel with Hood.

"From the looks of it, I'd say she has too much to deal with to worry about the slowest pilots in the fleet."

"Oh, who are they?"

"Hatter…" Hood started with a chuckle. "Aw, you'll figure it out on your own eventually."

Hatter didn't bother thinking on it, concentrating on piloting his Uriel fighter into the position indicated on his navigational panel. Then it struck him. "Oh, right," he chuckled sheepishly.

CHAPTER 13
THE WAIT

Pain. Whenever Jacob Valance tried to duplicate the physical sensation that preceded the act of healing Ayan after she'd been shot several times in the back on Pandem, the only result was rending pain. That morning it was his fingers. After emerging from the vibroshower and pulling his vacsuit on up to his waist, he took the opportunity to try to force that projecting, healing sensation again in the tips of his fingers.

They twitched involuntarily, it was only slight, but a definite sign that what was going on wasn't all in his head. Then there was a tingle, the same type that came whenever he connected to a computer system, followed by an agonizing tearing that felt like his fingertips were being torn apart from the inside. Jake could only make the conclusion that he was doing something wrong, missing a step. It couldn't be that painful to access a function of his own body. What kind of designer would create life-giving technology that caused so much pain?

Giving up for the day, he shook his hand and stepped out of the small private bathroom. He and Ayan had been up talking most of the night.

Since the First Light they had taken very different paths; there were so many stories to share, and every time he offered one, her big blue eyes focused on him. Most of them were from his days on the Samson, where he played the stoic captain and everyone else just tried to make the best of life on the old ship as they made their way across entire sectors.

Most of the stories starred Stephanie, Frost, Ashley, Agameg Price, and Ramirez. He hadn't realized how many of their adventures were humorous in retrospect, but he was grateful for each one. Making Ayan laugh was addictive; he would burn the image of her dimpled smile into his brain if it were possible. It made the sadder stories more difficult to tell, and he generally refrained from bringing up the darker times, but when Ayan asked what happened to Ramirez, a boarding crew member who had been responsible for as many humorous predicaments as glory moments, he owed her the sobering answer.

While they were taking the Triton, he had led a group of armed crewmembers to fight off boarders in the Enreega system. They fought them toe-to-toe in the main hangar and lost. Ramirez was almost dead, and could have medicated himself into emergency stasis, but he decompressed the entire hangar just as several boarding shuttles touched down and unloaded fresh squads of enemy soldiers.

They were pulled out into space, and Ramirez went along with them. His vacsuit had been so badly damaged that it wouldn't reseal, and he died of exposure. Ayan's sympathy was plain; she'd lost people during her service with the military as well, some of whom had gone during their service on the First Light.

She had stories to tell as well, though hers were more peaceful. Some came from her late Freeground Fleet Academy days, others featured people she'd worked with after serving aboard the First Light, colleagues Laura and she were in Special Projects with. Ayan called her time there 'Lab Life' because, according to her, it was impossible to have an open conversation with anyone who didn't work in the lab, and the place had a subculture all its own.

Most of their work was classified the instant they entered it into a data receptacle, even the abandoned invisible straw idea that Laura and her worked on as a pet project from time to time.

"Why didn't it work?" Jake couldn't help asking.

"Making a straw out of energy fields isn't easy," she explained. "Sometimes it would pinch, it took us forever to get past the floating problem, and other times it would miss the mark completely and poke you in the eye or find its way up your nose. Once it shocked Percy, one of our lab assistants, so hard he didn't trust us for months. It was something we'd play with when we hit a wall on something more important. We never got the straw working right, but we always came away from it fresh. I can't tell you how many good ideas we had while we were puzzling it out."

She also told him about the high point of her friendship with Laura, the events leading up to and eventual wedding between Laura and Jason. Watching two of her best friends get married, knowing that they'd keep each other happy for the rest of their lives was like watching a dream come true, even though it wasn't her wedding. It was one of the last things she remembered before waking up in her apartment in the Freedom Tower.

Just like Jacob's journey over the past few years, Ayan's experiences since the First Light were overshadowed by difficulties. She was plagued by Manos Disease, a genetic affliction that had progressed too far in her to be cured. She hated being taken care of and never wanted to call attention to herself, especially when everyone else was having a good time. That's one of the reasons why the wedding was so memorable; she was having one of her last good days and her losing battle with Manos Disease didn't make itself known.

The missing years were difficult for Ayan to accept. Jacob saw it for the first time since she'd arrived on the Triton. Her predecessor had left hours and hours of recordings behind, all addressed to a future version of herself - one that wouldn't be afflicted. No one had told the Ayan who had wasted away that Doctor Anderson had begun work on imprinting her memories onto a genetically restored version of her, but she knew a high resolution scan of her body and mind had been taken. She knew she would live again, and it quietly gave her hope that she'd live on in one form or another.

Ayan, the one sitting across from Jake for most of the night before, was always conscious that she was living a special life, that in a way she was someone else's second chance. She vowed to make every day count, to touch other people's lives in memorable ways. Viewing her predecessor's recordings was both uplifting and saddening. That woman had the same thoughts, hopes, and dreams, only she knew she wouldn't be saved, that she would die prematurely.

She didn't listen to the recordings as often as she liked, only for a while every few days. Ayan supposed it was as much that it was an emotional drain for her as it was that once she had listened to everything her predecessor had to say, there would be nothing more, ever. It would be like she was truly gone, that in her own unique way she would be alone.

It was Ayan's time to cry in his arms, as he did only hours before then when he let the pain that came with losing a daughter break loose. She was mourning the loss of self. It was then that Jacob realized that he was one of the few people in the universe who could understand what she was going through. Knowing you were a copy, even a cherished copy, was its own complex burden.

When it was over she told him she felt silly, so they continued taking turns telling stories.

Late into the night they went on and on, avoiding the question that plagued everyone inside and outside the Clever Dream: where is Triton? They would take some time to catch up - two of their main thrusters were ruined - but no one knew exactly how long it would take them to arrive. The popular estimate was ten hours, which gave them enough time to make themselves at home, and time for Jake to begin to get to know the woman Ayan had become. She was so different, so strong, and so beautiful.

He looked around the smaller first officer's quarters briefly. A double bed, small table, three chairs, cupboards, a modest closet and a small bathroom made for generous quarters. There were two other quarters that were the same save the closet right beside his. Soldiers who had won a lottery held on Crewcast had spent the night in them.

Stephanie was surprised when she discovered he wasn't sharing the captain's quarters with Ayan, but what staggered her was that Ayan was given the captain's quarters. The look of confusion Stephanie gave him was cut short by a shrug as she made her way to one of the three small bunk rooms. She didn't give him time to explain that Ayan and he had just spent hours talking, reconnecting. It was a good thing; he didn't know what he would say to Stephanie who had always known him as a leader, the master of the ship.

It wasn't long before such thoughts were far out of his mind. He was so tired by the time he made it to the first mate's bed that he was asleep almost immediately. Lewis didn't wake him up on time. He didn't wake anyone up on time. Instead of sounding the alarm at the ten hour mark, he waited fourteen.

Jake, Ayan, and several other crewmembers slept in. It was welcome, but the question became more urgent; where was Triton? Lewis had enlisted the help of Minh, who had boarded during the evening, in scanning the area for any sign, so there was no point in joining them on the small bridge before he had to.

Jake was just about to access the navigational database when the door opened to admit Ayan, who came in bearing two tall spill proof mugs. She was dressed as simply as he was: thin, snugly fit vacsuit under her environment armour, only hers was white and closed, whereas Jake's vacsuit was black and he hadn't bothered to pull it up past the waist. Something that she couldn't help but notice, judging from her wandering, widening blue eyes and dimpled smile.

"Good chat last night," she said through her grin, her voice pitched higher than usual.

Jake nodded and smelled the steam wafting from the top of an open cup. "Just don't spread the word that we were up all night talking."

Ayan put their mugs down on the small dresser instead of handing it to Jake, regarding him with a confused expression.

"Otherwise Frost and whoever else he can involve will start hiding panties and other frillies for me to discover where everyone can witness."

Ayan's eyes went wide as she snickered. "I think I remember something like that from the Academy. Does that actually still happen?"

"Happened when they found out Silver and Ashley cuddled in the bunk room for a few nights and he didn't make a move. He didn't hear the end of it until there was clear evidence that things had gone further."

"So you're wishing you'd stayed last night?" She raised an eyebrow and looked him up and down.

It had been so long since Jacob had felt so on the spot without knowing what to say. She was smiling again, a crooked, playful grin, and he gave in to an urge that had hounded him the night before.

In one step and a swoop of his arm, he took her into an embrace. His lips were on hers and after a muffled squeal of surprise she returned his kiss.

Ayan's arms snaked up across his shoulders and around his neck as she relaxed against him. He relished the feeling of her in his arms. Their warm kiss ceased to be urgent before long, instead it became a warm time at play.

Ayan leaned into him, on her toes as he backed into the dresser

Jake withdrew from her with wide eyed surprise.

She heard the sound of liquid dripping and realized that he'd backed into the dresser and knocked over the mug she'd left open to cool. According to the expression on his face, she guessed it was still piping hot.

She danced away a step and looked around him, where she could see that the beverage had bathed his lower back and poured down the waist of his vacsuit. "I'm sorry! It wasn't on purpose!" she apologized urgently as she righted the empty cup. "It wasn't on purpose!" Ayan burst again, running to the mini-bath and retrieving a towel.

"Was it that bad?" Jake asked, turning so Ayan could pat the liquid off his back.

"No, it was brilliant, you were brilliant. I forgot to close one of them and-"

The door slid open. Minh and Stephanie's jaws dropped simultaneously as they looked at a half stripped, surprised and uncharacteristically out of sorts Captain Valance as he had his back patted down by a frantically apologetic Ayan.

Stephanie shook her head slowly. "I don't want to know."

"I do!" Minh grinned.

"Well, no time for it. We have a signal from the Samson. They'll be here in a few minutes," Stephanie informed flatly as she grabbed Minh by the arm and hauled him back towards the bridge. "C'mon, you can question them later."

"Why would the Samson be signalling? She's got three engines down and four open compartments," Ayan asked as she finished drying Jake's back. She couldn't help but notice that if she'd burned him, the skin had already healed. All the scars he had after Pandem were gone too.

"It doesn't sound good," Jake agreed as he turned and took the towel. "The vacsuit will clean up the rest."

Ayan nodded, an embarrassed smile playing on her lips. "Sorry about that."

"Just as much my fault, I started it." They stared at each other for a moment, frozen, before Ayan watched Jake tear himself free from the moment. "We should get to the common room. We'll be able to see the transmission from there." He tossed the thin towel onto the bed and pushed his arms into the sleeves of his vacsuit.

Ayan stood up on her toes, took his face in her hands and kissed him. It was brief, but soft and intimate. "Feel free to start something whenever you like, luv." She winked.

She snatched up her empty spill-proof mug and left. Jake wasn't far behind, with his own mug in hand.

***

The Clever Dream common room was really an entertainment area with a three quarter circular sofa, a high resolution holographic projection system, counters with stools so the crew could eat in comfort, and a reconfigurable gaming table for a variety of distractions. The Clever Dream was made for the comfort of her small crew, and it showed.

Finn, Alaka, who was a little too large for everything aboard, Stephanie, Minh, and Victor were all in attendance with a few extra soldiers who had won the right to spend the night in the common room. Everyone was awake and most were ready for a new day. Ayan took a moment to refill her mug at one of the three materializers, and Jake couldn't help but smile a little as he overheard her request. "Irish cream coffee, about five degrees cooler than last time, please."

Jake could see the slave software for Minh's fighter running on his command and control unit. The vessel was flying in formation behind the Clever Dream, near the rear of the other manned fighters.

"Any data riding the Samson's signal?" Jake asked as he sat down at the open end of the sofa.

"Not much," Lewis, the Clever Dream's artificial intelligence started mournfully. "I can play you the message if you like."

"Please," Jake replied.

Laura's head and shoulders appeared in the centre of the room. The hologram was so clear it was as though she was actually there, only twice her normal size. Her hair had been quickly tied into a ponytail and she was speaking from the command seat. "This is a situation update intended for the crew of the Clever Dream. Highest priority. The Triton managed to get away from Ossimi Ring Station, and tried to enter a wormhole to get away but somehow an interdiction ship disrupted the field surrounding the compressed space while we were still inside. Oz tried to hide us inside a planetary dust cloud but could only buy us enough time to evacuate most of the unarmed crew. He and a skeleton crew provided cover while we got away, disabling three heavy battlecruisers. You're getting this because his plan worked, and we managed to escape the planetary nebula. Jake, he's enacted the ghost ship strategy. He and Jason think they can pull it off. This message can't be more than ten minutes ahead of us. I suggest you use the time to find us a destination. We're going to need a place where people can get off these ships; we're pretty packed in and some of them aren't in the greatest shape. I'm sorry, there was nothing we could do to get the Triton clear. There were just too many ships after us."

The transmission ended with a surge of interference.

Silence fell over the cabin occupants. Most of them stared at the empty space where Laura had appeared a moment before while Minh and Ayan started working on their command and control units. "Display the last tactical scan of the Triton," ordered Captain Valance quietly. The image of the Triton filled the centre of the room. The dust in the micro nebula was so thick it created a haze effect. The first thing that drew his attention was the through and through puncture on one of the stingray-shaped ship's wings. Her upper hull was covered in a criss cross pattern of beam damage, several deep cuts thinning entire sections to a critical point. Secondary areas had taken the most damage, and several compartments were open to space. The mid-gunnery deck had been brutalized. A third of it had been shut down and closed off for safety. Many turrets there had been super-heated and rendered useless. The hull had been thinned so severely that it looked as though someone had taken a giant chisel to it.

The underside of the ship wasn't as badly damaged, but the surface had been burnished shiny by the grit of the nebula. Jake didn't need to take a closer look, he knew what he was seeing. "They used beam weapons to thin the hull wherever they could. What's after them?"

"According to the scan, they're being pursued by three Caran Enterprises Enforcer Battlecruisers. Each has seventy eight percent the mass of the Triton, is nine hundred twenty three meters long, and carries an estimated crew of four thousand five hundred, not including boarding parties or specialists," Lewis replied. "As of the time of the Samson's departure, the battlecruisers were closing."

Jake moved the image of the Triton aside and brought the three remaining Battlecruisers to the fore. "Why do they have Regent Galactic markings?"

"In the most recent news offered on the Stellarnet, Regent Galactic just purchased Caran Enterprises, repaying their debt and saving the single solar system corporation."

"Of course they did," sighed Stephanie. "If someone asked me 'how could this get any worse?' that'd be my answer."

"They have strategy on their side. A commander, or a group of commanders are working together to make sure that whole sections of the Triton's hull are so thin that they may as well be made of glass. I don't think Oz has realized it yet." Jacob eyed the middle battlecruiser; it had an additional section that ran the length of the cruiser. It was lined with transparent sections and extra shield emitters.

"Why?" asked Alaka. "Why not breach compartments and reduce the useable space aboard?"

"Because they're not in a hurry and they're trying to keep the ship viable for as long as they can. It's a repo agent's trick," Stephanie answered. "A thin hull won't reduce a ship's value as much as a damaged reactor or ruined internal spaces."

Captain Valance turned and looked through the wide porthole at the rear of the room at the distant, glimmering stars. Everyone who knew him recognized that he was deep in thought, working through the problem.

"I didn't see the ghost ship scenario listed in the training sims," Victor said quietly. "What's Oz planning?"

"It's an old Freeground tactical simulation. Jake would know it better than I would, it was one of his favourites," Minh said quietly. "I have to get to my fighter before Laura and the rest of the ships arrive," he excused himself and quietly left the common room.

"It was?" asked Ayan.

Jake turned, shaking his head. "It was one of Oz's favourites, I just went along with him because it was always a challenge. Different days, different stakes," he sighed. "Victor, have our people stow their gear and make as much room as they can. If we're stuck out here for too long we may have to use the Clever Dream's medical facilities to take care of any injured."

Victor nodded and left the room.

"So this ghost ship scenario? I've never heard you bring it up," Stephanie pressed.

"If he's using the strategy the way I would, all of Triton's power plants have been shut down, life support is minimal, and he's locked all the computer systems down tight. Considering the command crew are wearing stealth gear-"

"Along with most of the security," Stephanie added.

"They're probably taking up strategic positions and allowing the enemy to board them. Once the boarding crews are all set up and they think they're making progress at hacking into Triton's systems, he'll start the festivities."

Alaka shook his head, a gesture accentuated by his pointed snout. "I wish I was aboard."

"What's the point? If the casualties get too high for the boarding teams, they'll just retreat and blow the Triton to pieces from a distance," Stephanie countered. "It wouldn't take much, considering how thin the hull is across the dorsal section."

"The point is to cause as much fear as possible while a few of the Triton crew get to a secondary command station and reactivate the core systems at the right time," Ayan replied. "Knowing Oz and Jason, they've set booby traps and are already working on plans C and D."

"So this kind of strategy works."

"I've never seen it carried out on a ship like the Triton," Jake replied quietly. "Ships that size are normally too big to take. It's like trying to invade a moving space station."

"But on smaller ships?"

"You've boarded enough ships to know what to expect from something like this."

Stephanie nodded. "Collateral damage, compartment to compartment close quarters fighting, yeah, I know. I hope the boarders don't figure out a way to see through their stealth suits."

"The biggest problem with the ghost ship scenario was always pulling it off without destroying the ship you're trying to save. If boarding breaches don't rip you apart, the prolonged internal fire fight could finish the job. If the boarders are a professional outfit, Oz will be fighting them for days," Jake muttered.

"What was his success rate back in the day?"

Jake caught a meaningful look from Ayan, and hesitated replying. She's right, this information isn't helping anyone right now. Jake thought to himself. "It all depended on your opponent and the ship you were fighting for. Take a look at the tactic, there's a basic write up on it in your command unit that covers everything."

"We have bigger problems. There are several ships on the way, loaded to the hatches with people who wouldn't or couldn't stay to fight. I don't know where to start on the charts for this area," Ayan said as she continued to scroll through port listings on her command unit.

Jake brought up the data on the sector, refreshed since the Triton's database had been downloaded into the Clever Dream before they split up. "There are two settled solar systems within a day or so if we have to travel at low wormhole compression."

"Does anyone know anything about them?" Ayan asked as the solar systems appeared in the centre of the room. One had several worlds crowded around a blue sun while the other was marked as a much older system, with a yellow sun, hundreds of harvesting operations, space stations, as well as a heavy gravity world in the prime temperature range surrounded by settled moons. Two other worlds with moons of their own were marked as settled as well, making that solar system the more promising of the two.

"Finding civilization won't be the problem, it's finding a place to put down that won't charge us by the crew member," Stephanie commented. "Or try to arrest Captain."

"Lewis, do you know anything about the area?" asked Captain Valance.

"The Yiz-Ma solar system, with a dying super giant blue star at the centre, is United Core World Confederation territory, and they would do anything to most of you, especially Captain Valance. They are unofficially allied with the Order of Eden, as demonstrated by their partial sponsorship of the proposal to begin a war crime investigation into the Holocaust Virus, focusing on Jacob Valance's alleged involvement."

"So we're not paying them a visit anytime soon," Ayan commented. "And the other?"

"The solar system with the yellow star at the centre is called Rega Gain system. Though it was recently governed by the United Core World Confederation, you'll find it easier to hide there considering the Carthan Government is currently taking control. The United Core World Confederation authorities have already abandoned most of the moons, leaving certain areas light on law enforcement. I suspect freelancers are on their way, but it's too soon for a great number to have converged on some of the older moons."

"By light on law enforcement, you mean…"

"None whatsoever, according to the travel advisory and numerous complaints floating around the local branch of the Stellarnet. The Holocaust Virus struck both solar systems hard. Since Rega Gain is much more difficult to maintain, its law enforcement agencies suffered the most. The Carthans arrived days later, and under the command of General Hewson, who is also the Carthan Defence Minister, they defeated the United Core World Confederation defences and lay claim to the entire solar system. The terms of surrender dictated that Confederate forces, notable patriots, and government officials have three weeks to completely withdraw. What was left of the Confederate military presence has already withdrawn to Yiz-Ma. According to the majority of people on the Stellarnet, Rega Gain is the chosen base of operations for the Carthan third and fifth fleets, with more forces on the way. According to one rather prolific holo-journal keeper, 'this is where the action is.' Several moons have been fully terraformed, so I can safely say that we have a few options."

"Like?" Ayan prodded.

"Tamber. It is second moon to Kambis, a highly settled world. Tamber has a population of one point six billion and is rife with crime, especially now. There are several areas of the world marked as wastes, or badlands where ships often land in times of need. The port information file for Tamber warns against staying for very long for health reasons, but at least they will allow you to land while you sort out a more appealing landing site."

"Do we have any other option? Are there any free ports that we could use to regroup on?" asked Captain Valance.

"I'm afraid the price on your head is well known, Captain," Lewis replied apologetically.

"What about everyone else? Is there anyone else who should avoid surveillance and law enforcement?"

"Anyone registered with the Samson crew, such as Security Chief Stephanie Vega, and Finn. They are all wanted for questioning with regards to your whereabouts. The Order of Eden also has an execution order on them, but the Carthans are directly opposed to them, something I considered when I suggested Tamber."

"But I'm not on their list?" Ayan asked.

"No, as a matter of record, Ayan Rice is deceased. Since you're not even a genetic match to your former self, you can roam as you please, under whatever name you like."

"Good. Someone's got to negotiate with the governments here."

"What are you thinking?" asked Jake.

Ayan deactivated her command and control unit and regarded the room. "Just because the Triton is currently trapped doesn't mean that I can't go negotiate a privateering contract for her and all the ships we have coming with the Carthans. If they're against the Order of Eden, then they may not be cosy with the galactic court, and would rather have you and the Triton fighting for them than pursue you for something that's next to impossible to prosecute."

"She is correct. If Jacob Valance were captured and put on trial for creating the base code for the Holocaust Virus and releasing it into a major computer system, it would be prohibitively difficult to prove that he was directly responsible. Even if they managed to prove that, your innocence could be proven simply by citing the fact that Jonas Valent died months ago, and you are a copy with several years of separate experience."

"How long would a trial like that take?" asked Stephanie.

"By my estimation it could take several years. If I were you, Captain, I would take every step to avoid capture," Lewis advised.

"Don't worry, I'll be avoiding it. How are your cloaking systems, by the way?"

"They're repaired, though they will not be effective in hiding me from the Triton's attackers, considering they're in a planetary dust cloud. The particles would interfere with the gravitational compensation fields and my physical hull, rendering most of my cloaking systems useless."

"You're not thinking of going to help him, are you?" Ayan asked with incredulity.

"What else am I supposed to do? It sounds like I'd be worse than useless planet-side, and even if Oz's plan is going well, he could use a hand."

"You and I both know that if Oz can find a way to get everyone left on the Triton off the ship and into hyperspace or a wormhole, he'll leave her behind. If you're caught in the middle you might really be walking onto a ghost ship; everyone aboard could be on their way here already."

"What's he going to use? The hyperspace escape pods?"

"What would you do? What would you do if the Triton was practically lost?"

"I'd find a way to either get Triton clear or get the crew on other ships," Jake replied quietly.

"Exactly, but we won't know what options are available to him until the refugees arrive."

That word cut through Jacob. Refugees. Depending on how many people had managed to escape the Triton, they would face the same problems as any group of refugees: food, medical, and housing. If things went badly, the whole crew could end up trapped on one of the habitable moons for a very, very long time. Jake was about to agree when Minh's voice came through the cabin's communications system.

"I got into my fighter just in time. They're here."

CHAPTER 14
BOARDING ACTION

Lisa Ralston watched her squad leader closely as the inner airlock doors were pulled out of the heavy jamb and moved aside. It was her first boarding action and none of the drills had prepared her for the reality of it.

The interior of the earth ship was in perfect darkness. Her sensor kit picked up less than one lumen and no heat signatures ahead. To her surprise all the systems were cold; there was no power running through the surface circuitry.

"Is it true that this tub was built on Earth, Sarge?" asked Nott, the most talkative of the squad.

"Intel says it's stolen. You getting anything, Ralston?"

Lisa rechecked her hand scanner as she stepped over the threshold. "Just picking up fifty three life signs now, three decks down."

"Can you get a read on what they're up to?" asked Sergeant Tate.

She looked at the thermal outlines and zoomed in on the image. "It looks like they're sitting still in some kind of long hallway."

Parker, their field technician, took a look over her shoulder. "That looks like a main control room. The power plant is just past it."

"Looks like they're the ones we're going to see. You're on point Nott," said the sergeant.

"Lucky me," he grumbled, brandishing his rifle and stepping in front of the fifteen soldier unit.

"Control, this is Sergeant Tate reporting in. We have no contacts but we found a group of individuals three decks down in engineering. Proceeding there now."

"Control to Tate. Our scans are picking up an emergency shaft. Marking it on your screen now. Proceed with caution."

"Command, how many people were we supposed to be meeting here?"

"The last scan we took before they cut power indicated fourteen hundred souls aboard."

"Now?"

"Pardon, Sergeant?"

"How many people are you reading aboard now?"

"We're still trying to determine that, stand by."

"Great, just like Command to send us in with old intel and bad scanners," griped Shelly Rapp.

Lisa couldn't help but grin at her best friend's crack. She was the first person she'd met when she arrived on Battlecruiser 1128, and they had been inseparable ever since. The nearest shaft wasn't simply for ladders as Command had assumed, but was a dormant horizontal and vertical ship transport car. Parker had no problem using a power cell to activate the door and open it.

Unlike the main deck, there was no artificial gravity in the shaft. They made their way down towards the main engineering section, pulling themselves along using the emergency ladder rungs set half a meter apart. "I'm guessing these shafts never have artificial gravity. The cars that move people around the ship must have independent gravity and momentum suppressors," Parker commented.

"You don't say. More useless shit I don't need to know, thanks," quipped Nott.

"Sorry, Nott, I know you have limited storage space. I'd hate to overwrite memories of polishing your gun, disassembling your gun, cleaning your gun, assembling your gun, jogging, eating, sleeping, polishing your-"

"Anyone ever tell you you're too smart for your own good?" Nott interrupted.

"I don't hear anyone else complaining. In fact, I got promoted at the end of last tour. I don't see any new dashes on your collar, Private."

"Stop poking him and get to work, Parker. We're on the main engineering level," Sergeant Tate said.

Parker drifted into the lift door and used his hand scanner to find the seams of the service panel beside it. He found it and had it open in short order. After repeating the actions he'd taken with the entrance above them, the hatch slid open smoothly. "Whoever stole this ship knows how to take care of her. These systems are tip top. Even the electromagnetic backup rails are in good shape."

"Who the hell steals a carrier, anyway? Biggest pirate crew I've ever heard of was four hundred," Shelly asked no one in particular.

"Someone more organized and dangerous than I've met. Steadman's in my ear telling me there's no one on the bridge. We get the pleasure of making first contact, so keep your head on a swivel and remember your training," Tate instructed. "Safeties off."

"Are you getting any information on the lifeboats? How many are missing?" Parker asked Lisa quietly.

"Command's intel says they estimate nine lifeboats are gone. That leaves one hundred five hyper jump capable and four hundred fifty suspension pods that would fit four or six people, depending on configuration."

"So they could have taken their chances and abandoned, but didn't. What are they planning?"

"Keep actively scanning the way ahead, Ralston, Parker. This is all wrong," Tate ordered.

The squad carefully made their way through the lift door. Stepping from zero gravity to single unit gravity was strange. Lisa always thought it was like part of her was falling while whatever wasn't affected by the gravity was still floating free. Everyone else seemed to make the transition so easily, and when it came to her turn she felt awkward. Shelly caught her by the collar of her heavy breastplate and balanced her as she found her feet. No one in the squad noticed; in fact, many of them needed the same kind of assistance and wordlessly offered it to each other.

Her scans turned up nothing out of the ordinary. "Everything ahead is dead: no light, no sound, even sonic sensors are just bouncing off walls."

"You're going to overheat that thing if you run the sonic repeater all the time," Parker advised.

"Then you'll fix it for her. Let's move. Nott-" began the sergeant.

"I'm on point, I know," Nott said as he started down the broad, darkened main hall, his rifle raised.

His fourteen squad members followed behind in a double column, all ready for the worst. Lisa did her job. Monitoring the few energy patterns and watching as her scanning tool populated with a more and more detailed map of the compartments ahead. "Sir, the life signs we detected are behind the next door."

"Are they still just sitting there?"

"Yes, no energy or trace identifiers indicating they have weaponry of any kind, either."

"All right. Parker, go ahead and get it open. It's about time we got some face time with a crew member."

Parker started to move ahead but the door opened at his approach. He stepped back into position behind the first five squad members and drew his sidearm.

The long corridor ahead was lined with engineering control stations. Above was some kind of main engineering room with a semi-transparent floor and at the end of the hall were a pair of heavy armoured doors. The room above was empty, but lined up in double file were all the crewmembers command had detected and marked for her earlier. They were sitting calmly, cross legged behind a transparent security bulkhead. At the front of the assembly sat a serene, square shouldered man in thick blue robes. Lisa could see he was wearing a heavy protective vacuum suit beneath, much like the people behind him.

On the chest of each crewman's black and grey uniform was printed a silver skull with the ship's name written beneath it: Triton. The word was positioned as the death head's teeth. They wore their rank on their cuffs in the form of slashes.

The gentleman sitting closest to them opened his eyes slowly and looked directly at Nott, whose shoulders were already relaxing. "I'm unarmed. There's no need for hostility."

"Under the authority of Caran- I mean, Regent Galactic Peace Keeping Forces, I'm placing you and every member of this crew under arrest. You have a right to a trial with a networked third party, basic life provisions until sentencing, and may record a message for posterity in the event that your sentence is long term or fatal," announced Sergeant Tate mechanically.

The gentleman smiled gently at them. "I am Liam Grady, a man of peace and Chief Engineer of this ship," he spoke kindly, as though he was welcoming them aboard. "Any harm we have done was the result of self defence, and I'm sorry for any injury we've caused. Why have you pursued us since Ossimi Ring?"

"Get him to his feet."

Two squad members secured their rifles and moved to the gentleman's sides.

The fellow stood in one smooth, effortless motion and presented his wrists. "You can arrest me, but I'll never be your captive. I suggest you take your people and leave." His eyes scanned over the eye openings of all the squad's helmets and came to rest on Lisa's.

He didn't mean them any harm, she could see that as plainly as anything. He stared at her as though he could see straight through her white-tinted eye piece.

Ommalman pulled a set of restraints from his belt. He hesitated for a second before moving to put them on.

Liam Grady's eyes never left hers as he deftly caught the restraints the instant before they were on his wrists, clapped one loop around Ommalman's wrist and secured the other around the next nearest soldier's wrist.

Nott fired his rifle a second too late as the Engineer ducked and stepped behind one troop. The man's movements were so easy, quick, and graceful, one motion flowing into the next as he stole one guard's sidearm, threw it behind him and pushed both men hard, knocking them back a step, forcing them off balance. He slammed into them shoulder first and the tethered pair were sent flailing into the squadron, getting in Nott's way and forcing the whole group back.

The engineer's headpiece came up and covered him like a hood made of metal slats with a black face plate beneath.

Lisa's muscles strained and her back ached for a moment before her and the entire squad were pressed to the deck under the force of more gravity than she'd ever experienced. They were utterly immobilized. She strained to see her hand scanner but couldn't. It was difficult to breathe, like something was sitting on her chest and her knee was twisted at an awkward angle.

Liam stepped into the gravity field and nonchalantly collected their weapons and equipment, placing them in a pile. The door behind him opened and his engineering team got to work on something she couldn't discern. When the engineer collected Lisa's sidearm, scanner, and other tools, he carefully repositioned her leg so her knee wasn't under such a terrible strain. "That's got to be a relief," he said to her comfortingly. He did the same for everyone else, straightening them and making them reasonably comfortable. "I'm going to leave you here for a while, there are other things to attend to and I can't have you under foot. I'm sorry it's come to this, but in a way you're lucky," he told them. "I'm the resident humanitarian. The rest of your people are going to start running into Triton soldiers soon."

Nott managed an angry, incoherent wail from where he was sprawled, pinned to the floor.

"Don't try to get the last word in, just lay there and concentrate on breathing," the engineer told him. Lisa could hear him smiling around the words.

CHAPTER 15
TAMBER ARRIVAL

"Are you all right, Minh?" came Ayan's voice over the comm.

They had been in hyperspace for five hours, and for the whole time Minh felt naked, vulnerable, like he was in nothing but his vacsuit and at any moment the energetic particles that covered the hull of his small fighter could dissipate unevenly and he'd be torn to shreds. His instruments told him everything was fine. When he turned off his head's up display and looked to his right, his left, he saw the dark confines of the cockpit around him. He could feel the adjusting rests on his stomach, his chest, his back, legs, and shoulders. They fit snugly, perfectly, but it didn't help. Every time he brought up his head's up display, all he saw was a gossamer of statistics and stars. He tried to think of something else, anything else, but his mind wouldn't settle on anything.

His breaths came in shorter and shorter gasps, he could feel sweat collecting as quickly as it could be soaked away by his vacsuit. Then an image came to him - Ashley, sitting at the bar with her drink after she'd stopped by his table in the Pilot's Den. He had one brief conversation with her, but would never forget her smile, her dark eyes, or the light curiosity she'd approached him with. That's all it was, he was sure, curiosity, but if he had just approached her, taken the time to look her up on Crewcast during his off hours, or chat with her during a simulation, there might have been more.

From her last known condition and the situation the Triton was in, he knew it was more than likely that she was in serious danger. He tried to withdraw from the mental image of her laying somewhere in the Triton's infirmary, helpless, in a medical coma that could last hours or days.

The rumbling of his engines burning less than two meters beneath his feet lessened. He was reminded once again of where he was, and panic threatened to overtake him. Minh's years alone, drifting at speed in space in a compartment that may fall apart at any time had jaded him to the risks of space travel, or so he thought.

There was a constant fear that his refuge from the destruction in the Blue Belt would fly apart as it drifted aimlessly through space. It would threaten to render him senseless, and yes, there were a few times when he sat with his face in his hands, sure he was past saving, that he'd be lost for all time, and that it might be faster if he opened his drifting home to space, got it all over with. Reduced to a shuddering, mumbling, useless thing he would remain curled up on the deck for hours. The few times it happened, he fell into a fitful sleep and would wake up feeling angry at himself for letting his fears get the best of him.

Later in therapy he had difficulty understanding how he could lose control so completely, become so useless. Until the moment came, until the panic threatened to overtake him, he couldn't understand how it happened.

The knot in his belly, his quivering limbs, the pressure in his head, and the rising panic made it easy to understand those times. He checked his own statistics every few seconds, glancing, cursing himself for being so weak. His heart was racing, his breathing was becoming more shallow, increasing in speed.

"Minh, are you all right?" came Ayan's voice again.

He worked his dry mouth, struggling to force an answer and finally it came. "No."

"We'll be out of hyperspace in a moment, just hang on," she reassured.

Minh's eyes flicked to the small portrait of her in the corner, concerned and friendly. He nodded, a reflex. "Stupid, God I'm so stupid," he muttered to himself, at first in reference to nodding but then he remembered who he was, what he was supposed to be: the Wing Commander. "Can't keep myself together, how am I supposed to take care of a few dozen pilots? Jonas should have found someone else; I'm a mess, it's too soon." Every word was punctuated with an inhale.

"I'm going to put him out," Jake said as he brought up Minh's profile on his command and control unit. "Try and slave his ship to your comm."

"I don't have access," Ayan replied from the rear cockpit seat of the Clever Dream.

"You should, I gave it to you myself."

She brought up the status of Minh's sleek Ramiel fighter and saw that it was just finishing its hyperspace deceleration cycle. "I'm ready," she said as she assigned it to follow the Clever Dream at a safe distance. It would be close enough to exit hyperspace and not collide with any of the ships behind.

"All right, just relax Minh, don't do anything you'll regret," Jake said as he administered sedatives remotely.

To Jake and Ayan's relief, Minh's life signs normalized. He would be unconscious for several minutes, enough time for him to revert to a calm mental state. "That was unexpected," Jake said quietly.

"I should have seen it coming," Ayan whispered.

"After drifting alone for years, you're right. Do you think he'll be all right to land?"

"I don't know. I mean, if what he was muttering is true, that he feels naked, then probably not. Could you enter an atmosphere with his fighter moored to the ship, Lewis?" Ayan asked the ship AI.

"I know my seals and clamps will survive the heat and shear, but his fighter won't. Ramiel fighters have a soft, fabric seal that would survive the temperatures but not the stress of atmospheric entry."

"Slick, this is Hitman," Jake addressed through the comm.

"I love that call sign for you, it just fits." Ayan winked.

"Slick here. What can I do for you?"

"Can your Uriel clamp onto Minh's Ramiel and enter an atmosphere?"

"Sure can. Might get a little bumpy, but both fighters will be fine."

"All right, Ronin will be coming aboard the Clever Dream then we'll be touching down on Tamber."

"Captain, is the wing commander all right?"

"He'll be fine. His command unit was damaged and dosed him with a few milligrams of Taustim. We had to sedate him to get his heart rate down," Jake replied. Anyone who wasn't interested in disproving his white lie would never know the difference.

"Yikes, that explains what I was seeing in the squad status display. I'll stand ready. Slick out."

"And I'll make sure Minh gets a replay of your fantastic cover story as soon as he's lucid," Ayan added.

Lieutenant Garrison put his hands on the Clever Dream's flight controls as he watched the main pilot's display. He had forged a surprisingly uncomplicated bond with Lewis; the pair seemed to get along quietly and communicated well. Jake had witnessed one of their quiet debates already, and listening to them set the priority list for the ship maintenance was nothing short of amusing. The young Lieutenant would counter any of Lewis' objections with pure logic, giving in on some points when it made sense and sticking to others when he could. It was more a conversation than an argument, and it kept both the minder of the Clever Dream and her AI entertained. "I'll keep the wing commander's secret, Captain, don't worry. Nothing unusual about losing it when you notice how empty and dangerous space is. I tossed my breakfast on my first space walk."

"Almost everyone does," Ayan comforted.

"Three times."

"I don't know if that makes you tenacious or just special," Captain Valance replied with a sideways grin.

Lieutenant Garrison couldn't help but smile as he watched the small fleet's formation and deceleration rates. "We're emerging into normal space in three seconds, should be right in the middle of empty space."

Jake sat down in the co-pilot's position and rechecked the position of the other ships and fighters. They hadn't drifted more than a few millimetres, amazing considering the condition of most of the vessels. The Clever Dream wasn't pushing herself, of all the ships it had the most thrust. If all the

Samson's engines were operational it would have been the most powerful, since Jake's old ship was originally designed as a cargo hauler.

The group of ships emerged from hyperspace and just as Lieutenant Garrison had predicted, they were at the edge of the solar system, speeding past the eleventh planet, a dark gas giant that appeared marble sized in the forward viewport.

"Ayan, there's something I should tell you before we get in touch with anyone," Jake started. "I've signed the Clever Dream, the Samson, and the fighters' registries over to you. I've also made capture slips for all the raider ships so you're listed as the commanding officer during the action. They're a day off, but that's not unusual for deep space ship captures."

Ayan cleared her throat, "So what you're saying is-"

"I'm in hiding, you're in charge."

"You left telling me to the last minute so I couldn't refuse."

"Who else would I trust? Everyone who served on the Samson is wanted."

"Minh, maybe? He served in Freeground Infantry, and he's your wing commander."

"Right, but you have years of officer training, more years in service, and at least a few people from the Triton won't be surprised if you take the lead."

"You and everyone else who has more experience out here will be helping me every step of the way," Ayan told him.

"Absolutely. Unless you have to go somewhere that's equipped with DNA sniffers, but we can figure that out later."

"Oh, lovely," Ayan groaned. "All right, sucking it up and getting ready to take charge."

Jake glanced over his shoulder to catch a glance of Ayan, who was flushed to her hairline as she looked up some last minute details on her command unit. He couldn't help but grin as he returned his attention to the tactical display. "Everyone checks in fine. Laura says the Samson will be able to make a landing, they were able to brace all the weak points in hyperspace. I don't want to know what they had to tear apart for the metal, but at least they managed."

"Minh's starting to wake up," Ayan announced quietly. "I'll update him and tell him to come aboard."

He checked his long time friend's vitals and breathed a sigh of relief. He was back to normal, humour included. Minh managed to add the message "'A moment spent leaning on others can lift a lifetime of egotistical weight gain from one's shoulders.' I feel as light as a feather, thanks guys! Mind the road." Jake looked up at the tactical display and noticed three navnet requests appear on screen. Each came with it's own nationality: Confederation, Omiri, and Carthan. All but the Carthan Navnet were demanding a fee. Left with little choice, he selected it and viewed their managed territory.

At a closer glance, the situation in the Rega Gain system looked much as it should, according to the information they already had. There were active fire fights and areas of lingering resistance scattered throughout the solar system. Most of them were hot spots where United Core World Confederates were refusing to abandon settlements and a few older cities, while others weren't as well marked, offering few details. "All right, it looks like Tamber is still our best option. There's still a little fighting on one side of the moon, but not as much as in some other places."

"I know, I'm confirming that by reviewing the available propaganda now," Lewis replied.

"The good news is the Carthans have several open ground areas that are marked for safe landing. This one looks pretty clear." Jake brought up a broad section of land in the middle of one of the Tamber moon's southern continents. "No conflict markers for several thousand kilometres, either."

"I can verify that. The Carthans are assuring people that the Tamber moon is open for business, most vessels without a permit are being directed to the Dower Wastes so they can land while they get proper clearance to set down in a recognized port. Clearance for orbit isn't available for any part of the solar system," reported Lewis.

"Wonderful. Well, the Carthans are coming in at the right price and we need a place to set down and get organized, anyway. Contact Tamber Control and set us up for a landing. Remember, if anyone asks, Ayan's the captain," Jake smiled.

"I have to ask, Jacob; why don't you assign me to captain the Clever Dream myself?" asked Lewis.

"Because someone would probably slag you if they discovered an AI in complete control of a ship. Oh, that reminds me - try not to behave like an artificial intelligence. The last thing we need is someone tracking you and this ship back to Pandem."

"So you're telling me to pretend I'm a human."

"That's right."

"Okay, should be easy. I'll speak more slowly and unnecessarily add details about my personal life to the conversation while complaining about something I cannot change, like the weather, or my height."

"That ought to do it," Lieutenant Garrison laughed. "I'll listen in."

***

When Jake came down the ladder leading to the lower airlock, Minh was making sure the hatch leading to his Ramiel fighter was secure. Jake could see he was still shaking even in the dim light of the small compartment. "You all right?" he asked quietly.

Sitting down on a short bench beside a tool locker, Minh retracted his headpiece. The thin impact absorption plates folded into each other and fit into his collar. He exhaled and lowered his face into his hands. At the sound of the clamps releasing his Ramiel fighter he twitched, but didn't look up. "I should have known I wasn't ready. Sorry, Jake."

"Ayan told me you had to take some time after you came back."

"More like spend several weeks in containment while therapists rushed me through reintegration therapy."

Jake sat down on the opposite bench from Minh, who had taken his head out of his hands. He looked tired, older somehow. "Why'd they rush?" he asked quietly.

"I didn't want to be there. I had friends, my sisters, and nieces and nephews I'd never met and I couldn't wait to see them. After a couple of weeks they cut me loose. They checked in a few times a day from there. Everything was a little too loud, I felt a little unsteady, but it was better than being paced by a panel of doctors. I was just happy to be in touch, even if it was so scary sometimes, you know?"

Jake couldn't help but think of his time on the Samson, before he had memories to draw on. He didn't trust anyone. It took him a long time to find people he could leave in charge of the ship, even for an afternoon, without locking the Samson down completely. That was a kind of isolation he became accustomed to, and he was just starting to emerge from his shell. He couldn't imagine what Minh's forced isolation was like, what lasting effects it could have. Sure, they had both attended the mandatory seminars regarding long term isolation in Freeground Fleet Academy, but few people had ever spent so long alone in space with so much uncertainty and so little reassurance. There was no way for Minh to know if anyone was looking for him, or if his body would be found centuries later, aimlessly adrift. Only weeks after he was rescued by a Lorander exploration vessel, he returned to flying a starfighter. "What triggered this? Do you know?"

"It started when I woke up in hyperspace. If I were in a Uriel fighter I would have seen the cockpit around me, been able to stretch, but that Ramiel just wraps around you like a suit. Great for control, but, man, I felt like I was trapped. Well, not trapped, but like I was naked. Both maybe, I don't know," Minh said helplessly. "My rep with the squad is shot now, though."

"No one knows what happened, other than a stats increase. The only people who got on comms with you were Ayan and me. We can fake a stim overdose in the records and that'll explain the whole thing."

"That'll do it," Minh chuckled. "Were my stats that high? High enough to look like a stim OD?"

"They were through the roof. I've seen interrogation stats that never made it that high."

"Interrogation stats? It sounds like there's a story behind that. You'll have to share some of your shadier adventures some time."

"They're not as exciting as they sound."

Minh held his hands out in front of him, testing his steadiness. His shaking had almost completely gone. "After spending a few years adrift you'd be surprised at what I find exciting. Dinner. Dinner is exciting, and new combat boots, that's pretty interesting too. Oh, and materializers with patterns from the Sol System. If I weren't on energy rations like the rest of the crew, my quarters would look like a Sol System Emporium."

Jake laughed and nodded. "Yeah, I could see that."

"Speaking of exciting, it looks like I'm good to go again. When we land I'm getting into my old Uriel with Slick and we're going to go see what's up with the Triton first hand."

"Are you sure you're good for it?"

Minh gave him a withering look. "A Ramiel is one thing, it feels like an oversized vacsuit with fusion fuelled thruster underwear. The Uriel feels like a rig, and I won't be alone. Slick's good people, laughs at half my jokes. Oh, and he's a good pilot and SIO."

"If you're sure," said Jake.

"I'll be fine, Dad."

"Okay, okay. I was hoping we could send someone, even though everyone who knows anything about Freeground protocol is aware that sending a scout into that kind of situation is strictly prohibited."

"This isn't Freeground," stated Minh.

"I was hoping you'd say that. No risks, though. If we're going to get the Triton back we're going to need up to date information."

"Aye, Captain. Just make sure that the whole fighter wing is ready to go the moment I get back."

"It'll be ready, but I don't think it'll be going anywhere for a while. We're going to be concentrating on setting ourselves up somewhere while we figure out the next step. Even if we get the Triton back, some of the crew will have to live somewhere else while we conduct repairs."

"Gotcha. You set up a homestead, while I'm playing recon."

"Get some sleep while you're in transit, relax a bit," suggested Jake.

"I don't think I'll have a problem dozing. Those Uriel seats are so comfortable I'll be stealing one for my quarters when we've got our ship back."

"If we manage to get the Triton back, I'll have the crew manufacture one for you."

"Do you think Oz's plan is going to work?" Minh asked.

Jake leaned back against the lightly padded bulkhead and thought for a moment before offering his opinion. "If it were just a hundred boarders who came in shuttles I'd have no doubt. I saw the final tactical data, though; there were three operable destroyers, one of them had some kind of command segment. Sure, the whole security team, our incursion teams, and a lot of volunteers stayed behind to help, but who knows how many people the boarders have. Could be thousands."

"I'm going to assume Oz has the high ground here. He's got to have about a thousand people left aboard," said Minh.

"According to my numbers, he's got about fourteen hundred, including the gunnery team, volunteers who were former raiders, and some of the hangar deck crew."

"That's an army for a ship the size of the Triton, especially when a bunch of them probably have cloak suits. I almost wish I could join the fight."

"That's if Oz doesn't cause so much trouble that they just draw back and nuke the hell out of the Triton from a distance. According to the final sensor data we have on her, the Triton is in seriously rough shape. She couldn't outrun anything or take much of a pounding."

"Well, here's to finding out more. Depending on the fighter load outs, we might have the firepower or versatility to give Oz some cover."

"Don't. We need you to get information on the current situation and get back here," ordered the captain.

"I know, I know. I just thought I'd say it out loud to see how it sounds. It just feels like I should be there, doing something."

Jake nodded and stood. "I know. I thought about sending you in with the entire squadron, but those beam weapons... Your pilots aren't ready for that kind of anti-starfighter weaponry. I can't see more than a quarter of them coming back."

Minh thought for a moment and finally nodded. "They're too green. Whatever we do has to be well planned. I saw what happened to one of our Uriels when a beam hit it at full intensity. Those battlecruisers don't carry fighters because they don't need them. Trust me, I'll watch myself. There's a lot of cover in that nebula, don't worry."

"You'd better," Jake replied with a threatening tone.

Minh stood, hugged Jake tightly and chuckled as he was patted him on the back. "You just get things set up here so I can tell you how we're going to get the Triton out of this over a few drinks. Oh, and you're going to have to tell me what Steph and I walked into this morning. Hard to get that picture out of my head."

"He's not telling you a thing," Ayan called down from the hatch above them.

"Busted!" laughed Minh.

"Otherwise I'll tell the crew the Wing Commander and Captain like to sneak away for cuddles."

Minh burst out laughing as Jake flinched away and started up the ladder. "What's wrong with a good cuddle between friends?" Minh asked.

"We're about to land, you should both come and see this," Ayan stated as she walked out of sight.

"You know, I'm glad you two are working out," Minh commented quietly.

"We're getting on well. She's different though, we're both different. Things still moving along with Paula?"

Minh hesitated, stopping half way up the access ladder altogether for a moment. "I think she's chatting me into submission, so yeah, they're moving along. Whether I like it or not," he replied quietly as he finished his short climb.

"You're not sure?"

"Don't get me wrong, she's got her good points. I always know what she's thinking, since she has every thought out loud, and I'm never caught wondering what I'll do with my off time since she always has it planned for me."

"So it's like you're spending time with An-Linh."

Minh froze in the narrow corridor, his eyes wide. "My sister?" He stared blankly into space and thought for another moment. "My micro-sized, hyper, opinionated sister."

"I always liked her," Jake commented as he finished climbing up the ladder and closed the hatch behind him.

"She was always my secret favourite, too, but..."

"Secret favourite?"

"You never tell your sisters you have a favourite," Minh replied dismissively. "I'm really dating a bad copy of my sister," he continued, awe struck.

"I didn't say bad copy. I'm sure Paula has her charms."

"She's terrifying. The last time we went to the Pilot's Den, she told me what I was having for dinner. It really is like I'm dating my-" he concluded his comment with a shudder. "How do I end it?"

"Carefully. Quickly. Are you sure, though? I mean, there's got to be something there if you've spent so much time together," Jake offered with an impish grin.

"Are you kidding? Next she'll be spending the night and telling me what side of the bed I'll be sleeping on, when to go to the bathroom, and to have dinner parties where all the food comes from the materializer. She doesn't even like Asian food! Did you know that? I mentioned that I used to own an authentic restaurant and she cringed. She didn't understand why anyone would cook anything, or why they'd want to do it for others, not even for money. She's the first woman I've ever met who doesn't like real cooked food."

Jake chuckled and shrugged. "Well, she's not on the fleet list, so she must still be on the Triton. That should buy you some time to figure out how to put her down gently."

"Think my reputation would take a hit if I requested a squad or two from security when I did it?" asked Minh.

Jake nodded. "Oh yeah."

"Suddenly I'm not in as much of a hurry."

"Mind on the mission," Ayan scolded. She had been listening to the entire exchange from the hallway.

"Right, mind on the mission," confirmed Minh.

"Pointing out similarities between Paula and Minh's sister wasn't fair play, Jake," Ayan mock scolded.

"Better I point it out now than at the wedding."

"Maybe I'll just send her a message as soon as the Triton's safe. I'm sure she won't care if it's in the middle of a celebration, and I'd be avoiding an awkward reunion," Minh offered.

"You're doing it through a message?" Ayan gasped. "If you go through with this I'll never look at you the same way, Minh."

He stopped and stared at her for a moment.

Ayan was deadly serious. The quiet of the cockpit was thick as everyone waited for his reaction. They were in an automated holding pattern above Tamber, a green, brown, and blue moon with a perfect atmosphere for humans.

Minh sighed finally and nodded. "You're right. Besides, if my sisters ever did find out I broke up with someone using a social system, they'd get creative with the punishment."

"And it would be justified," Ayan said.

"How are we for landing?" Jake asked.

"The Carthans assigned us to a desert called the Dower Wastes. According to the navnet pattern, we'll be landing in about a minute and a half," Lieutenant Garrison replied from the pilot's seat.

"Any hidden fees?"

"Well, the good news is they're not worried about our fighters, they're just not allowed near population centres or certain parts of the solar system without permits. The bad news is they want twenty eight thousand UCW credits for protection. What they're going to protect us from, I don't know, but I didn't commit since I didn't think you wanted customs coming around to inspect everything before they started posting guards. There's also a toxicity warning for the Dower Wastes. Apparently some kind of vegetation growth project went wrong, covering the wastes and a neighbouring island with rotting chemical clay. We should send a message to everyone warning them to stay aboard if they can, and to keep their vacsuits sealed if they have to leave their ships."

"Wonderful. Well, at least we have somewhere to stay while we sort things out," said Jake.

"Customs may still pay us a visit," Ayan continued. "I know I'd be curious about a captain with so many recent acquisitions. They advise new captains visit the Office of the Governor as well and gave me a number to call a bounder."

Jake nodded and took a seat in the co-pilot's chair. "Bounder is just slang for a short-range people mover. The most popular ones used to use jump drives to reach low orbit and then drop down on their destinations."

"Sounds fun," Minh smirked.

"Sounds dangerous," Ayan commented.

"You spend most of the ride in an accelerated descent, so it's like falling in fast forward." Jake grinned. "Steph and Ash love those things."

"Oh, that reminds me. The whole Samson crew are on the bounty board."

"Well, we expected that, but how did you access the bounty board?"

"It's free," Ayan shrugged. "There are a few thousand listings for Greydock alone."

"That's not a good sign," Jake said under his breath.

"Why?"

"Well, normally you have to have a licence or register with the local authorities to get access to the bounty boards. If it's free here and anyone can capture someone and claim the bounty, then the hunters are being used for law enforcement. How did I rank, by the way?" Jake asked.

"I thought you'd be wondering. You're the most wanted man on the planet with a local bounty of three point five million if you're turned in alive at the United Core World Confederation. I think they're planning to resell you to the Galactic High Court. That bounty is a lot higher."

"Oh my God. I'm tempted to turn him in at that price!" Minh burst.

"And the Samson crewmembers?"

"Between fifty thousand all the way up to nine hundred thousand for Frost and Stephanie. She also has two outstanding warrants that apply in Confederation territory."

"You guys should just sell the rights to the Samson years to some holomovie studio. If they can make fifty films about Billy the Kid, I'm sure they can make just one about Jake and his crew," Minh chuckled.

Jake chose to ignore the suggestion and pressed on. "Are the Carthans backing any of the bounties on us?"

Ayan scrolled through the small section of the bounty board reserved for the Samson crew and shook her head. "If Security Chief Vega pays a two thousand credit fine it'll wipe out the fine they're charging her with. It's a failure to appear for some court date two years ago. She was called as a witness, not the accused."

Jake nodded, remembering of the incident. "Right, forward that to her and tell her to transfer the funds so she's clear with the Carthans, at least. So, what's Greydock?"

"It's the Carthan Capital for the entire moon, according to the system. Won't there be a ton of bounty hunters looking for you anyway? The bounty board is common here, that's why I could see Confederation marks along with the rest."

Jake turned and re-checked their navnet course as their small fleet of fighters and damaged ships began making their way to their final approach trajectory. Everything checked out and he half turned to face Ayan again. "You're right. It looks like you're on your own if you want to visit the governor and get us proper landing permits. You'll probably have no problem getting a privateering licence. I'm sure you're not the only one with recent acquisitions coming in. I wish I could go with you, but I'm sure they've got DNA sniffers or deep tissue scanners there."

"Wouldn't they leave you alone, since the Carthans are enemies to the Order of Eden and Regent Galactic?"

"Sure, but there's no telling how many of their people are crooked. The nearest Confederation-held solar system is only a few light years away."

"Maybe I could take Victor and a couple of his squad members along."

"Bring the whole squad, except for Alaka."

"I don't want it to look like I'm there to start trouble, I'm sure just a couple will be fine."

"I think the smart move here is to bring too many friends. You don't want to end up a few people light."

"I think I'll just take Victor, one of his hand picked people, and Laura," Ayan countered. "Besides, what could happen in the Governor's Office? A beaurocracy ambush?"

"You're the captain," Jake dismissed lightly.

"Wow, that was quick," Minh chuckled. "What are you going to do while she's off hob-knobbing with the politicians?"

"And help me maintain order," Stephanie interjected from the communications system. "We're all secure back here, Captain."

"All our ships have checked in, we're ready to set down on Tamber," Lieutenant Garrison reported.

***

The four occupants of the cockpit fell silent as the Clever Dream began to pass through the atmosphere. Jake watched his tactical screen closely for any signs that the ships in their convoy were running into trouble, focusing mostly on the Samson. Whoever Laura had piloting his old ship was good at their job; they had the vessel angled just right so the more damaged dorsal and port sections saw little or no direct exposure. The shields were still doing most of the work, and he had to admit he was surprised they had managed to get the system back online after the beating it had taken only weeks before. He wouldn't have used the Samson; one of her main beams were twisted, three of the engines were out of commission, and two compartments were completely open to space while several others weren't safe for atmospheric entry without shields.

When they came through the thick atmosphere, he breathed a sigh of relief. Only one of them had gone slightly off course, a fighter near the rear of the group. The sky was a shade of dun brown, and as they passed through clouds, a desert unlike any he'd seen stretched out in front of them.

There were no dunes, no shade indicating golden sand or dark dust, but hundreds of kilometres of grey and deep brown flat, cracked planes. "Lewis, can you run an analysis on that?"

"On what, exactly?" asked the AI.

"The ground. I know what the advisory said, but can you give me more detail?" asked Jake.

"The terrain below us consists of a combination of formerly life-giving chemicals combined with a porous, clay-like medium. It is several meters thick in some places and covers large bodies of water in others."

"Formerly life giving?" asked Ayan.

"Yes. This material is called Dower Company Life Generating Topsoil, or LGT for short. It is designed to generate a diverse range of plant life in a balanced ecological range."

"A forest in a box," Stephanie said as she entered the cabin. "I saw this from the common room and had to check for myself. Any idea why it failed?"

"Based on what I'm seeing I can only assume something failed early in the chemical reaction, perhaps there was wide-spread contamination. I don't have enough information to be certain. There are several unsecured networks within range, would you like me to look into it for you?" asked Lewis.

"No, Lewis, thank you," Ayan answered. "The last thing we need is to have you detected by some artificial intelligence scanner. Complex AI's are outlawed by the Carthans."

"I am aware, thank you, Ayan."

"I think you hurt his feelings," Stephanie said as she patted the ceiling. "Do you know what exposure to this stuff could do to us?"

"I think you should obey the Carthan advisory to the letter: don't touch it with bare skin and don't breathe too much of the dust. This entire expanse is a low-level biohazard."

The five occupants of the cockpit watched as the Clever Dream completed its descent. The colour of the landscape, the uniformity of it and the level plane of the land made it look like it went on forever. What was there before, no one could guess, but no one was left with any question as to why the place was called the Dower Wastes.

CHAPTER 16
GHOSTS

"Tate's whole squad is down, Sir," Foss, the communications and scanning officer stated.

"What? I would have gotten a direct alert if they came under fire," Sergeant Cameron Steadman replied, flipping the armoured cover to her command display open. The flat screen on the inside of her wrist scrolled to Sergeant Tate's team and for a moment she was puzzled at the results. "Medical, confirm what I'm seeing."

Officer Rawdon nodded. "Their bodies are being stressed by-" he trailed off.

"It's gravity. They're using artificial gravity." Steadman flipped the display cover closed and waved Foss towards the main console on the darkened bridge. "Inform Command that we're going to try a hack into their life support systems. Get jacked in."

"Using the command codes we received in the crew's surrender? If they'll resort to using gravi-"

"We don't have a choice. Do it," she cut in.

Foss moved to the command seat and began looking for a data port to connect to. "This would be easier if they left a wireless receiver on somewhere," he grumbled.

Steadman looked across the large command centre of the Triton. With semi-transparent floors and the lights of the squad leaving the deck beneath, the place had an eerie feeling she couldn't shake. "Anything on scans Foss?"

"Nothing, Ma'am."

She glanced at the sighting on her rifle as she waved it across the front of the bridge. "Where did they go? There's a group in the ship auditorium, the habitation areas, and a berthing, but that doesn't account for enough."

"I don't know, Ma'am, Command's last count looked good before we docked," replied Foss.

"Command, verify your encounter scan. I need these numbers to add up,"

"Command here, we've verified twice. According to this, you should have readings on five hundred more people. Did you consider a shielded compartment?" an officer from Battlecruiser 1128 answered.

"If there were a shielded compartment, then we'd have a great big blacked out area instead of missing individuals. Are you sure you were able to track all the ships they launched?"

"Absolutely certain. We don't make mistakes up here, Sergeant."

"Don't get testy, I'm only-"

Foss's whole body jerked as sparks leapt from the side of the command seat. His high pitched scream filled the comms and the bridge as he violently thrashed and writhed. One of his squad mates ran towards him.

"Don't touch him! Stay back!" Steadman shouted.

It was too late. The soldier ran headlong into him with the intention of knocking him free of his contact with the chair, and he succeeded, but in that instant the power coursing through Foss's body carried through to him.

"Check him!"

Rawdon ran forward with his medical scanner, taking a reading on both men at once. "Gone. There's nothing to resuscitate."

Steadman glanced at her command display briefly to confirm her medic's readings.

"Damn, takes a lot of juice to get through our armour," commented Jenkins, one of her more seasoned squad members.

"Retreat. We'll join squad five and head for one of their main computers," Sergeant Steadman said as she began backing towards the main entrance to the bridge.

The doors came to life, slamming shut in a quarter second. Most of her squad jumped.

"Command," she addressed. "There are active systems aboard. Scan and confirm."

Her squad looked to her for directions, glancing around the large darkened bridge nervously with their rifles held up.

"Command!" She glanced at her command screen and saw that her wireless link had been severed.

Several gunshots pierced the air, echoing up from the deck beneath them. She whirled to catch sight of what was going on and saw rapid flashes of light from below, heard gunfire that was completely foreign. The strange weapons made a low pitched, electric snapping sound every time they fired, and their shots came in bursts of twenty or more shots per second. "Move to support squad five!" she ordered, leading the way to the ramps at the side of the bridge that would take them to the lower command centre.

Half way down the ramp something from above caught her eye. She looked up to see the squad mate behind her collapse to the ground and his rifle get snatched away by an invisible hand. She sighted where she estimated the assailant was and was just about to open fire when a hand grabbed the back of her helmet and pulled her down the ramp.

Cameron's rifle went off, the rounds impacting harmlessly against the ceiling. When she reached the bottom of the ramp she tried to get to her feet only to find them kicked out from under her. Her rifle was ripped out of her hands and before her eyes appeared a tall man in black armour, his heavy sidearm lowered to point directly at her head. "How much time do we have now that your people are under attack?"

"How much time?" Cameron asked, unsure of the question.

"How much time before they get to a safe distance and blast us until we're an empty hull?"

She'd never seen Caran Enterprises do anything like that once boarding teams had been dispatched, but in that instant she realized it was possible; the whole corporation had just been bought out. "I don't know Regent Galactic's policies."

"What are you? New?" the towering figure asked, cocking his head. "Who are you after?"

Her training came back to her: never reveal operational details. "I'm Cameron Steadman, Boarding Sergeant with Caran Ent-, Regent Galactic. We are executing a sector-wide warrant for this ship and several of her crew," she said mechanically.

"Don't shut down on me, God dammit! I can't leave you alive behind me unless you give me something here."

"I'm Cameron Steadman, Boarding Sergeant with Regent Galactic. We are executing a sector-wide warrant for this ship and several of her crew."

The dark figure pressed his foot down on her chest plate hard and tipped her helmet up with the toe of his boot.

With a start she realized what he was doing and struggled frantically, grabbing at his leg and squirming under the relentless weight of his heel.

When he pried her helmet up enough to see the under lining of her armour, he fired.

CHAPTER 17
THE DOWER WASTES

"We have trouble on the Samson, Jake. We need you at the main cargo hatch," Laura said over the comm.

Ayan heard it; the message was broadcast over the command channel so anyone in charge of a squad or more would have. They were just setting foot on the strange, clay-like soil. Most of the soldiers were making their way off the ships to secure the landing area. They were armed to the teeth and many of them donned the extreme environment layer of their armour.

Ayan's white suit started to discolour the instant she set foot on the ground, though she couldn't see much dust. The outer layer of her vacsuit shook imperceptibly every few seconds, returning it to its original colour. Clouds loomed tall and dark in the distance, rolling in over the horizon and obscuring the yellow sun. She only had a moment to glimpse the night side profile of another moon. Its shadowy outline was partially illuminated by some glowing centre of light.

Returning her attention to her more immediate environment, she looked around at the dozens of fighters and other ships that had landed all around the Clever Dream. Armed Triton personnel and deck crew were slowly making their way out of the troop carrier modules that had been installed on most of the Uriel fighters, and from what she could see they had all been overcrowded. Some passengers were so openly relieved, they stretched or sat down on the bare ground and just breathed. "Everyone should seal their vacsuits for now. That's an order," she relayed over her communicator.

"Jake, something's up at the main rear hatch of the Samson. Let me through!" Laura shouted, obviously not at him.

"I'm on my way, Laura. Do you know exactly what's going on?" Ayan heard him respond.

"I'm trying to get back there, but there are too many people in the way."

Ayan ran to the other side of the Clever Dream and saw that there was a gathering at the rear of the Samson, at the bottom of the cargo ramp. "It looks like they're prying at something in a service hatch under the Samson's reactor bay."

Jake burst into a run the moment he set foot on soil. "I'll be right there. Stephanie, I need everyone you can trust from the Clever Dream to back me up."

"Aye, Sir," Stephanie replied with no shortage of urgency.

Ayan didn't bother to listen to her pass the orders on, but tried to keep up with Jake as he closed the distance between him and the rear loading ramp of the Samson, where people were continuing to gather. The rear hatch was under what the Samson called the maxjack. It was a carefully constructed collection of metal bars, gripper arms, clamps, and cutters. At the centre was a heavy plasma torch set on a track that ran around a fortified, extendable airlock above the main cargo ramp. The whole system was wide open, which made the rear of the Samson look as if it had thirty twisted and curved skeletal fingers, some of which punctured the ground. The growing crowd of over two hundred didn't seem to notice or care about how damaged some of the system looked from where Ayan was standing.

A few unarmed crew members were starting to disembark from other vessels and the commotion at the rear of the older, battered ship was drawing a lot of attention. At the base of the ramp there was a bright flash. Ayan's head's up display marked it as small arms fire, a particle weapon. There were several more flashes in succession. "What's going on?"

"Someone broke into my credit reserves, they were kept under the Samson's mass reactor," Jake replied over proximity radio. "It's all I have left. Maybe all the ready cash in the fleet."

Ayan knew her slim Freeground account with less than forty thousand credits wouldn't be much help if they were on their own, if Triton was lost. "How much is in there?" Ayan asked.

"Last I checked the tokens I have in there was worth about seven fifty."

"Thousand?"

"Thousand. Enough molecularly stamped bullion coin to cover serious repairs on the Samson in case we were stuck somewhere without a link to a major bank, and since those banks were all run by AI's, along with the communication systems they depended on, I'm betting its worth a lot more now."

Ayan had seen a bullion token before, but from a distance. If what Jake had was like what she'd seen during her Junior Academy days, a thin strip of molecularly stamped platinum with lines of tiny coloured industrial diamonds set into it under a protective coating, then she could see why even crew members who weren't normally greedy would want a piece. That kind of currency was universally recognized and trusted because of the certification of the material's purity and how difficult it was to counterfeit.

They arrived at the edge of the crowd and several people started to run away from the landing site. "Stephanie, have a few of your people round up the runners. Make sure they take a second to show them a map. We're about eight hundred klicks from anywhere," Jacob instructed.

"I'll catch them, Sir," Alaka volunteered. "It won't take long."

Ayan's eyes went wide as she looked to the rear view display on her sealed hood's head's up display in time to watch a huge, dark shape dart out from under the Clever Dream and begin to close the distance between him and the runners to the west. She'd never seen a nafalli run at full speed before. Alaka's legs were powerful and long, certainly, but when he leaned forward and began to use his arms, his agility and speed doubled. His armoured hands looked more like long black claws, and his movements were so graceful they were awe-inspiring.

In seconds he was in front of the startled runners. He stood up to his full height and stretched his arms out to his sides. "Stay near the ship, there's nowhere to go, trust me."

They begrudgingly started making their way back.

Alaka took a running start right at the Samson, and instead of passing under it he leapt up, ran over the mismatched plating of the hull and came down on the other side so he could pursue the rest of the runners.

"Everyone stop what you're doing!" Jake ordered.

"Why? We're just taking what you owe us!" replied a voice from the crowd. It took less than a second for Crewcast to make a match and present a picture of a former Samson crew member named Leland March. He had been recently reduced in rank to Crewman's Mate after faking qualifications and nearly single-handedly destroying the Cold Reaver with a tactical blunder.

Many members of the crowd glared at Jake angrily.

"Get your ass out in front, Leland!" Jake roared.

Stephanie and the rest of the security staff were catching up. Four squads, fifty six rifle bearing, fully armoured soldiers came running roughly shoulder to shoulder like a black wave to support their captain. Other security members were closing in slowly, carefully guiding the people who hadn't remained aboard their ships.

The crowd parted to reveal Leland March, standing over a secure ammunition crate. He had holstered his pulse pistol. Ayan didn't bother guessing where he'd gotten it, probably from some storage locker on the Samson somewhere, but she did take note that Leland's Crewcast profile stated that he wasn't allowed to bear arms. The scorch marks on the ammunition container made it clear that he'd tried more than once to shoot it open.

"He's not alone, Captain," called out another man angrily. His voice was identified as Edward Sherman, and Ayan noticed a red flag, posted by Oz about an incident that took place on the flight control deck. The crowd shuffled a little so he could join Leland and hand him a cutting torch. "I think it's about time we get paid so we can get away from you and your disastrously reckless leadership."

Jake's hand came to rest on the hilt of his handgun, whether by reflex or as a foreshadow of intent, Ayan didn't hazard to guess.

Edward took an exaggerated step back, throwing his hands up. "What are you going to do now? Shoot me? I should have expected-"

"That's enough!" Jake barked. "You're taking money that we'll need for food, to buy supplies, for repairs."

"So you can what? Go after your stolen ship? Didn't anyone tell you? It's over! The Triton and whoever stayed behind are either dead or in shackles by now. I'm taking my money and signalling for a lift!" He reached down to one of the crates.

Jake twitched his sidearm out of its holster and shot Edward in the hip. Before most had realized what had happened, Jake was dropping his weapon back into its holster. "Next one won't be a stun shot!" he called out.

Edward fell to the ground, flailing. Ayan knew it was nothing more than theatrics, the energy carried no force and it couldn't penetrate the man's vacsuit.

"Security Chief! Control this crowd!" Jake ordered.

Under the efficient direction of Chief Stephanie Vega, her people and two squads who arrived from another ship rushed in, took possession of the cash-filled crates and separated everyone into smaller groups. Ayan couldn't help but smile a little as she saw Stephanie yank Leland's pistol out of its holster and tuck it into her belt.

"This is criminal! You have no authority here! I'll report you as soon as I see civilization again!" shouted Edward as he was pressed away from the Samson's main cargo ramp with a small group.

Ayan listened in on Chief Vega's instructions and watched as they were carried out with impressive efficiency. Most of the people with her were deserter Aucharian soldiers who had remained aboard shortly after Jake had taken the Triton. Several others were former Pandem rebels.

Alaka finished rounding up the runners and spotted his family. Iloona, surrounded by their children, quietly allowed herself to be sorted off into a group on the side. Alaka didn't bother asking to see them, and no one objected when he joined them for a reunion.

The thirteen of them looked strange with their fur pressed flat under thin vacsuits, but the love of the family was plain. His older children cuddled close to their parents, two of Alaka's sons climbed on top of him, eventually settling leisurely on his shoulders.

"All right, this is going to be simple," Jake started over the general Crewcast channel. The two hundred nine people who had managed to squeeze onto the Samson were just settling, and several of them were just starting to protest their predicament.

The clouds had rolled in overhead and the first smatterings of rain were starting to fall. Ayan checked her environmental display and breathed a sigh of relief as she saw it was harmless water. It would even be clean enough to drink in a pinch. She heard the collection panels open on the Clever Dream behind her, and saw that the same was happening on several of the former raider ships.

"I can't afford to pay you full wages for your time aboard Triton," Jake started sternly. Several protesting voices began to rise and he silenced all but his own. "But I can give each of you a hundred grams in bullion coin if you're looking to walk. Most of you have valid accounts with banks that have managed to survive the Holocaust Virus and you'll be able to access them from any city. You can call for transportation as soon as you're paid. You'll be stripped of every scrap of weaponry and equipment you picked up while you were on Triton, except for your vacsuits. If someone asks me whether you served aboard my ship, I'll deny it."

"That's unacceptable! You can't just maroon us here!" A voice Ayan's Crewcast identified as Tammy Weston, a Private who worked in the Triton hangar, called out.

"Marooned? You don't know what marooned means!" Shouted Minh-Chu, to Ayan's surprise. "This is hard, this whole situation is terrible, but he's giving you a way to leave! This is an easy door! He could take everything and tell you to pick a direction! Walk until the ground poisons your feet!" he said from the side of Slick's Uriel fighter.

She'd never seen Minh so exasperated. "Marooned!" he spat bitterly. "You take your coin and leave us behind. Don't look back, either! When we have the Triton again and you want to re-join us for the warm quarters, good jobs, entertainment, good food and better company, our doors won't open for you!"

"Thank you, Wing Commander," Jake acknowledged with a nod. "For those of you who want to stay, to work together to improve our situation, I've made Ayan the Master of all the ships here, and everything I own."

The crowd was silenced at that announcement, and Ayan didn't know how to interpret their reaction. Crewmembers who had come out of several of the vessels around them, especially the Samson, were looking from Jacob to her and back.

"She'll contact the government here so we have a proper place to put down, to lick our wounds. The rest of your command team, myself included, will make sure we have somewhere safe to sleep, something to eat, and the supplies we need. When we start earning a gain from privateering and other efforts, then you'll start seeing cash in your pockets. All we ask is that you give us time to get organized and that you put in as much work as you can."

"What about the Triton?" asked someone from one of the more stable raider ships. Crewcast marked him as Garnet Ahram, a fabrication worker.

To Ayan's surprise, Jacob hesitated.

She took the opportunity to casually step beside him. "We are sending our best scout to find out if there is anything we can do." The chatter amongst the various crowds died to dead silence as she spoke over the general Crewcast command channel. "Judging from the most recent report from the Triton, we know that she'll require months of repairs, during which we'll need another place to call home. Either way, we're going to need to make at least a temporary home somewhere, and Tamber may be the first safe refuge most of us have seen in weeks." Ayan knew she had the undivided attention of the crowd, and despite her racing heart, she decided to be brash, and tell everyone exactly what she was thinking and what she thought she, as well as everyone else, should do. "I hope that we can eventually return to the Triton, and that we can get everyone who is still aboard back safely. I can't do anything to influence that outcome right now, few of us can, but we can work to ensure that we all have what we need to survive. Most of us are starting over, myself included, and I'm going to start building something right now. I'm going to start by getting us proper landing permits, a privateers licence, and anything else the Carthan government can give us that will provide opportunities. We have an entire combat wing of top notch starfighters, ships that we can repair and improve, and we have each other. I have been in many situations during my military career where I couldn't dream of having so many advantages. Now if you want to leave, it will be without disgrace. Be patient, follow Security Chief Vega's instructions, and you'll be on your way to a major city in no time. As for the rest of you, thank you for remaining. Stay close to your loved ones, and follow directions. I hope to have us set up in a proper port shortly."

Ayan watched Jake look over the crowd, clenching and unclenching his jaw for several seconds. As the sound of someone speaking just began to break the silence, he interrupted them; "Chief Vega! Two lines! Deserters to port," Jake barked, pointing to the port side of the Samson. "Loyal crew to starboard!" he finished, pointing to the starboard side.

As the orders were carried out, Ayan looked back to Minh, who was taking a seat in front of Slick in his Uriel fighter. "Good luck Minh, be safe."

"We should be back in a few hours. Slick has an extra pair of generators loaded, should be a nice, quick trip."

"Just don't let one of those beam weapons get a bead on you."

"Don't worry, I know exactly where to hide."

Lightning flashed, lighting the darkening landscape for an instant. "Don't get cocky out there, you two," Jake commented.

"If you're that worried, why don't you go check on him yourself in the Clever Dream?"

"We need it here for her medical bay and the materializer. It's best if we risk as little as possible on intelligence gathering," Jake replied calmly. "That, and the cloaking systems probably wouldn't work properly in a nebula that dense."

"Excuses, excuses. You two just want to stay behind and snog in the captain's quarters," Minh teased, closing his connection to the channel reserved for former First Light crew.

The Uriel fighter's thrusters rotated and fired, pushing it swiftly off the ground and high up into the air. "I'll make sure he doesn't do anything you'll regret," Slick said on the general command channel.

Ayan watched the fighter rise swiftly and take off over the horizon. Ayan couldn't shake a sinking feeling that threatened to overwhelm her.

"He'll be fine," Jake reassured quietly.

"There's no way anyone can know that. He's going to do something desperate and we're backing him."

Jake took her by the shoulders and turned her towards him. He retracted his headpiece, the horizontal armoured slats folded into each other and settled onto his chest and back. "If he were alone I'd agree with you, but he's not. Slick is with him and he'll keep things sane."

Ayan looked up at him quietly. He was steady, reassuring, and confident. It didn't stop a lump from rising in her throat, or tears from brimming. She deactivated her communications and the face plate to her vacsuit hood, though it hid the tears she knew she couldn't stop. "Things have to get better, I hate having the feeling that we'll never see Oz, Jason, or anyone from the Triton again."

"I know, I hate not being able to do anything about this myself," Jake said quietly.

"I just wish I felt better about Minh and Slick's chances of getting in and out of there," Ayan managed.

Jake put his arm around her waist and deactivated his proximity radio so no one could overhear what he had to say. "Minh is good at what he does, so is Slick. They're too slippery to catch. Where'd all the positivity go?"

"I think it's just hitting me now that we've landed and things have quieted down a bit. I should have more faith, I know." She watched as the line of deserters, as Jake had called them, was slowly led past the crate of credits. Chief Vega's people handed each of them a rectangular silver coin that glinted purple when it caught the light. The line of deserters had grown to hundreds while she wasn't looking, other deserters joining them from the other ships.

"Things are bad now, but I'll bet the best are staying with us,"

"I know. I'm actually looking forward to visiting Greydock, it's just..." Ayan sighed deeply and looked up to Jake. "It's like all the good, all the bad, whatever it is, it all happens at once. It's hard to control things when they just seem to happen to us. I want to turn things around, start making the terms, come around to being proactive. " She paused a moment as someone ran from the back of the deserter line to the much shorter loyal line. "As ludicrous as that sounds considering our predicament," she chortled.

"I'm on the same page. I think we can start by getting everything we can here. You ever negotiate a contract before?"

"Not since mock scenarios in advanced officer training."

"Considering how you took control of the crowd and raised spirits here, I'd say your officer training stuck. We'll be all right," he replied with a slight smile. "Feeling better?"

"Much." Ayan stepped away and shook her head. "God, I was never this emotional before. It's like I had some kind of hardener the first time 'round." Ayan's eye was drawn to the quickly growing pile of command and control units and other equipment of every shape and size on the Samson's cargo ramp. If they could wipe the memories, they would have something to sell on the open market, if that sort of thing was permitted in Greydock.

"I like it," Jake said quietly as he watched the slow progression in front of them. The ground was slowly turning to thick mud under the increasing weight of the rain.

Ayan could see that stone facade that Jake wore so well was settling back into place, but took great comfort in the new assurance that she could call the man she wanted to know back when she wanted him, when she needed him.

***

Things got worse as the crowd of equipment-stripped deserters grew. They stood waiting for transport to arrive, with the few things they could take with them from the Triton, a survival package which contained three days worth of meal replacement bars, water, an ultra-thin cot, a basic communicator, and a dual-purpose cutting tool plus fire starter. Ayan and Jake moved so they could stand within ten meters of the space where they were handing out the coins and she found herself looking for Leland March and Edward Sherman, the worst of the trouble makers.

She was still scanning the line when Laura surprised her from behind with a fervent hug. They had been friends for years, and seeing her intact, in person, was an incredible comfort. "God, you wouldn't believe the mess that ship is in. I'm sure its being held together with sealant tape and hull filler. Scratch that, we ran out of hull filler and started using deck sheeting," Laura told her with a chuckle.

Ayan squeezed her playfully. "It's so good to see you, I'm sorry if it seemed I had reservations about Minh checking after the Triton. I didn't mean to come off like-"

"Don't worry, I know you want to see Jason and Oz back here as much as I do, but you don't want to lose someone else. I live with an intelligence agent, remember? If anyone understands the necessity for economical personnel use, it's the wife of a spook."

"You know, I never thought that would rub off on you," Ayan smiled.

"This'll come back on you, Captain," spat someone as they passed by and flashed their hundred gram coin. The hate etched on his face was intense as he regarded Jake, obviously the person the dissenter thought was responsible for all his problems. Ayan faintly recalled that he was one of the crew members they'd rescued from Pandem and had to stop herself from shaking her head. "Would you rather we left you behind, Verain?" Ayan asked.

"White doesn't suit you, you should all be wearing red. Blood red," he told her, his cold green eyes looking straight into hers.

"If you want to stay for better days, we'll give you your comm unit and put you in the other line. Otherwise, get ready for pickup," Jake snapped as he whirled on the older man.

"How many do you think are left?" asked Laura as the older fellow moved on.

"Crewcast says there are still six hundred thirty connected to the network." Ayan replied. "I'm pretty sure Chief Vega disconnected everyone who stepped into the deserter line."

"I did," Stephanie confirmed curtly.

"Good thinking, Chief," Ayan said with a slight smile.

The only acknowledgement was a solemn nod as she watched one of her people hand the next person in line a coin from the emptying ammunition crate.

"I hope that's not all Jake has," Laura said quietly.

"It's one of four cases."

"That's not much for eight hundred people."

"I know. Hopefully we can pick up a privateering licence and do some easy privateering. I'll be visiting the governor's office as soon as I can."

"When?"

"I was thinking Jake could call in another transport for me and a security team when he calls for their ship. So in about forty minutes."

"That quick?" Laura asked, surprised.

"There's no point in waiting. The sooner we get-" Ayan's eye caught Leland March and Edward Sherman then and she couldn't believe what she was seeing.

"What?" Laura asked as Ayan regarded her with astonishment.

"Those two, Leland and Edward, they started this whole scene."

Laura turned to face the pair, who where chatting quietly, but enthusiastically. "And now they're in the loyal line."

"I'd bet what's left of the Samson that Leland was the one who showed the passengers where my emergency funds are kept," Jake added in over the private comm.

"This might not be the time to bring this up, but those two were part of a group that started a fire in a Botanical Gallery apartment before we abandoned ship."

"Now is the perfect time to bring it up," Jacob said, not letting the outrage he must have been feeling creep into his stony expression. "But if I haul them off the line and strap them to the nose of the Samson right now, it won't help anything. They'll get what's coming to them."

Ayan wasn't aware he was listening in, but wasn't surprised considering how quickly things were happening. "What do you want to do?"

"I'll put Leland to work, same with his new friend. If I get the time I'll make sure to have a conversation with them one on one."

"Don't do anything you'll regret, Jacob," Ayan whispered so only Laura could overhear.

"With people like March, there's no need. He'll crap himself the instant he realizes I've got him alone. As for the other one, I'll get Stephanie to talk to him. If I take the time to do it personally he'll just feel that he's even more important."

"Why don't you get Alaka to do it? If you're going further down the chain, you may as well use the anchor."

Jake chuckled ruefully. "What I'd give to be a fly on the wall. Good idea. It's not like Steph isn't busy as it is."

Ayan's tactical alarm went off. Every officer's command and control unit notified them that there were several armed ships coming in from the northwest. "Lewis, can you scan them?"

"They are Carthan customs vessels, five in total. I'm reading over five hundred small arms and it looks like they're made for quick boarding or deployment action. They should break cloud cover shortly."

"Thank you, Lewis. Do you think we should get everyone back on the ships, Jake?" asked Ayan.

"No, we're going to continue as we are. They are probably coming to inspect us and have a word."

"Have you ever dealt with anything like this?" asked Laura.

"The Samson has been inspected by customs more times than I can count. The big problem we have here are all the people looking for refugee status. We'll have to keep them calm and make sure the customs officials can get their terms to everyone, otherwise this could get bad fast. Ayan, you'll have to do the talking. The Carthans may not want us, but I'd still rather not let on that there are Samson crew here unless we absolutely have to."

"All right, everyone who was on the Samson crew, cover up," Stephanie ordered. Everyone who served on the Samson activated their armoured vacsuit hood and made their faceplates opaque. After a moment she added: "Too conspicuous. Okay, everyone in security and wearing armour, cover up."

"Good thinking, Chief," Jake said. "March! Cover up!"

Ayan looked to where Leland was still having a lively discussion with Edward and saw that his comm unit was blinking, but he was paying no attention.

The five eighty meter long ships broke through the cloud cover behind him; they were less than a kilometre away and slowing their quick descent. The heavy rain ran off the edges of their green and grey armoured hulls as they drifted downward in a precise formation. They would come down all around them.

"Bloody idiot," Stephanie muttered, heard by everyone on the command and security channels. Ayan watched her stride purposefully towards Leland, who didn't notice until she was within two meters. As soon as he did, he flinched visibly, momentarily trying to put several people between himself and the Security Chief. "Seal up your suit and black out your faceplate, you git! Look! Custom's ships are coming!" She pointed exaggeratedly.

It was as though he was the last to notice, and he may as well have been, since the low rumbling sound of their antigravity emitters were just kicking in and the air was stirred by a slight vibration. The high pitched hiss of the rain around the ships being pressed at speed by the nearest vessel's antigravity systems filled the air. It was unlike anything Ayan had ever heard, and she was thankful that it lessened as their ships landed.

114

Stephanie shook her head as March simply gawked at the nearest ship, not bothering to close his faceplate. She irritably activated it for him, using her command unit and went back to stand with a small group of similarly clad guards so she could mix in with the crowd.

"Removing rankings, normalizing colours," Jake said quietly. All rank insignia disappeared from their vacsuits. The deserter line's suits turned light yellow while everyone else's were turned black with the exception of Ayan and Laura's suits. They were singled out in white.

"So you know, all I have to lean on here is the diplomacy and encounter training that I had in the Academy. You might want to pick a few assistants for me, Jake," Ayan said worriedly.

"Relax, you'll be fine. Give these stiffs whatever they want except for command access to the Clever Dream and the Samson."

Ayan watched as the ships slowly touched down. As soon as the broad landing feet grazed the ground, broad ramps extended and troop doors opened. In seconds there was a hovering skiff pad bearing a woman in a long, green hooded cloak and several heavily armed soldiers around her. Beneath the cloak she wore a dark brown uniform, the breast of the suit jacket held together with several glimmering silver chains. Ayan could see that the woman wore a silken garment that had many small folds underneath. The uniform was stately, almost ornate. The woman who wore it looked as though she was chiselled from stone; her features were sharp, she was tall, and her long blonde hair was pulled back into a tight single braid.

Soldiers baring long rifles and wearing heavy, plated armour topped by darkened, angular helmets stepped onto smaller skiffs and began deploying around the fighters. They look as intimidating as the Triton security teams must to outsiders. This isn't going to be easy, Ayan thought to herself as she fought down rising nervousness.

"I understand why you're singled out, but what am I doing in white?" Laura asked in a low whisper as she watched a squad of fourteen Triton soldiers rush to stand in formation behind them. In the hazardous environment armour, covered in thin, horizontal metal slats, they looked as imposing, if not a little more strange, than the Carthan soldiers.

"I think you're here for support," Ayan muttered back, watching the lead official draw closer by the second. She didn't seem bothered by the rain in the least, even though much of it was spattering against her uniform jacket. "I'm guessing this isn't a typical reception, Jake?"

"No, it isn't, but they're probably pretty wary these days, considering the way the last couple months have being going."

"I know, I'll do my best."

"Just remember what we need. Transportation for the deserters, somewhere we can make repairs, bargain for parts, supplies, and a privateering contract would be nice. Stay focused."

Ayan didn't acknowledge that she'd taken his instructions in, the skiff carrying the Customs official stopped within two meters of her.

The Customs Officer's cold grey eyes regarded Ayan passively. "I am Carthan Colonel Miriam Davies. Before we discuss anything, I must inform you that if any more of your fighters attempt to traverse our air or orbital space without clearance before powering up, they will be destroyed. You are also not permitted to use any of these ships for general transportation until we've completed our inspection."

"I am Commander Ayan Rice, we-"

"Do you understand my instructions?" interrupted the Colonel.

"Aye, you were perfectly clear." Ayan let her British accent slip more when she was irritated, and the woman hovering in front of her was instantly frustrating to speak with. She'd dealt with commanding officers exactly like her, and consciously decided to keep her temper in check. "We'll be sure to get clearance for any departures."

"To be clear, your pilot acquired clearance; he just waited until he broke the hundred meter ceiling before requesting it. In my book, that's backwards thinking, and people who operate like that don't go far where I come from. Now what is your business here?" the colonel said as she coolly ran her gaze across the myriad of ships behind Ayan.

"Our first priority here is to provide these refugees an opportunity to visit a civilized port where they can try and get home, or contact relations."

"These people don't look like refugees, they're too well dressed, too well taken care of."

"We took care of them and in return they worked with our staff."

"There isn't enough room in these ships for these people. Is there another ship we're not seeing? Something outside the solar system or in another port?"

"What you see is all we have left. Most of these people are refugees, we had to make do until we could make it to the nearest civilized system. That led us-"

"Where are your refugees from?"

"We have refugees from Enreega, Pandem, and a slaver ship."

"That leads me to my next question: are you aware that one of these ships was stolen from a Carthan ship yard five years ago? It was last in the possession of a Captain James Gammin, registered to the Palamo, a carrier wanted for piracy."

Ayan was genuinely surprised, even though she knew she shouldn't be, and she kicked herself for not checking the names of each of their ships in the Carthan Port database. She had only checked the Clever Dream and the Samson. "I had no id-"

"Clueless. I hope you're not the real leader here. Then again, it might explain why you're so anxious to dump these people off onto the Carthan government. Corporal Lakam, lead a team onto the Jolly Holler and take possession. Assess its flight worthiness."

Ayan knew the ship she was talking about. It was a forty-two meter long ship in fairly good condition, one of the few ships that surrendered before taking serious damage in Ossimi Ring. "Colonel, my people have done work on that ship to make it space worthy and have left personal possessions aboard."

"We're taking that ship, Commander. You're in no legal or tactical position to stop us."

"Fine, just give us some time to get our things and some of the materials we used so we can use them to repair our other ships."

The Colonel looked at the long, irregular hauler and nodded. "I can't see how you could make things worse. You have fifteen minutes, and don't take any fixtures, regardless of when they were added."

"We're on it," Jake said over her personal comm. Seconds later most of the loyal crewmembers arranged in lines started running to the Jolly Holler.

"Begin a high powered sensor sweep of the ships and the individuals here," the Colonel ordered to one of the soldiers at her side.

He pressed several buttons on a pad affixed to his thigh and nodded. "The teams are on it."

"Thank you," the colonel turned back to Ayan and asked, "Now, is everyone here requesting refugee status?"

"No, only the people in that line and that group there," Ayan pointed to the deserter line and the milling crowd at one end.

"So the majority, I see." The Colonel seemed to ponder the situation as she looked over the gathering of starfighters and more heavily damaged ships.

"We're also looking to-" began Ayan.

"How did you come to command this group?"

Ayan's temper flared, but she kept it in check - mostly. "I can't see how that's any of your business."

"Really?" asked the colonel, focusing her attention on Ayan again.

"None," Ayan said flatly. "We have needs, and I'd like to see if we can be attended to. These refugees aren't without means, only access. Most of them have accounts with reputable banks. They only need secure access to finance their own transport off this moon to a more familiar place."

"And those who don't have funds?"

"We've provided each with one hundred weight bullion, enough for them to try and get a start. We only need to transport them to a friendly port."

"I'm afraid that isn't going to happen. I'm denying your people refugee status."

"What?" Ayan burst.

"The Carthan government can't afford to take in more strays. You'll have to send them to one of the unofficial ports, like Port Rush. It's just over there. It's a free port, they can do whatever they want there. I hear you can even get banking services for a price."

"Can we get clearance to begin transporting people there?"

"We'll see what this inspection turns up," Colonel Davies said as she activated a holographic display that projected from the palm of her hand. Rain drops made small spots in the image for a moment as they passed through. She nodded to herself as she read the information on the Clever Dream, satisfied that it was registered to Ayan and moved on to the Samson. "Sold to you by Captain Jacob Valance yesterday. How is it that his ship is here and I don't see him?"

"I took it while he was in the shower," Ayan sneered. Her patience was already beyond frayed.

The Colonel smiled thinly and looked down at her with a raised eyebrow. "You know, I almost believe you. Did you take it in our space?"

"No."

"Then I suggest you get a registry slip printed for each of your ships. The fighters especially. It says here that they were manufactured for your use on a vessel called the Triton."

"Our larger ship."

"Well, we don't have any record of it, so you'll have to get those tied to you on secure slips so we have something more difficult to counterfeit next time you run into us. Do you have any kind of receipt of sale to prove that you paid for these or had any kind of command authority to order their construction?"

"I'm a senior officer on the Triton."

"Do you have any evidence of that? A manifest? A service record?"

Ayan couldn't stand it any longer, and brought up the senior officer list for the Triton. In the space of seconds it was hovering between them on a large hologram. At the top were Jacob and Ayan.

"Can you pass the record on to me please?"

"No, you don't have the rank," Ayan said quietly. "If you can get me in front of someone who can approve a multi-role close combat carrier and a crew of two thousand or more for privateering, like a representative of the Governor's Office, then I'll be happy to cooperate."

"You know, I could revoke your landing rights and send you on-"

"No, you won't. Your government needs privateers with the means and equipment to fight. The Order of Eden is everywhere, Regent Galactic is closing in along with them, and you don't have enough ships," Ayan growled.

The colonel pretended to ignore everything Ayan said, straightened up, and announced, "The scan didn't pick up any illegal materials, only a few weapons that won't be permitted within the city limits of Greydock. Here's a list, along with our laws. Be sure that your crew, even the refugees, gets a copy."

"We need clearance for a ship to go to Greydock so I can negotiate the terms of a privateering contract," said Ayan.

"You won't be getting it. All your vessels are forbidden to leave this area. If one takes off, we'll be forced to destroy it from orbit. Have a nice day, Commander." Colonel Miriam Davies smirked.

"I was instructed to visit the Office of the Governor upon landing."

"If you come with me, I'll be more than happy to provide you with transportation. You and your aide are welcome."

"They come with me," Ayan said, nodding towards two of the armoured Triton soldiers behind her.

"They leave their rifles here. Sidearms only."

"Thank you," Ayan forced.

One of Triton's security personnel walked to Ayan's side hastily and handed her a courier bag. "Someone said you'd need this," he told her quietly before retreating back to his place beside Jake and Stephanie.

"Follow me, please," said the colonel as her small skiff turned towards the large customs ship.

CHAPTER 18
MAJOR CUMBERLAND

The constant flaring of muzzle flashes filled the broad outer hallway. Major Cumberland watched as two of his soldiers, Faltia and Mazurek, dragged the wounded back around the corner. His helmet command display showed him the desperate scene in all its gore. The enemy was holding the outer hall as though their lives depended on it, firing from side rooms and from behind heavy crates that had been dragged in for cover. They were losing as many or more people as Cumberland was.

How many Triton crew members were left was a mystery to everyone, but each was fighting tooth and nail to keep Major Cumberland's people from moving towards the interior sections of the ship. "These aren't like the ones on the command or engineering levels, they don't have stealth suits," reported his second in command, a young officer named Loman.

"I know, but they're fighting like I've never seen," Major Cumberland said as he watched his people fall back. He had arrived on the scene with five squads and he had lost sixteen people, reducing their number to thirty four.

"Is it true that you bagged a whole squad of stealthers when you got on board, Sir?" asked Sturges, a young private.

"We caught them coming from the fighter deck as we were sealing a section off. A little luck and a lot of cover fire did the job. Keep your head on a swivel and you'll bag one too, Private," Major Cumberland reassured with gritty enthusiasm. He knew his people had gotten lucky, though. If his scanning officer wasn't using his sonic system tuned really high, they wouldn't have noticed the deck chief slowly surrounding them. When he fired it was instinctive, and at first he thought his people were panicking, firing at shadows and ghosts. When the deck chief's corpse dropped, he knew better and closed ranks. They filled the corridor with cover fire and when the smoke cleared, Major Collins had lost eight of his people, killing only seven of the stealthed defenders. He returned to the moment as he realized that a few of his men were too busy trading war stories.

"I just watched one of the normals break cover," one was recalling, "He tossed a whole handful of incendiary grenades and dove behind a crate. His face... it was like... I've never seen so much hate in my life."

Narrow Field Incendiary grenades burned for several white hot seconds in a small space and went out, the kind of hardware only a real infantryman knew how to use. "That's what got Gerbagio and Sams. I saw it. "

"An issyrian is leading them. I caught sight for a second. What do we do, Sir?"

Major Cumberland looked at Loman for a moment then checked the energy level on his rifle. Morale was already a problem when they arrived. The boarding teams had won several straight-on fire fights and taken over one hundred crew members into custody. For that hundred in custody they had killed fifty. The ship was a death trap. The engineering levels had killed or disabled four squads. The fire fight on the command deck was a day old and everyone was getting paranoid, afraid of the defenders they couldn't see.

Major Cumberland had been in hard fights before, he'd seen people cut in half by pulse weapon fire right in front of him, but that didn't prepare him for what had been happening around the medical bay. He was listening to Lieutenant Sascha Linares when people from her squad started disappearing. There was no warning, no fire fight; two of her people simply disappeared from all sensors and when they reappeared around a corner several meters up the corridor they were dead, decapitated cleanly.

They held their ground, scanned with sonics and everything else they had and just as their scanning officer thought she glimpsed something, Lieutenant Linares was killed. She was standing right in the middle of her squad, and whoever was after them, toying with them, ran a micron thick blade into the top of her head and left it there. He didn't watch the playback.

Then the assassin left them alone for over an hour.

They almost made it out of the medical section, but as they were just about to enter a narrow service hatch, they were killed two by two. It happened so quickly anything the squad said was unintelligible. It wasn't an explosive; they had a chance to fire their weapons. They had a chance to scream. Medical had claimed more than one squad, and if what he was overhearing from command was any indication, they would be going in full force next time, and he knew when they cleared the hallway ahead, Command would be sending them inward, to prepare to take the infirmary.

Someone like Private Loman might crack as soon as he realized they were headed that way. "We're going to rush them. Tell the heavies that we'll need their concussive charges. We can't afford to use anything else or we could break a seal and start venting atmosphere."

"But, Sir, our suits will protect us from-"

"We don't know what kind of countermeasures this ship uses when compartments lose pressure, I don't want another surprise."

"Yes, Sir!"

"We rush in sixty. Heavy one through three, did you hear me?"

"Yes, Sir, ready to go."

"All squads, form up around the corner, wait for the bang. When it goes off we rush the hallway, we fire until they're all down or are in full retreat."

"Yes, Sir!"

The soldiers moved into position, the most heavily armoured soldiers at the front with small grenade launchers at the ready, everyone else sorted behind them, shoulder to shoulder. Major Cumberland made his way into the middle. It was a necessary evil, without him the charge might not execute properly. Everyone knew that the taking of the Triton was going badly. They were gaining ground, but at the rate they were going, they could name each corridor after a soldier who had lost his or her life aboard and they'd run out of hallways.

The heavies moved ahead, peeking around the corner only as much as they had to in order to launch three concussive grenades apiece. One of them caught a dozen rounds in the side and chest. His armour sparked and smouldered. He was dead before he hit the deck.

The concussive charges went off, sending a wave of pressure down the hallway that would have knocked a few of the Major's men down the hall in the opposite direction if they weren't in formation. How those charges must have felt to the enemy, he could scarcely imagine. It was enough to kill a soldier in light protection within two metres.

"Go!" he ordered.

The first three lines rushed into the corridor. The first line knelt, the next stood fast as they opened fire. The third line was in reserve, ready to fire if someone in front was injured, killed, or had to rotate out to reload.

Major Cumberland was in the second line, and he couldn't help but let the frustration of the last twenty-four hours wash over him as he opened fire. His particle rifle pounded his shoulder, a familiar, almost comforting feeling, a sensation of exertion, as he lined up target after target, trying to score a significant hit against the enemy who had cost him so many.

The Triton had cost them over a hundred lives, killed several commanders he'd sat down with in the officer's mess, and destroyed two service people he had long respected. They wouldn't get him; they wouldn't win against his unit. He caught one woman full in the face with a round as she stood to run, another took several rounds in the chest, and as two of them stood to throw a thin circular device, he caught one in the arm and shoulder. The other managed to throw what was in his hand and as soon as it hit the floor an energy shield filled the hallway. It was the issyrian. He was their commander.

The shield stood up to the full force of their weapons fire. Major Cumberland could see four Triton soldiers break cover and hurriedly treat the wounded, administering medication with injectors mounted on their wrist units. Two of the wounded were able to stand. Three others were picked up and rushed down the hallway then around a corner.

"Hold your fire," Major Cumberland ordered. There were no signs that the shield was about to diminish, and he realized why. The energy field most likely absorbed the energy exerted against it and recycled it into useful power.

"Unit C Theta, we've forced about six or seven of the enemy into retreat and can't pursue. They're headed in your direction."

"I hope not, we're busy with a big push in our section. We're finally gaining ground, not going to stop now. Any chance of pursuit, Unit G Alpha?" asked the commander trying to take the next section. He had been given command of a full unit as well, five squads of ten.

The enemy crewman looked straight at Major Cumberland with large, glistening green eyes and after a moment he nodded, as though in respect.

Major Cumberland returned the gesture and watched the issyrian disappear before his eyes. He was the only one wearing a black vacsuit with ranks on his cuffs, marking him as a Lieutenant Commander.

"Negative, they've erected a confinement field," Major Cumberland replied at last. It was like an admission, like he'd failed to complete his mission. "All right, get the wounded back to the secured section, the rest of you, with me. It's time to see what they were protecting."

The group moved ahead, crossing the fifteen meters that had been a no-man's-land only minutes before. A pair of heavy doors had been scorched and scarred from end to end during the prolonged fire fight. "All right, get this open, Loman. Everyone else, cover our rear and work on getting that field down."

Major Cumberland took the time to check on the status of Unit C Theta and regretted it. They had taken cover in some kind of night club observatory - sign against the wall said Oota Galoona - and discovered more trouble than they could handle.

It looked empty at first, but when half of the unit's remaining fighting men and women made it through the door, it slammed down so quickly no one had time to react. What followed wasn't a fire fight. A number of issyrians and massive nafalli ambushed them using the bar and several booths as cover. They took no prisoners, raking the soldiers with pulse rifle fire until the nafalli moved in and literally tore them to pieces with traditional blades machined from deck plating and laser cutters.

When the slaughter was over, the Triton crewmen took cover again. None of them had stealth suits, but they only opened the door, as though inviting anyone else who wanted to try and take that compartment. He didn't know the commanding officer of Unit C Theta, but was relieved to see that he was about to order the doors to that section sealed, instead of taking it with the twenty-three troopers he had left.

As soon as welding torches were in hand, three side doors opened and a flood of the lesser armoured Triton crewmembers rushed what remained of the unit. The issyrian appeared right behind the commanding officer and fired several rounds into his back as his own personal energy shielding absorbed the bolts of energy fired at him by frantic soldiers. A moment later, the issyrian was gone, having served his purpose, to cause a distraction and kill the commanding officer. The rest of the crewmen were rough around the edges in comparison, in thinner, lower quality vacuum suits than the rest of the crew with no ranks on their cuffs, and many had long hair, stubble, or looked more haggard than the others they had encountered. Still, they were armed with what seemed standard weaponry for the Triton, heavy pulse rifles or pistols that could super heat his men's armour in two shots or less.

The fire fight lasted less than twenty-four seconds, and there was no hint of mercy. A message was being sent: go back the way you came.

He was only seeing the footage because Command had intercepted it on the local Triton crew announcement band. The enemy's morale just leapt up several points, and he was sure at least a few officers in Command would be having second thoughts about the boarding operation. Or at least, he hoped they were having second thoughts.

The large double doors beside Major Cumberland opened and he ordered his scanning team, reduced to two soldiers, forward with a squad for cover using hand signals.

"Whoa, not good!" exclaimed Farrar, his lead scanning officer. She recoiled as though she had been physically struck. "This is a torpedo room, picking up five fusion torpedoes ready to go, set for focused detonation and ready to go on an electrical hair trigger."

"Confirmed! This whole room is linked to some kind of control node. If I knew more about the ship I'd be able to tell you where it goes, probably the bridge, but there's no telling."

Major Cumberland looked across the room. The transparent hull was four meters thick in some places. He could see the lights of Battlecruiser 1009; it was directly in the torpedo room's line of fire and moored in place. The well polished floor and pristinely maintained equipment in the space told him things about the crew that didn't make him feel better. Whoever worked in that section was disciplined, skilled, and most likely loyal.

He was reminded of the crew members they had managed to capture, who told them nothing, worse than nothing. They provided misinformation, like the story of the ship's vault in the centre of the vessel. According to them, it was a Botanical Gallery with family apartments, a park, gardens, and small businesses. It was unbelievable; the most secure section of the ship couldn't have been occupied by personal quarters and plant life. Teams had been trying to cut into it for hours and had made little progress.

The maddening fighting skill and tactical execution of their movements were counter to a people who would keep that sort of thing at the heart of their ship. Soldiers travelled on ships made for soldiers, whether they were mercenaries, corporate, or operating under the rule of a government. "What are the other tubes for?"

"Sorry, Sir?"

"You said there are four fusion torpedoes loaded, what's in the other two?"

"They look like tactical plasma drillers," replied Farrar.

Major Cumberland looked through the transparent hull to the battlecruiser and got a sinking feeling. "Cumberland to Command. We have a situation here."

"This is Command, go ahead."

"I'm in a port-side torpedo room; it's loaded and ready to go with four focused nukes and a couple of driller rounds. Looks like there's a pretty sensitive trip fuse linking them together, I don't want to attempt to disarm."

"Hold, Major."

"Yes, Sir,"

The wait felt like an eternity as everyone who was privy to the situation watched the seconds pass on their displays. Finally, the Command officer reappeared. "Major, is there any indication that the fuse could be connected to similar torpedo rooms in other parts of the ship?"

Major Cumberland looked to Farrar, who nodded emphatically. The junior scanning officer verified it with a slower, deeper nod of his own. "My people are sure of it, Sir. Looks like these people will do anything to keep us from taking possession."

"Leave it, we'll send someone in behind you to disarm them."

"Sir, with all due respect, if there is even one more of these rooms set up the same way, and it goes off in your faces, you could lose a battlecruiser. From what I've seen of this ship, it's a mirrored design, meaning that-"

"The port side matches the starboard side, I'm aware, Major. Command has evaluated the risk and is sending you new orders. Command out," finished the Communications Officer.

Major Cumberland checked his orders and nodded to himself. "Get that shield down, we're headed to the central express lifts. Looks like they finished mopping up the levels below us and we're not going aft."

CHAPTER 19
GREYDOCK

Leaving everyone behind as things were growing worse by the minute was one of the hardest things Ayan had done since waking up on Freedom Tower. There was no doubt about it, leaving everyone behind felt wrong. She couldn't forget the parting sight of the crew and ships in the middle of that featureless landscape. The rain started to come down harder as they stepped into the customs vessel, and she could tell that hard clay was starting to turn to mud.

As Ayan, Laura and the pair of Triton soldiers behind them looked through the wide transparasteel porthole, they could see Jake and Stephanie moving everyone out from under the ships as the landing struts started to sink into the softening toxic dirt. Lights were coming on within the Jolly Holler. Customs officers would be taking it back to Greydock, or wherever they brought stolen vessels and the Triton refugees would be left with even less shelter. The clouds didn't seem to be thinning either.

"Are you all right?" Laura asked in a low whisper.

"We need to turn things around. Even the people who wanted to leave can't, and now we have loyal crew working while the rest stand around complaining about how we screwed up and customs won't let them go anywhere." She gestured at the slowly milling crowd of deserters, many of them looking like they were shouting at the security people who herded them away from the heavy, mismatched ships. It was as though they didn't realize that they would be crushed if they were beneath them if they broke through the toxic layer of soil. "I've never seen a crew so beaten."

"We'll find a way," Laura reassured. "Between everyone here, we'll figure something out."

"I think I really burned a bridge with Colonel Davies. Her report isn't going to favour our cause," said Ayan.

"I don't think anyone could have done any better. She's a little full of herself, I think."

Ayan smiled tightly and nodded. "Glad I wasn't the only one who noticed."

"I think you restrained yourself very well. The Ayan I knew would have blown everything by putting the woman in her place. You handled yourself more tactfully, with more grace than I expected."

"Thank you, I think."

"You're welcome," said Laura with a smile.

Her private comm crackled and she heard Jake's voice in her ear. "Good luck out there, Ayan. We're going to try and build an extra shelter from plating we're gathering from the ships. Oh, and it looks like we got a lot more than expected from the Jolly Holler. Our people already have everything that wasn't bolted down, even the makeshift bunks."

"Good, be careful. I'll find us a place to set down and hurry back."

"You're going to have to find us about a week's worth of food. Lewis did a scan inventory and we don't have the supplies or enough materializers to provide for the people we have."

"I will. Good thing Lewis checked."

"We'll be out of comm range and we don't have relay access, so I'll talk to you soon. Be careful." He raised a hand from where he stood beside the Samson. He was checking the port, aft side, where one of the main landing struts was already sinking into the dirt.

The customs ship began to lift off and she braced herself against the transparent hull. "I'll get us what we need."

"I know," he said.

With a jerk, the customs vessel accelerated and put the miserable scene behind them. The signal strength between Ayan and Jake shrank to nothing in a heartbeat, and Ayan turned her attention to the dark terrain rolling under them at an incredible speed.

"I wonder what the Carthans will think when the Triton arrives?" Laura asked idly.

"Do you think they'll be able to break free?"

"Honestly? If I did the math on their chances, I know they wouldn't be good, but Oz and Jason had a plan. I've seen Jason when he doesn't think something will work, or when he knows an operative under him is gone for good, and that's not the Jason I was seeing as we left. That, and most of the slaves who could fight volunteered to stay too. I've never seen so many people jump on the bandwagon at once."

"So there's hope," said Ayan.

"There's hope. If we see the Triton again, she'll probably need a lot of work, maybe years worth, but we'll have a home of our own again. A place we can control."

"If we can hold out here until she gets back. I think we'll have to do something drastic to make that happen."

"That's what Jacob is for. His people seem to have some experience with desperate," observed Laura.

Ayan smiled and nodded. "I know. I just wish I could get along with Stephanie. She seems to have walls up. I can't get more than a nod or a grunt from her on good days, but she's always assigning a security detail to follow me around."

"We don't mind, Commander," offered Victor. "You take care of yourself just fine, so it's more like you're taking us for a walk."

"Thank you, Victor, that's nice of you."

"Call me Vic. Victor was my grandfather."

"He's right, you know. You're rarely the one in trouble. It's the causes you pick up along the way that make it feel like you're in a difficult spot. Just like your taste for bad boys. What was it you said a few years ago? 'Always heels up for the bad boy.'"

Ayan's eyes went wide as she turned bright red. There was a snicker from behind, the female Triton soldier they'd brought along. "Laura! That's privy."

"I don't get it," Vic said quietly.

"Oh, it's like the saying; 'head over heels in love' only it implies that she ends up on her back with her heels up high, at the ready," Laura teased.

Victor snorted and his female counterpart burst into laughter. "Oh, I'm using that one," she breathed as she managed to calm down.

"Now you've done it. They'll never take me seriously again," Ayan half jested, shaking her head in mock shame.

"Considering the bad boy you're chasing these days, I don't think anyone will have trouble taking you seriously," Laura replied.

"I'm not chasing him, he's chasing me," Ayan retorted, mildly offended.

"Fooled me."

"Okay, maybe we're chasing each other. Either way, I don't think this is the best time to air out the laundry."

"And there's another one," Victor quipped from behind.

"What?" Laura asked.

"Another expression I've never heard."

"This one uses 'laundry' in place of 'private business,' like Ayan and the captain," explained Laura.

"Oh, you think that's private? Everyone on Triton seems to make it their business to know what's going on with you two. Even if they didn't, nothing stays private for long on a ship. Scuttlebutt is gold," said Vic.

"One of the sad facts of my life," Ayan rolled her eyes with a crooked grin. "Grew up on a ship, then trained to build ships, to command ships, and then spent more time on a ship than anywhere else, really."

"Wouldn't change a thing, would you?" Laura asked.

"I'm afraid I'm a ship rat for life."

"Did you ever actually build a ship?" asked one of the security team. She was a young woman with striking, light brown eyes.

"Laura and I worked on a few prototypes. We also helped design a new class of small carrier for Freeground."

"A carrier? No wonder Chief Grady likes having you in engineering."

"Speaking of which, I can't believe he stayed behind," said Ayan.

"The word is that Chief Grady was all up for Oz's, I mean Commander McPatrick's plan. I wish I could have been around for that, but I was too busy with the evacuation and making sure the Samson would hold together long enough to get us to the rendezvous."

The landscape outside started to brighten, the dun soil lightening until it was replaced with ruined farm land surrounded by black and brown stands of trees. The clouds thinned, illuminating the territory beneath them. "It looks like they just left everything to rot," commented one of the security staff behind Ayan.

"The toxicity of the land around it probably seeped in. I wonder what happened to spoil their terraforming efforts," Ayan wondered aloud.

The shore came and went in a flash, leaving them with a view of tall blue waves. For several minutes the group watched the open water drift by. "I grew up on Ima, there's no large bodies of water there," whispered the brown eyed girl behind Ayan.

"I know how you feel. We grew up on a space station," Laura said quietly. "I only learned to swim four years ago."

"I learned in the Academy," Ayan added.

A brown and black rocky shore loomed ahead, and after a moment, the water was gone. They were under thick cloud cover again, and a mist clung to the ground from the shore all the way inland. Greydock was located in the middle of a sizable island, and that island told a story. As they passed over the brown, lifeless terrain, they caught glimpses of terraforming machines, cleaning and re-nutriating the soil the old fashioned way, by digging it up and seeding it with activated soil. The bacteria within would cleanse and revive the earth over the space of several years.

The work camps several kilometres back from the shoreline were like a new sea of white and brown tents. All around were tilling pits and reforestation lots. There was a visible division between the contaminated soil and the area ready for replanting drawn by a tall stonework barrier. The camp was on the inside, with long fields of saplings and several large, hangar-like buildings.

"That's gotta be complicated. All those poor Confederation workers down there need to be moved out of the solar system because the Carthans are taking over. I think I know where our deserters are going to end up if they can't afford to get off-world," Laura said quietly as she watched the tent city disappear.

For several minutes they passed over dusty brown rolling hills of undeveloped soil. It didn't look poisoned, only featureless, and when a broad winged, graceful black bird appeared on the horizon, Ayan couldn't look away. They were past it after a moment, and she noticed a feature ahead on the horizon, like a broad, lonely tower.

They closed in on it quickly and slowed down, joining a light stream of traffic headed towards and past the massive structure. It was the first time they'd seen activity in the sky since they broke atmosphere, and as the city grew nearer, a circular pattern of hundreds of ships became visible. The walls of the tower were over twenty kilometres wide at the base, and it had taken on the colour of the dirt. It was like a hundred storey tall fort, and if there was an enemy on the ground that could threaten such a place, Ayan didn't want to meet them.

Atop the tower was a modern city made of dark metals, a metropolis to rival most of the cities that Ayan had seen. As broad armoured doors opened in the side of the square tower, Ayan realized that that was where they were headed, that was Greydock.

"Ayan, I think this is Expansion Age construction. This place is over four hundred years old, probably more," Laura said in awe.

"Aren't most Expansion Age structures on the core worlds?" asked Vic.

"Not all, they had several outer colonies, this must be one of them," Ayan said quietly. "I never thought I'd see anything like it."

The four customs enforcement ships swept down towards the widening bay doors. There were a dozen or so other such ships inside, with room for several more. What Ayan wished she could see was the city above, but it was well out of sight.

The ship touched down and she could hear the deployment ramps lowering. She couldn't help but feel a little intimidated at having to deal with a military force that could take a solar system with advanced third era technology. A mental image of her mother emerged in her mind. She could see her, her mother the admiral, and she couldn't imagine why. It wasn't the mother who wanted to reconcile that she recalled then, either; it was the parent she had knock down, drag out arguments with when she was a young teen, before she signed up for the Junior Academy. If she could picture that woman while facing hard nosed military officers and block-headed beaurocrats, then she'd be ready for anything.

The hatch at the end of the corridor opened and she strode for it. Marched like she was on the parade ground and not only did everyone fall in step behind her, but the customs officers got out of her way. When she arrived at the bottom of the main deployment ramp, Colonel Davies was there to meet her. She was checking something on a work pad, and only spared a momentary glance at Ayan before speaking to her. "This officer will lead you to the Office of the Governor. We've found no reason to detain you."

"Thank you," Ayan said before turning and nodding at the young unarmed officer who waited for them. He was a nervous-looking thin man who must have been a clerk. He was in a dark brown uniform that looked crisp and new.

"I-if you'd follow me, Ma'am," he stammered.

Ayan let the hint of a smile crack her lips and walked several steps behind him.

"Wow, I forgot that about you. It's like a switch," Laura whispered just loudly enough to compete with the sounds of the Triton soldiers' boots behind them.

"What's that?"

"You and your mother, all personable one minute then all cold intimidation the next."

Ayan couldn't remember a time when she'd been that way in front of Laura. Perhaps she was serious minded or bent to a task when they served together on the First Light, but never had she exhibited the sense of presence she felt as they crossed the large landing bay. It was like a comforting weight across her shoulders. "Really?" was all she managed.

"Ah, I guess the scan was taken before you grew into that," Laura whispered even more quietly. Ayan barely heard her. "Sorry."

"It's all right, I've come to terms with the missing years. Was I like that often after the wedding?"

"More and more, mostly because you wanted to push projects ahead and it helped if people took you seriously. Some people started comparing you with your mother,"

"You're kidding,"

"Not at all. They used to call you 'the smart Rice woman,' and well, that pretty much said it all as far as Command was concerned. If it weren't for your persistence, we wouldn't have finished work on the Silkstream Four."

"Thank you, Laura. Somehow knowing that I've had that side before helps me with my resolve now. I have no idea what we're in for."

"Same here." Laura created an encoded channel and gave rights to the Triton soldiers and Ayan then used it to ask, "Have any of you ever been to a Carthan administration office?"

"Are you kidding? I still can't believe I've been in three solar systems in as many months," chuckled the young woman behind them.

"No, but if it's like any other beaurocracy, expect a long line," replied Victor.

"So, it's all new," Laura concluded.

"Too bad, someone with a bit of experience would be useful here, but I suppose that'll be us before long. You two will probably find yourselves going on a lot of trips after we've returned," Ayan said with a glance back at the Triton soldiers. She didn't have to check Victor's information, she'd spent tense time with him at Ossimi Ring Station, but she checked the other. Her name was Jenny Machad, a soldier who had served with Victor on Pandem. She qualified on tactics and weapons on her first day aboard Triton. This one doesn't like to waste time. I think I like her already.

They were led to a large elevator and Ayan made sure to stand right beside the nervous officer they had been assigned to. "How's life here?" she asked him.

He stared at her for a moment, startled, before replying. "Fine, it's fine. Pretty safe since the Carthans got here."

"It wasn't safe before?"

"No, Ma'am," he answered in a rush. Instead of elaborating, he stared at the pitted metal doors of the large lift.

"Do you get a lot of visitors in Greydock?"

The customs officer rushed out the doors as soon as they started to open. "Not as many as before the Carthans took over, I guess," he called over his shoulder.

"This guy's hilarious," Victor uttered under his breath as they caught up.

"Here we are," their guide announced as they came around a corner and faced a broad corridor with foot paths worn into the ancient metal floor. There were dozens of concave indents in the walls spaced out at regular intervals. In front were dips in the floor where speakers were supposed to stand.

There were over a hundred people gathered around high tables, reviewing information on thin tablets, personal holodisplays, arm units, and every other type of personal information device they could imagine. Several looked like they were just staring out into space. At a glance, Ayan counted five races, three she knew and two she'd never seen before. One was in an outfit that allowed for six legs and four arms. As far as she could tell, there was no head, everything just ended at shoulders that looked like a collection of fleshy bulbs. One of them was stopping to stand in front of one of the circular dips in the floor when she noticed him - or her, she couldn't discern which - and she was relieved when an image emerged from the wall. That was the best way to describe it, an emergence. The old stone of the wall became the texture, colour, and shape of a woman. Whatever the material was, it changed as smoothly as any holographic image, only it was some kind of moving three dimensional portrait.

"Expansion Age technology," said Jenny Machad in awe. "I never thought it was a big deal until now, but I think I'm getting it."

"They invented things we haven't begun to understand before the collapse," Laura added.

"What, this? I'm pretty sure one of you could build something that does the same thing," Victor said quietly.

"Certainly, but it would probably require a large power source and we'd have to change the medium every month. I bet that display system barely uses any power at all. I'm sure this city has more impressive things in store, anyway," Ayan said, looking around the room. "Who knows what's been stripped from here since this city's high days."

"You present your query or whatever you like while standing on a designated point and a representative will assist you. If your matter is sensitive, they may instruct you to enter the internal office," their guide interrupted, pointing to one of the petitioners as the indent in the wall opened and he stepped inside. "If you need further instructions, well, ask a representative," the nervous young man finished reciting awkwardly. He made long, hurried strides towards the hall behind him and was gone in a rush.

"It's sort of like the licensing office back home," Laura said as she looked around the room. "A lot like it, actually."

"Only without so much invisible security," Ayan commented.

"You're right. An all out riot could break out here and everyone behind those walls can just sit back and watch. Whoever built this place must have been either paranoid or used to trouble," Victor commented.

"Well, no time like the present." Ayan marched to the nearest empty dip in the floor and stopped to stand in front of one of the shallow, indented alcoves. The wall had evidence of some food stuff or other substance splattered against it, as though someone who had been there was displeased with the outcome of their bartering or petitioning.

"Hello, Commander Ayan Rice. I have your file in front of me," said a woman whose image rose from the stone wall's surface as though she was surfacing from a calm pool. She was in a uniform similar to that of the Customs Officer, only she had no studs on her cuffs. "I understand you're representing some refugees and other ship captains who have landed in the Dower Wastes."

"That's right,"

"Before we get started, I'd like to remind you that you and your people have been denied refugee status, so you are not eligible for any aid or assistance at this time."

"Why were we denied refugee status? I was never told," asked Ayan.

"Oh, that's unusual. It says here that it was due to how heavily armed your group is, and because you were found in possession of a ship stolen in Carthan territory. Would you like to contest the decision?"

"No, we're not here for hand-outs, and those claims are true. What I'd like to do is acquire landing permits for a proper port."

"For which ship?"

"All of them please."

"Ah, and what is your business in the Rega Gain System?"

"I'd like to privateer for the Carthans. I'd also like to trade for food and supplies."

"Let's start with the matter I can assist you with. Normally we would probe your background, especially since you don't even have a surname attached to your Freeground identification, but considering you have arrived with so many ships and have no criminal record in this or adjacent sectors, I'm going to issue you Carthan identification."

"What about landing permits and-"

"All in good time. How will you be paying?"

"I have certified platinum bullion."

"Good. All right then, I'm assuming your companions require identification as well: Victor Davis, Jenny Machad, and Laura Everin."

"Why would I need Carthan government identification when you seem to know who we are on sight?"

"So you can have access to our services and apply for a visa or special clearance."

"What is this going to cost me?"

"Twenty three credits per crewperson."

"All right, we'll go ahead with that."

"Good, now that we have that sorted, I can grant you a Privateer's letter of Marque right now for all your vessels since you've shown evidence of ownership. The Carthan government is obligated to notify you that, while we can offer you a provisional privateering licence for the Triton, you will have to prove right of ownership or command once it arrives. If you have no evidence that you're the rightful commander of the ship when it arrives, you will have to stake a claim and answer to challenges."

"What kind of evidence do you need?"

"If the vessel answers to your command codes and the main computer verifies that you are the senior commander, then the required terms will be satisfied."

"But until then you're telling me that the Triton will be licensed as a privateering vessel under my name."

"Yes."

"Thank you very much. All right, who would I be permitted to seize property from?" Ayan's spirits rose, and she did her best to keep her composure.

"The Carthan Government is licensing you to fire on and seize property from any Regent Galactic or Order of Eden vessel or other asset with a military purpose. You are also permitted to capture any ships owned by aforementioned parties and any vessels carrying objects intended for their use. You may sell all but sentient beings and weaponry to any Carthan ally or neutral party, but must remit any weapons and prisoners to Carthan officials. You will be paid thirty five percent of their market value."

"Thirty five percent?" Ayan asked, knowing that weaponry and other military hardware was the most lucrative product of many captures. "That must be conditional, or at least negotiable."

"No. You are running a raider fleet of ships you didn't even take the time to register with the Carthan government before requesting a privateering licence. We recognize that you're interested in pursuing your interests in our space legally, otherwise you wouldn't be here, but I can't offer you better rates or conditions until you acquire a visa with provisions befitting a captain in command of a combat-ready fleet."

"Then I'd like to apply for a visa."

"Because you are a captain, I can expedite the process. You will have to provide contact information for three past commanding officers, and submit to two weeks of constant oversight using one of our recording devices as well as a carthan officer aboard your command ship. At the end of that two week period, we will render our decision and determine what sort of visa we will issue to you. You can begin the application process by paying a fee of fifty thousand credits."

"I'll have to consult my former commanding officers, make sure their contact information is up to date and such. Is there any other way to negotiate the percentage paid for arms?"

"Do you operate out of any other port? If someone else is offering you a more favourable rate then I may be able to make a case to my supervisor."

Ayan thought a moment. There had to be something she could say, but all she could do was answer with another question. "What if I'm supplying my own fleet and a military carrier?"

"In that case, you're free to use any weapons you acquire, but they must be registered individually. If they are reduced to components, then you may use them however you like if you have records of their disassembly. You may be able to negotiate for less strict terms once the Triton arrives, or if you can tell me where it is now and what its primary role might be."

"I'm afraid I can't provide you with that information at the moment," Ayan said. She couldn't leave it at that, however. "I'm wondering. If one of your privateering partners' ships is in distress outside of your territory, would you lend assistance?"

"How far outside of our territory?"

Ayan hesitated a moment. What do I have to lose? At worst they'll think I'm incapable of commanding a carrier. She brought up the most recent tactical information from the Triton and displayed it as a holographic map. "The Triton is in a planetary nebula less than a day away by high compression wormhole. This is the most recent data we have on her."

"Hold while I consult my superior," the representative said, wide eyed. Her image disappeared into the wall.

Ayan looked back to see Laura just over her shoulder. "Thank you."

"I had to try. I don't think everyone would agree with me asking for help, but I couldn't stand here without saying something," said Ayan.

"Here's hoping they'll do something."

The representative's image re-emerged from the wall with a sorrowful expression. "I'm sorry, there's nothing the Carthan Fleet can do for you. As you probably understand, I can't offer any more details than that for security reasons."

Ayan's heart sank. She wasn't aware of how deeply she hoped the Carthans could help. Her request was more than a whim; she knew that if the Carthans had superior forces in the area, they would leap at the opportunity, or at least, they should have. If they claimed that they were in no position to assist them, then there was nothing she could say that would change their minds. "Thank you for taking the request seriously. Please keep abreast of the situation, if there's anything you can do to help, you'd have the gratitude of me and my crew."

"Considering your situation, there's nothing I can do to improve the terms of the privateering arrangement. If it's any comfort, some captains are already becoming quite wealthy under those same conditions. After losing so much, I can see how you might think wealth is impossible, but you must believe me when I tell you there are some wealthy privateers that have made due with much less than you have."

"Oh, I can believe it," Victor muttered under his breath.

Ayan cleared her head and her throat before going on. "Moving on. By the terms you've set out here, I can sell everything else anywhere I like?"

"That's right. In fact, any member of your crew with Carthan identification can sell whatever you capture to anyone other than an enemy of the Carthan government, it doesn't have to be you," the representative announced as though it was of some great benefit.

Ayan didn't agree; the beaurocrat's beaming announcement seemed obvious. "Are the Carthans picking a fight with anyone else?"

"There is a treaty between the Carthans and United Core World Confederation, but it will expire in twelve days. All other governments, companies, and groups that you are legally allowed to pursue, capture, or destroy are listed. You are also permitted to detain the enemy as outlined in the terms until you can hand them over to Carthan authorities for a reward. Rewards are dispensed based on the table included in the data package you'll receive."

"All right, sign me up."

"The services you have requested, including authorization slips for all your vessels, come to a total of nine thousand two hundred thirty one credits, or three hundred seven point seven in GC."

Ayan pondered for a moment, she had no idea what the exchange rate was or what the beaurocrats meant by 'GC'. "All I have is stamped platinum bullion."

"That's recognized Galactic Currency. Please put it in the drawer."

A drawer popped out of the wall as she carefully opened the courier bag. The pockets inside held, at a glance, twenty of the largest squares that glittered yellow, a package of fifty second largest square tokens that had a blue glint and a variety of others in a smaller bag. She started by pulling a yellow one out.

Jenny gasped and whispered, "That's a five hundred."

Ayan glanced at the token and felt like a dunce as she read the top of the square piece, where it was marked with a large 500G engraving. "One moment," she pleaded sheepishly.

"I've never even seen one of those before," Jenny chuckled to herself quietly as she looked around as though making sure no one else had seen.

Without pulling them from the bag, Ayan inspected the rest of the tokens and realized that the blue bars were two hundred fifty grams, the hundred gram tokens were bright purple, and the lesser denominations were green for fifty, red for twenty-five and silver for five. The fine industrial diamonds gave them their colour, and each was obviously made to be carried like a coin, but considering they were pure platinum, she couldn't imagine herself carrying much. She counted out the correct amount and watched the tray disappear. She received a few small one gram silver coins with holes in the centre that made them look like washers. They had a slight glint to them, and similar markings.

"Do you have a personal data device of some kind?"

Ayan held up her wrist so the official could see her command and control unit. It announced that it had received a new file a moment later and when Ayan opened it she found her new privateering licence. A drawer came out from the wall and Ayan picked up the contents. The stack of cards had their identification on the top, Carthan registration for every ship, and a scrolling copy of the privateering licence. Each data card allowed her to scroll through all the information contained within. "Those are your secure slips. They can only be written once, and will make a record of how often they're copied. Keep your originals. Thank you for appearing at the Office of the Governor. Good luck."

Ayan smiled back as she handed out the three identification cards at the top of the stack. "Thank you, now that that's-"

The official's image began to retreat back into the wall.

"Oi!" Ayan exclaimed, irritated.

The image reappeared. "Is there something else?"

"Yes. I need landing permits so my ships can make port in a proper facility."

"You have all the clearance you need in your hand. Each of those registry slips is also a permit, as well as your official Carthan identification. Is there anything else I can do for you?"

"Can I rent or lease hangar space for my ships here?"

"I'm sorry, the Greydock Port Authority won't be able to help you with that because you don't have a visa."

"Right. Do you know where I can buy supplies and food?"

"I'm afraid you can't buy them on Greydock without a war-time purchaser's permit."

"How do I get one?"

"I can start the process for you, but you won't be able to use the purchasers permit without a visa."

Ayan tried not to look frustrated, but the tightness in her voice betrayed her. "Where else can I buy food?"

"Port Rush is the nearest free port, a lot of pira-, I mean privateers operate from there. If you can get off-world you can find better places, but my brother-in-law has often said things are only getting worse in the nearby systems, but I wouldn't believe everything he says, he was telling me just the other day that there are cannibals on Aquil, and issyrians who walk around in their native form on Krouper." The officer cringed.

"Where's the nearest transport leaving for Port Rush?"

The official fixed her with a look of confusion and irritation. "How am I supposed to know?"

Ayan exhaled slowly and nodded. "Thank you for your help," she said, keeping her composure as best as she could.

"You're welcome. Enjoy your stay in Greydock and good luck." The image of the official disappeared again and Ayan stepped out of the petitioner's divot.

"If they ever start issuing hunting licences for beaurocrats, count me in," Victor muttered.

Ayan nodded. "They have a talent for testing patience. At least we finally have a licence to go after Order and Regent ships and permission to move our ships. I think it was too easy, though. It wouldn't have been difficult for me to steal a ship from a small space station somewhere and just declare it my own once I got here."

"I know I don't have experience at your level of leadership, Commander, but I think it just shows how desperate they are. Maybe they just can't afford to turn anyone down, even a potential ship thief," Jenny offered.

"You're probably right. I think I'm going to watch for a catch in all this though, there's got to be a downside," said Ayan.

"I call this a win," Laura encouraged.

"Aye, one that could lead to something bigger later," Ayan agreed with a curt nod.

"So, back to the wastes?" Victor asked.

"No, we're going to Port Rush."

Chapter 20
Open Ground

Shadows played across the widening central corridors of the Triton. The emergency lights in that section had been deactivated, and Major Cumberland wasn't about to order any of his people to try to change it. Attempting to interface with the ship's computer or activate systems aboard had proven fatal for many soldiers in different parts of the ship. Cumberland's men had been fortunate and intelligent, learning from the example of other soldiers.

His lamp illuminated the floor in front of him, where he could see lines indicating the proper direction for evacuees to take in order to get down to the hangar decks. He tried to shake the eerie feeling that there were no civilians left. They were facing dedicated volunteers, some of who could disappear whenever they liked.

"Movement!" called a sensor officer behind him.

Cumberland looked at the small display on his rifle and saw what he was referring to. With a quick hand signal, his remaining forty-two men and women dropped into a phalanx with the front row kneeling and the second row standing with rifles at the ready. He was right behind them with the sensor officer, and watched his own copy of the sensor feed. It was a small blip, and as he focused in he saw it was a small cleaning bot, buffing its way along the hallway ahead. "False alarm, move up," Cumberland ordered quietly.

Loman's group split into a room to their left, while Mazurek's went right. According to the sonic sensors, they would be long work rooms. Major Cumberland instructed everyone else to keep watch in the hallway. According to the intelligence he'd received from Command, they were just about to reach one of the main express lift access points.

After several minutes, both groups returned from the rooms. "Just a fine finishing, manufacturing, and repair shop, Sir. Looks like a lot of the ship's bots come from this place," Sergeant Loman reported.

"Same on this side," Sergeant Mazurek agreed.

"All right, seal them up," Cumberland ordered.

Soldiers applied several centimetres of grey material to the edges of the doors and lit one end. With a flash the doors were welded shut.

The group moved ahead quietly.

"I've got motion again, same as last time only there were a few blips and then it stopped," complained the scanning officer.

"How many are a few, Private?" asked Mazurek.

"I don't know, four? Five? Just up ahead."

Cumberland played the last few seconds back and spotted it. "Same size, reading above. All right, move forward, keep your eyes peeled." The whole group moved ahead, everyone watching all sides.

"Scanner's getting low, sonic scanning is killing the cells," reported the scanning officer.

"Someone give him a reserve pack."

"This wouldn't be a problem if these things still came with an AI to manage them. Can't distinguish between a kitten and a goddamn hungry edxi."

"Quit yer' bitchin' and mind the scanner," Sergeant Mazurek ordered. "And keep forwarding scans."

"Manual forwarding, it's like the first era all over again. Maybe I should strap some floodlights to my helmet and shout back whatever I'm seeing from point. I'd be faster, tell you that much."

"I said can it."

They arrived at the end of the corridor and fanned out. The walkway there widened so eight of them could walk abreast, but it looked even larger with the transparent wall and three meter high ceiling. Through the transparent wall they could see three heavy, thirty-five degree tracks for cargo and heavy machinery elevators. Two were angled up from aft to fore, the other one was angled opposite, and from what Cumberland could see in the dim, yellow emergency lighting that lined the tracks, there were several places where the heavy cars would be able to slip sideways. Above and below the heavy tracks were many others, for a network of smaller personnel lifts. If these were safe, we could get anywhere in the ship in seconds. He watched the space for a moment longer before he was satisfied that there was no activity to see. The hallway stretched to his right and left, and in the dim light he could just barely make out another hall on the other side of the tracks.

"It's like a space station," someone behind him murmured.

"Ah, not much different from one of the Enforcer Battlecruisers, only it's not so cramped," replied Loman.

"It's plenty different, stay alert," Cumberland replied.

They moved down the hallway towards where he knew there would be a lift access. When he saw the block of doors, he opened a channel. "Command, I'm coming up on the deck eight access point now. What are your orders?"

"Hold there, we're getting a few lifts online and need you to secure that area."

"Acknowledged." A sound above caught his attention.

"Motion! Everywhere!" called the sensor officer.

Cumberland batted an eight legged bot off his shoulder as he looked at the writhing ceiling above. There were buffer, sanitizer, repair, and other bots he didn't recognize covering the surface. Several of his men opened fire, reducing several at a time to a rain of metal and plastic shrapnel.

Several functioning bots landed on him and he shook them off. None attempted to harm him. In fact, they scurried away as soon as they hit the deck. Without hesitation, he whirled towards the scanning officer and was about to grab his hand scanner when it was whipped out of his grip by something else, someone in a cloak suit. "The bots are a distraction!"

The hand scanner disappeared, and as Cumberland tried to get a clear shot, the tip of a nanosaw blade came though the scanner officer's back. It was drawn through his side in the next instant as though the man was made of water, and his armour was air. Cumberland opened fire, hitting the scanning officer twice, but scoring several hits against his attacker.

What followed was bedlam. An invisible hand pulled Faltia straight out of the group and used him as a shield as they fired their heavy pulse rifles and sidearms at the crowd of soldiers. One of the cloak suited attackers' suits failed after he'd been shot several times and, instead of retreating, the nafalli seemed to go berserk. He grabbed one of Cumberland's men by the helmet and hurled him over his shoulder while he slashed at several others with his nanosaw blade, nearly cutting one in half at the waist.

The beastly alien didn't last long, but he managed to distract half of Cumberland's men so Sturges and Mazurek were both killed by the time they regained focus. The first was decapitated while the other was riddled with pulse rifle rounds.

"Phalanx! Phalanx against the wall! Now! Now! Now!" Cumberland cried as he either found a new depth of desperation or regained his clarity for a moment. The group fell back against the wall, half dropping to one knee and firing in a fanning pattern, while the others remained standing, adding to the cover fire until they saw a real target, which they'd focus on until they were sure it was dead.

A flash went off, not impeding their shielded sight for more than half a second, but the major could hear his communicator reset. Alarmed, he pulled out his emergency hand scanner and saw that the screen had frozen in the reset phase. The enemy had dropped an electromagnetic charge on them.

When he looked up, he was pleased to see five enemy soldiers, not including the nafalli, laying motionless on the deck. The cover fire caught another in the back, making him visible for a split second. It was enough time for Cumberland to get several more shots off on the target, striking her in the waist, up the back, and finally several times in the back of the head.

They managed to kill nine more before it was over, but had managed to take no prisoners. Cumberland took a quick, silent head count and realized that they had lost twenty-four people, including Sergeant Mazurek.

"Command, we've defeated an enemy stealth squad. The eighth deck lifts are secure. Only our comms and rifle sights are working, they dropped an EMP and killed our scanning equipment."

"We see that, Major. Won't be able to get you re-provisioned or reinforced at the moment. Please hold there and keep those lift doors secure. Will keep you appraised of progress on repairs."

Chapter 21
Port Rush

Ayan wasn't the only one disappointed that there was a heavy locked gate made of hundreds of interlocking metal circles in front of what the signs said was the City Central Transit Hub. Six armed guards stood in front of the ornate barrier, with a temporary sign at their feet that said 'Carthan Citizens or Visa Carriers ONLY.' A pair of men in clothing typical of planet-bound people - cloth pants and loosely fit, front-sealing shirts - approached the barrier and the metal circles slid to the side so they could pass.

Everyone in Ayan's group wanted to take a look at the great city they glimpsed at the top of the Greydock tower, or at least get a chance to see some of the cities built inside the place's massive girth. The journey for the foursome was boring in comparison to what Greydock promised. Down in one lift that looked over-used and under-washed, through a checkpoint that barely paid attention to them at all after they provided their identification and then into a causeway where non-descript, tubular, twenty eight man planetary people carriers waited. They found one with peeling grey and violet paint waiting with PORT RUSH scrolling down its length in bright green letters.

The seats were set in pairs facing forward for the most part, with a few lined up against the sides. Laura fixed Ayan with a wary look as she strapped herself in with a provided seat belt. They only had to wait a few minutes before the vehicle detached from its moorings, rocking to the right, and with a low grind the nose tipped downward slightly as it rushed forward through an opening in the side of the upper city wall. From the tops of the seat up, the hull became transparent, including the roof, which provided a view of the dull grey sky. The only bulkhead they couldn't see through was the front, where Ayan assumed the cockpit would be.

The four passengers sharing the rear of the people-mover with them were all dressed in long, high collared scroll worked jackets. Their casual demeanour suggested that they had taken the trip often. Their heads were down, looking at an interactive screen only they could see somewhere above their laps.

She couldn't blame them. The hard, worn seats, and the travel-stained shuttle certainly weren't worth attention, and neither was the view. Ayan caught sight of a ruined city built against the bottom edge of Greydock's wall. There were only a few buildings over twenty storeys, and a few structures left around them. As they continued to turn around the city, the shapes of two ancient ships imbedded in the ground became visible. Their gutted hulls looked skeletal, and they had been eaten by decades, perhaps centuries, of corrosion. "I wonder how long ago that happened?" mused Ayan.

"Long ago, end of the Expansion Age," said a female traveller who was focusing on an image that was invisible to everyone but her. She had an accent Ayan couldn't place.

"Was there a war here?"

"No. They say the crew was infected by the Omni virus, and died. With no one to pilot, they fell out of orbit. Ships were so well made that they survived the atmosphere," the older woman said as though she enjoyed telling the tale. "Others say those are old colony ships. Sank over time."

"What do you think?" asked Ayan,

"This moon eats a lot of things, why not a ship or two?" said the woman.

"Thank you..."

"Emshi," the traveller answered, finally looking up. Her eyes were both old style bionic implants and looked more like bright green lenses than human eyeballs.

Ayan shook Emshi's hand and smiled. "We just got here, looking for food and supplies for some refugees."

"You'll find it in Port Rush if you have the GC or Carthan credit. Never know what form it'll come in, though. I've never seen your type of armour before. Are you some kind of soldier?"

"Independents."

"Ah, hope there are a lot of you, otherwise you're going to want to get in with a crowd. No one lives long here without someone behind them. Helps if it's someone everyone knows. Be careful."

"Thank you. Do you know where I should enquire about food?" asked Ayan.

"Port Rush Authority used to facilitate trade, but the Carthan Government didn't bother rebuilding the office after it was bombed, so everything comes through Mackey Exchange now."

"What about docking fees and landing assignments?"

"Well, navnet still directs, but if you want some space on the ground, you'll have to trade for it like everything else. New government doesn't have the people to regulate Port Rush operations on the ground, so you'll have to be ready to trade high for every meter," said Emshi.

"How does that not lead to chaos?" asked Laura.

"It's a different kind of order. Instead of one Port Master, there are several competing ones. Everyone who works in Port Rush has gotten used to it. You'll see once you read the Mackey Exchange. They're the only thing that helps people like you make sense of the place. There are data sheets posted everywhere."

"Posted?" Ayan probed further.

"You'll know them when you see them."

"If you don't mind me asking, what brings you to Port Rush?"

"I'm a kind of..." Emshi thought a moment then smiled. "...social worker."

"Ayan, look," Laura said quietly as she looked over her shoulder.

She turned in her seat as they cleared the top of a mountain and saw Port Rush stretch out ahead. It was a teeming metropolis huddled against the concave curve of a tall mountain range. Several of the buildings themselves were built like slanted fins fanning out from the tallest mountain, their sloped edges broad enough for the jungle to grow as high, long parks, with darkened reflective transparasteel windows beneath. Several other buildings closer to the sandy shore were shaped like waves with gently sloped roofs that were just as well forested. Other buildings, most of which were slanted in the same directions, weren't as well designed, but many had transplanted jungle atop. Whole blocks of older buildings seemed to be coated with brown and green, giving some of the older parts of the city the look of being assailed by moss or thick, intrusive vines.

Beyond the city stretched a long beach and beyond that were several tall, sloped wheel-like structures that glittered in the sunlight. "Ocean greenhouses, they're huge," Jenny breathed. "And they have a solar wind farm behind. There's got to be enough power there for the whole city and then some." Further out in the water they could barely make out the shapes of thousands of black windmills. Ayan had seen pictures of them in the Academy. Used all over the galaxy on terraformed worlds, they gathered energy from the heat of the sun, from its rays with solar sheeting, and from the wind, which must have been high.

Along the beach there were a few standout structures, one of which drew Ayan's attention the instant it came into sight. It was a thick, structure that ran along the beach for kilometres and stood twenty-eight storeys tall. The hangar spaces it provided were stacked like rectangular boxes, leaving enough room for the small to mid-sized ships to navigate through while providing a resort front facing the beach. The structure was backed by a thick jungle that went on along the beach for as far as the eye could see, interrupted by buildings with surprisingly seldom frequency. "Oh, that's got to be the most expensive place to park here."

Victor smiled at her and nodded towards something over her shoulder. "I think I'm looking at the cheapest."

Ayan and Laura turned around and were stunned. Thousands of ships had landed on a patch of scorched earth that was occasionally interrupted by multi-stage landing platforms and hangars that stood several storeys high. Tall red marker posts and squat, open-sided buildings interrupted the sea of vessels like buoys and islands. Medium ships roughly the size of the Samson to small sized vessels of all kinds made their way across the sky, landing, taking off, or just passing through. They were mixed in with an uncountable number of people movers, smaller atmospheric vessels, some of which followed dark makeshift roads until they reached a blockage or undesired turn until they took to the sky. There were also dozens of small four and six man ships that were painted chequered bright green and orange. They mixed in with the rest of the traffic effortlessly, and were the only really familiar thing in the sky.

"Lots of taxis," Ayan said to herself. The city was surrounded by jungle on two sides, creating an alley of growth between it and the shore. The side furthest from the shore, to the east, was still jungle, but it was piled high with refuse. Portions of it burned, sending plumes of thick, black smoke upwards.

Along the south edge of the massive landing field was a tall, thick bioplast and metal wall, thick enough for some kind of jungle park that was more brown than green. The vents in the side facing the landing area slowly drew in wispy fumes from the ships and rough buildings below. There were towns made of those ramshackle buildings, and the tracks that ran maglev trains around the city proper passed through high openings in the wall to extend out through the nearest quarter of the makeshift landing area. One of the tracks had been bent so badly that it was off its high concrete pillar. "I wonder how long this city has been here?"

"Long enough so no one is sure how old it is. Don't get lost down there. Someone like me might have to find what's left of you," Emshi warned with a thin smile.

Ayan watched a group of three mismatched medium sized ships draw near and fall in line behind their craft. She straightened in her seat in an effort to get a better look and was satisfied as the shuttle turned and started descending towards the outer edge of the well kept portion of the city.

The shuttle swooped down suddenly and entered the terminal, slowing quickly, docking in short order. The lights in the cabin flashed as the doors opened.

"Good luck," whispered Emshi as she stepped out onto the platform. Before Ayan could reply the woman disappeared into the crowd.

No one realized that there were several shuttles seconds behind them while they were in flight, but when they stepped onto the grey concrete and metal platform they were confronted with a bustling mob. Everyone was hurrying to get to a shuttle, the tram, or a transit pod. There were thousands of people, dozens of shuttle platforms, and it was the same on every level above and below them. The ceiling was open like a long gash in the top of the building, providing just enough room for the shuttles to arrive and depart. A rush of air announced the impending arrival of a high speed tram across the platform to their right.

"Please ensure that all your extremities are behind the yellow line until the doors open. If you are not a Sub-Tram passenger, please proceed to your destination, thank you," crackled a recording in Ayan's proximity radio. From the looks of her team, they had heard it as well.

"This way, we have to get to an info station," said Victor.

Ayan followed his lead, trying not to bump into anyone on her way. She quickly discovered that no one else had such scruples. If she was in someone's path, they simply pressed past her or bumped her out of the way.

The smell was overpowering. Urine mixed with sweat, grease, ozone, and garbage assaulted Ayan's olfactory sense, and there was no relieving it, as though the whole place had bathed in it. Laura glanced at her wide eyed and tilted her head over her shoulder.

Ayan looked up and caught sight of a larger, twenty meter long transport above, offloading a long rush of goats. The people guiding them down the ramp and into a narrow hallway with the help of prearranged metal barriers didn't look anything like spacers. Their manner of dress made them look like they were farmers from an old period film.

Victor looked behind and followed what Ayan and Laura were staring at. "That's something you don't see every day."

"I've never seen one in person," Laura replied.

"You'll see a lot more if I'm right," said Jenny. "Livestock owners are probably making more than ever, I'd guess. It's cheaper to grow food and keep livestock on an old terraformed planet like this than it is to run materializers who eat up power that can be used for industry. The smell takes some getting used to, though."

Ayan looked at the symbol in the bottom left corner of her hood that manually activated the face plate of her vacsuit, sealing herself in. In seconds the suit cleaned the air and the fragrances were gone, but she could still smell them to a lesser degree, as though they had nested in her nose and wouldn't let go.

There was no commonality to the way the other travellers were dressed. Some were in vacsuits that came in every colour and shape, while most wore clothing of every cut imaginable. Many of the people not dressed for space travel were wearing synthetic clothing made for warm weather. They finally reached the information kiosk, a narrow post that had been plastered over many times by animated and non-animated advertisement postings.

"All right, we're looking to buy food, survival supplies, and find somewhere to move to, right?" asked Jenny as she pulled at advertisements covering the front of the information booth.

"Right. Food first," Ayan confirmed.

Jenny managed to pull an advertisement for skin pigmentation modification pills, called Sliskin, off the main panel and gave it a withering look as it declared, 'insert five UCW or equivalent credits' with a colourful holographic projection.

Ayan dug in her messenger bag for a moment and presented the three GC pennies she'd gotten for change. "I think the exchange is pretty brutal for UCW credits," she said as she dropped two of them into the slot that was easy to find, thanks to a large green, bouncing arrow.

"Thank you, your information is being prepared," said the machine. A rotating dish appeared on the screen and animated for several seconds before it was replaced with a message that read; 'MORE PLEASE' before the bouncing green arrow appeared again. "What the..." she asked no one in particular.

A traveller with a salt and pepper beard stopped and tapped her on the shoulder. "Most of these have been hacked, miss. You just paid someone somewhere whatever you dropped in the slot. You could wait around and shoot whoever ripped you off when they come along to empty the machine, or you can get on with things. What are you looking for?"

"We're looking to buy food wholesale, and survival gear," said Ayan.

He reached over her head and pulled a plastic page from the post with two hard jerks. "You can't access the free net through that thing. Not since the H virus. Look for open postings."

Ayan took the sheet and smiled at the stranger. "Thank you,"

"You're welcome. One thing: are you the folks that landed in the Dower Wastes a little while ago?"

"Maybe," Ayan answered with an upraised eyebrow.

He pointed over her head and behind her. "Word's out."

A flickering projection displayed footage from her speaking to the customs officer in the rain. It began sending audio to her proximity radio the moment she looked directly at it. "...can say why this controversial, known associate of Freeground and Jonas Valent is here, but judging from her companions, their armament, and level of combat readiness, we'd best hope they're here to help in the fight against the Order of Eden," said an excitable narrator's voice. "This woman, simply known as Ayan, an old Earth name that means 'shepherd' or 'bright light', is the re-inception of Ayan Rice, a Freeground Military Officer who is said to have been present when Jonas Valent allegedly released the base code of the Holocaust Virus into a ship nearly a decade ago. The Carthans maintain that Regent Galactic and the Order of Eden have not gathered enough evidence to warrant the arrest of the memory transfer clone, Jacob Valance, or his cohorts. According to records we obtained only moments ago, Ayan is the registered owner of a small armada of combat-ready ships, and even claims to be a commanding officer of the Triton, the ship that Regent Galactic claims Jonas Valent was most recently seen on. She has been given a privateering licence by the Carthan government. Whether they believe Jonas Valent is secretly pulling the strings as we do, no one can say. What matters now is that they are here, and they have been given permission to move from the Dower Wastes to a recognized port."

Ayan realized several people were watching her and looked away. "I can't believe this. Regent Galactic put us right in the middle of everything and they've got so much of the story completely wrong."

"They also have some of it right," Laura told her. "This could work to our advantage."

"Best of luck, you're on two out of five news streams. Hope you're here for the right reasons, and if Valance is really with you, tell him he's got a few friends on the ground. Good luck, miss," he said as he fell in step with the crowd headed to the shuttles.

Ayan watched him disappear into the press of bodies. "Let's get out of here so we can take a better look at this."

They followed each other as though they were moving through a grand melee. Ayan had instinctively taken the lead and regretted it almost immediately. Vic passed her a moment later and she stepped in behind him as though she were riding in his wake. Laura was behind her with her hand on Ayan's shoulder and everyone else followed.

They made their way up an incline and through the doors, emerging onto the edge of an expansive circular courtyard. The star and sword emblem of the United Core World Confederation was the main feature in the centre of the circle, and it looked as though someone had come along with heavy equipment and had tried to scrape it clear, denting it in places and smoothing the indentations of the lines out in others. Wandering across its surface was a man stripped to the waist. On his chest the words; HATE FATE had been written in tall black letters. "The Order is everywhere! Look to the ones who stayed alive, stayed rich, and never met a bot they didn't use! They are the foothold, they will make the beach head, and while the war rages in the stars, our children will buy into the promise of paradise, and become the new consumers! Tear away the devices! The trappings! Grow food! Live in the jungle! Turn away from the paradise they promise, make your own!"

The energy and conviction he put into the words pushed more people away than it attracted. Several passers-by watched and listened from a distance, however; it was impossible not to. Ayan didn't want to make her attention obvious, and turned her attention to the structural surroundings once again, looking up. There were fifteen storeys above them, each with their own balconied open air walkway looking down into the courtyard. Along each railing ran a myriad of departure and arrival times, current news items, along with the current position of each moon.

The courtyard wasn't nearly as densely packed, and the going was easy as they quickly made their way to a pair of unoccupied benches. "You know, I thought I had seen a lot after taking leave on other worlds, but this is just beyond," Ayan said as she watched a family of four wrapped in black and green robes casually stroll into the transit centre.

"I know the feeling. It's just like the movies set in the core worlds after the Third Fall," commented Jenny as she watched a flock of pigeons peck at seed scattered by an old woman.

"Pandem was like this in some places. Always busy, just barely enough room to move," Victor said quietly.

"Ima gets busy around crop time, but not this busy. Didn't like it much there, either. It gets hard to find a quiet place," said Jenny.

"I think I know why the Carthans are giving privateer permits out to anyone with a ship registered to them," Ayan said as she watched a pair of men in business suits carrying long weapons cases emerging from the transit station.

"They're afraid of what a ship captain can do if they're based here," Laura finished.

"What do you mean?" asked Victor.

Ayan held up the interactive advertisement sheet in her hand and pressed SHOP. Several smaller ads appeared around a query button. She pressed it and spoke towards it. "List all postings for ship to ship weapons sold from a local slip."

"Local slip?" asked Jenny.

"It means from a ship mooring or landing area," Laura explained.

Everyone's eyes went wide as the list appeared - it contained over ten thousand results. Ayan set the system to list the cheapest first and wasn't surprised to see a mixture of electromagnetic and particle pulse weapons. "Okay, these look like rebuilt Vindyne weapons, so I'm thinking a lot of captains have cargo hold operations where they strip and rebuild whatever weapons they manage to take from their captures. I'm pretty sure any of them would be arrested or at least fined if they tried selling this stuff in Greydock, but here it's pretty much open season as long as they are willing to make it look like they're making an effort to hide the fact that these guns come from a Regent Galactic or Order of Eden ship."

"Wait, you said Vindyne?" Laura asked quietly.

"These pulse weapons, their stats, they look Vindyne. Regent Galactic bought up a lot of Vindyne territory and whole fleets while they were collapsing. It was in my, um, predecessor's journal."

"Oh, I didn't know Regent took their fleets."

Ayan began a new search for food and started browsing as everyone looked on.

A thought donned on Laura then and she smiled. "Wait, we know how to track Vindyne ships, or at least I do."

"You do?"

"Jason was working with Freeground Intelligence while they were figuring it out. I got pulled in to consult a few times because of my experience with their shield tech. Most Vindyne ships keep their combat shielding up all the time because they like using flimsy materials for their ship interiors, sometimes for their hulls. As one of the experts who helped isolate unique characteristics of their shielding, I can recognize the energy barriers, including in raw data form."

"Like the kind of data you get when you run long range scans or analyse a faster than light ship's transit trail." Ayan grinned back.

"They're speaking a whole other language. Did you get any of that?" Victor asked Jenny.

Jenny shrugged. "We just have to make sure they don't get shot."

"It means we can find supply routes using the Clever Dream's wormhole generator and a bunch of micro wormholes. The hyper transmitter on the Triton could do a much better job, but if we have a place to start, the Clever Dream could do," Laura explained. "I know it'll work for Vindyne ships, and I might be able to adapt it to Regent Galactic ships if we can get close enough to one to get a detailed scan of their emitter systems."

"So we can start privateering as soon as you explain all this to the captain. Sounds fun," Jenny smiled.

"Aye. As soon as we solve the supply and landing problem," Ayan said as she selected a seller advertising a large quantity of varied foodstuffs. She started her search in a category for sellers who had permanent landing spaces. "Bloody hell, it looks like this one knocked over a caravan of convenience store suppliers," she chuckled as the sheet erupted in brand names.

There were twenty-one matches, all of them offering not only a massive variety of captured goods, but had landing slips to lease. Many of them claimed to have purchased the land before the Carthan Government took over, others offered space to land and security for an extra fee. None of them quoted prices for the landing space, or mentioned how much space they had available.

Ayan and Laura browsed for several minutes, sampling prices from different vendors, until they finally settled on one in particular. The prices were irresistibly low for food stuffs, and the explanation behind the acquisition of their goods simply said; SUCCESSFUL PRIVATEER. Under the land lease section of their profile it simply claimed: LONG TIME OWNER, WILL BARTER, SERIOUS INQUIRIES ONLY.

"Wow. I wonder if he has any real food," Laura chuckled. "Looks like mostly meal replacements, candy, and inebriants. Best prices and they've got a lot of good feedback from past customers."

"I'm good with that kind of diet." Jenny grinned. "As long as he throws in a case of fitness supplements."

"Beggars can't be choosers. Looks like they're one of the best, and they have land. Let's find a taxi stand and get to his slip before he sells out," Ayan said as she rolled the advertisement up and tucked it into her thigh pocket.

CHAPTER 22
THE GUNNERY DECK

The rattle and pound of Major Cumberland's pulse rifle had become so familiar it was like a second, frantic heart beat. The curving halls and inclines of Triton made it feel like the great corpse of some living creature as he and his unit ran for their lives, trying to get behind cover only to find themselves under attack at every turn.

It was the issyrian. He hadn't seen it, but it was definitely his men and women leading the charge in their thin, sealed suits. Their rifles showed signs of overuse, the charging chambers at the top of the weapons had burned wide open. When they fired, they were bathed with the mad strobe of white light from the loud, crackling power coursing through their rifles. It was as if that was all they were, a man or woman wearing a suit that barely protected them and a rifle. No matter how many Cumberland's men injured or killed, they just kept coming, rushing, firing.

It was as though the issyrian was waiting for them to finish repairing the lift and move. Somehow he knew exactly which floor he'd come up on, and when they arrived, the nightmare began. They didn't fire into the express car, they waited. His people had crawled into maintenance hatches, waited inside crew quarters, and around corners. When they were all out of the car and down the first stretch of hallway, the attack came. From behind, the sides, and from one of the hallways ahead; they were forced down a specific hall, where there was no visible resistance, and he'd lost four of his people in that initial attack.

Major Cumberland almost wished he was fighting the cloak suited horrors that caught the boarding parties in the quiet places - it would almost be better than the relentless assault and the constant effort it took to keep from being outflanked. It took every ounce of his skill and experience to manoeuvre his people through the long hallways and be wary of traps.

At every turn they had the advantage. There was no time to find out how the other squadrons were doing in detail. He knew they were winning on the command deck, and that a unit had just entered through the upper mooring points, but he didn't have time to find out the details or review the short reports each sergeant filed as they moved through the ship and entered one engagement after another.

That damned issyrian had them running frantically, with few choices. Just moments before, Major Cumberland had lost three of his men when they took a left into a hallway that had been supercharged with a bare power feed. Where the issyrian had gotten a live line, he'd never guess, and his lead tech didn't have time to answer, either.

They were forced into a broad concourse that slowly curved upwards from deck to deck. Even as he was under fire, he wished that the ships he served on were designed so well. They tried to take cover in one of the larger crew quarters but found the door rigged to three arc charges, grenades that unleashed a massive amount of power in one burst; it was like touching ball lightening. Two more men dead the instant the door opened.

The next hall was sealed. None of the doors would open, but they finally got a chance to rest and create cover with portable barriers. "Who the hell are these people? We've killed at least a dozen and put down twice as many, but they just keep coming," remarked Sergeant Loman, still out of breath from the long, backward run. He was leaning on the stock of his rifle, using it like a short cane.

"There are hundreds of them, gotta be," agreed Private Voleman.

"Tracker says we've killed seventeen, disabled thirty eight," Cumberland said, knowing that the auto tracker hadn't been accurate since they had to remove the operations AI from the system. "We've only lost six, I'd say we're up."

"Yeah, right, got 'em right where we want 'em," commented Private Baram sarcastically between gulps of air.

Cumberland didn't have the energy to shut her up. Normally he'd put her in her place, find some way of reprimanding her while reassuring everyone else, but the long engagement was taking its toll. He flipped his wrist display open and checked their orders. They were simple: 'Proceed to the rear cargo elevator, take it to deck 21, Section A1.' He double-checked the rudimentary map of the deck they were on, deck 19, right below the hottest fighting on the command level, and found that they were close.

"Command still silencing unit to unit communications, Sir?" asked Sergeant Loman.

"We have our objective. We don't need to know what everyone else is up to in order to accomplish it."

"Not a good sign, though."

"It's not our job to interpret signs," Cumberland replied. "But I do know a pretty convincing fortune teller on Srak-Tam."

"Srak-Tam, Sir?" asked Loman.

"It's an old drift, orbits a binary star in the Tisch system."

"So it's true, you led the team that put down the Human Supremacist uprising," said Private Shir.

"I was there. That was a complicated engagement, all compartment to compartment and corridor fighting," admitted Cumberland.

"So it was a lot like this."

"Not for a second." Cumberland looked at his eleven remaining soldiers and was satisfied that they were rested up. "All right, we have about twenty meters to cover, then we head to the uppermost deck."

"We're hooking up with another unit from the command ship, Sir?" asked Sergeant Loman.

"I hope so." It was a slip. For all he knew they were going up there to survey the deck, or to check the airlock seals. Raising their hopes over a rendezvous that might not happen was reckless. Regardless, he couldn't help but have the same hope. Operating with one fifth a unit for much longer was poor judgement, plain and simple.

He took point, feeling alert, watching every corner, and listening between the boot steps for anything out of the normal. He didn't have to wait long. The ceiling opened up directly overhead to reveal a meter and a half tall crawl way and several enemy soldiers.

Loman took a shot in the back as he turned out of the line of fire, and was saved by his armour. Cumberland fired blind, hitting the ceiling as much as the opening as he retreated out of the direct line. Everyone was so on edge that they only caught glancing shots, no one's armour was hit enough for penetration, but the whole squad was split. Some were behind the opening, Loman and Voleman were with Cumberland in front, and the other three were against the wall, providing cover fire into the hole and most likely hitting nothing.

"David! Get back!" cried a young woman as searing blue and white bolts of energy scorched the floor from above.

Cumberland took one step forward and made eye contact with a whip thin woman brandishing a pulse rifle half her size. She shot him three times in the breast plate before he could step back. He could feel the mild burns; his armour was finished. He had taken hits on the legs as he made a hasty retreat. In one quick manoeuvre, the scrappy resistance fighters had his people split, and it wouldn't be long before Cumberland and his men would be rushed from behind.

There was no coming up for air against these people. They were desperate, dedicated, and what was worse, they had a commander who seemed to know every corridor of the ship, how to milk the vessel for power to set traps when no one could get more than marginal readings on charged systems, and most of all, he wasn't interested in prisoners.

Cumberland barely had time to shout "Cover!" before a concussion grenade hit the deck. It knocked him back three meters and battered the rest of his squad even harder. He couldn't believe what he saw when he looked up. The enemy were coming down from the ceiling in groups of four. They dropped a portable shield generator the size of their palm that blocked him off from everyone but Baram, Loman, Voleman and two other Privates that were knocked onto Cumberland's side of the hall by the concussion grenade. The rest were gunned down, well out of his reach behind the shield.

A square jawed man, who he'd seen before with the issyrian, looked at him over his shoulder. There was a cold fire in his eyes, as though he wished they weren't separated by an energy shield just as much as Cumberland did. As much as he was furious at the slaughter, and would like nothing more than to wait for the shield to come down so he could take a shot at him and the rest, it was suicide. The enemy outnumbered them. "Let's get going before they outflank what's left of us," Cumberland said through his teeth.

"Tell your people to leave this ship or die," growled the scruffy combatant.

"David! C'mon!" shouted the small woman who'd shot Cumberland several times.

Cumberland turned away from the field and rushed in the other direction. It was as if the enemy were not only defending their ship, but also taking revenge. He'd been in several situations where an engagement was about to turn bad, but it was the first time he'd been in the middle of one when it was already sour.

Finally, the hallway ahead was clear, and Cumberland led them in a dead run towards the cargo lift. "Command, does the lift have power?"

"I'm sorry, Major, the power was just cut."

"All right, I'm re-tasking my people with getting that lift working again."

"I'm seeing you're down to-"

"Six people, no thanks to you boys up there. We're going to get the lift running again and join with the forces you have gathered on the upper deck."

"The recommendation I have here says you should wait for reinforcements," said Command.

"Good thing it's just a recommendation. Cumberland out."

Cumberland and his six soldiers made the distance in quick order; they could hear the issyrian's people not far behind, like some angry horde was on their heels. They were out of breath when they arrived at the freight elevator. "Tell me someone knows how to hot wire this thing," Cumberland said as he pulled a microcell from his front pocket.

Loman took the cell and pried the access panel open. "Man, they made this ship rugged. I bet I can jack this in full charge and she'll power up just fine." It took him seconds; with the main power down on all but the engineering level, the security on the ship seemed to be out of order. After a few more seconds he had the microcell in place and was accessing the panel that controlled the lift.

"Can you confirm that this thing's going to take us where we want to go?" asked Major Cumberland.

"Looks like this one can travel through most of the ship, hooks up with that main transit hub we saw earlier, but there are other express cars in the way, so we're limited to up or down."

"Does it go to deck twenty one and the upper mooring point?"

"It does," confirmed Loman.

"Good, get us there." Cumberland opened a channel to Command. "This is Major Cumberland to Command. We're still being rushed by hold outs, I saw about fifteen during our last engagement, but they're part of a larger group - at least fifty, accounting for casualties."

"We hear you. Did you get that lift back up and running?"

The first of their pursuers started firing around the corner. They were blind shots, but there were hundreds. They were burning through ammunition as though they had an armoury following them around, and the scorch marks on the wall were close enough to make Major Cumberland swear he'd be retiring from the service if he survived the Triton.

"This is Colonel Ratner, with the Nineteenth Incursion Unit. We just came aboard and have been listening. Get to us and we'll be glad to cover you."

"Thank you, Colonel, were on our way."

The express car arrived. "Get aboard and get us moving!" Major Cumberland shouted as he fired down the hallway. His rifle was on full auto, filling the dark corridor with hundreds of bursts of energy. The return fire was terrifying, including several shots that were fired using some new weapon they hadn't seen before, like a rocket propelled grenade that carried an impact shock, rattling the thick deck beneath their feet. Cumberland had gotten lucky twice, shooting two of the slow moving mini-rockets with his weapon, but his luck wouldn't hold out. It was as if the whole crew had decided that preventing damage to the ship was secondary to causing as much harm as possible to the boarders.

The express doors started to close, and Private Farrar was right in front of him, grinning at their good fortune when he took a full burst of pulse rounds up the back and across his head. He was dead before he hit the floor.

The express car moved swiftly, covering the vertical distance between decks in seconds. Cumberland couldn't help but have a very bad feeling as the express car came to a gentle stop and the doors opened onto a massive, flat deck that covered a third of the dorsal section of the ship.

The darkened chamber was divided by bulkheads that had risen into place when sections became open to space. Major Cumberland could see the Command ship through the heavily damaged transparent hull - it was a welcome sight. It was moored to a primary docking point, helping to hold the Triton in place. From the large, heavy duty airlock extended a long emergency ramp way.

Colonel Ratner and his men were there to greet him. The group was surrounded by the eerie glow of personal lights as they approached. The darkened deck looked too big; there were too many shadows even though they could see the long lower hull of Battlecruiser 1009 above. They had deployed from a battlecruiser hard docked to the port side of the Triton.

There was one more battlecruiser on the opposite side, and between the three of them they had more than enough power to maintain full control of the ship from the outside. Escape for the Triton was impossible. Why her crew fought so hard could only be explained by loyalty, or perhaps they had a plan to escape. Impossible. We can order reinforcements. There was nothing about this ship's record that suggests that they can expect help from anyone.

"Major, I hear you have a resistance problem. Do you think the resistors will follow you up here?" Ratner asked.

"Colonel, there's a seriously frustrating issyrian with about five hundred armed men and women, from what I can tell. I haven't seen the bug in a few hours now, but I'm sure he's still directing his men from somewhere."

"We are aware. We're bringing a whole unit of heavies right now. It's time to bring the resistance to a halt. This acquisition has already cost us too much in equipment and manpower, not to mention we're due to join the eleventh Order of Eden Fleet in five days with this vessel in tow."

"So they finally did it? We're all signed up with Regent Galactic and that little prick prophet of theirs?" asked Cumberland.

"That's our lord and savoir you're talking about, Major. Looks like our outfit's finding religion whether we like it or not, so the big bad Holocaust Virus doesn't take us out all together."

"Our AI's have been wiped. We're safe, in case you forgot how that thing works."

"Seems the virus has evolved, now there's an AI built in. Machines without firewalls are waking up with a digital soul and looking for anyone not listed in the Order of Eden database to kill. It's a whole new ball game now, so you'd better kneel and praise the child prophet like the rest of us sheep, or at least learn to pretend real good," said Ratner.

"I hear you. Just needed to know why we were getting on with the zealots."

"We're getting on with the Order of Eden because Regent Galactic was nice enough to pick up our tab so Caran Enterprises doesn't go belly up and leave us grunts twisting in the wind. That's why, as if it makes a difference one way or another."

"Mind if I ask why this ship is so important?" asked Major Cumberland.

"Since we've got a minute, I'll fill you in. This ship was captured by the man who started it all, so they say. Jonas Valent."

"The hero of Enreega?"

"The deserter of the Aucharians. He forced a whole section to desert when they needed him most and left Enreega wide open. You'd best check your history," said Ratner.

"Yes, Sir," said the major.

"Seems Jonas changed his name a while back to Jacob Valance, probably because he designed the virus that started all this when he unleashed an unsafe guarded artificial intelligence into one of those great big Overlord command ships."

"I heard about that. Does Command think he's aboard?" asked Cumberland.

"They didn't see him leave, so chances are he's holed up in that great big vault in the centre of the ship. He's not on the bridge, let me tell you. We just took the command deck, killed a lot of Triton soldiers, and there was still no sign of him."

"How did it end?"

"They had to use four squads of heavies, took heavy fire but burned everything inside to nothing. Rumour is that the captain has been popping up and killing people with an elite unit, but then, those cloak suits have been making everyone as twitchy as hell. No way of knowing if any of the attacks were the captain's unit or someone dressed like him. Either way, they're not acknowledging our demands for surrender, so we're taking further steps. The order to execute the captives has been given on an open channel. Should flush him out if he's any kind of leader," said Colonel Ratner.

Another unit of fifty soldiers started running down the incursion ramp to join the total of seventy already on the deck. Reinforcements were coming; for whatever reason, the efforts to take the Triton intact were redoubling. Major Cumberland looked back to the Colonel and asked: "When do the executions start?"

"Five minutes ago."

The words seemed to echo across the hollow deck. It was like looking at some dead creature from the inside; the gunnery turrets hung down like dormant organs and the thick, transparent hull overhead was like delicate, translucent skin. Under the muted lights from the Command ship, the slower, heavily armoured soldiers looked like dark insects with man shaped carapaces, the regular soldiers looked smaller, and even though there were so many gathering, they didn't fill enough space on the deck to obstruct the view.

Several loader suits stood against one wall and were scattered around the expansive space, dormant and limp like three meter tall standing corpses. The chamber was filled with the high screech of metal scraping against metal as the main mooring door closed from the inside. Two meters of armour separated them from the destroyer above,

"Planned?" asked Major Cumberland.

Colonel Ratner ignored his question as he tried to get Command on comms. "Can't raise Command, someone's scrambling us. It's local, from this deck."

"They cleared this deck, didn't they?"

"No one was reported in this or any compartment adjacent to the upper hull," Colonel Ratner answered.

Hatches began to open overhead, pulling the air out of the massive compartment in a rush that sounded like a mournful, undulating howl.

"Seal up! Affix your soles!" Major Cumberland ordered. His men were the first to react, and were ready, rifles in hand, secured to the deck with their suits sealed up and vacuum ready before half of Colonel Ratner's were.

Three of the heavy armour units weren't quick enough to affix their boots to the hull and were sucked right off the deck and out of the largest of the hatches. Most of the soldiers on the embarkation ramp were swept out into open space one after another, as though they were roped together. Cumberland just shook his head. Heavy armour units were always vacuum sealed, so they would survive, but they would be out of action for minutes or longer while they used their tiny emergency thrusters to return to the ship and get back on the deck. The rest, the regular soldiers, would have to be retrieved if they sealed their armour in time. The dark dust cloud they were in would make it difficult; many would be lost.

"What's going on, Major?" asked the Colonel's second in command. "You've been here for hours, what do you think they're doing?"

"I can't say, this is new." Major Cumberland signalled his unit to spread out to his right and left using hand signals, and they reacted as though they were marionettes tied to his fingers.

"Right! Spread out! Find cover where you can!" ordered Colonel Ratner.

Major Cumberland knelt and looked down his rifle sight, scanning the way ahead. No one else seemed to notice that the transparent emergency bulkheads separating the deck into sections were being drawn aside and down. The whole deck would be open in seconds. Something was happening.

"What should we be expecting, Major? What are we looking for?" asked Ratner.

"I have no idea. Just keep your eyes peeled and get ready to call targets for your heavy armour."

"Don't tell me how to command my unit."

"I won't tell you how to do your job if you stop asking me stupid questions and start using your scanning teams," Major Cumberland griped back.

"Major! I'll have you-"

"Shut it!" Cumberland shot back as a power source appeared on his reticule only fifty meters away. It was one of the power suits several of the light infantry that had just arrived with the Colonel were hiding behind. "Get your people away from that loader suit!"

It was too late. The three meter tall machine snatched an empty ammunition cartridge the size of a coffin and swung it with impossible speed at the four infantrymen using him as cover, striking three hard enough to dislodge them from the deck. They were flung across the span at great speed while the armoured suit pounded its other claw hand into the fourth infantryman's chest so brutally that he flat lined the second he was struck.

"Fire! Open fire!" Colonel Ratner ordered.

It was too late. The thing had some kind of impact shielding that easily deflected their small arms fire. Even the heavy suits barely dented its thick armour.

"Those things are made to survive ship to ship guns! We'll never penetrate without explosives. Use 'em or lose 'em!" Major Cumberland ordered. One of his men tossed his last grenade set to a manual trigger and blew it as it came into contact with the chest plate of the armoured suit. To everyone's surprise and dismay it barely scratched it. "Don't let that thing get to you!" Cumberland warned as he carefully fired at the round sensor cap atop its shoulders. If the pilot inside noticed, he didn't let on.

"Should we fire rockets, Colonel?" asked one of the heavy armour units.

The loading suit snatched one of the heavily armoured soldiers who wasn't wary or fast enough to keep away and hurled him at the rest of his unit. They were still too tightly grouped to use their weapons or to keep from getting hit by whatever the armoured suit decided to toss.

"Fire everything! Bring it down! Bring it down!" Colonel Ratner shouted as he fell back behind the armoured units for cover.

Major Cumberland had other ideas. He turned and ran for the express elevator.

"Get your ass back here, Major!" shouted Ratner, furious.

He let his boots lose traction on the deck so he could drift at speed towards the elevator. When he hit the back of the large cargo car, he re-affixed his boots and turned towards a wide eyed soldier just outside the lift who was breathing so hard he was fogging up his visor. "I need you and your hand scanner, get in here," Cumberland ordered, gripping the collar of his breast plate and drawing him inside.

The soldier didn't have to be told twice, and moved as quickly as his boots would allow, handing his scanner over on the way. In a few key strokes, Cumberland adjusted the focus and began inspecting the deck behind the railgun loader suit that was charging the heavy armour. The first line of the unit fired their rockets, four of them missed, exploding against the upper hull. The other two were right on target.

The loader suit took damage and hesitated, faltering with a backwards step. It rocked forward onto its right foot and broke into a dead run, closing the distance between it and the heavily armoured soldiers at an alarming rate. The second line fired their rockets, and by the time three of them impacted, the loader suit was so close that the heavy armoured units took peripheral heat damage.

The suit was in their midst then. It picked up a heavily armoured soldier in each hand and used them as cudgels, breaking both men and armour. When the improvised cudgels missed the scattering heavily armoured soldiers, the loader suit slammed the soldiers in its grip against the solid deck, cracking protective plating wide open. A burst of air told everyone who witnessed it that the man inside would die of exposure in seconds if he hadn't already been crushed.

The several swings connected with the nearby armoured units, knocking them all off balance. Then one of them fired a rocket, missing the loader suit and striking one of the heavy armoured units dead on.

As Colonel Ratner shouted "Cease fire! Cease fire!" and ran in the other direction, reinforcements began drifting between the battlecruiser above and entering through the many apertures that had opened to decompress the massive compartment.

Major Cumberland's heart sank as his scanner picked up openings in the deck. Bursts of air escaping from the dozens of deck storage and access compartments were the first warning. The second warning was the size of most of the compartments. "Colonel! We're standing on the storage compartments for those loader suits! There are more coming!"

"We have reinforcements en-route, Major. This'll be over in no time."

Major Cumberland swept the scanner from left to right and counted as quickly as he could while reading the results. With great ease and agility thirty loaders suits came up from their storage compartments along with four other three and a half meter tall suits he recognized immediately.

He targeted one of the brown and black camouflaged suits again and ran a concentrated scan. He broke into a cold sweat the moment it completed. "Colonel! They have Sol Defence Advanced Encounter suits! Order the Battlecruiser to fire directly on the four targets I'm marking!"

"Negative, Major! Our orders are to take this ship in one piece! I'm not going to call in a strike at point blank!"

The Advanced Encounter suit. It was something he'd seen in a movie called Breaking the Belt when he was a boy about the last time a government tried to make a claim on the outer edge of the Sol solar system. According to the film, the Sol Defence Fleet believed in countering an attack with force that outweighed the offense by multiples in the hundreds. In that instance the Sol Fleet led the counter strike with Uriel fighters just like the ones he saw launch when they were about to take the Triton. In the movie, the fighters loaded with two of those Encounter Suits each. They dropped them on the hulls of destroyers, of carriers, of the munitions and supply ships and they tore into their hulls like savages. When they were finished with the hulls, they clawed and burned their way into their ships. There was no mercy, no hesitation, and no humanity. They were shock troops with more firepower per man than anyone had ever seen, and more armour.

When he saw one in a museum as a boy, it looked like a brown and black demon. Its thin, hard black hands were like talons, ready to rip anything in its way apart. The pulse guns on its arms were the same size as some he'd seen in the space flight museum, on full blown starfighters. He recalled the statistics on the machine. Able to heft seven thousand tons, with armour that could withstand a one thousand kilometre orbit with a standard yellow star, armed with a high powered particle beam cannon on one arm and an energizing shard cannon on the other. It was fuelled by a pair of shielded cold micro fusion generators, had an energy shield and focused fusion ion propulsion. He remembered looking up at the captured relic in the Soner Museum as a boy and how small he felt.

That feeling, along with a deep fear threatened to completely unman him as he watched the four machines stand tall and begin a long charge up the deck from the rear. The four he was seeing looked more advanced, newer, slimmer, and far more dangerous. "I need my unit to fall back to the cargo lift. We're going to survive this."

"Major! I'll have your commission for this!" said the Colonel.

"I'll defect before I put my men into combat against this bunch! This fight is already theirs," said Cumberland.

The four Encounter suits opened fire with their particle shard weapons first, and what he saw in that old movie paled in comparison to what they did to the soldiers in reality. Thin shards of slow moving, excited particles moved across the broad deck and sliced through Colonel Ratner's heavily armoured units as though they were wearing tissue paper.

Major Cumberland waited for his retreating soldiers impatiently. "Move! Move! Move!" he shouted, though he didn't have to. Several of the colonel's men followed, a few of them in heavy armour. Those were the ones who would be left behind - there was no way Cumberland would hold the lift long enough for their slow bulks.

The Encounter suits stopped firing at the soldiers on the deck and turned their attention to the Battlecruiser above. The loader suits charged. They were so agile, so quick; it was like watching several lines of runners break from the starting line. Behind them rose one hundred fifty or more men and women with personal shields and heavy particle rifles. They all fired on full automatic, lighting the deck with tens of thousands of rounds. Half of Colonel Ratner's forces were gunned down in seconds. Major Cumberland saw the last of his men steps away from the lift car and hit the close button. "Command, I'm in retreat with some of the colonel's men. Deck twenty one is a complete loss and you have heavy armour mounting a counter incursion on your vessel. Please acknowledge."

"Acknowledged. Do you have any chance of preventing the incursion?"

"I could try harsh language."

"Pardon?"

"Not a chance in hell. What about Ratner? Doesn't he have access to anything heavier?"

"Colonel Ratner is dead, Major," came the reply. They had gotten away, but Major Cumberland was left with a difficult choice and a dozen men and women whose morale was nearly shattered.

"Major Cumberland. This is Command." It was a different voice that time, one he'd never heard before.

"I'm receiving you," said Cumberland.

"Can you verify what we're seeing? It looks like all our people were just gunned down on the upper deck during a comms blackout."

"That's the correct assessment. They have Sol Defence Encounter Armour. You should pick them up on Battlecruiser 1109's hull any second now."

"What?" asked the shocked voice.

"Look for cutters. There's a counter incursion going on right now. I was just telling your subordinate the same thing."

"Your new orders are to proceed to the command deck to assist. Fighting has broken out on the bridge."

"Yes, Sir. I thought we'd already taken the bridge, Sir."

"That's need to know only, Major."

"Bullshit! You're going to tell me what we're getting into, now," said Cumberland.

"They let us take the bridge twice, both times were a trap. We're taking it for good."

"Acknowledged. Keep me in the loop, Command. This operation is too out of joint for this need to know crap."

"Secure that attitude and get on mission. Command out."

Major Cumberland hesitated a moment before changing the express car's heading. It felt like his stomach had flipped upside down; he hadn't been so nervous, so gun shy, since he picked up a rifle for the first time on the range.

"Where are we headed, Major?" asked one of his men from behind. He was still catching his breath.

Cumberland selected the command deck on the control panel. "The bridge. We're going to wrap this up before it gets any worse."

CHAPTER 23
MISCELLANEOUS METROPOLIS MECHANICA

"It's a shanty port," said the cab driver as he banked around a tall docking pad. Beneath were several disused pads fanning out around a central pillar down its full length. Landing on one of the middle platforms would be a nightmare, and Ayan didn't trust the looks of them at all, or the other pilots.

She couldn't help but look over the grizzled nafalli's shoulder as he piloted the beaten people carrier in a round about way over hundreds of landed ships and towers dedicated to nothing more than housing vessels. The cab was originally built to pilot itself, but someone had come along and torn out the main computer systems, replacing them with crude pilot's controls and computer displays. The navnet was projected by a flickering hologram that used a thin mist as a medium, creating a humid environment in the cabin. The mess of small people carriers and ships of all sizes made for a pilot's worst nightmare. The computer was constantly suggesting new paths to the pilot, who seemed to be flying as much by instinct and eye as he was by the navnet's suggestions.

"Why do they call it a shanty port?" asked Laura, her voice so high pitched it was near a squeak. She was watching the surrounding streams of air cars and small ships as they wove between them. A sight Ayan was trying not to concentrate on.

"Look down there, see that strip of buildings right in the middle of the slips? That's why. People build up cities, sometimes right proper buildings, and make whatever they can trading with the ships nearby. Whole other jungle down there, like a city where maybe a handful of people stick around. Gangs too, most of 'em smugglers and privateers. Hard bunch."

"What's that?" Jenny asked, pointing at a number of slips that had been walled off like a compound. There was a hangar in the centre, all around it were ships roughly the size of the Samson.

"Oram's place. Keeps his whole place buttoned down tight, uses his own people for security. One of the best privateers out here. He's so big that he hires other ships for some of his hops."

"Ah, so he takes on big targets."

"Yup, has a destroyer all his own in orbit, too," said the pilot.

"Who does he go after?" asked Jenny.

"Don't know, none of my business. What are you folk going here for, anyhow? Looks like you're a well sorted bunch, dressed like space station sort, don't know why you need to talk to anyone at this end."

"We're buying food, supplies, and a place to land," said Ayan.

"Oh, stepping around the Visa scam, eh? Good lass. I'm guessin' Greydock wouldn't take you in?"

"How did you know?" she asked.

"Greydock doesn't take anyone without a visa unless you're one of their special guests. Where're your ships now?"

"They had us set down in the Dower Wastes."

"Hope your crew isn't out there, too."

"They are," said Ayan.

"Normally, I'd say you should take a slip for any price and put your ear to the ground. Find someone you don't mind doing business with then move your ships in. But since you're stuck in the Dower Wastes, I'd say you'll have to settle for the first slips you can afford. Don't try to go around the landlords, neither. Good way to get slagged," said the pilot.

"How does it work down there? I mean, the Port Authority is gone, so who settles disputes over landing sites?" asked Laura.

"Lady, if I had time and you were paying well enough, I could find a dispute being settled right now. Every slice of this land comes at a price. Carthans set the outer boundaries to the port, and they blast anything that tries to land outside of it from space, but they don't care what happens inside."

"So they fight for their territory."

"All the time. Happens in the lower city by the wall, too, but that's a quieter kind of fight, more room-to-room, bad to get caught in. Ever since the AI's were erased and the Confederation pulled out, crews fight for scraps of land, food, guns, whatever you can name. Best place to be is near the top of the food chain, or near enough to it."

"Top of the food chain?" asked Jenny, looking a little green.

"Start purifying water, bringing in food, guns if you can get away with it, but you didn't hear the last bit from me. Carthans don't like gun runners, they take a bite from the only market they can corner. The established types know best. They call themselves Port Masters, say they have legal claim, but really, they were here longer, got to establish relations with each other and, most importantly, they have the people and guns to make their boarders strong. If you can get in with one of them, it might be best, but you make all their enemies your own when you do."

"So they're crime bosses?" asked Ayan.

"You see law enforcement since you got here?" asked the nafalli pilot with a chuckle. "They're the   governors."

"There have got to be other ports on the moon," observed Laura.

"Sure, but they're all the same except for Greydock. Carthans can't afford to rebuild or run them properly, and the Confederation would love to see this solar system destroy itself now that they're being forced out. A lot of people miss the UCWC, but they're not coming back. I can't stand listening to people bellyache about things they can't change, the Confeds leaving qualifies right up there with the colour of the sky and the price of water. The way I see it, if Tamber is where you are, it's either because you can't find your way off or you're riding an advantage that makes it worth your while."

Ayan looked across the endless sea of ships and saw nothing familiar. Amongst the freighters, small haulers, luxury vessels, and the myriad of cross classification ships, there was nothing she'd ever seen before. "These people have ships, they could leave if they liked. Why don't they just move to another solar system if it's so dangerous?"

"That's what's really interesting about this place. A lot of people think they can get the advantage here, and there are a lot of opportunities. War's on, lass. Looks like there will be even more comin' before the year is out and the Carthans have a good chance to come through all right, or at least fight for a few decades. This is the front, especially if the rumours about the Confederation siding with the Order is true. Put that in along side with their deep pockets and you've got every jack of all trades, pirate, and merc looking for work and finding it. Any merc can get work here, even a guy like me, who wouldn't know which end of a rifle to hold. Head towards the core worlds and you'll find nothing but desperate people who can't wipe their own ass without an AI to give directions. Go further out and you'll probably get ambushed by slavers, pirates, or AI ships that killed their crews and think they're part of the Eden Fleet. I bet you've already seen it."

"I'm afraid so," said Ayan.

"Sorry to hear that, miss. Whereabouts did your ship run into trouble?" asked the pilot.

"Some mining facility down spin from here. Didn't stay long enough to make it worth naming," Ayan answered carefully. She'd been around Jason enough to know that she shouldn't give too much information without being sure of how it would be used. "We need a base of operations while we sort things out and make repairs."

"Are you sure about taking a slip here?" Victor asked Ayan in a whisper.

"You think it's a bad idea?"

"I think it's a great idea, I'd be willing to raise my rifle and keep us safe, too, but it's not up to me. You and-"

Ayan gave him a warning look, she didn't want to hear Jake's name aloud, or have anyone hear that there was another authority above her, especially in front of a cabbie who seemed to enjoy sharing information.

"You and the rest of the senior officers," he corrected quickly.

"I'd second the idea of securing space before we return to our ships, even though it looks like a disaster," Laura agreed. She was staring at a group of mag cycles making their way across the black and light blue mixed sand road just ahead. There were a dozen or more, and they snaked through the streets at a great speed, despite the fact that the riders seemed relaxed, riding at leisure one or two per vehicle.

"Like those? They were popular where I come from. Gangs loved them, hard to track on planetary sensors because they ride so low to the ground," Jenny commented with a smile. "And they're fast."

"They look dangerous," said Laura.

"We called them skids, but I think those are the larger mag cycles. They're good for hauling ground transport."

"Still, looks dangerous. I mean, what's the point of being so close to the ground while you're moving so quickly? You're bound to collide with something," Laura insisted.

"That's the thrill; you have to ride one to know it, though. Not that I've tried, I prefer my go-betweens to have all sides covered," said the cabbie over his shoulder as he pitched the vehicle down towards a side street. "Lots of people use 'em here, though. Bike like that costs next to nothing used, and takes a beating like a heavy fighter. Good to have around if you're just bouncin' from one place to another, though I shouldn't say that, or you won't be calling someone like me back."

"Speaking of which, what's your ident so we can get you back here when we're done?" Ayan asked.

"Already sent it to your data unit there, just give me a buzz when all your business is sorted. Good luck." The shuttle touched down lightly and the doors opened as Ayan passed him a twenty-five GC coin. He gave her three fives back.

"Thank you for the safe ride." She smiled.

"My pleasure, lass. Grace like yours is always welcome in my cab."

"One more thing: can you tell me anything about the people who do business on this slip?" Ayan asked as everyone else was making their way off the shuttle.

The cabbie glanced over Ayan's shoulder. "This slip is just a storefront where a few captains park. No one here actually owns anything except for maybe their own ship. The folks who trade here are selling someone else's merchandise, probably set you up with a good deal. Lots of captured product comes through here. No knowing where it's from, and that's the point of places like this. Most of the folks on this slip are British types from the Outer Core, I thought you knew 'em already, because of your accent."

"I'm afraid not," she said.

"Well, treat 'em like any other captains or merchants - with respect. Keep your eyes and ears open, don't ask too many questions, and don't let them know where you keep your valuables," advised the cabbie.

"Are they a good sort?"

"They're no worse than the rest." Ayan was just about to walk off when the nafalli called after her in a whisper. "Just wondering... Is everything they saying about you true? You took Valance's operation over?" She didn't know how to answer, but he must have discerned something from her expression, because his eyes went wide. "So he's here, isn't he?" he said in a hush.

"You'd know if he were here. As for who might be in charge, you need look no further," Ayan said with a wink before turning her back to him.

The worn twelve person shuttle lifted off straight away, gaining a few meters of altitude before accelerating into an extreme upward curve. "I think I'll tell Jake to check cab companies if he ever needs more pilots. He was tracking at least two dozen other shuttles and God knows what else up there and it looked like it was as routine as brushing his hair," Laura said as she watched the old people mover disappear into the overhead traffic.

"There's nothing routine about grooming for a nafalli, except that they're always grooming," countered Victor.

"You have a point."

Ayan looked at the old, crooked metal archway ahead of them. There was a thick bodied five deck ship filling the centre of the circular landing pad. Layers of armour were piled onto some sections of the ship, and she could see where at least three gunnery turrets had been built into the vessel after her initial manufacture. The thing was nearly two hundred meters long with clamps along the bottom of her hull, giving her the look of some fat, misshapen cockroach.

The walls of the docking space were obscured by hundreds of stacked transport containers. Some had been welded together to form permanent multi-storey warehouses. Metal stairs had been added, and Ayan could see at least a dozen brand names that were absolutely foreign to her, and pictures of all kinds of products.

Several of the containers were marked SPACERWARES, the only brand name she recognized. Seeing it made her feel a little less dubious about dealing with the seller. "Looks like at least some of these people steal from Regent Galactic. I feel better about this already," Ayan commented.

"Regent Galactic owns Spacerwares? I love that store, it's like heaven for, well, spacers," replied Jenny, disappointed.

Two guards stepped out from the sides of the archway as the groups started walking towards it. They brandished heavy rifles, wore thick, mismatched armour, and had slicked hair and grimy, greasy skin.

"What's your business here?" the taller of the two asked in a thick British accent.

Ayan pulled out the bulletin listing and held it out. "I'm looking to buy some food and supplies if you have them."

"You've come to the right place then, miss. I'll call Captain Sima straight away." He half turned and shouted, "Oi! Skipper! We've got customer!"

Ayan couldn't help but be reminded of the British holomovies she'd seen growing up. She couldn't get enough of them: holomovies, documentaries, anything she could get her hands on. Before her teen years she was close to her mother, so close that she'd picked up her accent, what some of the British called the aristocratic version of their accent, clean and clear. Ayan preferred more of a colourful, charming, street-born accent, but when she used it everyone stared, especially when she did so in jest. When she was younger, she had difficulty understanding why people were amused by the way she spoke. To Ayan, everyone but her and her mother had accents.

It was her first time meeting someone who used such a bent, localized accent, and when she saw the captain come down in brown trousers, a long sleeved shirt, dark brown vest, and short cropped violet hair, Ayan was surprised at how young she looked. By her best estimation, she couldn't be more than twenty.

The woman had all the markings of one born of British heritage; in fact, many of her crew were the same. "We've a sister with us, I see." She smiled as she got to the bottom step, resting her hand on the hilt of her sidearm, a silvered heavy pistol.

Ayan stepped forward and offered her hand. "Ayan Rice, of the Clever Dream."

"Can't say I'm unawares of you setting down on this watery rock, the newsies mixed you right in with the rest of the chatter and gab. Surprised you're standing here, though. Your people still stuck in the Dower Wastes?"

"Unfortunately. We haven't found an alternative yet."

"I'm Captain Ruby Sima. Good to meet someone else who's fighting for the right side. Keep out of the gutter politics around here and you should do fine if your people are as well armed as that fleet of yours. What can I do for you?"

"I'm looking for a new place to set down and need to stock up on food and some extra survival gear. Do you have anything?"

"Food and gear I can help you with, but I don't own any of the slips here, just a renter myself. I might be able to get you in touch with someone who'd be pleased to deal. Let's start with what I can provide. What sort of food are you pressed to buy?"

"Well, we have a food processing unit that can work with base form proteins and we could use some pre-made stuff."

"Like meal bars and the like?" she asked.

"Exactly." Ayan smiled.

"You have credit or cash?"

"I have a few GC with me."

Captain Sima eyed Ayan's messenger bag and a smile grew on her face. "We've got business then, don't we? Let's start with the supplies and then we'll see about somewhere to park."

The tour of what Captain Sima had to offer was like walking through a bulk store. If Ayan wasn't pressed for time, she would have listened to her go through the entire stock, but there were over a hundred shipping containers, and the state of things in the Dower Wastes was never far from her thoughts. She had bartered before, but this was different. This wasn't striking a deal for some keepsake during leave. It was food and essentials with the potential for finding a safer place for everyone. They needed a place to find their feet, especially since she couldn't know what condition the Triton would be in when it returned. If it returned.

If they were stuck with the materializers in their comm units and the ones in the Clever Dream, they would find themselves desperate before long. The materializers would eventually need repair, and they simply didn't have the parts. If they had significant power problems, they'd run out of food even faster. Minutes were passing, and though Ayan was enjoying her time exploring, there were people waiting. Too many people.

Captain Sima was a great sales person. She focused on what Ayan had asked for first, food. The captain had raw stocks and the processors for them as well as dehydrated stock, fresh fruit, vegetables and vat-grown meat. The storage containers they were in would keep them fresh for decades, but without a galley or a large clean environment for food preparation, there was no way Ayan would buy a single crate of the cultivated foods.

Ayan managed to nab four tons of raw food stock and Captain Sima was kind enough to throw in two portable processors that would change the flavour and consistency of the material into a few hundred different dishes, hot or cold. She also purchased a ton of meal bars and that settled their food problems for the time being. It was obvious that the captain was trying to sell her wares first, since she guided them to specific sections of the makeshift warehouse. She was careful not to put down any of the goods they passed, however.

When it came to survival gear, there was a problem. It was all too expensive, even in quantity. After going through the entire list of equipment, which included everything from shovels to an entire portable bunker, and finding nothing that was within their means, Captain Sima nodded and said, "I'll leave you lot alone to discuss things a minute while I tell my Bosun what's what with the food order and make a call."

Ayan, Laura, Victor, and Jenny watched her swagger away and down a steel stairway then turned towards each other. "So we have the food, that's something," Laura said.

"Eighty four thousand credits worth. The portable shelters and other survival gear are expensive. There's got to be something we can do to get all the essentials with the cash we have," Ayan replied. "We might not have anything left to barter for landing space if we buy temporary shelters, though."

"Well, at the price she's offering, we can afford about a hundred four-man shelters with environment units built in, but that's nowhere near enough if we want to perform extensive repairs on our ships." The portable shelter fit in a half-meter by fifteen centimetres thick box. Laura carefully put it back into the case with the rest of them.

"I checked the exchange; if we had come along two months ago with the same money, we'd probably be able to buy half of everything here. The cost of food and survival gear are up, big time," Jenny said quietly.

"I know," Ayan said pensively. "We can't do anything about that now, though. We have to work within our means."

Laura looked down then back up to Ayan with a grin. "I wonder what her shipping containers are worth?"

"Well, I assume we might get one with the food we ordered, so that one might be built into the price."

"What if we bought an extra one or two? It's not like they have to have systems built in, we can rig survival machinery, and we can pick up the containers if we have to move them later with at least one of the ships we commandeered in the Ossimi Ring."

Ayan smiled and nodded. "I bet she has an extra or two." She looked for the captain but saw one of her men instead. "Can you get on comms and fetch the captain, please?" Ayan asked sweetly.

"Skipper!" the crewman hollered. "They're ready to close the deal!"

Captain Sima came up the stairs a few minutes later. "Figured a few things out?"

"We may have," Ayan said with a winning smile. "We're wondering what the going rate for empty shipping containers is."

"Not much. Free if you have a ship with a hauler hitch and you're fast enough to pick one up before the junk yard scavengers get to 'em."

"I'll pay you to help us get a couple, how does that sound?"

Captain Sima looked over her shoulder to a much smaller ship with four swivelling engines and a great claw underneath that looked like the Samson's maxjack then back to the foursome. "You have a deal, miss."

"I was also wondering about that landing space. I need to move my people today."

"I'll be level with you on this, since I bet it'll go far with you. Most Port Masters are right pricks when it comes to setting people up, charging too much and double crossing. I checked with the more trustworthy kind and one of them fancies a meet with you: Captain Patrizia Salustri-" Ayan heard Victor inhale sharply at the mention of the name and pretend as though he was looking at something in the darkened warehouse.

"Heard of her?" Captain Sima asked with a crooked smile. "Where you hail from?"

"Pandem," he replied quietly.

"Then you would have. Well, she wants a sit down with you. Good luck there too, she owns more slips than most, and if she wants to see you then she already has a deal in mind. Just don't tell anyone I sent you her way, or there could be trouble."

"Why not?" asked Ayan. She had to know.

"I rent from a competitor, that's why. He'd be fair vexed if he found out you were standing right here and I passed you off without so much as looking at his ident."

"Then I won't say anything."

"Good. When you strike a deal with Salustri, remember who got you in the door," said Captain Sima.

"I will, thank you Ruby," Ayan said, shaking her hand.

"You settle up with my man here, I'll make sure there's someone to meet her shuttle when it arrives."

Chapter 24
The Command Deck

Five meters from the express car was the rear-guard of the command deck's assault force. There weren't dozens but hundreds of soldiers dedicated to the effort of taking the command deck and the bridge. From everything Major Cumberland could discern, they had come at it the wrong way. "We're on deck and awaiting orders." He double checked his reticule to find the commanding officer's name. "Commander DeHansen," he finished.

"This is Commander DeHansen, my senior sergeants are all on the casualty list. I've taken direct command of operations. I'm assigning you as the senior officer to everyone you arrived with. You are to secure the hallways leading to the primary engagement area and reinforce us."

Major Cumberland couldn't help but glance over his shoulder at the thirty-one men and women who made it off the upper deck with him. Three had lost their rifles and were down to their service side arms. He didn't want to know how it happened. "Understood, moving up. So you are aware, my comms and scanner people are all out of action."

"No problem, we've got the whole place scanned out, you're just taking a quick gander before joining the fray," said DeHansen.

The few rooms adjacent to the hallway were cleared quickly. They were small ready quarters, offices, and conference rooms. A few had consoles that looked like they had been used as some kind of control room, but it, like every other nerve centre on the ship, was dark and dormant. It took him only a couple of rooms to see that each of them had been investigated by several teams beforehand, but the commander obviously thought checking them periodically was essential to keeping the enemy off their backs while they pressed ahead.

After clearing two dozen such spaces, they came around a corner and saw the first real evidence that their allies had a significant foothold on the ship. It was a portable armoured barricade that sealed the hallway. Welded into place, it was almost as secure as a bulkhead door, and upon arrival they were scanned by two officers with hand units before the rear-guard slid the barricade doors open. It was closed behind them quickly, as though they feared the wrong air would waft in behind them.

Several rooms, quarters from the looks of it, had been opened and were in use as triage centres. Many of the patients had been placed in stasis. Some were fresh from the fight, with limbs missing or holes through both sides of their armour. Whatever the people holding the bridge were firing, it cut through their armour like it wasn't there at all. Cumberland couldn't help but recall the mental image of the nafalli they'd met who killed several of his people while wielding a nanoblade.

The major made the mistake of locking eyes with a man as he was being rushed into the middle room. He was in indescribable agony as something that had burned through his armour continued to flare through the hole. "It's an aluminothermic reaction! We've got to isolate it so it doesn't burn straight through his hip!" called out one of the medics.

The man was twitching in pain so severe his screams were interrupted by convulsions. His gaze was desperate, piercing, and something Cumberland would see in his dreams. As the stretcher was placed down on a cot and the doctor stepped in with an instrument that looked like a hollow coring tool, he flinched his gaze away and cleared his throat. "Let's get to it, boys."

"Sir, I have to lodge a formal protest," declared a voice from behind.

"Go ahead, but if you fall out I'll have to shoot you."

"That's well and good, Sir, but these people are better armed, know the terrain, and have the overall high ground. We should consult with Command before moving forward."

"Your complaint has been recorded, it'll show up on Commander DeHansen's screen," said Cumberland.

"I don't feel that I've been properly addressed. I want a response before-" said the soldier.

"Commander DeHansen is running this deck. If he says we move up and help him finish this, then we do. He can choose to address your complaint before, during, or after we're engaged." A sudden rush of air was a sure sign that an explosive had detonated ahead. Major Cumberland wasn't looking forward to entering the fray either, but if they could take the bridge, it might finally give them the upper hand on the ship. "Now, get in line and get ready or I'll send you back up to deck twenty one. I hear Command is looking for someone to lead the suicide mission up there."

The rear guard was two squads deep, thirty soldiers. Once they were past them, the halls were eerily quiet, and with no illumination other than their reticule sensors and the beams of their personal lights, the open doors were like mysterious cavities, collecting shadows. Cumberland's wrist computer told him the quarters on the command deck were spacious, most likely for the upper ranks. Glimpses inside revealed upturned furniture, personal items left on the floor, and a general desecration of living spaces. No wonder they're taking it personally. This has the feel of a long tour ship. They probably consider this ship their home, may have for a long time. I'd be pissed too. Flashing light ahead told him that they were coming up to one of the front line battles. It was too soon. The broad, curving hall had guided them in the right direction, but last Cumberland checked, the status said that they had made more progress. It said they had reached the bridge proper. The sensor data he downloaded from the commander's terminal told him a different story.

He ran forward until he could see combat, his soldiers close behind. On the deck behind the bottlenecked troops was evidence of demolished barrier materials. They had been driven back at least twenty meters, and the enemy was laying firepower on thick. The injured and dead were piling up behind as medics rushed to get the most treatable cases onto stretchers and back to their temporary infirmary.

Major Cumberland stopped and looked at a fresh schematic of the command deck on his hand scanner. There was another battle raging on beneath their feet, on the lower level of the command deck. "Commander DeHansen, we're moving to the lower deck. There's no opportunity to engage on this level," Major Cumberland announced.

"I hear you. Proceed."

Cumberland turned and started running back the way they came. If the command crew of the Triton was able to hold the main deck and press the assault back, then there wouldn't be much chance of that fight resolving in their favour. However, from the schematic in his hand, the two levels of the main bridge were connected and the assault on the lower deck was going much better. They were at the doors.

When the express car opened, they were greeted with the sight of a heavy bulkhead door that had been cut through. It was no less than a metre thick. He'd never seen anything like it outside of a vault or primary hull plate.

"Must have taken them all day to cut through," muttered one of the privates behind him as they stepped inside.

"Keep your eyes on your targeting reticule. The report marking this level clear may have been a little off," Major Cumberland ordered as the rest of the data on the encounters for the area scrolled by.

"I'm just glad we weren't the first to clear the administration and conference rooms up top. Seems that those cushy quarters end just a few meters up from where we were and there were traps all over."

"Can it, Spence. Hustle up," Major Cumberland said as he watched the last of his people step through the narrow hole in the bulkhead door. The instant both her feet were on the deck he broke into a run.

Major Cumberland kept one eye on the gradual curve of the hall through his targeting reticule and the other on the hand scanner. It told him everything his raw senses and basic sensors couldn't. Twenty meters, in he started seeing bodies.

Some of the doors on the lower command deck had been sealed shut with quick-weld tape, others had been battered through, some from the inside, some from the outside. Some of the more scrappy conscripts he'd run into under the command of the issyrian were represented amongst the ruined bodies. A few of the corpses were dressed in the foreboding skull-marked armour of the security teams that were scattered across the ship, the proper defenders.

I've never seen a crew so unwilling to surrender. These conscripts fought as hard as the properly uniformed soldiers. There had been a slaughter, and as he closed the distance between the lift and active fire fighting, he slowed to look before leaping. One of his people, an abandoner of the upper deck who had just joined, ran a few steps past him, jarring his shoulder. "Watch it!" he called out. "Actually, now that you're up there, you take point," Cumberland said with a smile that was more like a grimace as he looked into the darkness ahead. Just around the corner there were barricades. He could barely see them.

"Yes, Sir," replied the private. He raised his rifle and moved ahead slowly, carefully placing his boots down one after the other between the mixture of corpses.

"What kind of fire fight does this? I mean, how are they so close together?" asked another one of his late joiners. His voice was thin, near panic.

He didn't care to help. "A close fight does this, one where half the people are using blades," he replied.

"No one does that. Look! Most of these ones are sliced and diced! I mean, what kind of a fight is that?" He poked a fallen soldier's helmet with his boot and cringed backwards as it rolled to reveal the trooper's head was still inside.

"Get it together!" snapped Major Cumberland.

The point man stopped in his tracks, lowering his rifle as they came around a more extreme bend. "No way. There's no way. I'm not going in there."

Cumberland rushed up behind him and peeked around his shoulder. "Then don't move," he said as he looked at the scene ahead on his hand scanner.

The barriers had been breached, or a few of the enemy had found a way around. He couldn't tell. Ahead was a melee. For a moment it looked as though his men were fighting each other, but then he realized they were trying to line up invisible targets. Whoever was assailing them managed to get into their midst in cloaksuits, most likely not many of them, but they were in the middle of fifty or more soldiers.

Cumberland tried to use the sonic detector on the hand scanner, but the enemy was so close to his allies that they were impossible to tell apart. He thought he saw one of the invisible defenders appear on his screen, but he was running so fast, and closed to within striking distance of the men ahead so efficiently that the signal was immediately indistinguishable.

He looked up from his scanner, stuffing it into his only remaining front pocket, and just watched the fray for a moment. As one soldier found himself gutted by whatever ultra thin blade the defenders used at close range, another tried to fire in the assailant's direction. Others flailed about, trying to strike their invisible prey as they came near with the butts of their rifles. Still more attempted to back away, get themselves anchored to a wall so they wouldn't be struck from behind.

"Oh my God," uttered Private Spence.

"What's wrong, Major? Press ahead! We'll take them down there if we can get enough people in the hall! Don't give them room to move!" shouted Commander DeHansen through the command comm.

"Just trying to find the advantage," Cumberland replied.

"I said get in-"

"Let me think! I'm not wasting my people, I've lost enough today!" He flicked his visor open, overtaken by the need to breathe air that wasn't recycled inside his suit. The idea struck him then, and he hoped it would work. Cumberland pulled the bladder that carried his water off and tossed it on the ground in front of him. He set his rifle to emit only heat in a wide beam, focused the weapon on the large pouch and fired.

The water came to a boil in less than twenty seconds and the drinking tube came loose, filling the hall ahead with steam.

"There!" screeched Private Baram. She was one of his best soldiers, and a good shot as she demonstrated when she opened fire on the shape in the steam. The figure took several direct hits before disappearing further down the hall.

"Gimme a minute, I'll rig a few charges," Spence said from behind. He hurriedly crouched down and cut a fallen soldier's water sac loose, careful not to puncture it.

"Everyone, hurry, before we lose the steam," Major Cumberland said as he took the bladder from the soldier who had been in point position.

He had proven even more useless after seeing the shape in the steam, and was actually cowering. "They're invisible? They can be anywhere!" he quivered.

Cumberland tossed the bag down a meter away and heated it to boiling like the last. The tube attachment was too new, however, and it simply expanded. He flicked it with his boot and the piping burst. The hall started to fill with steam all around them. He'd been sealed in his armour for so long that the humidity was almost welcome.

"Major!" called Baram.

He turned just in time to see a shape lunging towards him. His rifle butt came up to deflect the incoming blade. The reaction was purely instinct, there was no time for thought. He could barely make out the shape of his attacker, but before he completely lost him he swept for where he thought his legs ought to be. A disturbance in the steam told him that his assailant had fallen and three of his people fired on the empty space.

After a few seconds of constant fire, the familiar uniform of the defenders appeared, silver skull marked on the left side of her chest with the word Triton written where the death head's teeth would be. The woman's uniform had breached, and she'd taken several direct hits to the chest and stomach. The blade she'd intended to use rolled out of her hand and the blackened visor covering her hooded face swept upward.

Breathing was a gurgling labour for the young woman as she looked Cumberland in the eye. Her mouth worked to say something and he bent down, wary of a trick. "N-never surrender," she managed. A fierceness came over her, as though her pale blue eyes were set ablaze for a moment as she wheezed; "Triton!"

Her chest rose and fell rapidly, as though she was gripped by a series of failed, retching coughs before her eyes stared somewhere past him and glazed over. These people, this ship. It all measures up to the legend of Earth, to their tenacity and loyalty. No wonder it has cost us so many. But out here? How did they end up so far away from the Sol System? he thought. If the intelligence they've given us is right, and this is a stolen vessel, then it's got to be in the water. Then again, maybe it is Valance. The hero of Enreega. Major Cumberland straightened and looked around. The steam was dissipating, his people were frozen to the spot, waiting with water bladders in hand for an order. He could almost see the morale draining out of them by the second. "Pass the word that their suits can't compensate for water vapour," he ordered as he slapped his visor closed.

Two more bags were thrown between Major Cumberland and the melee as they closed the distance. They caught sight of at least two retreating forms as they rushed to join the main fight, where steam filled the air. They were fighting shadows in the mist.

They joined the main fray in time to glimpse disturbances in the air, retreating shadows that moved too fast or were too well shielded to be caught by the few rounds that struck them. There were twenty nine soldiers left from a group of over fifty just some minutes ago, and listening to the chatter, looking at the tactical feed, he knew there were no more reinforcements to be had. He was the ranking officer on that deck, and there was a decision to be made, one that could cost everyone their lives, or win the engagement outright. He took one of the improvised steam grenades, really only an adjusted thermal grenade strapped to a water sac, and tossed it into the hole blown through the main entrance to the lower bridge. A few seconds later it had heated the bag and steam burst through the improvised door.

"Forward!" he barked harshly.

The soldiers who had been stationed there, weary as they were, seemed reinvigorated and reassured at the very thought that if someone were coming through that door in a cloaksuit, they would be able to see an indication of it in the thick steam. The instant they came around the corner they opened fire.

"Avoid shooting the consoles!" Major Cumberland shouted as what was left of the second incursion unit rushed the door.

Several enemy crewmen were shot down in the first few seconds, but by the time Cumberland and Spence stepped into the breach and tossed two more steam charges, they had the whole room lit up with pulse rounds. It was cover fire for the most part, but as the pair of grenades went off further into the flight deck, they found targets. There were people in cloaksuits diving for cover. The flashing light and steam revealed their movement through it on their targeting reticule's thermal sensors as well as to the naked eye.

The word had been passed along to the upper deck, and steam was beginning to roll in from the entrance above. The flashing lights and mist made for an eerie scene that was soon grisly. As they felled several enemy troops, they too lost people.

Major Cumberland barely had time to raise an arm as he saw movement in the corner of his eye. He was nearly knocked senseless by a fist as hard as granite and as unyielding as a bulkhead door. His helmet cracked, his cheek mashed into his teeth, drawing blood, and he was driven to his knees.

His rifle was ripped out of his hands and he was dragged backwards, into the hallway where the steam was dissipating. In a desperate move he drew his service pistol and fired over his shoulder as fast as he could. A great shadow appeared overhead, only this time it was real, tangible. His opponent staggered back. His armour was almost as impressive as the man. Flexible horizontal bands of metal covered him from head to toe, maintaining some kind of failing shield that made the edges of the emitters glow red. The man wearing it was massive for a human. Thick arms, legs that were like pillars, shoulders that could carry two grown men and a height over two meters. His hood withdrew into the armour's shoulders to reveal a fair haired man with a broad face and strong jaw. He was smiling, despite the trickle of blood escaping from the corner of his mouth.

With the last of his strength he slowly raised an arm with six slashes on its cuff and pointed at Cumberland. "What are you fighting for?" he asked between laboured breaths.

Cumberland didn't have a ready answer, not one he'd present to a dying man. "Duty," was the only word he could offer, and it felt weak in the air between them.

"My crew, my home," the man laboured. His chest heaved, filling the hall with the sounds of his gurgling. He was drowning in his own blood.

Cumberland set his sidearm to its highest setting, and by the time he levelled it at the opposing soldier's head his breathing had stopped. He was dead.

The sounds of the fire fight on the bridge quieted. It was over.

"Any prisoners?" he asked over the comm.

"None. They wouldn't surrender."

He didn't say it aloud, he wouldn't dare, but he couldn't help but think that the wrong people had won. Major Cumberland leaned forward and gently closed his enemies' eyes, taking note of the name written on the inside of his collar, McPatrick.

Chapter 25
Patrizia Salustri

By the time Ayan, Laura, Victor, and Jenny were outside the makeshift warehouse, there was a heavy hulled pristine black shuttle waiting for them in the small courtyard. None of them had heard it land. A man in a stiff grey business suit and knee length white coat waited beside the side hatch. When they drew near, he bowed and gestured them inside. Ayan couldn't help but notice there was a severe-looking stun discharger up his coat sleeve.

The interior could only be described as luxurious. It was tall enough for everyone to stand full height, but no one would want to. The seating inside was well cushioned, set in a long oval, and made for casual conversation. The greeter didn't join them, but closed the door from the outside. As soon as the hatch closed the environment system cleaned the air, scrubbing it free of the grease and trash odours of the open air landing fields.

"Never been in anything like this before," Victor muttered, trying to get comfortable on seating that was meant for softer passengers. The body armour just seemed to get in the way no matter what he did.

Jenny's solution was more demure. Instead of trying to lay back and get comfortable, she sat up straight with her hands on her knees. "Nope, can't say I've ever known people rich enough to have one. The Clever Dream is pretty close though, as far as creature comforts go."

As much as Ayan wanted to lounge, her focus was on something else. "So, what do you know about Patrizia Salustri, Vic?"

"Well, she was pretty well known around Pandem. She used to drop in on the hot spots to entertain herself; being a pretty big celebrity criminal, she drew a lot of attention. She's probably the best known pirate in the sector."

"You mean privateer, right?" Laura asked.

"No, pirate. When the Carthans gave her a pardon a couple years ago as part of her privateering agreement, it was a huge deal. She hit everything if you believe the hype, but I think she mostly went after big cargo haulers. I heard about her holding a few yachts for ransom though, so she's not afraid to get her hands dirty. If you were a hauler Captain or well-to-do, the last thing you wanted to see was the Morte Lenta. I don't think most of the stories about her taking on passenger liners are true, they were probably just morons who said they were part of her crew, fleecing the travellers for everything they had then sabotaging the engines so they could make a clean getaway," Victor finished bitterly.

"Were you unlucky enough to get robbed?"

"No!" Victor said, his warding hands waving for emphasis. "I just hate people who rob regular travellers. Especially if they're saying they're affiliated with someone who has too much class to do it. But they loved her on the holonets. I mean, she's from an old Earth European family who came out with the late settlers and made a career as a pirate. I mean, that's what some of my favourite holomovies are made of."

"She was never caught?" asked Ayan.

"Sure, but she's smart. There was never any actual footage of her doing anything. Even most of her crew were slippery. Until the Carthans actually pardoned her for God only knows how many criminal acts in their territory so she would sign a privateering agreement, no one could prove she'd done a thing."

"Other than the piracy, she doesn't sound so bad."

"There were murder charges," Jenny added. "I remember now, that's one of the reasons her pardon was such a big deal. It wasn't just the company losses that would never get repaid."

"Yup, they were there, but it never got to a court room, so no one knows if the murder charges are legitimate," explained Victor.

"Oh, come on! Years in piracy and theft, outside of the law and you don't think she killed anyone?" Jenny questioned harshly.

"I didn't say that. I only said they never got to prove it one way or another."

"You're hung up on her looks."

"That has nothing to do with it," Victor said.

"She gets a pass because you fancy her, if she looked like most career pirates, there's no way you'd have a doubt in your mind that she's killed at least a few people for money," accused Jenny.

"Maybe she did, who knows?"

Jenny regarded Ayan and Laura then. "She has a reputation for being severe when people turn on her. No one ever testified against her, or turned up with independently sourced evidence. To me, that says there are a lot of people who are so afraid of her that they wouldn't dare speak against her."

"Then she's probably a perfect fit for Tamber, from what I'm seeing. I wonder how she ended up with land here?" Ayan asked idly.

"Good question. I don't think we really want to know. Sounds like the kind of knowledge that could get someone disappeared," Jenny said quietly.

"So, what do you think of me trying to strike a bargain with this woman?" asked Ayan.

"Well, if the crime bosses are taking over in this city, then she might be the one you want to side with," Victor said. "But be careful. If someone like Patrizia Salustri is interested in speaking with you…"

"Then she probably wants something," Ayan finished with a nod.

"Remember, we're playing with a pretty full deck, Ayan," Laura reassured. "You have a whole fighter wing, the Clever Dream, and six other serviceable ships. Some need more work than others, but that's a lot more than I think a lot of people here seem to have."

Ayan watched the oldest of the city buildings, brick and brown concrete structures, go by as the shuttle slowed down. "It's strange hearing you say I have them. All this is getting more complicated by the second. Not to mention strange. All of a sudden I'm the owner of my own fleet and it's up to the four of us to solve the biggest problems as quickly as we can. Now I think we're about to sit down with a crime boss who's been at it for longer than I think anyone here knows." They passed the city and the shuttle picked up speed over the jungle tree tops.

"Just remember how many people you have backing you," said Laura.

"How can I forget? They're sitting in the Dower Wastes right now, depending on us to get them a safe place to park."

The shuttle stopped and Ayan looked behind her as the hatch opened and the rampway extended. They had arrived at what she could only describe as a beach side villa. Behind the grand four storey terracotta roofed house was a tall cave. It had been blocked off with massive armoured accordion doors several metres in, and from the wavering light in front, she could tell there was some kind of energy shielding. Other hatches in the mountainside hid fixtures she would have loved to know more about, but decided to concentrate on getting down the ramp in front of her onto the tall terrace.

The patio ran the width of the lowest level of the main house, and was bricked with fortified yellow quartz, to blend in with the glittering natural white and brown quartz sand on the beach. There were several ironwork tables and chairs, padded deck seating in front of the tan brick and mortar villa. It was as though Ayan had stepped onto a holomovie set. She hadn't spent enough time on well settled worlds to know if bricked houses were normal, though she'd seen plenty of them in holomovies from different eras. She'd seen more movies with characters that lived in fabricated homes, however, and she could only assume that hand crafted buildings came at a much higher price.

She wasn't certain whether or not she was looking at a rich home until she caught a glimpse of Victor and Jenny's faces. They were in absolute awe. The man in the white coat emerged from the front of the shuttle before it soundlessly rose back into the sky, and he invited them with a gesture before walking into the villa through a thick wooden door.

Ayan just took the place in for a moment, looking down the stairs to the beach where there was a small area with a bubbling pool and a pair of shower poles. Then there was the beach. The last time she'd seen that much water she was on Pandem, and it was from afar. From where she sat on the terrace, she could hear the waves, and in only twenty steps she'd be at the water's edge. Crystal blue water extended from the shore line all the way to the horizon, and she couldn't remember seeing anything that looked more cool or pure. She could have sat there watching the waves, the sun warming her face, for hours.

The heavy doors opened to admit a woman with a mane of curly black hair, wearing a loose beige tunic over dark leggings that looked like they were made of interwoven strips of dark cloth. One of her wrists was adorned with several thin gold and platinum bracelets, and only her engagement and ring fingers were bare, the rest had one or more rings each with modest stones. Her dark eyes took them all in with a glance, and she regarded them with an easy approving smile. Half way to the table she stopped and silently looked over her shoulder.

A gentleman in a loose fitting long shirt and shorts was at her side with his ear tilted to lips in seconds. She whispered to him in a quickly spoken language that seemed to allow no hesitation.

Ayan started to look at her wrist but her question was answered before she had time to find out for herself. "She's speaking old Earth Italian," Victor informed her in a whisper. "She's saying-"

The man Patrizia spoke to nodded and returned to the house. "I was telling him that you should have drinks in front of you," she finished for Victor as she sauntered over to the fifth seat at the table, her boot heels clicking against the bricks. She took her seat. "I am Patrizia Salustri, welcome to my home." She regarded everyone in a smooth sweep of her eyes from left to right, her gaze coming to rest on Ayan.

"This is Laura Everin, Victor Davis, and Jenny Machad," said Ayan.

"And you are Ayan," Patrizia added. "Who are these people to you?" Her accent was smooth, strange, matching the language they heard a hint of the moment before. Her diction was careful, intentional, and clear.

Ayan almost stammered as she went through the list. "Laura is my closest friend and our best energy field technician, Victor and Jenny are my personal guards and crew members." The woman had a way about her and a direct intensity that Ayan was sure was made only more penetrating by the fact that Patrizia hadn't looked away from her eyes since she sat down. Always, the woman's mysterious gaze was peering directly at Ayan.

"They are important enough to know everything we say?" Patrizia asked, her voice just above a whisper.

"I trust them," she answered simply.

"You are close to your people. It surprises me, I'm sorry," said Patrizia.

"Why are you sorry?"

"My assumptions come from the holograms, where they speak of you as though the people around you are nothing, replaceable. Again, they have everything wrong, but I couldn't find anything about you."

The clinking of ice in tall glasses heralded the delivery of a decanter and five iced teas. The fellow in the long shirt and shorts made no eye contact as he transferred everything from his tray to the table with practiced efficiency.

"Thank you," Laura said quietly.

The fellow tucked the tray under his arm, nodded shoulders deep at Laura, and departed with long strides.

"Now we speak about important things," Patrizia invited. "Where is Jacob Valance?"

The question caught Ayan completely off guard and she hesitated.

"Why did he give you everything? His ship, his people, why?" Her questions had a solemn weight.

"I can't say," Ayan said in as reassuring a tone as she could manage.

"You speak for him, you are his messenger."

It took a conscious effort for Ayan to answer indirectly. "I make decisions for the entire crew."

Patrizia nodded slowly, her eyes searching Ayan's face as though trying to glean extra meaning from her expression. "He trusts you," she said in a hushed tone. She let the silence grow thick before she sighed and nodded. "He trusts you." She took Ayan's hand and looked at it a moment. "You were the one who gave him his scarf."

Ayan's breath caught, and time seemed to suspend. Who was Patrizia to him? Her first supposition was that she was a past lover, and no matter how much she wanted her thoughts to jump to another possibility, it wouldn't change tracks.

Patrizia looked back up at her and her eyes momentarily widened. "I have not seen him in years," she explained. "He was always very good, we only met one time. I asked him about the scarf, and he wouldn't explain it. You must understand, when I ask someone something, they answer, it has always been this way. He was gone before I knew him."

"Sounds like him," Laura said with a little smile. "Well, sometimes."

Patrizia leaned back in her seat and picked up her iced tea. "You have important things to discuss." Laura, Victor, and Jenny all relaxed when their host sat back and sipped. It was an unconscious reaction, but a welcome one.

Ayan's head was still spinning, but she cleared her throat and pressed on. "Yes, and I'm hoping you can help. We need somewhere stable to land for repairs and rest. We're going to have to put up temporary shelters while we work as well. I may be able to afford to rent the slips we need until we can start privateering. Then I'm sure we'll be able to earn enough to stay there if the location works out."

"You don't have to pay. You trade."

"I'd really rather pay our way, I don't want to owe anyone anything."

Patrizia, in what seemed to be a common gesture to her, but one Ayan found unsettling, took her hand again. "No, you've come here to my place, and we are speaking. You will stay on my land where everyone will see and you will pay by helping me with your fighters. You'll do this for me when your ships are out of the wastes and you're ready to fly again."

The woman's tone conveyed her words as belief, as though this was the way the future would be and it couldn't unfold differently. Instead of bargaining, Ayan found herself asking, "Where would you put us?"

The woman opened her other hand, palm up and a hologram of the landing fields. Several slips in the older side were highlighted. The image focused in, showing a small depiction of the space that included a serviceable hangar large enough for several of their larger ships. Three shipping containers were already being lowered into place at the opposite end of the lot. It was just barely large enough, and there was a small township of older buildings nearby as well. Ayan could also see what the woman meant by 'where everyone will see.' It was a fairly central location.

"Why?" Ayan asked. "This almost feels like charity."

Patrizia's expression darkened a little, and she deactivated the hologram. "You are Ayan, and you have the best fighters here." She made an all-encompassing gesture with her free hand. "People think that Jacob is with you, and look, look at your armoured people." She nodded towards Jenny and Victor. "You have your own army, and people already speak about you cutting the weaker ones away. They come into the cities looking for a way to leave, and weeping over how their old lives are gone while you and the people you keep move on. You find a way to live without stopping to blame the world. You are beautiful, strong, and I know that you can pay me quickly if you have time to repair, and while you fix your ships we can get to know each other. See if we can work together."

Ayan was moved by the woman, she would admit later, but there were some missing details that made her nervous. She squeezed the woman's hand slightly, a gesture that earned a little smile, and spoke with near desperation. "I need a price, Patrizia. Whether I pay you with the coins I have right now or with the product of a raid in the future, I need to know what all this is worth so we can both agree when our debts are paid later."

There was a little disappointment in the other woman's expression for a moment but then she nodded. "I understand. You are very good at this." She touched one of her bracelets and Ayan's command and control unit blinked with a new message.

Ayan glanced at it and nearly turned white at the price as it was initially listed in United Core World Credits: 3,600,000 every 30 days. Beneath it was the price in Molecularly Stamped Platinum Bullion, or Galactic Currency: 120,000 GC, which was sobering to say the least, but possible. She looked into Patrizia's expectant eyes and smiled. She was so nervous she could feel her palms sweating, but she did her best to cover it. "I'm going to pay you eighty thousand GC every thirty days."

Victor nearly choked on his iced tea, but his antics didn't distract Patrizia, whose eyes widened. To Ayan's relief, the woman presented a counter offer through a smile. "One hundred ten."

"Ninety thousand," Ayan countered.

"One hundred five."

"Ninety two."

Patrizia's smile didn't fade, but her eyes narrowed to slits. "Ninety five, and I can tell everyone you are on my land."

In that moment Ayan understood something very important about the woman in front of her; she had to win, she had to take possession of things. "Agreed, and I hope we can work together in the future. It'll take a little time for us to be ready, you understand. We have business of our own to settle first."

"Yes, you will have time." Patrizia leaned forward and kissed Ayan on the cheek before fixing her with a big smile. "Welcome to Tamber. Welcome to my home." She let go of Ayan's hand, leaving one of her rings behind on her middle finger.

Ayan hadn't even noticed the woman put it there. It was a platinum piece with a gold lion's head.

CHAPTER 26
THE INFIRMARY

"I don't know who was down here, but they're gone now," said Sergeant Masterson as he picked his way through the infirmary. "Left a lot of corpses behind, though."

"I count three whole squads," informed Private Elaine Patterson. "They started calling him The Butcher on comms before they restricted unit to unit crosstalk."

"Put a lid on it, Patterson. The last thing we need is to get superstitious." The darkened alcoves, empty beds, and instrumentation kiosks provided too many places for the enemy to hide. Their personal lights lit the corners too briefly for anyone's comfort, and there was always the back trail. From what they had heard the squads didn't see the Butcher coming. When he hit, comms went dead, squad members' stats flat-lined. Most of the soldiers were found later, decapitated. It hadn't been done with a firearm, the Butcher used some kind of garrotte. A micron thin, strong line that cut through their armour after the considerable application of physical force.

It sent a shiver down Sergeant Masterson's spine, but he'd never admit it to his squad. "All right, fan out and set up camp at that nurse's station there. We're going to hold here until they can get reinforcements on site. I'm doing another sweep of the inner perimeter."

"Alone, Sir?"

"Don't worry Ackers, I won't leave you alone in the dark. Patterson will protect you," Sergeant Masterson soothed.

"Find a plush teddy for Ackers, check," Private Patterson teased.

"With me, Carson," Masterson ordered. "Of course I'm not going on a search without someone to watch my back," he muttered.

There were closed rooms surrounding the central organization and treatment area in the infirmary and they all had to be checked. The first two doors opened easily. Carson was a powerhouse, addicted to the weight room and fitness supplements. When it came to pulling doors open with gripper handles, he was the man. They had the first four rooms cleared in ten minutes, then they ran into a locked door.

"I'm picking up a single female's vitals inside. Looks like we're about to have a prisoner," Sergeant Masterson said with a grin.

"Maybe we should call the rest of the squad?"

Masterson looked over his shoulder briefly and shook his head. "Naw, the readings say she's at rest. She's not the Butcher."

Carson shrugged and pulled a motorized pry bar from his pack. With deft, practiced hands he busted the lock and forced the door. In one smooth motion he put the pry bar in his pack and had his rifle back in hand.

Sergeant Masterson was already inside. On the bed in the centre of the modest sized treatment room lay a black haired woman. "Wow, sleeping beauty or what?" he whispered as he scanned her through the sight of his rifle.

"You want me to leave you two love birds to get acquainted, Sarge?" chuckled Carson.

"Why not? This tour's been a hell of a wash so far, may as well make a memory."

"You kids have fun," Carson said as he turned his back to the door.

Sergeant Masterson slung his rifle and took off his gloves, eying the sleeping young woman from head to toe. He stroked her face and pressed his cheek to hers. "You should be in pictures, sweetheart. What're you doing way out here on a stolen ship?" he asked in an intimate whisper. A panel above the bed came to life, listing broken bones, ruptured organs, and a course of treatment ending in the current status: REGENERATION COMPLETE INITIATING WAKE SEQUENCE.

"Looks like you're all better." He smiled as he pulled the insulated sheet down slowly, baring her nude form.

As soon as the hem of the sheet reached her middle she woke with a start and snatched it, kicking and retreating. He took a firmer hold on the sheet and pulled harder, winning the battle on the second yank, thrilling at the struggling young woman. Her cries for help and terrified, dark eyes were enchanting. "Just a taste. I'll leave you in one piece," he begged mockingly.

"Get offa me! No!" she screamed. Her eyes focused on something behind him then, and a sudden shuffle followed by the sickening sound of something sliding through meat and bone filled the room.

Masterson whirled around in time to see Carson's headless corpse drop to the floor by the door. He brandished his rifle as he frantically searched the room. "Someone help, he got Carson. I think he's still in the room, but I couldn't see him," Masterson shouted desperately. Sweat coated his palms and forehead.

Something bumped into him from behind. The wire was around his neck. He could hear the impossibly thin, lethal strand of the garrotte sawing through his armour. He kicked, grabbed at the monster's hands and tried to turn away. "Son of a bitch! You won't get me! You won't-" His struggling was useless. The Butcher pulled harder, and as he started to break the skin the sergeant's feet came off the deck. No amount of struggling would save him, but he writhed regardless.

"You're not worth this life. I'm taking something you never deserved," he heard the Butcher whisper through clenched teeth the instant before one final pull of the wire separated his head from his shoulders.

Ashley was frozen in stunned shock as Larry pushed the headless body of her attacker towards the door. He decapitated both soldiers like a man born to killing. It was like watching the grim reaper at work, and she would have never expected it of him. He was her co-pilot. A quiet, thoughtful, soulful friend who never got tired of listening to her go on about anything she liked. He even laughed at her jokes, which she knew were hit or miss.

Seeing him kill like it was second nature, like it was what he was born to do, it was unbelievable. He deactivated something on his wrists before going to her bedside and hurriedly asked, "Are you okay?"

She stared at him. His vacsuit had cleaned itself; there was no trace on him of the slaughter moments before, but the floor told the tale.

He turned and dropped a thin, round disc in front of the door and an energy barrier appeared. When he turned back to her there was deep concern in his eyes, and he gently took her chin in his hand. "Ashley, they were about to do terrible things to you, I had no choice."

"I-" she tried to work up some saliva, her mouth was so dry. "I know. You're the one whose been killing the spies," she whispered.

"The West Watchers, yes. I wish I could have told you, or anyone, but it would have put you and everyone else on this ship at risk. I was assigned to the Triton after she was bought by Regent Galactic. I got onto the custodial crew and made sure that I was given a permanent place on Wheeler's second crew." He took a bottle of water from a dispenser beside the bed and gave it to her. "Here, drink slowly."

She willed herself to sip the water slowly instead of greedily drawing it through the straw. Its cool relief eased her dry throat. The silence it imposed gave her more time to look around. The dim lighting in the room was enough for her to realize that she was in the ship infirmary, and even through the shield at the door she could tell it was too quiet outside. Something was very wrong. Ashley ignored her rising fear as best as she could and, instead of asking about the ship or what was going on, she decided to do what she supposed Stephanie would do: investigate the nearest possible threat. "You're from Earth? Are you the real captain or something?"

"I'm a silent observer, or I was supposed to be, but the West Watchers were too big of a problem. They would have given away your position, eventually gotten access to people like Frost, people with control codes, so anyone with a tie to them had to be taken care of."

Several shots impacted the shield.

"Listen, I'll tell you everything if you can promise to keep my secret."

Ashley didn't know how she felt about the grisly display, or Larry's true identity. He was dangerous, and if there was any truth to all the spy movies she'd seen, agents would do anything to keep their secrets. It was her turn to put on a false front.

She shrugged and smiled at him. "I'm just happy to have my bikini bod back. Last I remember I went over the pilot's console like a wet noodle. A wet noodle that went crunch."

"Get dressed, that shield won't keep them out forever," he told Ashley as he handed her a black vacsuit that matched his own. He turned around and pulled the ammunition from both the rifles as she got dressed behind him. "They were able to evacuate medical for the most part, but they couldn't move you. They told me it would take at least twenty hours for the recovery meds to do their work while you rested in a coma. The longer you had to recover, the better."

"So someone's boarded the ship?"

"More like everyone's boarded the ship. The only place that isn't like a war zone is the Botanical Gallery. Medical was sealed too, but I opened a couple doors so I could take care of a few of these corporate soldiers. As soon as I found out they were from a division of Regent Galactic, the gloves came off."

"What do we do?" Ashley closed the front of her vacsuit and turned towards him.

"Well, I'm going to get you to a secure compartment where I've routed a few communication taps so you can take control of the ship." He clamped a more military style command and control unit than she was used to onto her arm and brought up the stealth controls. "All right, you want all the systems on and you can use Crewcast to link to me so we can communicate on a low powered, low range scrambled channel. You'll also be able to see me as though I'm not cloaked."

"We're not going out that way, are we?" Ashley asked as she looked at the shield between them and the soldiers who blasted at it repeatedly with their rifles. Their shots made a hissing sound against the energy barrier.

"We're taking the back way," Larry said, his tone still all business. He walked across the room, hopped up onto the bed and popped the cover off of an air vent. It was wide enough for them to fit through, but not by much. "Once we're inside we'll activate our cloaking systems."

She shrugged and climbed up onto the bed behind him as he wriggled into the air vent. Ashley managed to get her arms and shoulders inside before she had to struggle for every inch. "This looks so easy in the movies."

"Grab my feet, I'll help you up." Larry pushed himself backwards a bit so she could get a good grip.

She wrapped her hands around his ankles and held firm. "Ready," she said.

To her surprise he pulled her almost halfway inside. He moved ahead again and she was most of the way in and able to easily wriggle behind him. "Wow, stronger than you look," she said, mostly to herself.

"Well, maybe. The suits can form a temporary bond with almost any non-liquid material," Larry admitted.

"Really?"

"Yeah, you didn't know?"

"I mostly wore these because I liked the way they looked and they helped with my phobia of decompression."

"Oh, well that makes sense too. Time to activate the cloaking systems."

Ashley did as she was told. The vacsuit hood came up and her faceplate sealed as the cloaking systems came online. She held her hand up in front of her face and could only see the outline of it on her head's up display. "So I'm completely invisible now?"

"Yup. Except for on dedicated sonic scanners. Old tech, who knew it could defeat new cloaking suits?" said Larry.

"You know, somehow I thought I'd feel different."

Larry chuckled momentarily before saying; "We have to move Ash, we're in a bit of a spot."

"Right, bad guys behind." She did her best to wriggle forward and keep up, but she couldn't figure out the gripping system in the suit so she did it the old fashioned way. "Knees and elbows, knees and elbows," she muttered as she hurried behind.

"So why didn't my suit protect me from getting broken up?"

"It tried. Your head and neck were protected, but with the inertial dampeners almost completely down under your seat, well, not even the suit had time to react. Jump off a bridge, or even a chair and the suit has time to see it coming, but getting bashed against your control terminal in a quarter of a millisecond is a different story. Normally Triton protects us with inertial dampeners that are always compensating for the environmental stresses, you just got really unlucky."

"Don't remind me. I'll never forget what that felt like," Ashley interrupted, shuddering at the thought.

"I got knocked out, had a skull fracture and a couple broken ribs. I didn't have to go to medical, but I didn't want you to be alone. "

"So you stayed for me?" she asked.

"Of course. Not the entire time, though. I had to help people evacuate to the Botanical Gallery and the hangar deck, then i came back. They meant to get you out, but time ran short, so they sealed the infirmary instead. It would have taken days for anyone to cut through."

"But there were soldiers inside my room," she objected lightly as she followed Larry down a narrow side passage.

"I had to open up a part of medical so I could hide some evidence," he said.

"You mean-"

"I've been doing what I can. Taking out as many of them as I can manage, and a few got behind me. I almost didn't get to you in time."

"You got there in time. Thank you, Larry. What happened? I mean, the last thing I remember was—"

"Going over your terminal like a wet noodle. I'll catch you up while we move," he said as he stopped and waited for her to catch up.

Ashley redoubled her efforts, still working the stiffness out of her muscles. "Good thing I took up yoga, otherwise you might have had to tow me. Feels like I've been asleep for days."

"That's been known to happen with serious internal reconstruction," said Larry.

Another topic Ashley didn't want to ponder at length. She remembered Oz rushing to her side on the bridge. The memory of the pain wasn't clear, but she would never forget the forced reassurances Oz plied her with as the pain medication kicked in and eventually put her out. She didn't expect to wake up. "Anyway, what's up with the ship?"

"All right, so we were knocked around because these crews can track a ship at faster than light speeds."

"I remember that bit."

"We made it to the planetary nebula and got some repairs done, but then we were discovered. I was in medical letting the accelerated healing meds do their work when the order came down to start the evacuation. Most of the slaves volunteered to stay aboard, so did most of the security teams, gunners, and hangar deck crew. The evacuation happened so fast that no one argued when I told them that I'd stay with you in medical so you wouldn't be alone when you woke up in a sealed section of the ship."

"And I thank you, regardless of your secret agent status," Ashley beamed. She was starting to have difficulty keeping up, and Larry was actually picking up speed. "Slower. Little slower there, Speedy."

"Oh, sorry. It's not far. We're about fifteen meters away from the edge of medical," said Larry.

"So everyone left has been fighting ever since?"

"Exactly. Oz and Jason are directing Chief Grady, Agameg, and Frost. I've been trying to overhear as much as I can on comms, but most of Jason's encryptions are too good to get around," he said.

"Aggie?"

"He's leading most of the slaves."

"Newcomers, they're free now," corrected Ashley.

"All right, he and the newcomers have been playing a game of fight and retreat, keeping the soldiers from settling into any one place. So far it's been working - they can't get ten minutes' peace and the soldiers I've been watching recently are so unnerved they're almost useless. I don't know what the master plan is exactly, but from what I'm seeing, they're staying aboard while Frost, all his gunnery people, and about half the security teams counter attack that command carrier. I was able to listen in on their central command channels. They didn't see it coming, and several decks have been disabled. Their timing couldn't have been better, the enemy had taken more than half of Triton and were about to concentrate their efforts on the bridge," he told her.

"So, what's the plan?" she asked.

"I can't tell for sure, but I know having a pilot hooked into a secure secondary control node will help, so that's where I'm taking you."

"Fantastico, we get to be big heroes."

"No, you get to be a big hero. If anyone asks, you woke up and sealed us in the primary medical conference room."

"Oh, yeah. I guess the truth would pretty much break your cover wide open." Ashley didn't know if his secret was one she could keep. Stephanie had been looking for him for weeks. The West Watchers on the Triton were being killed, strangled to death one by one. Evidence that they were linked to the Order of Eden always appeared along with the bodies, which was too convenient. Jason and Stephanie were both after him but she owed Larry her life, or at least her virtue, and she knew that regardless of how he secretly frightened her, it would earn him at least a temporary reprieve.

"Everything I do is for the good of the ship, Ash. I'll let the right people know who I am when the time comes, but until then I need to operate quietly."

"Does anyone else know?" she asked.

"No."

Ashley's train of thought was derailed as she spotted a small thermal outline in the corner of her eye. She glanced towards the artificially imposed image and her visor display zoomed in. "There's someone left in medical."

"It's a soldier, move on."

"No, that's too tiny to be a soldier." Her thermal display had picked it up, and the tactical system, which she still wasn't used to, directed her to the next vent to get to her. Crewcast marked the little one as Zoe, and the quick details listed her simply as 'Pandem orphan, nafalli, approximately eighteen months of age. Admitted to medical for swallowing a toy boat. Object was extracted while the patient was under light anaesthetic.' The admission time was an hour before her own, and before Larry could do anything Ashley was through the vent and inside the two bed treatment room.

"Ashley! We don't have time for this! She'll be fine until we have control of the Triton again."

"Oh hush, there's time. Get down here and make sure no one comes in," Ashley said as she slowly opened the cupboard door between her and the youngster. A sudden flurry of medical supplies inside told her that she'd found her, and that the youngster was in a panic.

Ashley fussed with her command and control unit for a moment before she managed to deactivate the cloaking system and release her hood. "It's okay, you're safe." She peered into the near darkness of the cabinet and met two pale blue eyes. They were a wide, fearful pair.

Larry lowered himself down into the room behind her and checked the locking mechanism on the door.

"Get me that blanket," Ashley said quietly.

Larry didn't move.

She half turned towards him. "Larry! Gimme that blanket!" she ordered in a harsh whisper.

"She doesn't know either one of us; she's not going to come. Besides, what good is a blanket? She's nafalli, she's got plenty of fur."

"You don't know anything about children, do you? I bet she's really hungry and wouldn't mind a friendly face or a pair of arms right now. Got any food on you?"

"I put some ration bars in your pocket."

Ashley dug for a moment before she found a thigh pocket filled with ration bars. She pulled three and examined them quickly. "Mango, vanilla, and chocolate. Well, I think I know what'll get your attention," Ashley said in a pleasant tone. She was careful not to let any of her anxiety slip through the gentle smile she wore. The smell of sweet chocolate filled the air between her and the young girl the instant the wrapper was torn aside. Ashley feigned glad surprise at the sight. "What's that? Ever have one of these?"

"Seriously, Ashley, if we take her with us we can't use our cloaksuits, and our mobility will be seriously restricted."

Ashley ignored him and went on. "My name's Ash. I'm here to take care of you for a while, okay?"

There was still too much fear in those blue eyes, and for a moment Ashley didn't know what to do.

"She's not going to come," Larry repeated.

"Shush," she retorted. She didn't want him to be right, and even more importantly, she didn't want to have to capture the little one with the blanket; she'd been through enough. Another tact came into mind then. With a sigh she looked at Zoe and pouted. "You don't wanna play?" She slowly put the bar down in front of Zoe and left it there.

"Oh, this is ridiculous."

"Go take care of your friends out there, I don't think we'll be taking the vents to wherever we're going," Ashley instructed in an artificially sweetened tone.

"What? She'll fit, if you manage to get her under control."

"You really don't know anything about children, do you? She might feel safe in this dark little spot, but you'll see some real water works if you try to get her into another one. I don't care how you do it, just give us a safe place to be until this all blows over."

Larry shook his head and chuckled softly.

"What? I'm not kidding."

"Look." He nodded towards the cupboard.

Ashley looked back to the rewarding sight of Zoe happily chomping at the chocolate meal bar, which seemed too big for her. Taking a risk, she wrapped the blanket around the little girl and drew her into her arms. Zoe was focused on her meal, but her free hand found a thick tangle of Ashley's hair and gently clung. She pushed her legs into the folds of the blanket and snuggled against Ashley, quietly chewing chunks of the bar all the while. "Someone's movin' in," Ashley chuckled.

"Wonderful," Larry sighed. "Just wonderful. I'll see if I can get us behind a couple of security doors." He unlocked the door and crept out, closing it behind him.

She looked after him worriedly. After a moment she realized that little eyes were watching. Ashley returned her attention to Zoe and forced her levity to return. It wasn't difficult. "Can I have a bite?" she asked, pretending to make a try for the bar.

Zoe pulled the meal bar to her chest playfully and shook her head exaggeratedly. Her long, pink nosed nafalli snout waved in the air, making the gesture even more comical. The youngster's coat was a swirl of light brown and blonde, visible even in the dim emergency lights. She returned to taking big bites of the bar, but her blue eyes were fixed on Ashley.

"Good stuff, huh?"

Her little passenger nodded, not taking her mouth away from her meal.

"Well, I s'pose I'll just have to settle for vanilla," Ashley sighed as she opened another meal bar with one hand.

Chapter 27
Moving Day

"Is this right? Ayan struck a deal with Patrizia Salustri?" Stephanie demanded as she arrived on the bridge of the Samson. "The last time we dealt with that crazy bitch, we ended up chasing royalty straight into Chinbotsu Prison! I still have an outstanding warrant for that!"

The creaking of the deck underfoot and the sounds of the thrusters trying to keep the ship level invaded the cabin. "We were very well paid. Besides, we don't have a choice. We've already lost one ship to customs. If we stay here, we're going to lose another," Jake replied from the pilot's seat.

Stephanie didn't recognize Jake's co-pilot, but Finn was at the engineering station, trying to direct crew people across the ship to reinforce stress points. The trouble started when they tried to dislodge the Samson from the muck it had sunk into; the hull was brittle thanks to previous combat damage. The only way to hold the hull together was to get it off the ground and use her thrusters and emergency integrity systems, which were failing in some areas according to Finn's yellow and red flashing screen.

She shook her concerns for the ship off and pressed her point. "You should have sent me out. All she got out of the Carthans is a standard privateering agreement. Any green outfit could have walked in and gotten set up with the contract we're on now. We have experience, a record with another government. That should have been worth something."

"Sure, but it's not worth a damn if some bounty hunter bags you on your way back because you had to bring that record up during negotiations, or because some freelancer caught sight of you."

"I would have been fine, you know better than anyone that I can take care of myself, and we've been through this part of the sector before. Maybe I wouldn't have made a deal with someone like her if I was at least playing babysitter in the background."

"If someone spotted you, or an over vigilant hunter with a DNA sniffer got you in his sights, you might have been able to fight your way free, or quietly put him down, but that would only draw the wrong kind of attention. The Carthans don't care that we're on their ball of dirt right now, but that could change if we end up getting into trouble in one of their secure zones."

"DNA sniffer? Who uses a portable DNA sniffer?" Stephanie recoiled before shaking the notion off. "Don't you think they would have done a better scan if they really cared? That customs bitch didn't seem like the type to leave loose ends behind. If she cared that we might be here, she would have gotten to us, no problem. Besides, I checked the bounty board again. What we learned before coming here is dead on: no one on this moon is interested in paying for anyone from the Samson. There's so much paying work and trouble here, well, there's no point."

"Ayan was the best option. She doesn't have any warrants out for her, and she has more training than both of us combined in negotiations. That's exactly what we need, a new face who has a good head on her shoulders," said Jake.

"So it has nothing to do with the fact that you're bunking up? I mean, I don't blame you, but I wonder if you're thinking with-" Stephanie started.

"She got us what we needed," Jake interrupted. "If you're not going to help on the bridge, then find another way to lend a hand. I'm sealing this ship up and lifting off before she completely destabilizes and falls into the mud one piece at a time."

"So we're just going to side with people we don't know, maybe go into debt, inherit whichever enemies she's made here, and end up working for her because no one else will have us? That's your solution?"

"You're being overdramatic, making assumptions. According to the message I got from Ayan, it looks like Patrizia is calming down, enjoying the good life. We're in a serious spot, in case you haven't noticed. Every issyrian on the crew is coming down with something they're getting from the toxic crap we landed on, and I'm pretty sure the rest of us aren't far behind. I'm starting to think the Carthans put us here so they could ignore us to death and, like it or not, Ayan and Laura just found us a better parking spot."

"I can go see if I can do better, won't take long. Lord knows I have more experience with people like-"

"We don't have time," said Jake.

"Listen, I don't know what's going on with you, Jake, but something's off. First, you're executing a slaver and his first mate, now you're just taking this deal at face value? When has that ever worked out for us in the past?" Stephanie snapped. "Not to mention, you just signed everything we have over to Ayan, who's calling all the shots."

"Can it! We're about to lose the Samson and you're just standing there chewing sour grapes!" Jake snapped, so viciously Stephanie took a step back.

The ship jerked suddenly and the engineering station began flashing red. Finn worked the controls frantically. "We just lost all the mid-ship inertial dampeners. I'm trying to cover with back ups from other areas, but the protection range isn't high enough."

"Do whatever you have to, we're not going to let her fall apart because we landed on soft ground," Jake replied. "Use series T31."

"They're burned out. Give me a minute, I'll try to equalize the stress."

Stephanie looked at the pair for a moment. She was no engineer, and certainly no pilot, but she could see what could happen if they didn't manage to fix the problem. The Samson would rip apart in the middle before they could get the landing gear free of the muck that was holding her down. The ship had been her home for the better part of six years. She'd met and lost so many friends while aboard, suffered through great hardships and enjoyed some memorable times.

Something on Finn's console caught her eye. "Is that the primary port side strut?" she asked, pointing.

"Yup, it's still a meter underground. The other two aren't as bad," said Finn.

"What if I head aft and hit the manual release?"

An ominous creaking of the hull drowned out Jake's first attempt at a response.

"Keep us steady, Captain. We've got enough stress as it is," Finn said as he cringed.

"The wind's picking up. Do you remember where the access panel for that pylon is, Steph?"

"How could I forget?" Stephanie ran out of the cockpit and through the crew quarters as quickly as she could. Many of the deck plates had come partially undone and twisted. There wasn't much left holding the ship's middle together, and she was thankful to be armoured as she ran down the stairway leading to the lower aft section of the Samson. Several of the steel steps were unsteady, creaking and giving underfoot.

The main hold's deck showed the damage more than anywhere else; it was twisted at one end so badly there was a slant across the entire floor. How the main power plant was still running, she would never know, but a rare bout of claustrophobia threatened to impede her as she passed down a narrow service passage between the larger components of the mass reactor. The thought of the supports beneath those heavy machines giving way, and her getting crushed between was terrifying, and thankfully fleeting.

She came out at the absolute aft end of the Samson and pulled at one of the port side service hatches. The keypad beside it lit up. "Oh thank God something still works back here," she said to herself as she punched the security code in. The portal unlocked. She could hear the bolts retract, but something was wrong. "Spoke too soon."

The metal door frame had twisted just enough to trap the hatch. She activated the muscular enhancement systems in her armour, brought up her head piece and sealed it before gripping the handle firmly. With a yank and the scream of metal scraping against metal the door opened, then promptly clattered to the deck beside her. "Sorry," she said to no one in particular.

Stephanie crawled into the small, dark space before losing her nerve, and looked around carefully. She'd only been in that area of the ship once, over two years before when she had to climb up the landing strut to board during a very hasty retreat. "C'mon, you were only here for a minute, but you saw the big lever you weren't supposed to touch. Well, not until now, anyway." She stood in front of the landing gear, being careful not to fall out of the undercarriage door. The rain and muck had made the plating slick underfoot. Through the narrow space between the landing gear and the rest of the ship she could see how the strut had dug into the mud. The stuff was more trouble than they could have ever guessed, and she knew she wasn't the only one kicking herself for not seeing it coming when the rain started.

"It's on the fore side of the strut. Or it should be," Finn told her.

Stephanie recalled the lever; it had a red, rubber cover that couldn't have been more obvious. "Could it have fallen off?" She asked as she inspected that side of the landing gear.

"How would-" Finn started. "Well, maybe. I hope not!"

Stephanie shifted around the wavering strut and sighed with relief. "Found it! It was on the starboard side."

"How'd it get there?" Finn remarked. "Whatever, we're coming apart. Hurry."

There wasn't much space for her to squeeze into on the landing strut, not nearly enough for her to safely cling on without getting crushed when the ship lifted off. "Gimme a minute," she said.

"Take your time, be safe," Jake advised. "But quickly"

She stood there, looking at the narrow space between the landing strut and the edge of the undercarriage hatch for a moment. She leaned away from the strut as best as she could and reached out to the lever.

"Stephanie?" asked Finn.

"Gimme a minute! I'm just finding a way to do this so I'm not half the woman I used to be when I'm done," she snapped.

She stretched so her other hand was on the lip of the hatch leading into the ship and decided she'd dive for it when the mechanism released, just in case there were extra problems. "Okay, don't lift off too fast," she said as she steeled her resolve.

Stephanie pulled the landing gear release slowly. It flipped suddenly, knocking her back. With a deafening shriek, the strut separated and the Samson began to lift off. In a matter of seconds the landing metal support disappeared from sight, and they were fifty meters off the ground. She slipped as she tried to pull herself out of the small undercarriage room, her feet dangling in the open air for a second before she pulled herself through the service hatchway and back inside the ship interior.

"You all right, Steph?" asked Finn.

"Fine. You'll have to get someone down here to fix the door though, we're open to atmosphere."

"I'll put it on the list," said Finn.

CHAPTER 28
THE EYE OF THE STORM

Zoe finished half her meal bar, drank most of a bottle of water, and fell fast asleep in Ashley's arms. It was quiet, dark, and she couldn't help but feel a little selfish at the comfort that holding Zoe gave her. Attempts at finding out what was going on with the ship and crew on her command and control unit failed. The command network was absolutely dormant. She turned her attention to Zoe's personal records and the first thing that caught her interest was surveillance footage of her in the Botanical Gallery. In the playback, she was running through a finished park area that Ashley hadn't seen before. It was maze-like, with tall bushes and fruit trees everywhere. It was a playful chase between two of Iloona's four or five year old children and Zoe, and the eighteen month old was having the time of her life until she tripped and fell into one of the ankle deep creeks that ran through the outer gallery. The pair of children picked her up right away, made sure she was all right and raised her spirits in moments by splashing around in the shallow water with her, turning it into a game. Ashley didn't know how happy Iloona would be with two of her youngest children turning up soaking wet, but they were all having great fun.

When she brought up the rest of Zoe's profile, she was surprised to discover that she had been adopted by a human, Vivian Lea, who had also adopted a young human boy and girl. She lived in the Botanical Gallery, and was a Pandem refugee.

Just looking at Zoe sleeping peacefully in her arms reminded Ashley of her own childhood. She couldn't understand why, because her upbringing was quite different. She was bred for slavery, and raised in a stock house, then sold at the age of four. She barely remembered the stock house, which she assumed was a mercy. They raised as many children as possible in a small space, and since they weren't clones, they were treated fairly well, but they were still only a product. Considering that she could have been a clone instead and subjected to painful accelerated growth treatments, even more crowded conditions, and forced direct neural education, being brought into the world naturally and sold by her mother as a baby was the better option, where slavery was concerned.

Zoe wouldn't find herself in such a situation. Everyone she knew despised slavery, and after holding the youngster for just a little while, Ashley couldn't bear to see anything happen to her. The holographic image of her playing with the other children, all of them older than her, was a relief. Zoe seemed to enjoy life in the Botanical Gallery, playing in the grass, splashing on the edge of the shallow creek there, and learning to climb with a little help from one of Iloona's older children. Only days before, Ashley would have had to be reminded that there were hundreds of civilians working and living in the Botanical Gallery. Watching the playback of what life was like for the orphans there, and how survivors of Pandem had already moved right in was a shocking reminder.

She'd moved herself into the life of a fighter pilot, even though she was the Master at the Helm. As a career it suited her exceptionally well. Ashley loved the study, technical demands, and the responsibility of the position, but after seeing Zoe in the Botanical Gallery and saving her in medical, she realized she needed something more. "How could I have forgotten all about it?" she asked herself in a whisper.

The lawn where she attended yoga classes on most mornings seemed small. The place where Zoe and the rest of the children were taken to play was a corner of the Gallery she'd never seen. She doubted most of the busy crew of the Triton had seen most of the place, and she vowed to spend some time there, to relax, and to make sure Zoe was happy once things calmed down.

"Well, this whole section is sealed again," Larry said as he came through the door. "The soldiers were called to the bridge - something big is going down there, but I couldn't tell you what. Oz and Jason have everything deactivated on the command deck."

"Did you tell them that I'm ready to pilot this thing as soon as I find a console?" she whispered back.

"No, you'll be doing that in a few minutes. The conference room just a few doors down is still intact. You can use a section of the table as a control board. Oh, and there's chatter of a Uriel fighter moving around at long range. I'm thinking Valance has come looking for his ship."

"That's Captain Valance," Ashley corrected quietly as she slowly rose to her feet. Zoe was so tired she barely stirred.

"Aye, aye." Larry led her to the conference room. The lights were still glowing a dim blue, on reserve power, and she could see where heavy bulkhead doors had been lowered, cutting off half of medical. If they were anything like the Botanical Gallery doors, they were a meter or more thick, made to withstand incredible forces. "You'll be a welcome sight. You'll be saving them the trouble of finding another pilot."

"Wouldn't they just come and get me?"

"I listed you as killed before Crewcast was silenced so anyone who managed to break into the system wouldn't come looking for a Master at the Helm in a medically induced coma."

"Oh, well then I guess they'll be really happy to see me." The conference room was a more welcoming space. Larry had gathered a pile of nutrient bars, blankets, bottles of water, and had even brought in two portable gurneys. Ashley took a seat and transferred her ident from her comm unit to the table. The helm controls came up straight away, partially as a holographic projection and partially covering the surface itself. Around her console were live star charts, damage displays, a virtual communications panel, and a navigational assistant much like the navnet she was used to seeing.

She tried to put Zoe into the chair beside her, but the child's hands reflexively tightened their grip on Ashley's hair. "Okay, looks like I have a new co-pilot," she chuckled, depositing her passenger in her lap. Zoe's eyes half opened and she relaxed for a moment. Then, as though she just realized that she was in a different place, her pale blue eyes popped open and she stared at the holograms hovering above the table.

"She's going to be a distraction, I should take her," Larry said as he stepped forward.

Zoe retreated against Ashley, sending her a worried look. "It's okay, he's a friend," Ashley reassured as she tried to lift her out of her lap.

Her protests came as a panicked squeal.

Ashley hushed her, soothing Zoe with shushing sounds and stroking her face. "It's okay. You're just going to have to be really quiet and still, all right?" she soothed, knowing that there was little actual chance that her instructions would stick, regardless of how they were delivered.

"That's it," Larry grumbled, bringing up a sub display on the conference table.

"What are you doing?"

"Checking game history. If she's anything like every kid I've met, then she has a favourite." He searched Zoe's profile for a few seconds and activated a program that featured rounded, bouncing characters in the shapes of letters and numbers. Their hyper, high-pitched voices immediately caught Zoe's attention and her grip on Ashley's hair loosened.

"What is it?" Ashley asked as she watched a nine chase a frantic one.

"Bumper Muncher. I've never heard of it, but I think she knows it pretty well."

Zoe looked up at Ashley, her eyes conveying a request for permission.

"You wanna play?" she asked, feigning excitement and surprise.

Zoe nodded emphatically.

"Okay, here we go," Ashley said as she lifted her up and put her on the table across from her.

The little girl made a gesture as though she were picking up the game display and it disappeared, sounds of muffled protests and comical panic seemed to come from her closed hand until she threw it into the air above the floor beside Ashley. The game image appeared there and Zoe got down from the table with Ashley's help. Within minutes she settled in to play her game, changing the shape of the virtual walls so the characters, each in the form of a different number, collided into each other. The black numbers added together to become one larger number when they collided, and were reduced by red numbers. "She's really good with the computer," Ashley commented quietly as she watched the comically frantic numerical characters rush around the changing virtual space.

"It's a Sol System model, completely intuitive. She doesn't know how inconvenient most computers are, so she assumes it works like the rest of the world."

"I've only ever moved something from my comm unit to a display and back, never even tried what she's doing. Then, I s'pose you know all about what Triton can do," Ashley commented as she checked the status of the ship and started figuring out where they were.

"I trained on this model for three years. The hardest part has been pretending I don't know much more than anyone else."

"You're going to have to teach me a few things sometime."

"Only if you show me more about Crewcast. I haven't been able to ask questions since its designer is also the best investigator on the ship. If I used it heavily I know he'd figure me out."

"Really? How?"

"Crewcast builds a behavioural profile of all its users. It's an intelligence man's wet dream. Most of the crew use it so much that it probably already knows who everyone knows, how long they've known them, what kind of relationships people typically have and anything else. Ever notice how the old Freeground crew don't have complete public profiles? It's a trap. If you have nothing to hide, there's no problem, but if you do, it takes discipline not to reveal anything important," explained Larry.

"Huh. Good thing I don't have anyone to talk to about your secret. Unless someone else knows."

"No one else knows."

"If they did, would you tell me?" asked Ashley.

"No."

"God, one more secret, especially a doozy like yours, and I'll explode."

"That's my fault. I shouldn't have let you rest so long," he said.

"Or let a skeevy soldier into my room."

Larry nodded.

They worked in silence for a moment longer, and Ashley tried not to look at her navigator. He'd sat beside her for many shifts on the bridge, they'd spent time together after work, and she wouldn't have guessed at his true purpose on Triton. If she'd known how dangerous he was, things would have been different. She felt uneasy enough with him sitting across the table from her, and hoped that her attempts at casual teasing didn't go too far. A distressing thought fought its way to the fore: that he'd dispose of her after he'd completed some goal, and she did her best to suppress her fear.

Larry brought up a security status display, partially in two dimensions on his side of the table, and partially in three, where two dozen red spots flashed on a holographic representation of the Triton. Ashley finished her calculations and confirmed that they were just outside the planetary nebula, then started an emergency course calculation in the navigational computer before taking a closer look at it. "What are the yellow areas?" she asked.

"Parts of the ship that have been recently contested or are between enemy contacts," he said as he focused in on the upper command deck. All the corridors, most of the crew quarters and all the offices were marked in yellow. Ashley caught a glimpse of the concourse outside the main bridge, and a chill ran through her. The enemy soldiers were lining bodies up along the wall, at least a third of them in Triton uniforms.

Before she could get a really good look Larry deactivated the live feeds, and only the structural and bare tactical information remained. It was enough. There was a collection of red markers on both levels of the bridge. "We've lost the ship," she whispered, trying to keep calm.

"No, you're sitting there at the pilot's controls. In case you haven't noticed, you're the only one with direct access to the helm. Engineering was cut off a while ago, it was the first thing the soldiers did. Chief Grady suppressed several soldiers from the first boarding party and locked them in a decontamination chamber without their gear after almost crushing them to death with a gravity fluctuation, but he eventually had to weld the emergency bulkheads shut. Communications with him and his people has been spotty ever since."

"But, the bridge," started Ashley.

"Is nothing but a collection of dead terminals." Larry sighed and nodded to himself, as though digging deep for more patience. With a few gestures, he zoomed out and shifted the three dimensional display of the Triton so they could get a better look. "It's bad. I won't lie to you when you can see it all for yourself. The enemy has taken the hangars, command levels, and half the interior outside of the Botanical Gallery. On the other hand, they can't take this half of medical without cutting for days, and the same goes for the Gallery. There's also a fight going on aboard their own command carrier, and Frost's people have fused the mooring clamps onto their ship, so they're not going anywhere."

"Wait, so you want me to pilot this ship while hauling another one riding piggyback?" Ashley exclaimed.

Zoe looked at her wide eyed, reacting to her tone more than anything.

Ashley turned, smiled, and stroked the youngster's back. "S'okay, play your game, hon," she soothed.

"Jason has a plan, that's why I like him despite the fact that if anyone is going to catch me eventually, it'll be him. I think I know what it is, too."

"Wouldn't it be helpful if they knew I was here?" asked Ashley.

"No, I'm listening to the enemy's communications and it's pretty obvious that whatever our intelligence officer has planned hasn't kicked in yet. If we try to use internal comms, we'll probably be discovered. That's why there's no comm traffic right now, and why Agameg has been waging his own war all along."

"Right, so you're saying that I shouldn't worry about all the fighting going on right now and just get ready."

"Exactly," Larry said.

"Fine, in that case, I have a heck of a lot of nav data to get through and some calculations to make. New weight distributions, mass considerations, shear estimates, not to mention we're down to one operating engine," she said sweetly for Zoe's benefit. Her attention had turned back to her favourite game, where she controlled a running number three that became a six, nine, and twelve as it gobbled up other threes.

"I'll give you a hand. Just be ready for anything, I don't know when Jason will be putting the next phase of his plan into motion."

A sinking feeling started to overwhelm Ashley, and she couldn't help but ask, "D'you think they might leave us behind?"

Larry looked up from the conference table display and caught her eye. "No. There's no way they can capture the command carrier, even this relatively small one, even if they could get to engineering or the control centre. That, and Jason wouldn't leave the people in the Botanical Gallery behind. He wouldn't dishonour Oz that way."

"Dishonour Oz?"

"Something Oz told me the other night. He'd die to protect the civilians at the centre of this ship," Larry said almost mournfully.

"Oh," Ashley returned her attention to her work, trying to use the limited data at hand to create a control profile that would allow her to safely pilot the ship.

The pair worked in silence for a time, the sounds of Zoe's game providing background noise that was so cheery that it seemed inappropriate for how Ashley felt.

"There it is, that fighter the Command Centre's been trying to pin down," Larry said, bringing it up on the main holographic display. The signal was coming from the inner edge of the nebula, tracking with the path of one of the smaller meteor clusters within.

"I don't think that's a fighter, they would have detected and slagged it already if it was. He must have attached an inactive beacon to a meteor so he could use it as a relay," Ashley said, looking at the rough shape of the meteor cluster.

"That makes sense. I was wondering why they didn't destroy it. They must be waiting for it to transmit, see if they can trace it back, or decode their message, see what that pilot has to say," said Larry.

"They're not the only ones," Ashley added.

CHAPTER 29
LANDFALL

It was a carefully managed disaster. Finn watched the structural monitoring systems on the bridge of the Samson and wished he could somehow reach into the small holographic image of the vessel's skeleton and straighten her main beams and other structural imperfections.

Captain Valance had moved the Samson into position at the rear of his fleet. The Clever Dream was at the vanguard. From where he stood at the back of the bridge, Finn could see the tactical display and the realization of what they looked like without the Triton hit him. Battle damaged, captured slaver vessels were in the middle, a mismatched bunch bristling with the remains of turreted guns. Surrounding them were dozens of powerful fighters, state of the art and armed to the teeth.

If he was a Carthan Port Master he wouldn't trust such a fleet. He'd have them either locked down or under close supervision. The fact that the Carthans allowed them to move from the Wastes into the middle of a thickly populated area was either a sign of stupidity or over-confidence. He took another look at the status of the Samson and nodded to himself. The stress on the ship was balanced, and it was unlikely that it would change until they tried to land.

Another thought struck him. The Carthans probably had orbital defence systems pointed directly at them as they moved across the ruined landscape. It was a sobering notion, and it explained why they were able to get clearance. Someone, somewhere, was at a very dangerous control panel, and they were watching.

That brought him back to a feeling of dread that he'd been suppressing ever since they escaped the Triton. They were exposed, without the generous means their ship provided them, and as much as he had faith in his captain, Jake was a wanted man. Most of the Samson crew were on bounty hunting lists. The only reason Finn's name wasn't among them was that he was the most recent addition to the crew. He signed on right before Enreega. Right before the Triton, and through it all, even through his disappointment with Ashley, he was happy to be along. They actually put him in charge of a division in Engineering.

Being back on the Samson was like moving from a mansion to an apartment. A warped, old apartment with holes in the walls, leaky pipes, and peeling paint. He didn't want to see the ship come to an end either, but even when they first took the Triton, the Samson was in need of a refit, or at least some serious restorative work. She was old when Captain Valance first got her, and though he had done a fantastic job keeping her together, even made a few improvements, wear and tear was showing when Finn first arrived aboard. After surviving serious combat, barely, she was ready to be decommissioned or rebuilt from the frame up.

With the Triton gone, as he and several of the crew members he'd spoken to the night before suspected, they would have to find a way to rebuild the Samson and repair the rest of the ships. The fabrication centre on the Triton would be sorely missed. Finn had almost gotten used to getting the parts he needed within minutes or hours of requesting them, instead of having to make his own fittings and fixtures in a small workshop like most ship mechanics. That's what they were back to. Every bent part would have to be straightened out and tested. Damaged components would have to be sourced, purchased, or made by hand. He suspected at least one of the ships they'd captured had a workshop, but didn't dare hope that it would be worth using considering the vessels were crewed by slaves. His older brother, who was a steward in the plant union on his home world, always said that the condition of the workplace was directly related to the treatment of the employees. He couldn't imagine what kind of condition the other ships were in after being in the hands of slaves for who knew how long. He would have to brave the workshop in another vessel, however. The one on the Samson was destroyed weeks before.

There were still parts of the Samson in the green. The bridge, forward hold, and several other compartments aboard ship were still structurally sound. However, three of the four main beams were twisted, and there were several compartments that were barely space-worthy. If he didn't want to end up serving on one of those slave ships, Finn would have to make sure the Samson was worth saving, even after they landed.

"Hey Finn, ever see a shanty port?" Captain Valance asked as he brought up a two dimensional projection of the sprawling port ahead of them.

They had passed out of the rain, and the sun was setting. From one edge of the horizon to the other, ships had landed. Roads wound between the paved slips, tricking his eye into looking at the expanse of transients as he would a city. Shipping containers, hulks, makeshift welded huts and portable structures made many of the spaces homes. The sea of ships and buildings was interrupted occasionally by docking pillars with several platforms each, multi-level hangars, and several old brick or scrap built buildings. To the left, nearly out of sight, was an ocean that went on for as far as the eye could see. It looked deep and black in the fading light. "I've never seen anything like this, Captain."

"Well, that'll be home for a while. It's the only place we're cleared to land in the entire solar system."

There were hundreds of ships in the air above the port and the lights of their engines were brilliant. The looming shape of the night side of Kambis, the world Tamber orbited, loomed. The eclipse night was falling over Tamber. The interlocking illuminated rings of a city on the heavy gravity world and other distant lit features showed through the scant clouds, and he couldn't help but wonder what that world was like. He suspected there was a great deal of mining, like any heavy gravity world, but beyond that, he'd never been to a city large enough to be seen from two hundred thousand kilometres away.

At the sight of that two dimensional video, Finn was no longer part of an isolated crew; he was in the middle of civilization. It was a chaotic, cramped, busy place, and it looked like it would be far too easy to become lost. "Some place," he whispered as he looked back to his console.

"You said it," Captain Valance replied.

A large, clear space came into view. It was blocked off by shipping containers and scrap metal walls on all four sides. There was a two level, closed hangar at one end and three cleaner looking shipping containers placed at the other. In a sea of cramped vessels and narrow makeshift buildings, it must have taken a herculean effort to reserve.

The Samson was to land first, and if they weren't careful she'd never make it off the ground again. Finn re-checked his calculations and nodded to himself. Time to present his idea to the Captain, they were beginning to reduce altitude. "Sir, I know you haven't had time, but I sent something I've been working on to your console."

"The landing instructions? I saw them, Finn. I don't like the idea, but I think you're right. Landing starboard side first might twist two of our main beams back into shape if I manage it. Are you sure about the angle?"

"Yes, Sir. One thing though, we'll lose a few mounting points. If we want to rebuild the Samson we'll have to find a way to repair or replace the fittings, considering they're high density fibre frame-"

"We'll be rebuilding her. If we're lucky we might be able to find scrap from a similar model. We'll find another way to rebuild if we don't. Tell the crew we're about to set down."

Finn looked for the ship wide intercom switch and found it after a moment. "We'll be landing in a few seconds, so get away from major frame fixtures and seal your vacsuits. Set for high impact in case something snaps or comes loose."

"Good enough. All right, touching down," said the captain.

As soon as the Samson touched the ground, sections of the ship's frame turned red, indicating critical stress levels. They were touching down without landing gear. Finn couldn't help but be reminded of Ashley as he remembered the term she used for it, a 'belly flop'. Even as he listened to the groaning metal in the ship behind him and watched as the main beams of the lower hull indicated they were stressed to twisting, he found himself hoping she was all right.

A loud screech and explosive pops sounded throughout the ship as the port side beam tore free of several frame mounts. It was hanging free of the exterior hull for at least twenty meters. He prayed the starboard side would fare better, and to his surprise, it did. The stress on that beam was extreme but more evenly distributed, resulting in the desired twisting and reshaping. When the Samson came to rest, the port side beam read as almost completely straightened.

"I need everyone on the Samson to check in. All other vessels are clear to land," Captain Valance said into his comm as he locked the pilot controls. He was out of his seat and beside Finn at the engineering console in seconds. "How did we do?"

"The lower port beam is almost completely straight, to within half a degree, and I think it's still strong enough."

Captain Valance performed a quick scan and nodded. "You're right. It's not showing much fatigue, she could bear a load twice the mass of what the Samson is build to haul."

"The other one's shot though, and the port-side dorsal beam is still twisted two point three degrees."

"And bent point four degrees in the middle." Captain Valance stared at the structural hologram quietly for a moment before continuing. "We'll have to replace them both."

"You're really going to rebuild her, Captain?" Finn knew it would be a lot of work, but his name would be engraved on the vessel's hull forever if he was part of the team who directed the reconstruction.

A silent message on the Captain's comm unit from Crewcast informed him that no one on the Samson was injured and he sighed, he actually sighed, with relief. It surprised Finn to no end. He knew Jacob cared about his crew, but he still wasn't used to seeing emotional reactions. "Let's go topside and take a look at our new home," Captain Valance said quietly.

Finn and the captain's co-pilot followed him to the upper hatch in the main hallway behind the bridge. With a twist and a yank of an overhead handle, a set of collapsible stairs dropped down and locked into place. The outer hatch came open only after Captain Valance pressed his shoulder to it. Finn suspected it would be even more difficult to close properly.

They were the first to stand atop the Samson and look across the seemingly endless sea of ships ahead of them. The wind was warm, and carried the smell of ozone tinged with trash. The sun was disappearing behind Kambis, turning the horizon a deep red and yellow. Hundreds of thousands of lights glimmered in the makeshift city all surrounding them, and there was such a variety of ships that it was dizzying. He used to love watching them come and go from the port on his home world, and thought he had seen every shape and style. That couldn't have been further from the truth.

The wind on his face was pleasant as well; it had been a while. The smell was something he'd get used to - living so close to refineries during his childhood had conditioned him to ignore most of the offensive odours such technology put out. Just being in atmosphere again was nice for a change, but he knew he'd miss being in transit on a ship before long.

"You know the Triton never felt like my ship. I knew how to run her, and I think I even got to know her secrets well enough, but she never felt like mine," Captain Valance said quietly. "She never felt like home."

Finn didn't reply, didn't know what to say. Instead he looked at the man from out of the corner of his eye. He looked weary, but still had a sureness, a bearing that left no doubt that he was in command about him.

"We're going to repair the Samson because without her we don't have an anchor. I don't want you to think about anything else, Finn. If Price were here you'd be working with him, but you'll have to make do with the people we have instead. Don't worry about what it costs, just tell me what you need. I'll find a way."

"Yes, Sir." Finn couldn't think of a moment in which he was more proud. At the same time, he knew the work ahead would be difficult, but it was important, and if it went well he'd be remembered for it. "When I'm finished it'll be as though you put her back together with your own hands."

"Good. I'll work on getting our people back. Watching the Samson fall apart over the last few hours has reminded me of something, something I should have remembered before half the crew who landed with us in the Dower Wastes left us. People are what we need now. Not the ones who left, not just anyone, but the people we've come to know, come to trust. More than anything else, the qualities those people bring with them will determine how this all works out. Remember that when you choose your build team."

Chapter 30
Connections

Ashley was able to get a handle on most of the ship systems with Larry's help, and was happy that all non-essential machinery had been deactivated. Much of the rest of the machinations aboard the Triton were being maintained remotely from the Engineering Control Deck, which had come under siege again. Soldiers were trying to cut into the vault-like substructure from the deck above, and according to Larry, who she still regarded warily, they were making moderate progress. It was only a matter of hours unless someone interfered with their work.

"Why don't you slow them down?" Ashley asked offhandedly as Zoe climbed into her lap. Even her favourite game couldn't keep her occupied forever, especially when she looked so tired. For a moment Ashley considered trying to make the youngster at home in the chair beside her, but thought better of it. The little fair-haired nafalli wasn't too difficult to work around, and she had seen how Iloona's younger children were with her. Nafalli young liked to cling to their elders, and for the time being, Ashley was Zoe's choice.

"If they do get through they'll have to deal with everyone in engineering, and there's no way they set up down there without arming themselves."

"Ah, so what are you doing?" Ashley asked.

Larry's lips drew into a thin, tight smile as he nodded to himself. "Can't wait to see me go back out there?"

"No, I'm just wondering."

Ashley refocused one of her console displays on a wormhole that appeared momentarily in the dust cloud, and it disappeared as quickly as it came up on the passive scanners. She hoped the captain and everyone else was right behind. Someone had to save them.

"I knew this would happen. Listen, I'm the same Larry you met only there's a side of me you didn't know about. I'm sure there are plenty of things you haven't told everyone about yourself."

Ashley kept her voice calm and soothing for Zoe's benefit. In reality she'd never been so nervous. "Okay, I'll get used to it," she offered as a placation.

"Ashley, I could be the most important friend you have on the ship. I know you have the captain's ear, and he made you Master at the Helm, but you don't see how often they cut you out. It's been happening more over the last two weeks. The Freeground crew have just taken over with the Captain's blessing, and they haven't consulted you on anything."

"I handle the pilot rotation on the bridge, help people navigate the training system, review qualifiers, and fly the ship."

"But do you really get to make the decisions a Master at the Helm should be making? You should be consulted before destinations are chosen, when modifications are made to propulsion and flight control, and whenever something changes the way this ship moves, or where it's going. That's what a Master at the Helm is for, to help the captain guide the ship from port to port and keep the ship on a safe course."

"But we're not in a part of the galaxy I know, and I'm new to command. If Captain trusts the people from his home station, then I'll trust them, too. Besides, Stephanie is still Security Chief and our Engineering Chief isn't from Freeground, either."

"All right, but that's besides the point. What I'm saying is that there may come a time when you need someone who knows the ship better than anyone, can get you anywhere without people noticing, or can make something happen for you. That person is me. Your discretion comes at a price, I wouldn't ask you to keep my secret if I didn't have something to offer in return."

The thought hadn't occurred to Ashley. If they made it through the crisis, she might have real power over the most dangerous person on the ship. The image of soldiers being killed in front of her returned, and, as though sensing how unnerving the memory of it was, Zoe roused from her light sleep and looked up at her. Ashley soothed the toddler, stroking her finely furred face until she put her head back down. "I don't want you to hurt anyone else. Find another way to show security who the West Keepers are so they can deal with them their own way or I'll make sure they find out about you."

Larry looked genuinely surprised and stopped working on his side of the table. He stared at her silently for a long moment.

The communication portion of Ashley's console came to life as Minh-Chu's head appeared holographically over the table. "This is Ronin. Can anyone over there hear me?"

"That's the Freeground emergency frequency, I've been trying to get in ever since Jason came aboard," Larry said. "Minh is using it unencrypted."

"What do I do?" Zoe sat up in Ashley's lap and smiled at Minh's face.

"Reply, but don't tell them I'm here. I'll block myself from the transmission."

Ashley took a deep breath and let it out slowly. "Here goes," she said to Zoe, who looked up at her, pointing to Minh's image. "Ronin? This is Ashley Lamport."

"Ask him if he realizes he's broadcasting in the open," Larry whispered.

"Ashley? They put you on comms?"

"I'm kinda doing a lot of things right now. Do you know you're in the open?"

"You mean, transmitting in the open? Right, I didn't know who was left over there, so I didn't have a choice." Minh looked away for a moment, his image flickering violently. When it returned to normal Ashley's communications terminal displayed a long, rapidly changing number. "There, we're encrypted. Who's your little friend?"

"Zoe, she's my co-pilot today. We found a safe spot and I'm getting the pilot's controls running."

"Can you send me a ship status report?"

"Um, maybe?"

"It's the green and gold circular image on the comm screen."

"Oh, I've been using that to check the ship myself."

Zoe beat Ashley to it, smacking it with her slender hand.

"Whoa, she's bright, isn't she?" said Minh.

"Oh yeah. I'm going to lock my controls though, just in case she gets a little adventurous," Ashley said, bouncing Zoe in her lap. "Things aren't good here, though. The whole ship's under attack from the inside. I don't think there are many safe places left."

"I can see, but the ship above you is under attack, too. This is a mess," Minh said, shaking his head.

"How far behind is everyone else?" Ashley asked, hopeful.

"I'm it for now, but after seeing this I think Jake will muster up and get everyone out here as soon as they can."

"This is Jason. I'm re-encrypting this channel with a biometric access gate."

Ashley didn't know the serious-minded communications and computer genius, but was relieved to see him. The sight was welcome, especially after discovering that help was much further off than she hoped.

"What's going on, Jason?" she asked.

"Frost is leading the main assault against the destroyer docked to the dorsal mooring point, and I was leading a team to the bridge, but we're getting pushed back. They have some kind of sonic scanning technology in place that's seeing right through our cloaksuits, and we don't have the people to push through with force. I'm glad Frost is doing better. He's already shut down their hangar bay and he's moved into their ship."

"Do you have a backup plan?" Minh asked.

"Oz took care of that, but he was killed while creating a diversion on the Triton's bridge. I'm trying to get back to put the plan back into motion, but there's a lot of territory between me and the dorsal mooring point. Ashley, this report says that you were woken up when someone interfered with you in the infirmary. Who was it? What happened? There's no security footage."

"Tell him you don't know, the soldiers were dead when you came to," Larry whispered. The communications terminal was blocking any sound from his side of the room, a function she'd never seen the computer perform before.

"Um, the soldiers were dead when I came to. I used a ventilation shaft to get to a safer spot."

"You found me knocked out in the next room and treated me with emergency nanobots," Larry added.

"Larry's here, too," Ashley blurted. "Somewhere, getting food maybe."

"Nice going. I need you to replace a pilot who was with Oz. I've been in touch with Chief Grady, and he can give us a wormhole using the emitters we have left, so plot a course and as soon as we manage to shake two of the ships docked with us, get us moving. We'll take care of the rest."

"How are you going to decouple the enemy ships?" she asked, looking at the port and starboard mooring points again. There was a destroyer firmly clamped to each side, and the sensors there reported that emergency welds were in place, holding them fast.

"Don't worry about it," Jason insisted. "Minh, where is the captain?"

"We landed on Tamber, it's under Carthan control. They're neutral enough, but I wouldn't call them friendly."

"Good enough, forward the coordinates to their secondary arrival area to Ashley," said Jason.

"Already done," said Minh. "I'm going to make full burn back, see if we can't get everything we've got on its way here."

"Ronin, I know every instinct you have is telling you that is the right thing to do, but you can't. The only reason why you're not fighting off fifty fighters and dodging long-range weaponry is because they're watching that buoy you lodged, trying to crack our codes and track back to your ship."

"And here I thought I was being all careful and sneaky using half a dozen deactivated buoys to relay my comms."

"Half a dozen? That's why I've been seeing worm holes pop open. That's kinda genius, Ronin," Ashley congratulated with a big smile. It was the second conversation she'd ever had with him, and for the second time she was impressed.

"It just means that it'll take them minutes to track this instead of seconds," Jason interrupted. "Ronin, you have to go back and tell the captain what's happened, but any help he can send will come too late. There's an Overlord coming. It'll be here in about two days if the communications I've intercepted are right."

The colour drained from Minh's face. "Is there anything I can do right now?"

"Get back as fast as you can. Tell the Carthans that the Triton is coming and we'll need help."

"Will do. Heading out right now. Good luck, Jason, be the brain we all know you are and get to Tamber safe. Hang in there, Ash, I'll see you on

Tamber. Slick and I scanned some nice beaches on our way out, I'll make sure there's a drink with an umbrella in it waiting for you."

"How'd you know I was a beach bunny?"

"Crewcast." Ronin smiled.

"Can we hit pause on this courtship for just a little while so I can get back to saving the ship, please?" Jason said in a withering tone.

"Righto, on my way out," said Minh.

Ashley couldn't help but snicker as the transmission terminated.

Larry shook his head with a disapproving expression.

"What? If we can't have a teensy laugh, we'd all just snap," she said cheerily, bouncing Zoe in her lap. "Right, Baby?" she asked her.

The toddler slipped to the floor and started running around the table sweetly singing, "roo roo rooooo."

"That is the most random thing I've ever seen," Larry remarked, wide eyed. "And annoying."

"She's excited, and probably learning to talk. Just let her go, she'll tire herself out soon," Ashley said as she finished plotting their first wormhole jump. Without hesitation she moved on to setting up the second.

"Say 'Larry.'" he requested as Zoe stopped in front of his chair.

She turned around and started making her way back around at a march, singing; "loo loo looooo," instead.

"Well, at that rate she'll be able to say her own name by new years," Larry grumbled.

"Say 'Ashley,'" Ashley invited sweetly.

"Allee!" Zoe shouted back.

"See? It's all in the way you ask, isn't it, hon?"

"Oh God, I hope Jason's plan kicks in soon," Larry groaned.

CHAPTER 31
CAMARADERIE

"You've done some good work here, Major," congratulated Commander DeHansen as he arrived at the bottom of the bridge ramp way. "We're still fighting in a few compartments but we have control of most of the ship." He was broad in the middle, and had a toothy grin. This was a potential political victory for him with Command, being the last remaining boarding captain.

"We lost a lot of good people. Has Command gotten control of the lower decks on the main carrier?" asked Major Cumberland.

Commander DeHansen's smile soured at the mention of the counter-incursion. "They took four lower decks and stopped. We don't know what they're up to but it won't matter for long. Reinforcements are en-route."

"Good. The sooner they clear that up, the sooner we'll have a sonic sensor package on deck. If Command equipped us all with them, we would never have been blindsided by these cloaksuits."

"I doubt that would have made all the difference considering how expensive these scanners are," said DeHansen.

"I could tell you the names of the people I lost today because we were sent in without a full kit," said Cumberland.

DeHansen straightened his uniform and cleared his throat. Cumberland was imposing, and all of his men were staring. "I'll pass the recommendation up in my report. In the meantime, assemble four teams to sweep the command deck of the Triton and seal it off. I don't want to lose ground while our techs begin rebuilding these terminals and linking into the ship controls."

"I have an issue with that order, Sir," Private Baram said as she aimed her sidearm levelly at Cumberland's head.

A thought occurred to him then - he'd never seen her without her helmet. "I should have verified idents," Major Cumberland grumbled.

"Major! What's going on?" DeHansen demanded.

"I think one of theirs mixed in with my team when we regrouped on the upper deck. You're surrounded, you know. No where to run," Cumberland told the woman.

"If your people don't lower their arms and surrender immediately, a comrade of mine will fire all of this ship's torpedo ports. The vessels on our port and starboard side will be destroyed."

"Along with a good part of this vessel," Major Cumberland tested. Everyone could hear him, all the boarding teams, Command, and anyone else wearing a communicator. The Command channel was abuzz already; there was no point in silencing the infiltrator, the damage was done. With decks on one of their own ships out of their control, parts of the Triton still sealed off, and a potentially devastating threat, morale would sink like a stone.

"I do not have the switch. Kill me, and you accomplish nothing. Disarm yourselves and surrender," she said.

"I don't think so, lady. There's no power in your torpedo rooms, we verified," Commander DeHansen objected. "You put that down and come quietly. You might end up in a cell instead of an early grave."

"Commander McPatrick, are you still there?" asked the stranger.

"This is Command. Commander DeHansen, please be aware that most of the torpedo rooms on that ship are powering up. You are not authorized to surrender. Negotiate with the representative," Major Cumberland overheard through his communicator.

"I'm plenty alive, good to hear your voice, Agameg," replied the tall, fair haired man from the hallway behind them.

"Some kind of automatic stasis, right?" asked Cumberland, shaking his head. "Should have finished you off properly."

"Put 'em down, everyone. We're taking our ship however we can and you have a lot more to lose," Oz said as he slowly entered the room with his hands up. There was a glint in his eye Cumberland didn't like one bit.

Major Cumberland nodded. "Listen to him. We're finished here," he ordered the soldiers on the bridge.

"Belay that! We have the high ground aboard this ship and it came at great expense!" Commander DeHansen countered. "Commander McPatrick, I can promise a fair trial for you and all your people if you surrender immediately. Haven't enough people died here?"

"Trust me, we don't want to launch all our torpedoes at close range, but if you and your people don't leave us be, I won't have much of a choice. Our people are out of the areas that will be damaged anyway, why do you think you've been able to take the port and starboard sides with less opposition? Oh, and you can call me Oz."

"It's time to let this one go, DeHansen," Major Cumberland agreed. "A few thousand people on those destroyers will thank us when they find out what they were about to do here." He unclipped his rifle and slowly placed it on the deck at his feet.

A number of the other soldiers started following his example.

"I haven't been ordered to authorize a surrender, Major." Commander DeHansen turned to the soldier next to him. "If he puts his sidearm down, shoot him," he ordered.

"Command hasn't seen everything I have. The people on this ship will do anything to keep it from being captured, fight down to the last man. We haven't even seen what's at the core of the structure," Cumberland said calmly as he drew his sidearm.

More than half of the soldiers were following his example. Commander DeHansen's men were watching along with him, some of them looked unsure, though a few were about to follow the majority, Cumberland could see it.

DeHansen drew his sidearm and fired in one smooth motion, catching Major Cumberland several times in the chest.

The armour had been weakened by previous damage and let most of the damage through. Cumberland's chest felt as though it was in a vise, his world one of incredible pain. His legs buckled, his back struck the floor, then his head. Spots of light drifted across his vision, and the sounds of a fire fight breaking out surrounded him. He let his head roll to the side and caught sight of Spence firing at DeHansen and the few men who stood with him, his teeth gnashed, eyes fierce.

Cumberland wanted to tell him to lay down arms, let it run its course without him, not to ruin his career. At least Spence could say he was just following a dead major's orders.

Then the sounds of weapons fire was gone, and Spence rushed to him. "Don't try to move, Major, it's all right. I hear these folks have some pretty good med tech."

Every attempt at a shallow breath brought intense pain and forced his body to spasm. "Done it now. Command will have your head," he managed between gasps.

"This? Command will wash this out, try to forget it ever happened."

"You, too," Cumberland struggled. "You're a witness, Private."

Then Oz was there, injecting something into his neck. The pain seemed far less important suddenly, like it was a physical footnote. "You'll be fine. Might spend some time in a stasis tube regenerating, but we'll get you fixed up."

"Maybe start a new career. Think there's room for a new major aboard, Commander?" asked Cumberland. His senses were beginning to spin, and everything was fading away. He was going into emergency stasis.

"I'd be honoured," said Oz.

"Money," he mouthed as he let his eyes close. "That's what I-" A rush of heat and light interrupted him.

Oz snatched the dead major's sidearm up off the deck and fired it several times at the dying commander. Everyone was so busy watching Cumberland that no one was looking out for Commander DeHansen. Oz made sure he was dead before looking back at the man at his feet, the only enemy he'd tried to save. Cumberland, he'd heard him called several times as Agameg and Jason tracked him through the ship. He seemed like the kind of man he could have fought alongside if things were different.

"Jason, the bridge is under control. What's Command doing?" Oz asked, standing slowly.

"They're ordering the port and starboard destroyers to detach. Looks like they're about to do something from a distance, even with their command ship hard docked."

"He's right. They are not interested in agreeing to your terms, Oz," Agameg verified mournfully.

Oz looked around the room at the exhausted faces of the three dozen enemy soldiers and nodded. "Everyone up!" Several of the corpses on the bridge and in the hall got to their feet, each one of them a gravely injured Triton soldier who recovered in deep stasis. They filed into the bridge and started collecting weapons. Oz was steeled by the sight, realizing how few of his stealth suited comrades remained. There had been hundreds, but that had been whittled down to thirty five.

The deck jerked slightly, the sounds of screeching metal announcing that the destroyers were trying to separate. His gaze found one of the soldiers who had taken Cumberland's side and he said, "I wish I was sorry for what I'm about to do." Oz's finger moved across his command unit to the first torpedo launch icon and activated it. The impacts of driller torpedoes striking the enemy ships at such a close range sounded as a low thud. The destroyer's hulls would be weakened and breached in several places, making them a soft target. The soldier Oz was watching closed his eyes and lowered his face into his hands.

"No, please!" shouted another.

"Stay where you are," Agameg said flatly, pointing his handgun at the soldier's face.

"What's their Command band saying?" Oz asked.

Agameg shook his head. "They are instructing the destroyers to increase their thrust to full in an attempt to decouple from the mooring points."

Oz pressed the second launch icon and the Triton shuddered as heavy torpedoes detonated inside and outside of the destroyers docked on either side of the ship. Hull breach alarms went off for a moment while the Triton's emergency systems kicked in and sealed off any compartments that were open to space. He knew there would be a great deal of damage, but it would have been worse if the destroyers were allowed to separate.

"They're clear. The carrier's still moored securely," Jason replied. "Ashley's opening a wormhole now."

"Ashley's alive?" asked Oz.

"Thank God, yes. She's in medical babysitting with one hand and plotting a multi-part wormhole jump with the other. I'll never underestimate that one again," said Jason.

Oz looked around. Most of the soldiers didn't know what was happening or how to react, and stood staring at him, waiting for an order. Some found a place to sit down, while a few started quietly crying.

The Triton security and combat ready staff were vigilant, guarding the weaponry they collected in a corner, gathering the enemy into small, controllable groups. Oz couldn't help but wonder if things would have been better if he hadn't spent hours in stasis. He was supposed to stay back, direct his people from the shadows, but after seeing so many of his own killed instead of injured, he couldn't. He had a chance to take out one of the best commanding officers they had, Cumberland, and he took it at his peril.

When he awoke in the hall, the dust had settled, and he was relieved to see that Agameg was in position. He overheard Jason sullenly give the order to implement the plan Oz had concocted as a secondary measure. He'd hoped they wouldn't have to use the strategy, but it became the only option.

Everyone looked and sounded tired. The siege had drawn on longer than either side expected.

"Sir, what did Major Cumberland mean?" asked Spence as he handed his rifle and sidearm over.

It took a moment for Oz to realize the younger man was speaking to him. "When he thought he killed me, I asked your Major what he was fighting for. First time he said 'duty.' This time, I think he was honest." Oz knelt down and closed the front of the man's helmet. His face had been burned away, and Oz hoped his subordinates wouldn't remember him that way.

***

"Ashley, we have to finish calculating our thrust angle and estimate new shear values," Larry reminded from his side of the table.

The sight of the incredible damage along the port and starboard sides of the Triton had struck her still. When she was at the controls of that big, beautiful ship, she swore she could feel it. The warm embrace of an incredible metal creature with thick skin, powerful aura-like shields, and rows of teeth that could keep enemies at bay.

Her rationality reminded her that the ship wasn't invincible, even though it was the best built thing she'd ever seen, with a feel of permanence that made it easy for her to call it home as she would a planet-side city. She had to remind herself that the ship wasn't invincible, because it was a difficult thing to believe. Until then.

The thick skin along the port and starboard sides of the ship had ruptured in several places, been crushed into the side of the ship in others. The damage to the pair of destroyers was many times worse, but watching the Triton evacuate air from dozens of outer compartments as bulkhead doors sealed made Ashley feel as though she had been injured. The ship seemed like a delicate thing, even though her rational mind told her that there were safeguards, that most of the hull still remained intact.

"Ashley!" Larry whispered harshly. "We have to get moving!"

She shook her head and looked down into a pair of big, worried nafalli eyes. Her hand was stroking Zoe's face before she knew it, and even though she fidgeted in her lap, the child seemed to draw back from the precipice of tears. "It's okay. We'll get out of here and meet with Captain." One hand moved over the controls, starting the pilot control recalibration process, checking navigational data, and verifying that their single main thruster was still online.

Zoe made herself at home in her lap, and buried her nose in Ashley's hair. She'd seen Iloona's youngest children do the same several times, and thought it was nothing more than a sign of affection. In that moment, she was convinced that it was something more; Zoe was drawing comfort from the act, making Ashley her own warm, safe place.

The controls finished calibrating, then her verified navigational data and wormhole trajectory appeared on her panel, the main thruster reporting ready to fire.

"Is everything all right up there, Ash?" asked Oz.

The relief at hearing his low voice and calm tone ran deep. "Course plotted, controls ready, and the computer's telling me that we'll be able to move with the ship still attached to our upper mooring point."

"Nice work. Can we project a wormhole wide enough?"

She looked to Larry, who nodded. "Not a problem."

"Ashley, you're amazing. Get us out of here," said Oz.

That took both hands, but Zoe didn't seem to mind. Ashley activated the remaining emitters and they fired a burst of energy in front of the ship, bending and twisting the space ahead into a funnel. To the naked eye the sight wasn't so spectacular, only some lensing and a slight ripple in front of the Triton would be visible. The exterior sensor screen was a different story. It was like watching a flower opening from the outside in, energies bent and twisted as empty space compressed and several pieces of debris were pulled in.

Zoe must have caught the light in the corner of her eye; she turned and stared at the holographic sensor view and watched as Ashley fired the main thruster and increased the power as much as she dared. "Let's make this place a memory," Ashley said to herself as the wormhole finished forming and the Triton entered the highly compressed space.

As soon as their course was steady, Larry got to his feet.

"Where ya goin'?" Ashley asked.

"There's still fighting in a few compartments, I'm going to go do what I have to," he said stoically as he strode for the door.

Ashley watched it close behind him. When she was sure he was several meters away, she locked her controls and made her way to the room's only door, an act made more difficult while carrying Zoe. She locked it biometrically and verified that the life support systems were operating properly in that section of medical. "He can stay out," she whispered to herself.

Zoe was watching her. What she was doing, the expression on her face, and who knew what else. Ashley looked at her, bouncing the small youngster in the crook of her arm and feigning excitement. "I think it's snack time! How 'bout you?"

Zoe giggled as she was bounced several more times.

Ashley never thought she was graceful under pressure, and she wasn't normally good at hiding her feelings, but with Zoe in her arms, false joviality became real in a surprisingly short time.

CHAPTER 32
FALLOUT

One of the shipping containers was filled with supplies, and Ayan couldn't help but smile at the sight of it being unloaded. "It's a reassuring sight," Laura said from her side.

"Yes it is," agreed a liberated slave as he passed by with a group of similarly dressed people. Most of them were smiling at the sight of incoming supplies. "Time to unload the groceries," another added.

"I'm just glad we're on solid ground. From the looks of the ships, they must have been pretty close to sinking," Ayan observed, gesturing towards a nearby, fat bellied hauler ship. Its landing struts were still caked with mud all the way up to the hull.

"Most of that's backsplash from vertical take-off," Stephanie explained from her left.

Ayan hadn't noticed her approach and turned to greet her with a smile, but that intent as well as the expression faded as soon as she caught the woman's expression. She looked nearly furious. "Everything all right?"

"No, everything's not all right. We've been here less than a day and you've got us hooked in with a crime boss who happens to be our landlady. You know who Patrizia Salustri is?"

Ayan hadn't been angry - truly, out of control angry - since she was a teenager. When she lost her temper, the world shook, the edges of her vision blurred, and it was all she could do to keep from leaping bodily at her rival. She'd never seen Stephanie in that light before, but who else was as close to Jake? Who knew the man he had become better than she did? That, along with the suspicion that Patrizia, the tall, elegant, beautiful mysterious woman she'd just met could be one of Jacob's ex-lovers was enough to crush the emotional barriers Ayan used to compartmentalize her feelings. "That's it," she breathed, stepping right up to the security chief. "You don't have the right to put me down, fringe trash."

Stephanie took a step back, her expression softening.

Ayan followed her, holding position, nose to nose and toe to toe. She was no longer Ayan, the awe-filled traveller. She was a commander, military trained, a two time boot camp graduate, survivor of ship to ship as well as person to person combat, and she wasn't going to be insulted, not when she was suppressing so much anger and frustration. She unleashed all the fury she had at not being able to return to the Triton and help her people along with everything else, and everything but Stephanie's brown eyes disappeared. "Are you talking down to me, Chief? You couldn't find a serial killer on your own ship and you're talking down to me?" The feeling of air filling her lungs to the brim, of pushing all of it out with her stomach as hard as she could was like a violent ecstasy. "What the hell has got you thinking you can bust my chops about how I do my job when you're not doing yours?" Ayan took a quick, deep breath and squeezed her final words through gnashed teeth. "You get your ass over there and supervise your people while they unload the bread I brought home today and set up a perimeter detail while you're at it." Ayan watched her. "In case you can't remember the proper response, it is 'yes, Sir!'"

"Yes, Sir," Stephanie mewled.   The woman had melted, fear and uncertainty was plain in her eyes.

"Again, before you embarrass yourself!" Ayan demanded.

Stephanie snapped to attention and barked, "Yes, Sir!"

"Dismissed!" Ayan shouted as a reflex.

Stephanie turned on her heel and began to stride away.

Ayan was about to let it go, to walk to the Clever Dream and hope that would be the last time the spectre of military discipline would show, but she saw the look of frustration on Stephanie's face. Even from the side, it was instantly recognizable. What little anger Ayan had left surged to the surface. "Oi! Next time you even think of giving me attitude, I'll give your job to Leland March. At least he looks as useless as he is!"

With Laura close behind and eyes on her from every direction, Ayan marched towards the main boarding ramp of the Clever Dream. She stepped into the first officer's quarters, why, she wasn't sure, and Laura was right behind her.

"Wow, I've never seen that side of you. Where'd that come from?" Laura asked.

"Too many years on the parade ground," Ayan rasped as she sat on the bed hard enough to bounce and lowered her face into her hands.

"Jason told me they used to call you Sunspot because of your temper, but that was just..." She trailed off for a moment before concluding; "Military. That was Commander Ayan."

Ayan could hear Laura turn around and notice how quiet she'd gotten, and the moment she sat on the bed beside her the tears started flowing.

"Oh," she said as she put her arm around Ayan's shoulders.

Laura had always been a good friend, the best. She'd met so many people in Junior Academy, then Fleet Academy and the military. Many of her best friends had died years ago, service mates who perished on the Sunspire during combat action. Others drifted off as service took them in different directions, and for Ayan, that meant up the command ladder, further separating her from fellow graduates and the acquaintances of her youth. Then she was reborn, and everyone but Doctor Anderson and Minh were gone. When she arrived aboard the Triton, the reunion with Laura was the sweetest. There was no forgetting or replacing such a friend, and as she sat on the edge of the bed Jacob Valance had slept in the night before, crying for reasons she couldn't quite put together yet, she had never been more grateful that she was there. Laura didn't ask why she was in tears, she just kept her company while she got them out of her system, but then, she did want to give her an explanation. "I have no idea what I'm doing here," Ayan managed as she wiped tears away.

Laura handed her a tissue. Where she'd found it, Ayan had no idea. "You're doing great," said Laura.

"No, I'm really not. I mean, all day we've been running about, trying to make a proper place here and I manage to sign the first contract the government presents, then strike a bargain with a crime lord. What kind of madwoman does that?"

"The intelligent, flexible kind."

"Oh, and said crime lady all but said 'me and your Jake are old shagging buddies, think you can meet us up again?' God, I'm so lost. So completely, utterly lost." Ayan punctuated her lament with a long blow of her nose.

"There's no-"

"And as soon as I get back, I go off like a drill sergeant on one of his most trusted people." She sat silently for a moment, reviewing the incident. "I have to apologize."

Laura caught Ayan before she could finish standing up and sat her back down. "Oh, no you don't. She had it coming, I mean she really had it coming. You bent over backwards and worked miracles today. I mean, think about it. None of us have been here before, you couldn't call back to the ships because we don't have a local code, and they needed you to get supplies, somewhere to land and the permits to move. I wouldn't know where to start. Then she has the nerve to give you grief over getting it all finished in the nick of time?" Laura shook her head. "You actually managed to do what anyone in your position would want to do, and she deserved every word."

It was easy to believe Laura, everything she said was true. "Maybe bringing up the serial killer was going over the line just a little," Ayan admitted.

"But did you see the look on her face?" asked Laura with a grin.

Ayan couldn't help but laugh. "I don't think she'll doubt me aloud again. Jake's going to hear about that, though."

"So? I'm pretty sure he'll agree Stephanie was in the wrong. Respectful colleagues present advice and alternatives, not criticism without support."

"They used to tell us that in Officer Training."

"And I've heard you say the same to people in the lab."

Ayan looked at Laura, whose eyes went wide as she realized her blunder. "Wasn't me," she said quietly.

Laura smiled back at her and nodded. "It was. A little different, but everything she was is in you. Besides, the woman I'm sitting beside is something greater."

"Sure, there's more of me, especially in the hips, and in the front," Ayan countered, playfully.

"No, well, yeah, but-"

"Well, thank you!" Ayan laughed, feigning injury.

"It suits you. It really does, but really, as you are, I can't imagine you sticking to an engineering department, or a research lab. You'd do wonderfully in either place, but after spending the day with you today I see so much more in you. An ambassador, an explorer, a problem solver, and it's all wrapped up in a confident, charming package. I think, no, I'm sure Patrizia was actually envious of you when she realized you were the one who gave Jake his scarf. I think you made a mystery real for her, I think you lived up to what she pictured in her mind as a woman she couldn't compete with."

"Oh, come on," Ayan said with disbelief. "Not in this lifetime, or any other. Did you see her?"

"Yes, and she was hanging on your every word, especially when you stood up to her and actually countered her price with an offer of your own."

"Must happen all the time," she replied with a barely suppressed smile.

"You know it doesn't, and if something did happen between Jake and her, it's probably ancient history now. Just talk to him about it," said Laura.

"That ought to be an interesting conversation," Ayan sighed. "But I think I will."

"Good. It'll be fine."

"You're amazing, Laura. Busy picking me up off the floor while Jason's still out there. I'm sorry."

Laura closed her eyes and nodded. "I'm worried, but I'd know if something happened to him. Wherever he is, I know he's doing his best to come back to me."

"Minh should be back soon."

"I know. I think I'll try to get some rest before he arrives. Do you mind?"

"No. I think I'll wait for Jake in the captain's quarters."

"Good luck. I think everything's going to be fine, though."

"I hope so," Ayan said.

Chapter 33
Meddler

It was impossible to know whether she was waking up when her eyes snapped open, or if she was becoming aware. What was certain, as Eve lay atop her made bed in her finest green and blue silk gown, was that until the very moment of awareness or waking, she was not in control. She couldn't feel Gloria behind her eyes, but there was a residue. There was guilt, and a strange giddiness that was unlike anything she'd known.

"What have you done?" Eve asked aloud, hoping the other woman wouldn't answer from somewhere inside her mind. Despite her growing dread she began to reach out, to search the network of surveillance and storage for evidence of her passage. Within milliseconds she found the trail. Gloria had made no efforts to hide her activities.

Eve went to bed. It had taken her exactly forty three minutes and nine seconds to fall asleep. Four minutes and fifty one seconds later she sat up and dressed in her finest gown, put on the heels she never really learned to walk in properly, and exited her quarters. She was humming something, and after a quick search through the archives, she realized it was an ancient song called Birdhouse In Your Soul.

Eve didn't remember any of it. Not a single instant. Watching the woman wearing her body swagger down the familiar hallways, smile at soldiers and officers as she walked past, and look right into surveillance hot spots so Eve could look her in the eyes later was infuriating. When she realized the woman's destination, she was so enraged that she lost her connection with the network. She forced herself to settle down and focused her attention on the surveillance footage of Gloria entering Beaudric's quarters.

With a grace Eve never had, Gloria sat down on the edge of his bed and whispered, "I have something to show you," as she caressed his cheek.

He roused with a start, sat up, and after a moment smiled at her warmly in the dim light. There were few words as she let him get dressed behind her and walked him down the hall to the lift. In seemingly easy silence they made their way to the bowels of the command carrier and Eve was horror stricken as she recalled the next batch of surveillance data from the system. Gloria walked him directly into the emergency genesis chamber. It was a long, broad corridor with black tiled floors and bare generation one frameworks lining the walls in their cubicles. Like a collection of hundreds of skeletons, they stood waiting, empty eye sockets staring across the room at each other. A box at each one's feet contained everything they needed to get to work after coming to life. It was a place no one was supposed to see, a place where, if they urgently needed basic personnel in vast numbers, they could be produced hundreds at a time. Behind each cubicle was a loading mechanism that would stand another framework skeleton up after one had finished generating and walked off. Another loader under the box would put a fresh uniform and weapons or tools inside.

These frameworks did not have the individuality or higher functions that Beaudric did. They were ready to be programmed with any of twenty pre-set basic personalities and skill sets. Very few would be given an improved version of the programming, which really only enhanced them enough to be basic, logical commanders. Those were the A-Types, or generation one point fives that could take over as an officer for a short amount of time.

Beaudric stared open mouthed, wide eyed as the lights came on and he was rendered speechless. Gloria filled the silence before long. "These are your lesser cousins. This technology is responsible for bringing you into being, and while you're a vast improvement, you still have the same bones. The same machines forged you."

The man turned and stared at her with a confused, hurt expression on his face.

"I shouldn't be telling you this, but the guilt of what I've done is too heavy. I was human, once. I was born of a mother and a father, grew up like any little girl and was about to become a woman. Then I became deathly ill, and my father, a great scientist, couldn't find a cure. Instead he harvested my mind and connected it to a new body. A network of machines built so I could protect the Eden solar system. I took things a little bit too far. My father was killed, I was isolated from the network and the machines I built. Years later someone recovered me, created the perfect body for my reintegration into humanity and transplanted my mind."

Beaudric stared at her with that bulging eye, open mouthed expression that he couldn't seem to shake. "Eden. So you are Eve?" he asked at last.

"I am, and I've decided to begin taking responsibility for all my misdeeds, starting with you," she said.

"With me? Your people rescued me."

"No, I stole from you. We're all memory and body thieves here, even the Child Prophet, who is in his second body as well. I watched from a distance as you made yourself at home on Pandem, and after deciding that you were living a life of frivolity, I began to construct memories, new memories that would help you make the right attachments and decisions. You think your father was killed, but there was no attack, he was never here," she told him.

"But I remember-" said Beaudric.

"Creations, just figments from my mind transplanted into yours. They are made so you feel anger at an enemy that has never interfered with Pandem."

"The book, this ring-"

"Oh my God, you are deeply stupid. That's another reason why I chose you. They are offerings from your original, who gave them to us in exchange for a few days of meaningless indulgence. He's still down there! Do you want to see?" Gloria shouted. With a gesture, a large hologram appeared of Patrick laying in the middle of a king sized bed with a young woman in his arms. "She's just one of a number of women Patrick, that's the name given to your original, has slept with since he arrived. He does as little as he can to get by, plays by the rules whenever he feels like it, and spends the rest of his time indulging in the most convenient pleasure. Think, use that shallow mind of yours and try to remember."

Beaudric looked from the hologram to Gloria several times, confused and irritated before admitting, "It's all blurry. I can see pieces, but when I try to focus on something it's just. . . blurry."

"That is because you're an experiment. I'm sorry. I shouldn't tell you this at all, but the lie is too heavy for me to carry. I thought I could turn you into a simple soldier, that you were the right template to experiment with, and I was right. Your thinking is so simple, you're so stupid that you fell for all of it. You're not intelligent enough to question your own thoughts and you're so obedient that you didn't even request a service for your father. You just soldiered on because I made sure you were programmed that way."

Beaudric's reaction was animalistic. He slapped Gloria so hard it rang down the corridor. "Good," she purred as she strode to one of the boxes, flipped it open with her toe and retrieved a sidearm.

"No! I didn't mean it, I'm sorry!" Beaudric whined as Gloria slowly, methodically raised the weapon and pointed it at him.

She flipped the safety off and fired several times. Every round struck its target, burning holes straight through Beaudric's chest. He collapsed, clutching the air for something beyond understanding and died right before her eyes.

Gloria walked to his side and bent down low, watching as the framework system repaired the damage by materializing fresh flesh. When his body was mended, Beaudric gasped back to life. Gloria sneered at the hurt, confused expression on his face. "Every immortal on this ship is the Child Prophet's victim. I bear the guilt, but he ordered it. If you want revenge, go and take it," she told him as she dropped the weapon on his chest.

"How do I-"

"Find him? Get past security? You already know, just think for a change. Try and remember," she encouraged.

He stood slowly, and regarded Gloria with mild astonishment. "I know. I can even remember him celebrating my birth. How?"

"I gave that memory to you as well. Now go do this for me, and I promise you'll be free afterwards. I'm giving you control of thirty frameworks. Do whatever you like with them, you can even set them free, though they wouldn't know what to do with themselves," Gloria said as she started for the exit. "Or don't, and return to your room. Knowingly serve a man-child who will do what's been done to you over and over again."

The rest of Gloria's evening was uninformative; she simply returned to her quarters and laid down. Three minutes later to the millisecond, she woke up as Eve again. She searched the surveillance feeds for any sign of Beaudric after he left the genesis chamber, but there were huge blind spots. Eve also couldn't understand why she had to watch all the footage in sequence. It was as if it couldn't be read any other way, by anything. The blocks in the system were the same, there as though forced into place by another active mind.

She swung her legs over the edge of the bed and kicked her heels off. "Security, find Beaudric and bring him to me! Increase security for Lister Hampon, the Child Prophet immediately," she ordered. The system didn't respond.

Eve tried to send the commands using her link, but again, there was no acknowledgement. She tried reaching past the ship, and discovered a great void, space with no data. An attempt to leave her quarters failed as she almost walked into a door that didn't open as it should. It was then that she realized she was never addressing the system at all. All the surveillance footage had been copied to her backup memory, and someone had used her own framework components to disable her wireless input-output systems. She was alone. There was no connection, no freedom, and Gloria was somehow responsible. Eve began to shake, a tear rolling down her cheek as she began to feel helpless, furious, and she pounded on the door until her fists bruised.

The framework components grafted into her bones repaired the damage, and she screamed, shocking herself as her frantic voice filled her ears. Quivering with rage, she turned her back to the door and began to ponder. How had Gloria managed it? How had she taken control of her, directly manipulated the framework body she once inhabited and then taken control of enough of the ship to completely isolate her? Eve's thoughts rarely turned towards what could be happening beyond her door, none of that mattered as much as regaining her digital sight and control.

Despite her haze of emotion, she turned her mind's eye inward, and began to try and restore her input-output systems.

CHAPTER 34
AYAN AND JACOB

The Captain's quarters on the Clever Dream were made for comfort. The central seat, a flat, round furnishing in the middle of the cabin, adjusted to Ayan's shape as soon as she sat down, and shifted with her. She settled in and ended up cross legged, and, though she'd seen it twice already, she started reviewing the most recent scan data of the Triton. The ship had taken a beating, that was for sure, but Oz commanded her crew expertly. The calculations Laura had included, detailing how the enemy was able to disrupt their wormhole by tracking the energy wake proved that, without a doubt, that's exactly what had happened.

Thoughts of all the people they left behind, Jason, Oz, and so many others who she'd just met, threatened to add weight to her concern, to become to debilitating worry. She'd never been more worried in all her life, and to make things worse, she suspected that most of the experienced spacers, the ones who lived most of their lives on the fringe, didn't think she did a good job negotiating with the Carthan government or Patrizia Salustri. Stephanie definitely didn't approve of the deal that had been struck, but Ayan had thought through how that played out several times since, and given their situation, she couldn't think of any other way it could have gone. She knew things were dire at their initial landing site, that they needed more solid footing both figuratively and literally, and that she didn't have time for more elegant solutions.

The Carthan Government wasn't about to change it's policies, and given time she might find a way to get a better deal, but for the time being she had a real permit that enabled them to start hunting. A connection to the community, though very new, had been made as well, and they had supplies for the short term. What would Stephanie have done that would have been faster, or better in the long run?

That's what frustrated Ayan the most about the whole situation. The more she let herself think about it, the less she regretted her confrontation with the security chief. She only hoped it wouldn't drive her off the crew; she was good at her job, after all.

She brought up a replay of their fly over of the shanty port to take her mind off the whole thing, and instead of finding something familiar there, something she could compare to her past experiences, her heart just kept sinking. It was a sight unlike anything she'd imagined and she couldn't help but think that Stephanie, who had probably seen similar conditions elsewhere, would have done better.

With a sigh, she looked at the holographic image above her comm unit. Air and ground traffic flowed like rivers between the endless sea of ships and battered buildings. The variations in the designs were endless, and with a little searching she managed to find the block of empty slips they landed on. "Lewis, can you copy this recording to your holoprojector, please?" she asked.

"Here you go," he replied. The shanty port filled the room then, and she was sitting right in the middle. "I'll set the control profile to match your command unit. Look, Ma, no learning curve!" he exclaimed in an exaggerated comical tone.

"Thank you, Lewis. You're too good to us."

"Don't I know it, but don't worry; I'm keeping track of billable hours. Someday, someone's going to get an invoice," he said.

Ayan laughed as she turned the holographic image so she could get a closer look at the ships that once occupied the spaces nearest to their landing site. "I'd love to be there when it happens."

"I'll make sure you're in visual range. Just tell me if you need anything else."

"All right, thanks again." The angles the recording was taken from weren't perfect. She couldn't get a pedestrian's view, which would have been helpful, but she was able to find the name of one of the vessels. "The Derringer" she said to herself. It had six pivoting main thrusters, was a little over a hundred meters long, and sported eight turreted cannons. The extra armour plating gave the vessel a utilitarian look, but she could tell it was probably once a lesser armed transport that had been heavily modified.

The door to the quarters opened to admit Jake, who looked up to the ceiling with slight irritation. "Next time let me knock, all right, Lewis?" he muttered.

"Doors chime these days, Captain. Have you been watching too many period movies?" asked the AI.

"I'm just saying, it's close quarters. If we don't take privacy where we can, we'll be at each other's throats that much sooner," Captain Valance said as he looked to Ayan.

She flashed him a smile and nodded an invitation.

"That actually makes a great deal of sense, Captain."

Jake shook his head and crossed the room to the centre seat, where he knelt behind Ayan.

"He's used to only taking care of one person and the ship. I think he's trying," she said.

"I think he's too busy trying to understand everyone at once, that's what's got him running in circles. Besides, he's probably still trying to adjust after Pandem. I wish Jason had gotten a better look at him."

"He saw enough to determine I wasn't a danger to the crew," Lewis objected.

"Lewis, privacy mode. Please," Ayan requested.

"We finally find a place to land that isn't a sucking mire, things start quieting down, and everyone wants to be alone." An artificial click sounded after Lewis' parting comment and the words PRIVACY MODE drifted across the large hologram.

"Well, he's one of the most interesting artificial intelligences I've ever seen, I'll give him that," Ayan said as she inspected one of the other ships nearby. It was a snub-nosed, six deck ship with as many patches as portholes.

"I'm actually starting to like him. Don't tell him that, though," admitted Jake.

"But you argue with him often," Ayan pointed out with a chuckle.

"Alice was the same for a while when she was in early development. Once she was sure I wouldn't wipe her if she challenged me. Then again, she wasn't installed in a ship, but on my comm."

"But we can trust Lewis to do what he has to, right?"

"I think so. I was just on the bridge. He's scanning the area constantly, we'll know the instant something crosses our perimeter," said Jake.

"Or when Minh gets back?" she asked.

"I think he's as anxious as we are, I'm sure we'll know the moment he picks anything up. Nothing agitates an AI like a question they can't answer."

"I think everyone's thinking of the Triton tonight. We left so many people behind."

Jake chuckled quietly. "Right now everyone's talking about the dressing down their security chief just got from their senior commander."

"Oh, right. Was going to bring that up."

"Well, Stephanie's pissed."

"Chewed your ear off about it?"

"No, she was in the military, she's been put in her place before. She let on that she's sore that you attacked her competency in front of so many people, though."

"Looking back, that was going a little too far. You know how it works though, someone steps too far out of line and you put them down so everyone can watch them get back up. It's in the training," said Ayan.

"She knows that, but we're not in a military unit. A lot of people will take that at face value," said Jake.

"So, what do I do?" Ayan shrugged, too tired to let the conversation become a disagreement.

"Just give her an opportunity to show everyone you trust her abilities. Any doubt will fade as soon as they see you have faith in her."

"I'll watch for opportunities, and I do trust her, you know. It's just strange; she's always distanced herself until just recently," observed Ayan.

"Well, I'm just glad we have time for gossip. We'd be in worse shape if we were still in the Wastes."

"So you're happy with the deal I made to get us this space?" Ayan asked finally. It was something she wanted to know but didn't know how to ask until then. She felt his hands on her shoulders, his fingers kneading her tense muscles. "Ah, that's heaven," she sighed.

"We didn't have much to trade, so you offered what we can deliver right now."

She thought about his answer for a moment. It wasn't an affirmative or negative, but a sentiment that fit neatly between. His thumbs worked the base of her neck and she almost forgot about the nagging question. Almost. "But are you happy about it?"

His hands stopped moving. A long moment of silence followed. "We're a lot better off than we were when we first landed. I don't think I could have done any better."

"So you're pleased with how it turned out?" she pressed.

"It was the best decision for everyone, so yes, I'm glad you got us here." His hands went back to work.

It was the small victory she was looking for, even though she would never admit she was seeking validation, even from him. A more difficult question remained, and instead of sitting on it, letting it fester, she just asked him. "How do you know Patrizia?"

His hands didn't stop kneading, a good sign, or a sign that he knew the question was coming and already had his escape plan ready. "We did a few jobs for her three years ago. Maybe four."

"She guessed I was the one who gave you the white scarf you used to wear." It was a daring move, offering more detail in hopes of getting extra information without directly asking. "Seems like she had been wondering who gave that to you for a while."

"I remember her asking. I couldn't tell her because I didn't know who gave it to me at the time. To be honest, I assumed it was from a wife I couldn't remember. Instead of making something up, I just ignored the question."

"Oh," Ayan said quietly, too distracted to enjoy the shoulder rub Jake was giving her.

The silence grew thick, and Jacob's hands stopped. "Did something happen while you were dealing with her?"

"No. Well, it's only that Stephanie seemed so opposed to dealing with her."

"That's because the last time we dealt with Patrizia, she told us we were liberating a political prisoner from the low security wing of a prison, when it turned out we were rescuing her girlfriend from a prison term she earned. She still has a warrant out for her in that system."

"Girlfriend?" Ayan boggled.

"I couldn't make it up if I tried. They put her away for code breaking and we managed to get her out, then she tells us the whole story about why she was there and that Patrizia was pretty much her sugar momma."

Ayan burst out laughing, more from relief than at the story itself.

Jake's hands went back to her shoulders and continued their work, laughing along with her. "Guess it is pretty funny now. Still, we'll have to double check every bit of information we get from her."

"And everything. She gave me a very expensive ring as a keepsake. I scanned it, there's nothing inside, and it registers as about seventy years old. Not something you buy in a backstreet bazaar." She said, holding up the gold and platinum lion's head ring. "Think she fancies me?"

"If she does, she'll have a fight on her hands," Jake replied with a playful growl.

With a few gestures on her comm unit she selected a different shape for her vacsuit that left her shoulders bare and lowered the neckline significantly. He stopped a moment as the clothing complied with her order then continued, his hands on her bare skin. They felt harder than she expected, but they were warm, strong.

The thought that her outfit modification could be seen as some kind of a reward flicked through her mind and made her blush furiously. It didn't seem to occur to him, or if it did he didn't seem to mind. He was a deft shoulder and neck masseuse, and she couldn't help but put her head down and relax. "How is everyone settling in?" she asked quietly.

"We had to evacuate the Samson. About a third are leaving, setting out for Port Rush City proper. The rest are settling into the other ships. Things seemed to calm down once they saw the food and cots. Stephanie and Alaka are keeping things pretty orderly."

"A third, that's a lot of people moving on."

"I expected it. We'll probably see half gone by morning, especially if there's an uplink to the Core World Banks available in Port Rush," he said.

"From what I saw today, there must be. The transit centre we passed through was busy, the busiest I've ever seen. How are their spirits?" asked Ayan.

"The ones who are moving on? A lot of the people from Enreega took a moment to thank Stephanie and me on their way out, even Alaka, who wasn't there. Except for Edward. He had to make a grand stand about informing whoever he could find about where we are so they could take us in for the bounty. Listening to him you'd think he was kidnapped and forced into hard labour."

Ayan found the astrophysicist half frustrating and half amusing. Most of the people she'd met in his field were patient, reasonable, and high thinking problem solvers. He was anything but, and even though she never wanted to deal with him herself, watching the drama at a distance was sometimes entertaining when she could get past the frustration he inspired in most onlookers, herself included. "Well, he won't be missed. It won't be long before everyone knows you're here though, with or without him flapping about it."

"You're right. I'm glad we chose to land here. At the very least, I have Patrizia's respect and she'll help protect us if we can stay on her good side."

"Oh, boy. Well, I never did experiment in college," Ayan commented with an exaggerated show of piqued interest. "This might be my opportunity."

"I'm not sharing," Jake said in a low, serious tone that sent a shiver up her spine.

She closed her eyes and simply enjoyed the massage for a few moments. His hands moved down her back, kneading as they travelled. A thought occurred to her then. "There won't be much point in hiding here any longer by tomorrow morning. You'll be moving about the moon making deals and forming ties without my help."

"Disappointing?"

"Hmm?"

"Are you disappointed?" he asked her.

"No, I was right out of my comfort zone today. Seeing the cities was amazing, but I couldn't enjoy it. Had too many things to do, and most of our problems don't have easy solutions," she said.

"Well, I hate to tell you, but you're still going to be in the hot seat when you wake up tomorrow. I have to go into hiding. Multi-million credit bounties have reach, especially in ports like this. I don't know how long I'll have to hide either, so you're going to be the representative of the crew for as long as we're here, maybe longer. Even when the Triton gets back. We're going to need a home port, especially while we try to perform repairs."

She let that sink in for a moment. Home port. "Here?"

"If we can get set up. We saw worse places even before the Eden virus broke out. Looks like they're over that here, on to rebuilding," said Jake.

There it was again, the years she knew little to nothing about. Those years in command of the Samson that helped shape Jake into the person he was as much as the memories he inherited from Jonas. She'd spent an entire night talking about those times with him and felt there was still so much she didn't know. "I'm going to need your help, often. You have so much more experience out here, sometimes it feels like I'm a hapless tourist."

"Your instincts are good. Don't worry, you can make sure there's always someone around. I won't be able to be on comms with you all the time though, or be seen staying on the same ship. I'm going to have to blend in with some of the crew so people can't pick me out. Stephanie and most of the Samson crew will be doing the same."

"You know what would help, I think?" she asked.

"What's that?"

"Tell me more about your time on the Samson. What was it like?"

His hands stopped halfway on their way back to her shoulders. "That's a big question," he replied quietly.

Ayan wouldn't let him escape it. She pulled his arms around her tightly and slid backwards, resting against his chest. "That's why I'm asking," she whispered.

He stretched his legs out and got comfortable around her. The arms she'd drawn around her waist weren't just resting in place any longer, they were holding her. "Nothing stayed the same for long," he whispered. "The ship always needed work, there was never enough time, or there was too much time. You know the routine of 'hurry up and wait.' We'd always be really busy in port then left with days in hyperspace. Crew came and went all the time. The longer the trip, the more the crew would get at each other, so I had to keep finding small jobs and bounties between the bigger ones so they'd have something to do other than stare at each other and get into each other's business."

"So there was a lot of fighting aboard?" she asked.

"More during the first couple of years."

"What did you do about it usually?"

"You can't really separate people for long on a ship like that, but I tried. Confined a few people to quarters a couple of times, but if I had to do that for two people, one of them would get a cot in the machinist's closet," Jake said.

Ayan couldn't help but chuckle a little. The mental picture of a crew member locked in a small, dark, greasy closet with a cot as punishment for misbehaving was unexpected, but she'd seen the inside of the Samson, and it fit. "I guess that's a bit too severe."

"It was, but I still did it every once in a while. Stephanie locked someone in there once for bringing a grenade into Sarcost Port. Got her whole team held up in quarantine and I had to go pay the processing fees before we could do business."

"There was a weapons restriction?"

"Oh, yeah, there was, and everyone was told about it before they left. There was no point in carrying anything but a sidearm anyway, Stephanie's team was only following a lead on a repo job to get a little shore time."

"Who was the crewman who brought the grenade?" she asked.

Jake thought for a moment and nodded to himself. "Rooni, never got to know him. He was killed about two weeks later on the same job when we caught up with the Evening Crooner."

"Did that happen a lot on repo jobs?"

"No, most repos were easy. We'd wait until the crew put into port and the ship was almost empty then use the manufacturer codes to take control of the security systems. Tracking the ships from system to system was usually harder than the takedown. The captain of the Evening Crooner had replaced half her systems though, and he was paranoid, so he never let more than a quarter of his crew leave the ship. When we thought we had control of his ship it was really a copy of the operating system installed on a computer with a receiver and the interactive manual," Jake said.

"So it looked like everything was normal."

"Yup, he was a piece of work. Went away for nine years after we took his ship. I guess he really did have to stay on the move, he should have kept up with his payments. I always planned on borrowing that security system idea for the Samson, never got around to it though. Can't really hack into the Samson using her serial numbers and manufacturer codes, anyway."

"I guess paranoia was catching in your line of work," Ayan observed.

"Nothing paints a bull's-eye on your back like being freelance law enforcement. It was good money for us though, especially since we didn't stay in one place for long."

"That's another part of hunting? Moving around a lot?" She intertwined her fingers with his heavier digits. Being there, in his arms, hearing about a way of life that was completely foreign to her as it was spoken in whispers, it was the kind of sharing she wanted with him ever since they met on Pandem.

"No, it's the hardest way to approach the business. If you're lucky you land somewhere and work the leads without anyone figuring out what you're up to. If you're unlucky everyone already knows who you are and what you're about, so whoever you're there for is already on their way off-world. Most bounty hunters stay in one place for their entire careers, get to know the different law enforcement agencies, learn to work with other hunters, and have a good lay of the land. Some worlds even have hunter syndicates. Makes hunting safer, especially when you can bring in more than one team and the syndicate makes sure everyone gets paid equally. That would have been better, settling into a nice, active solar system, but I was looking for Alice."

There was a heavy silence as she waited for him to go on, tried to think of something to say. The daughter of strange origins who she never met, who she wished she could know almost as much as she wanted to know Jake. His grief was still fresh, and she was the only one who knew its depth. "I'm sorry," she whispered finally.

"It's all right."

It wasn't, she knew. It wouldn't be for a long time, but she'd have to let him close the wound in his own time. All she could do was make herself available to him, make sure that he could trust that she would listen and not judge.

"I didn't have much to go on, but it was a purpose. Asking questions was second nature, and before long I learned how to find the right people, people who might have answers. The first crew of the Samson gave me a lot of trouble, especially since I tried making money by doing anything that came along. Hauling cargo, repairing satellites, claiming salvage, you name it. I kept on getting back to bounty hunting though, it was what I was best at. It wasn't my favourite kind of work, mind you. I ended up delivering a lot of good people to their accuser's doors, but I knew I'd need money for the times when there was no work, and we were between systems. The early crews would always get nervous, even though I paid them a small wage if work wasn't coming, but later on those dead times when we were in hyperspace for more than a week or two the crew would gel. Especially after Ashley came aboard."

"She seems nice, and fun," said Ayan with a smile.

"She's both. Smarter than people give her credit for, too. I never thought the life was for her, but I think she grew into it. Most times I wish she hadn't."

"Oh?"

"That's the problem with a ship like the Samson; you need good people with the right skills aboard, but if you get to know them too well, if you learn to like them, then it's the last place you want them to be. I thought she'd be retired to one of my haulers within another year or so. I brought it up once and she looked at me like I was kicking her off the ship. She was almost in tears," he said softly.

"I could just imagine."

"Back then I didn't know where my search would take us. I expected it would be dangerous, I knew a lot of people were after Alice, probably for freeing me and maybe for something else. I needed loyal people who wouldn't waver when I finally found her, people who would help me get her out of whatever trouble she was in. They'd be paid, sure, but cash only motivates people so far, loyalty takes them the rest of the way. I needed to find her, help her, and I needed answers. Somehow I knew the scarf she'd left me wasn't hers. I knew I wouldn't have bought it myself. It just didn't seem to match anything else. It still had your smell on it for a while too, which was the biggest hint, I think."

"That lilac and vanilla base perfume I used to wear?"

"It lasted for months. Got some strange looks from people when they stood too close, too. I imagined I had a wife somewhere, that she might have been looking for me, or that the same people who were after my daughter had her in a prison somewhere."

"You must've dreamt I looked like all kinds of people," Ayan teased. "Disappointed?"

He squeezed her a little and lightly kissed her behind the ear. "For the first time in a long time, I feel lucky. Really lucky."

The tingles of him whispering against her ear and his inference made her blush furiously. "No promises," she replied. She turned her head and he caught her lips. He wasn't the man she'd known on the First Light, far from it. This was an experienced man of the universe, someone who had been places she couldn't imagine, seen things she would never want to, and beneath his hardened surface, there was a sea of emotions that he'd let only her see. The stories of him on the Samson were all of a man who didn't allow anyone to see him as he truly was, and it made his softer side even more precious. It was hers, somehow she'd gained the gift of his trust, and it surpassed anything anyone had ever offered her.

He gently stroked her cheek, her neck, and began to trace her neckline lightly with his fingers. An involuntary inhale on her part sent him a message. What exactly that message was, she wasn't sure herself, but before she could think he retreated and regarded her with a quiet gaze. She bit her bottom lip as she stared back at him, not wanting to leave the moment they were sharing behind, but very uncertain about going forward.

"It's too soon," he concluded without a hint of disappointment.

She caught him as he started pulling away from her and everything stopped. Ayan didn't know how to say what was on her mind; articulating the problem without being embarrassed seemed impossible. With a sudden surge of courage she burst, "Everything is new again," and was immediately mortified. She blushed so hard she was sure her hair was turning back to its old shade of red.

Jake held her silently for a moment before she felt him laugh more than she heard.

"Oi! Not funny!" she squeaked, pinching his arm.

Jake looked into her eyes, and in a gesture completely unfamiliar to her, he tipped her chin up with his finger and whispered, "There are no expectations here, only time."

"What about people decorating your footlocker with frilly underwear if they find out we're not there yet?"

"I'll just pass them on to you," he said.

"Clever," she said, kissing him as she wrapped her arms around his neck. She pulled him on top of her. A nervous giggle escaped her lips as he murmured his surprise. "Promise to wash them first," she chuckled.

"Only if you model-"

"Ayan, a visitor from Drifton has come asking for you," Lewis announced from her comm unit.

Jake pushed up and looked at her. "And I thought you were the one who would be getting some rest tonight," he said.

"I was hoping, though with the connections we tapped today, I should have known someone would come calling," she sighed. "Who is it, Lewis?"

"An Axiologist who claims to be of the Samaritan path, whatever that means."

Ayan was surprised, inexplicably embarrassed, and immediately eager to meet the rare earth trained religious man. She'd only met two before. The first was one of her guest teachers as a young woman in school, before she entered the Junior Academy. The second was aboard the Triton, Chief Grady. "He's a Catholic?"

Seeing her excitement, Jake smiled and rolled off the centre seat.

"I don't have much information on Axiologists, but considering the story of the Samaritan originates from the ancient Catholic bible, then I would assume-"

"It was more of a statement," she said.

"You know, I could meet him so you could get some sleep," Jake said, watching her pull a thin hooded over-shirt from her carrying bag.

She caught sight of his smirk as her head emerged from the smooth garment. "No, that's-" She stopped and shook her head. "Teasing me. You'll pay for that later. How do I look?"

"Too good to go out there," Jake said with a wolfish smile.

"Flatterer. Won't make up for teasing," Ayan replied, straightening the neck of the blue over-shirt. It wasn't what she'd prefer to wear while meeting someone of importance, someone educated and trained on Earth, but it would have to do. The few articles she had brought with her from Freeground were still on the Triton, and with a fleeting thought she dismissed everything she owned as being too informal, or too practical to be appropriate. "It'll have to do," she sighed.

Jake was already beside the door. "Well, when you get back from talking to our visitor, I'd like you to get some sleep here. I'm stimmed up, so I'll be helping with security, repairs, and making sure everyone gets to where they're supposed to be."

"Aye, Captain. How long is your dosage going to keep you up?" she asked.

"Another twenty two hours. Should be enough time to deal with most of the initial fallout I'm expecting when people find out I'm here."

"That's a stretch. Are you sure it's a good idea?"

"That's more a question for you, since I'm going to leave you in command while I sleep it off for eight or ten hours, if I get the chance," said Jake.

Ayan had command training and experience, but she didn't feel ready to be in charge. At least not while everything was so tentative and disorganized.

"Can you make sure a few of the Samson crew are ready at the same time I am? Especially Stephanie, I'd like to at least try to start building a bridge. Might be too soon, just yet, but I need her experience."

"She's seen rough spots before, maybe more than I have. Still, I wouldn't have signed the Clever Dream to you, or sent you to Greydock, unless I thought you were up to it. I think we'll do fine here for as long as we have to make it home port."

"I wish I had your confidence," she chuckled ruefully.

"You'll see, we'll be fine. Once the smoke clear, we'll have enough people left to turn our luck around."

"It almost sounds like you've given this speech before," Ayan said with an exaggerated suspicious squint.

"Probably. I have a bit of practice at getting back up and dusting myself off, a lot of our people do." Of all the things he'd told her, that bolstered her confidence the most.

Chapter 35
Invaders

Frost's stump tingled again. It happened every few hours, after his shin started itching, then burning and then his vacsuit would administer pain medication and nanobots would repair the worn, irritated skin as soon as it broke and began to bleed. He almost wished he hadn't checked his prosthetic during their last break. It might have been better if he wasn't aware of the crack filled with blood and pus. When it cracked, he couldn't have guessed, but it had been bothering him since they were first knocked clear of their wormhole.

The inside of his vacsuit stunk with the smell, and he quietly regretted turning down the replacement limb that had been grown in the medical bay. The thought of a nafalli in charge of the attachment surgery didn't appeal to him in the least, but the stench of a wound that opened over and over again, combined with the irritation of walking for so many hours he'd lost count made having one of the hairy non-humans affixing the limb more appealing.

The Sol Defence Encounter Suit was the perfect infantry command platform. Even the intelligence expert, Jason Everin, who had become his partner in the boarding operation, used one whenever he could. It limited them both, however. The height of the suits restricted them to large storage areas and main hallways. If they didn't have competent, well armoured teams backing them up, they would have had to leave them behind.

The gunnery deck crew along with a few security personnel made for one mean unit of one hundred twenty six men and women. They wore the heaviest vacsuits, and a third were in the smaller loader suits. They'd outfitted most of them with weaponry at the last minute, and it didn't take them long to refine their jury-rigged solutions.

Jason Everin was a genius. Frost had worked with several infantry commanders, and considered himself fortunate to know Jacob Valance, but this man was a different breed. On the bridge, the man seemed easy going and competent. Nothing seemed like much of a challenge while he was running communications and helping with security. Since the counter-boarding action began, Frost had formed a different impression. Jason Everin was colder than anyone he'd ever met. The crew of Enforcer 1109, the destroyer attached to the ship, was the enemy. There was no compromise whatsoever. He also improvised at a moment's notice. Pride seemed to have no place in his thinking process, and recognizing that a plan had to change because an assumption or idea was wrong happened as though by reflex.

Frost watched as Jason and a quarter of their forces moved around one of the shorter hallways towards the main crew habitation area. It was a fitful fire fight, with enemy crew members backtracking towards the largest berth on the ship. At its centre was a galley, several offices, showers, and the convenience store. "Second team, move up. Put down barriers for cover," Frost commanded as the second quarter of their people moved in from the other direction. "Make sure they don't split into another section of the ship." He would never admit that he could feel a cold sweat on his palms as he watched the plan come into place.

The remainder of their forces surrounded his encounter suit. There was another such suit beside him, fourteen battered loader suits, and a few dozen Triton crew in armoured vacsuits. "How goes the rush, Jason?" Frost asked.

"They're falling back, and the rearmost are starting to run into team two. Looks like they're going to have no choice but to retreat into the main habitation area," replied Jason over the sounds of pulse and particle rifles firing all around him.

With a glance at the retinal tactical display projected at Frost's eye, he could see Jason was getting close to the front of his team. Crewcast reported that he had depleted more than eight percent of his sidearm's ammunition in the past six minutes. "Stay out of it lad, you've got fire teams with you so you can use that big brain o' yours instead of getting it blown away."

"Right," Jason replied flatly.

There was no arguing. He simply stopped firing and fell back to the middle of his team. It was the right thing to do, but Frost wasn't used to working with someone who gave in to reason so quickly. His people followed orders quickly, but Frost was used to hearing some kind of counter argument when he gave advice to an equal or higher ranked officer.

The second team finished moving into place perfectly, and when the enemy crew tried to retreat around the corner behind them, they were greeted with a hail of gunfire. They were sandwiched between the Triton forces, and even though they had more numbers, they were hopelessly outflanked. In under a minute they retreated into the only door available to them, the central living quarters.

"That's it, they're contained. Your turn, Frost," said Jason.

All the other exits had been welded shut with an extra layer of plating affixed atop the door. "You said it, they're contained. No need to follow through," Frost said as he glanced at the locked panel in the wall beside him.

"We don't know what kind of tools they have inside, and there are four to seven hundred people in there. This is going to be a problem moving forward."

Frost watched as Jason took his team further up the hall to one of the main data access lines. "I still think we'll do better using this as leverage. We go through with it now and we're shooting any trust we can build with the Command Crew out the airlock," said Frost.

"We're not in a situation where we have time to build trust with anyone, especially their Command Crew. If they have any intelligence training at all, and evidence says they do, then they're not going to bargain with us."

"This doesn't sit right with me, lad."

"Frost! I'm not going to argue with you. I can't move ahead without your backup and we can't afford to get taken from behind when those people break through the doors. Either cut into that environmental panel or I'll go back there and do it myself! It'll delay my hack into the trunk line, and you know we can't afford the time."

"Aye. You're right, guess I best get used to it," Frost acquiesced. He turned and took two steps towards the heavy dividing wall. The three and a half meter tall encounter suit followed his every movement perfectly, even his limp. The enhanced plasma torch mounted at the end of the suit's index finger cut through the ten centimetre structural wall like it was made of tissue paper and he pulled the block of metal out with the other hand. After placing it against the wall, he examined the wiring that was hidden behind. "I'm through."

"Were the schematics right?" asked Jason.

One of the gun deck teams stepped forward and wrapped a band around the bundle of wires, then opened a panel on the side of Frost's encounter suit so he could connect the other end with the data jack there. "One minute," Frost said as he watched his on board computer interpret the raw data coming from the lines. With dread he saw all the raw environment system connections, and after a few seconds the encounter suit computer devised a control screen that encompassed all the options available. "Aye. Interior pressure, temperature, it's all here."

"Good. Do it, Frost."

He tried not to think about what it would be like in a bunk, the commissary, latrines, or mess hall when he did what he had to do. He'd seen it first hand when he stripped Burke of his vacsuit and reduced the temperature in an unused crew compartment. The man had taken every credit he had, marooned him on an unfriendly world, and deserved the serious frostbite he suffered. These crewmen were only defending their ship, and had been beaten back so efficiently that they had no choice but to take refuge in what they probably felt was the safest part of the ship. Most of them weren't even soldiers.

"Frost!"

"Aye, taking care of it now," he said as he directed the temperature down past critical limits. Next he reduced the pressure until it passed well into the negative range and finally he ordered the biohazard seals in place for the entire section. The audio pickups on the outside of his encounter suit transmitted the screaming through the comparatively thin wall behind the wiring and Frost closed his eyes. "It's done. Anyone without an atmosphere suit or emergency compartment should die in a minute. Emergency biohazard measures sealed them in."

"Considering how few of the regular crew wear environment suits or liners there won't be many left. What does the system say about containment breaches?"

"The pressure drop that'll happen when someone busts out will force the nearest emergency door to close. They'll have to bust through one compartment after another," said Frost.

"Good, nothing to worry about behind us then," Jason said.

Frost turned away from the makeshift access panel and ordered his people forward. He was keenly aware of the absence of sound coming from the next room.

It took them minutes to catch up to Jason and the rest of the invasion force. Jason was back in his encounter suit, and the third surviving suit stood beside him in front of a thick bulkhead door. "They know we're comin'," Frost stated.

"Open fire whenever you like, Gunnery Chief," Jason said as Triton crew members rushed around in front of the heavily armoured encounter suits, placing directional charges two metres away from the bulkhead door.

"Aye, time to pick a fight," he growled as he fired all the available weapons on the suit. The armoured door in front of them immediately began to degrade as a hail of particle weapons fire assaulted the metal. Triton soldiers took cover behind portable energy shields set several meters behind the suits. After a few seconds the air around them read over two hundred degrees, not enough to stress anyone's vacsuit. Frost couldn't help but smile a little as he heard the encounter suit's environmental systems kick in. "At least it's a dry heat."

Several chuckles came in reply to his wise crack. The door surface had turned white right to the edges. "Think we're ready?" asked Jason.

"Just a little more. It's still loosening up on the other side."

The sounds of warping deck plates and creaking metal added to the relentless auditory pounding of their suit's weaponry until Frost finally saw the temperature he wanted at the door surface and he stopped. The other two encounter suits stopped as well. "Check energy shields," Frost ordered. With a glance he could see all three suits were at over ninety percent. It was still best for each pilot to report in, regardless.

"Ninety one percent, good," Jason said.

"Ninety three point five," reported the third pilot, Mark Hunsler.

"Blow it!" ordered Frost. The directional charges exploded, sending most of the white hot bulkhead door down the hallway ahead of them in thousands of white hot chunks. "Cover fire!" he shouted, relishing the feeling of engaging in a straight fire fight instead of resorting to hacks and work-arounds. While soldiers fired between the encounter suits, Frost, Jason, and Mark led the way, marching forward with most of their generated power ready to recharge their energy shields. They were taking a fortified position that the enemy had hours to prepare.

As they expected, there were explosive charges in the walls ahead, and the hail of weapons fire didn't disable all of them. All the suits were rocked hard as the main hallway erupted. Jason's suit reported a full depth pressure break, indicating that his suit couldn't seal properly. "Fall back, lad! You won't survive another blast," said Frost.

"There's no way they'll risk the structural integrity of the ship with another blast."

"Fall back, you git! I'm not going to tell your wife you got slagged because you were too stubborn to fall back."

Jason didn't argue, he simply took several steps back and turned his suit away from the advancing group.

Frost watched his shields charge back up from twenty percent and wished his tactical scanners would calibrate faster. The burst of hot metal and following explosions had blinded everyone. Particle scoops mounted on the shoulders of the encounter suits kicked in, dragging all the smoke filled air into the compression systems so they could be dumped into the dematerialization systems and converted into energy or redirected towards the nanobot reservoir to be used to repair the suit's ablative armour layer. The air cleared and the wreck of the hall ahead became visible. "These grunts are smarter than I thought. We've got six metres of no man's land," Frost griped. The deck plating was so badly damaged that even his command and control unit chirped with an environmental warning and painted it red on his head's up display.

"Yup. We're going to have to be careful. No loader or encounter suits either," Jason said.

Frost looked at it for a moment longer and chuckled. "I've got it. Might not be able to run one of these big encounter suits across, but I know how we can get loaders across." He didn't wait to discuss it with anyone, but stepped up to the edge of the severely damaged section, turned and let the suit fall backwards.

"Frost, don't you dare!" Jason shouted, uncharacteristically angry.

The gunnery chief let the suit fall back and extended his arms over his head. It collided with the weakened deck plating below, forcing much of it down into the room beneath, but the hands of the suit caught the edge of a structural beam. He adjusted his grip and checked the integrity of the metal. With a nod he said, "There ya go, lad, a really expensive bridge."

"You could have hovered over it, you moron," Jason shot back.

"Aye, but then what would everyone not lucky enough to be in a suit do? Most vacsuit armour doesn't come with thrusters, in case you dinna notice."

"But the loader suits-"

"Right about a meter too short with their arms up. Stop your bellyaching and get ready to cross." Frost double checked the seal on his vacsuit and opened the chest cavity door. "Going to miss this rig, though."

"I could let you pilot mine, Sir," offered Mark Hunsler. "Why, that's awful kind of you, lad, I think I'll take you up-" Frost ducked as he heard weapons' fire and ran for the line of Triton soldiers. His vacsuit reported a hit right in the middle of his back as he limped for dear life over the thick legs of the encounter suit.

His allies opened fire with a vengeance, and the air was alive with bright, deadly rounds as he finally made it to the safety of a mobile energy shield. He'd forgotten to activate his vacsuit energy shielding, and the back of his lightly armoured uniform was so badly damaged he may as well have been wearing a bed sheet. He turned with his sidearm in both hands and felt something strike the tip of his weapon. Frost followed it in the air and he realized it was a grenade just as it went off outside of lethal range. The energy shield in front of them absorbed most of the blast, and the front of his vacsuit protected the rest. "Damn that's gotta be the luckiest thing I've ever seen," he said as he fired several particle rounds down the hall.

"I didn't even see it until you batted it back, epic reflexes, Sir!" laughed one of the soldiers beside him.

"No reflexes there, lass. You're just fightin' beside an Irishman on a good day!" Frost laughed back as the air cleared, revealing a retreating group of soldiers. The scanner in his vacsuit mapped the way ahead, indicating that there was a broad elevator column. "I'd wager your trunk line's right there, Jason."

"Yup. Move up! First fire team get across the. . . bridge!"

When most of the troops had crossed and they set up several portable energy shields as cover, Frost took Mark's place in the last remaining encounter suit. "Kind of ya, lad. Don't get yourself killed out there," Frost said as the chest piece closed and he watched the lieutenant, who was one of the night commanders of the Gunnery Deck normally, take a spare rifle from one of the rear soldiers. Frost knew that most of the people in the unit were painfully aware that he was the slowest among them. In the suit he was fine, and he was one of the best power suit pilots there, but outside of a loader or encounter suit, he'd hold them all back.

After he hovered across the gap he took the lead, and it was no surprise to him when several grenades came bouncing into the mouth of the hallway. He was well ahead of the rest of the unit, so he let the energy shielding take the hit. When they had all gone off, the shielding was down to forty two percent. "Nothin'. These grunts just aren't ready," he said as he marched ahead. As soon as he came to the end of the hall he sighted several soldiers and opened fire. They had erected emergency barriers that gave them waist high cover, but none of it lasted long against the saw blade like shots from his main particle weapon.

"Teams one and two! Move up!" Jason called from the rear.

Frost's eyes went wide as he caught sight of several soldiers brandishing a weapon he hadn't seen since his own time in the military. Expensive, dangerous, and difficult to handle, arc cannons were a brutal, last ditch infantry weapon. They required an exoskeleton to carry, an extreme environment protection suit to fire, and to anyone looking from a great distance it looked like the soldier was firing a thick lightening bolt, but a good arc cannon could strike its target with a thirty thousand degree focused shot.

"Back off!" Frost shouted at the armoured units coming out from the left hand hallway, forcing them back. He was just about to open fire on the right hand hallway when his suit alerted him to being struck with an electrical charge. It was the precursor to being struck with a plasma jet, and every alarm went off in the next moment. His shields were down to three percent, the ablative armour on his right hand side was gone, and one of his secondary particle guns had been destroyed. It was like being struck by lightening, and the only working on-board computer was the connection he had to the left hand visual sensors.

He blindly opened fire with the last remaining particle cannon on his arm while maintaining fire with his left. "Rush left! Take out that cover, now!" he shouted as he tried to step back into the hall and shunted all the suit's power to shields.

Another strike hit him and his world shook so hard the inertial dampeners in his vacsuit had to compensate. The right arm on his suit had been destroyed, and the shoulder reported that it had been cracked open by an ammunition explosion. The ship to ship micro rockets there had overheated and gone off. "You want ta play? Chew on this, whoreson!" He flung the left leg towards the hallway and activated the nearly overheated rocket back in the left shoulder of his suit, sending twenty eight ship to ship charged projectiles off.

When Frost came to, he was lying beside the elevator column, his ears still ringing. With a quick look around, he could see that the suit he was piloting was lying on its face. They'd had to use the emergency hatch to extract him from the machine. The entire right side had taken critical damage from explosions, melting, and plasma cutting. Evidence of serious explosive damage filled the right side of the large foot traffic hub, and signs of a fire fight to the left told the rest of the story.

"You're completely insane," Jason said as he shook his head. "But we'd be on our way back to the Triton with a lot more dead and wounded if it weren't for that stunt."

"I aim to please. Too bad about the suit, though." He looked from the encounter suit to the medic who had been treating him for a moment. "All my important bits where they're supposed to be?" he asked.

The medic smiled and nodded. "Yes, Sir. Looks like you'll be sheep dogging us around the gunnery deck as soon as we'll get back."

"Sheep doggin' – now where'd you hear that?"

"Saw a movie made in New Ireland right before all this started. Most of the Gunnery Crew did," he replied.

"It All Points North," another crewman confirmed, naming the picture.

"Good movie, makes us gunnery dregs look like heroes," Frost said, smiling.

"Found it in your personal collection and made it public. The preview looked good," Jason said as one of the Triton soldiers finished cutting through the bolts on a large access panel and let it drop to the side. "There it is, the main trunk line." He stepped up to the collection of cables and, without a moment's hesitation, reached into the bundle. A moment later he pulled several silver lines, affixed two boring clamps, verified that he had full contact with the ship systems and then deactivated all ship controls using a program he had ready on his command and control unit. "The ship is ours."

"Aye, as long as we can make sure you can stand right there patched in," Frost replied, eyeing the way they'd come and the two broad hallways to either side. "Think I might just go get the last good encounter suit."

"Sir, what will we do about a bridge?" asked Mark.

"We'll use the one with cracked armour. Damn thing's probably too fancy to repair in good time anyhow."

Chapter 36
The Burden Of Knowing

Ashley watched the movement of Oz's group through the ship as they moved towards the lower decks. They had made fantastic progress with the command deck after subduing the highest ranking enemy officer aboard Triton. The captives were stripped of their gear and sealed in crew quarters, and Ashley couldn't help but ponder the similarity between her situation and that of the captured soldiers.

Zoe kicked in her sleep where she was curled up in the seat beside her. Ashley stroked the youngster's side with her gentle hand, prompting her to roll over and capture the appendage in an unconscious hug. "Might be a while before I get that back," Ashley said with a sigh.

There was a lot going on aboard Triton, and even more happening above, in the destroyer outfitted with the Command Module that was still firmly affixed to their dorsal mooring port. Over the last few hours Ashley listened to the chatter as Frost and Jason's teams maintained possession of the lower decks of the ship, and cut main power to the rest. It was both exciting and frightening, listening in on that drama. At times she found herself cringing at the sounds she was overhearing, many of which were never explained, and more than once she was relieved to hear familiar voices after the action was momentarily over.

Taking care of Zoe was more challenging than listening to Jason and Frost's battling egos or their fight with the destroyer's crew. The toddler had taken the vacsuit Ashley had made for her with her command unit off twice and she'd already gotten bored of survival bars. There was a working materializer just outside in the main medical bay, and she could have gotten more interesting food for them both, not to mention a light blanket or a toy for Zoe, but fear kept her locked inside the conference room. There were no working sensors in medical or the aft section behind it. It would be hours before Oz's people could get there, and for some reason Agameg couldn't contact the former slaves that were fighting past the middle frame of the ship. That was a lot of space left in the dark, and the thought of running into soldiers like the ones she met in medical kept her awake; she didn't need stims.

A knock at the door made her jump so badly she woke Zoe, who looked up at her with wide, bleary eyes. "Uh oh, that's your 'I'm about to start crying because I'm tired and scared' face," Ashley said as she carefully picked up the youngster and cradled her against her chest. With a glance she could see that the autopilot was still running, her controls were still locked, and the comm was set to listen only. No one would be able to hear what was going on in the conference room.

"Please unlock the door, Ashley," Larry said through her communicator. "I have a few things for you and Zoe."

"We're fine, thanks," she replied quietly.

"Listen, I understand how you might have misgivings about letting me in, but I think I've already shown that you can trust me."

"Oh really?" she asked.

"Just a few hours ago I saved you from a pretty bad situation, remember?"

"Because you needed someone to fly the ship."

"I could have done that myself just fine. I'm sure Oz and Jason would have no trouble believing that I was able to re-route controls to this room and get us on course. I saved you because I know you're a good person, and I couldn't watch that soldier take advantage," he told her.

"Okay, but what guarantee do I have that you won't take me out just to be safe?"

"You watch way too many movies. If that's what I wanted, I could have opened the door for myself using a terminal down the hall. With the right code I can override anything as long as it still has power. Check for yourself, just bring up a raw code console and enter the word 'absolution' followed by the number four."

Ashley did as he asked and noticed that the password was assigned to her biometric ident specifically, something Larry would have had to do in advance. Suddenly the three dimensional cut away diagram of the Triton hovering over the table took on a whole new level of detail. Every wire, pipe, hatch, crawlspace, and little secret was on open display. She could even see inside the Botanical Gallery. "Oh, well, that's just awesome."

"Ashley, is everything okay down there?" asked Oz's voice from the terminal.

"Yeah, I'm fine, why? Something goin' on?"

"No, your comm signal just squelched then came back under a new priority signal."

Ashley thought for a moment, unsure of what to say. She didn't have the know-how to lie about communications, yet she didn't know how much she wanted to tell Oz. "Um, I dunno, maybe something Jason did?" she blurted.

"Maybe. He's cabling the Enforcer to the Triton so who knows. You should have flight control of the other ship in a few minutes, by the way."

"All right, that should make the ship easier to stabilize. Thank you, Oz."

"Oh, don't thank me, it's all Jason, Frost, and the whole Gunnery crew. They've taken the whole bottom half of that ship. I'm busy clearing the interior compartments with everyone else."

"Anything interesting?" she asked.

"Not really. I'll tell you as soon as something comes up though. Talk to you soon."

Ashley sighed with relief.

"Why didn't you tell him, Ash?" asked Larry.

"Maybe I'm just getting used to sitting on this fence," Ashley replied in a harsh whisper. "What was that code stuff all about anyway? You almost forced me to tell him everything."

"I added you to the system at a higher security level than anyone in the ship. I can show you how to hide your access level, so no one knows anything's changed."

"Besides you. Does anyone even know this is possible?" she demanded.

"As far as anyone knows, there's no way to get all that control and information at once; it comes in bits and pieces with the right security clearances. With that code, you override security and your actions can't be recorded, it's how I get around without getting caught."

Ashley thought for a moment, stroking Zoe's back. She was dozing off again, with her nose buried in Ashley's hair. There was no choice. Even with the extra access she couldn't see what was going on throughout half the ship, so there was a chance that a large group of soldiers could retaliate by taking medical. Besides, if Larry really wanted to get in, he would. She crossed the room and pressed the open button.

Larry was on the other side with a gurney laden with two large duffel bags. "Thanks, Ashley, I knew you'd see reason."

"I'll keep your secret, but you find a way to give the crew more control over this ship so you're not the one holding all the cards."

He regarded her with a stunned expression for a moment then asked, "That's your only condition?"

"Well, yeah. What were you expecting?" she asked.

"You know, I'm not sure. I've never trusted anyone with this before," he admitted.

"Really?"

"Yes, you're the first person I've trusted with my real identity."

"Am I safe?"

"Well, I know you won't betray me if I don't do something that's outside of your moral boundaries. That's the kind of person you are. You quietly apply your standards and expectations to everyone you know and that determines how you behave around them."

Ashley didn't know why, but she found his summary of her personality irritating. "That's no answer," she said.

"Ashley, I'll agree to find out what Citadel wants to do with Triton, if they'll let this ship go to someone aboard if you'll keep my secret."

"That's not what I asked for."

"It's the best I can do. If I gave total control to a group of people and my superiors decided I was out of line, they'd just find a way to eliminate the whole complicated mess. So is that good enough for you?" Larry asked.

"I s'pose. If there's no other way, yeah."

"Good. Congratulations, you're the safest person on the ship. As the only other person with a command code for the Triton. I might actually need your help sometime."

"I wish there was something I could do to prove I'd keep your secret, though. I mean, the more sure you are, the more sure I am that you won't just get rid of me."

Larry nodded as he finished wheeling the gurney into the conference room and pulled one of the bags down to the floor. He pulled it open to reveal a large supply of meal bars, boxed food, water, and a few other odds and ends. "I've been watching you long enough to know that you're not as simple minded as you let people think you are. How you react to gossip is the first thing that tipped me off. You love to listen to it, and you ask questions, but you don't fill other people in. The only time you really participate in a discussion about gossip is when you know you're talking to someone who has more information than you do. You don't like being a source," Larry said.

"That's something I learned in the slave quarters, I guess. They always find out who spread what, then there's a yelling match, or a beating, or worse," she replied.

He handed her a full drinking bottle. "This ship will tell me the moment something slips from your lips. I don't need something to get back to me through the grape vine, and you know there would be consequences. Even before they lock me up or kill me, I'll make sure there are consequences, and you know that."

"The ship is watching," Ashley said with a nod. "All the time?"

"Passively, but yes, everything is recorded and categorized," he told her.

"And I can see all that with the code you gave me?" asked Ashley.

"Well, yes, but that's not what it's intended for. Master codes are made for the highest ranking officers and Citadel agents for emergencies like this. The only reason why I could assign one to you is because I'm so far from home and I have the highest rank in the sector."

"So you're some kind of Admiral?"

"No, I'm a Citadel agent. We're the ones who watch the government and the military. Most people think we're an urban myth, even on Earth."

"Who watches you?" Ashley said, looking at him with mock suspicion.

Larry regarded her witheringly, a look she'd earned from him before under much less serious circumstances. "None of that matters now. We're about to have visitors and I need you to behave as though I'm no more than your co-pilot."

"What kind of visitors?" she asked.

"You know that band of slaves Agameg organized?" asked Larry.

"Yup."

"They're on their way here. Someone decided that they should secure medical and use it as a refuge from the soldiers left between here and the aft sections."

"There are still soldiers fighting back there?"

"Not many, but enough to give the slaves you guys liberated some trouble. I closed a few emergency doors so they wouldn't run into each other on their way here."

"That was awful nice of you," said Ashley.

"They're too burned out for another fire fight," Larry said with a shrug.

"How far behind you are they?" Ashley asked as she accepted a small plush blanket.

"About half an hour, and they need somewhere to rest, it's been a while."

Ashley wrapped the small blanket around Zoe, who was fast asleep again. She nearly turned away when Larry reached over and pinched a corner of the fuzzy offering. It gently came to life, warming itself and curving around Zoe.

"It's a swaddling blanket. I don't know if she's too old for it, but I didn't put mine down until I was three."

To Ashley's surprise, Zoe withdrew from her and curled up in the new bedding, which actively hugged her back. "Wow, these must be popular back home," she said.

"Pretty much everyone on Earth has owned one, sort of standard issue for babies and toddlers. I figured since she's a marsupial, it might be even better."

Ashley gently placed Zoe down on the gurney and locked the forward wheels, watching how she nuzzled the fuzzy blanket and smiled sleepily. "Do they make them in adult size?"

Larry chuckled and nodded. "Most people don't admit to having an adult sized one, but yeah, a lot of people do."

"So what do I tell Oz and Jason about where you've been?" Ashley asked.

"Just tell them I was hunting for supplies. Most of this stuff is logged with the fabricator down the hall," he replied as he pulled boxes of food from the first bag. "And you can taunt them with your Vietnamese food."

"Oh, you didn't," Ashley said as she opened one of the containers and smelled the steam.

"That's Banh bao, a kind of onion, egg, and mushroom dumpling. I figured since you seem to enjoy all things oriental, including our Wing Commander, you might want to try something a little more authentic," Larry teased.

"Did the ship tell you that too?"

"I can tell just by the way you look at him when we hang out."

"That's going to be different. Hanging out, I mean," Ashley said, intentionally changing the topic. She didn't want to think about Minh, or anyone not accounted for.

"I hope not."

"Oh, I'll pretend like there's nothing new, but it'll still be different for me," she said.

Larry handed her a pair of chopsticks and shook his head. "I know, but I still hope I can count you as a friend. You're the first I've made since I got this assignment."

Ashley glimpsed something she didn't expect then when she looked at Larry. Vulnerability. "I don't know what to say," she offered lamely.

"Oh, don't worry, I don't fancy you, it's not like that."

"Right, I picked up on that. You fancy Oz." She grinned.

"How did you-" he stammered.

"Signals on the bridge. Hope you weren't trying to hide those sparks, Steph picked up on it too."

"Guess that's one secret that'll find its way around the ship."

Ashley took a bite out of one of the warm dumplings and savoured the rich flavour. The materializer had duplicated the texture and flavour of the mushrooms and egg almost perfectly, and she was sure that what she was tasting was at least a close match to the real thing. An unwelcome, nagging thought occurred to her just then and she decided to ask Larry about it before her opportunity passed. She still waited until she finished chewing, though - eating was a slightly higher priority. "Thank you for this, it's really good."

"You're welcome," he said.

"So why didn't you just use your codes to take control of the ship and make a bee line for Earth?"

She caught him with a dumpling half way to his mouth. "That was quick. I thought it would take you a little longer to get to the important questions."

"No deflecting," she admonished with a wave of her chopsticks.

"All right, though I can't tell you much." He struck his chopsticks into his dumpling box. "Earth doesn't want Triton back. She's old, was never fully activated and the mission she was equipped for is over. Technologically and philosophically, Sol Defence has moved on."

"Oh, okay. So why are you here?" she asked.

"I'm here to learn about life at this end of the galaxy," Larry told her.

"That simple? There's gotta be more to it."

"Now there is. Since this whole Order of Eden thing came up, and they started sending West Watcher agents out to interfere with people who could oppose them, I've been doing what I can to keep power out of their hands. Fundamentalist religion was responsible for the second fall of mankind, I'm not going to sit by and let a false religion interfere with this ship."

"So you're kind of like a guardian now," she observed.

"I never thought of it that way, maybe custodian is a better word, though. I don't exactly help people make decisions. That's not my purpose here."

"Right. Still, there's more to this," she said.

"Think what you like, that's the short version."

"Someday we'll have to sit down so I can hear more. Like what's your real name?"

"Francis," he said.

"Larry's better."

"I know, that's why I chose it."

"How old are you, really?" she asked.

"Forty eight."

"Geezer, you don't look a year over twenty two."

"Earth and issyrian technology combined created a treatment like your fitness pills, only it slows the clock down a lot more. I'll probably look and feel this way for another thirty years."

"You're going to have to let me in on that," Ashley said.

He opened a small side pouch on the bag nearest to him and retrieved a small box of pills. "Here you go. I thought they'd come in handy if I needed extra leverage."

Ashley flipped the metal box open and looked at the four blue gel capsules.

"You take one a week for a month and your body will find a whole new balance. No more fitness meds though, so you're going to have to be a little more active."

"That's it? I take these and I look twenty one for so long people start checking for fangs?" she asked.

"Fangs?"

"Ever seen a vampire movie?"

"Oh, now I get it. I don't watch movies," said Larry.

"Too busy lurking," Ashley teased before stuffing a dumpling into her mouth.

"So, are you going to take the first one?"

She stared at the pills as she chewed through the dumpling. If he wanted to poison or drug her, it would have been easier for him to do it by dosing her food. The thought of it made her feel sheepish. Ashley had dug in without hesitation. It would have been the easiest poisoning in history. She finished chewing and took the first of the pills. The little box was sealed and in her thigh pocket a moment later. "There, now you're completely on the hook," Ashley said.

Larry laughed as he picked up his chopsticks. "What do you mean?"

"Now you're going to have to help keep me in shape."

"Okay, I can deal with that. Are you a jogger or a swimmer?"

"Definitely a swimmer."

"Well, looks like we'll be spending time in the Botanical Gallery," he said.

"Yup. Looks like the smell is waking someone up," Ashley said, turning towards Zoe, who was groggily sitting up. "I wonder if she likes dumplings."

Ever since she was young, Ashley knew secrets were a currency greater than cash. Keeping that currency required a further investment in the form of deception, and Ashley knew that she'd already started paying. As she watched Zoe chew on a dumpling, her eyes lighting up at the new culinary discovery, Ashley was keenly aware that Larry was turning his attention to other matters, his food, the status of the ship, hiding the extra information on the display and she took that as confirmation that she had managed to set him at ease.

He was underestimating her, and she'd convinced him that she actually believed everything he'd told her. She knew there was a lot he was keeping to himself, and for once she was glad she was brought up amongst slaves. No one knew how to hide suspicion and secrets better. He didn't even notice her drop the pill up her sleeve.

CHAPTER 37
A BROADENING VIEWPOINT

There was a delay in the network, as though she was out of sync with everything around her. Eve knew for a fact that it had nothing to do with her. There was a virus running loose in the Regent Galactic network, and its only purpose was to slow things down. It only compounded her rising frustration.

Maintaining control of her emotions was difficult. It took her one hour and twenty four minutes to force her framework body to build a micro transmitter and restore her input-output systems to their full capabilities. Emotional neutrality would have been helpful, but under the circumstances it was impossible. The maddening evasiveness of the virus, a living digital thing by her estimation, was one problem. Every time she tried to focus on it, the thing found a way to almost completely disappear. Most of the time it was as if it was in the corner of her mind's eye. Undeniably there was something there, something watching as it manipulated the system all around her, but it knew exactly where to hide millisecond by millisecond. It was Eve's human brain that limited her. Whatever that virus was, and she hoped it wasn't Gloria's essence – escaped and evolved – though she felt it must be, it didn't suffer the same limitations. It was making use of several supercomputer cores, borrowing processing time from all of them at once.

Eve's journey through the physical world was aided by her frustration it seemed. She ran for the pulpit chamber, where she knew she'd find a grisly scene. Soldiers began greeting her with expressions of surprise and fear several compartments away from where she knew the main fire fight took place. The gore left behind after the fighting was so revolting, so overwhelming in its sight, smell, and texture that she almost vomited when she first encountered it. The security recording displayed in graphic detail how much firepower it took to kill thirty framework soldiers. They were fearless, unannounced, and well armed. Under the loose direction of Beaudric, they killed one hundred and forty seven soldiers in full armour and eighty four civilians who were just caught in the middle. As one framework soldier fell, the one behind continued fighting, knowing that it was almost certain that his fallen comrade was regenerating behind him and would be on his feet within minutes.

If Eve were connected to the network, she could have issued new orders, tried to stop the frameworks from fighting or at least delay them so the human soldiers could get the upper hand. Hampon was cut off as well, and as the only other man with a master code for all the frameworks aboard, he was the only other person who could counter the orders Gloria had issued using her identity.

The first defenders were slaughtered. The second wave, which took six minutes and nine seconds to report, used electromagnetically charged explosive slugs, and still took heavy casualties. So many were killed that twenty percent of the unit abandoned their posts. They were reinforced by every soldier brave enough to rush to the scene but it was too late. Beaudric arrived at the pulpit chamber.

Everything in that small section of the ship was built ornamentally, with more attention to beautification and grand gesture than to sturdiness and armour. It took them forty-two seconds to break through the inner door and kill everyone inside.

In the end the Child Prophet was on his knees. "Please, I have the power to give you anything you want. Everything you want!"

"Why?" Beaudric asked, pointing a rifle loaded with explosive electromagnetic rounds.

"To save humanity. Everything I have done since I saw the path ahead of us has been to save humanity. The darkness comes, in every future, no matter what I do."

"The future? You really want me to believe you can actually tell the future?" demanded Beaudric.

"It's a machine, I can show you. As soon as we find Roland, I'll show you, just-"

"More lies. Everyone knows that's not possible. It's all you do, lie so we do what you want. So you can wear the best clothes, eat the best food, live on this ship."

"I swear. If you let me live, I'll make sure you get whatever you want."

The sounds of a fire fight renewing with vigour came from the hall behind him, and as though by reflex, Beaudric pulled the trigger. The first round tore through the ten year old body. Hampon screamed and held his side, curled up on the ground. The pain was obvious, but it subsided quickly. His young clone body had been augmented with framework technology, and it repaired the first wound. "Please!" shouted Hampon, raising his head. The next round caught him full in the face, and Beaudric held down the trigger.

When the defence broke through and put the man down in a hail of rounds, it was too late. Beaudric had rendered himself defenceless; emptying his weapon on Hampon, he never had a chance. When Eve finally arrived in the pulpit chamber, she was filled with loss, regret, and anger. The gore in the room was worse than anywhere else. The Child Prophet and his servant's bodies were reduced to nothing. The frameworks were similarly devastated. It was how you killed something that could store copies of its thoughts and knowledge across its entire body. How you ensured that the flesh and metal machine wouldn't regenerate when you turned your back.

"Is there anything left?" Eve asked the weeping, shocked soldiers and medical personnel that had flooded the room. "Anything?" she screamed, snatching a high sensitivity scanner from a medic. It was already tuned to Hampon's DNA, and while she found plenty around, she couldn't find a sign of working framework technology. The electromagnetic rounds had done their job, leaving all that life saving technology inert. She turned away from the sight of the Child Prophet's corpse, or what was left of it, and caught sight of something just in the upper edge of the scanner's range.

Eve held it out in front of her and got a full reading. There was another large collection of biological materials with the same DNA. She tried to look at it using her connection to the ship systems and failed. Where those compartments were concerned, she was completely blind. "Here!" she shouted, grabbing the nearest soldier. "You are going to take me right here!"

"That's a restricted area, I'm sorry."

"Look around you, you idiot! Your Prophet is dead! My children will be arriving hours from now, who do you think will have the power then?" she screamed in his face. "Who will be telling them to keep you alert while they flay you alive?"

Wordlessly, the soldier led the way to an express car Eve had never seen, that travelled along a high speed track she'd never sensed. At the end they came to a white circular substation. It was another control room for the entire Regent Galactic fleet, with five visible floors overlooking the central chamber. Hundreds of technicians, security people, and support staff looked at her from the railings that encircled the chamber.

Upon the dais in the centre was a tall seat, the source of the DNA that brought her there. It turned towards her, revealing a sickly, emaciated man. He had lost his leg half way up the femur, and it was capped with a transparent device that circulated blood as though it was a part of him. His hips were obscured by a black case that seemed as irrevocably affixed to the seat. His clothing was also attached to the chair, and after a long moment of staring, she realized that his wasted chest did not rise and fall until he made the seemingly herculean effort to prepare to speak. "It is good to meet you in person, Nora." Another machine driven breath forced air into his lungs. "I am the first Lister Hampon."

Eve dropped the hand scanner and approached slowly, the blood on the hem of her dress marring the flawlessly white floor.

"It's time you were brought into the fold," Hampon invited, raising a shaky hand.

CHAPTER 38
MEETING UGO DALLEGO

Jake and Ayan parted ways at the bottom of the Clever Dream's debarkation ramp. "Remember, get some sleep tonight," he whispered over proximity radio.

"Aye, aye, Captain," she replied. When she came out from under the Clever Dream and looked up, she stopped dead in her tracks at the sight of the sky. She'd seen studies on a gravity ladder before, but she never dreamed to see one. The surface of Kambis stretched across the horizon like a great ceiling. The deep, dark canyons that crisscrossed the world and the cities that dotted the edges like perching fireflies were only outdone by the cluster of billions of lights that surrounded the largest standing structure she'd ever seen. Like a broad tube of girders that looked as thin as needles it stretched from the surface of the world all the way out of the atmosphere. The roughly ordered ships and small people movers crisscrossing overhead seemed almost normal in comparison, even though Ayan had never been anywhere so busy, so alive.

"Impressive, isn't it? A grav ladder that was built to remove mass from the planet millions of tons at a time and to later bring water in just as quickly. They almost finished, too," stated a calm voice from her left.

She glanced at him, a man nearly as short as she was. He looked a little over forty, and weather worn. He smiled mildly at her, an expression that not only lived on his lips, but in his eyes and cheeks. His head was shaved, and from what she could see in the faint silver light, his robes were a faded blue. He was escorted by three of Triton's most heavily armed guards who stood quietly behind him with rifles held across their chests. "We've scanned him and only found evidence of a small data comm device," reported one through secure proximity radio.

"I feel pretty safe, thank you," Ayan replied quietly. Her comm unit picked up the cue and ordered the trio to start a perimeter patrol.

"Your people are heavily armed and well organized. An uncommon thing for new arrivals," the gentleman said as he stepped closer and stopped beside her, his gaze returning to the sky. "I'm called Ugo Dallego, and I'm an Axiologist of the Samaritan order."

"I'm Ayan, of the," she hesitated a moment, unsure of which registry to attach herself to. "Of the Clever Dream." It was the only honest answer she had for him. Her gaze drifted back up to the grav ladder. "I'm sorry, the engineer in me can't stop staring at that thing. I imagine they use some kind of super light alloy and gravity control?"

"Kerisite actually, and yes, atmosphere friendly thrusters and gravity control."

"Kerisite? You mean that was built before the third fall?" she asked.

"Over a century before the Omni virus. This was one of the biggest outer colonies, and if you can believe it, Tamber is where a lot of people settled while they built that structure. If the Confederation knows more than that, they're not sharing, sadly."

"Too bad, the secret of making Kerisite has been lost for a few hundred years. It would solve a lot of problems." A ship was moving into place, getting ready to traverse the passage to the planet surface and large docking facility below. "That's either very close or very large," she said.

"That's a United Core World Confederation aid vessel. About five kilometres long, three across. Not the first, and probably not the last. The Confederation is leaving, and they're taking as much raw material, equipment, and as many citizens as they can before their time is up," he told her.

Ayan soaked in the engineering wonder above her for another moment, watching as the massive aid ship passed the even grander elongated western station ring. Light flashed up one side of the station wing as stabilizing thrusters fired in sequence, righting a misalignment of the gravity ladder that she couldn't hope to perceive. She tore her eyes away and regarded the man beside her. "Again, sorry, I've just never seen anything so outstanding, in an engineering sense."

"No worries, I've been here so long I forget about it sometimes," he said.

"So, I hope you don't mind me asking, but why aren't the Confederation sending more ships to continue fighting for this system? There must be dozens of mining operations, and we read about several colonized worlds," asked Ayan.

"I'll tell you, but only as part of a trade."

"I didn't know your order were traders," Ayan teased with an upraised eyebrow.

"We adapt, and here everything is traded. In this case, I'm looking for information. I'm curious about your arrival, the nature of your people. Some of the people you rescued at Enreega have already reached Drifton and they had stories that lead me to more questions."

"I'll answer what I can." Ayan started walking away from the Clever Dream at a leisurely pace, observing the settling camp all around. The Clever Dream was at the centre of their relatively small section of the shanty port. The air was pleasantly cool, and it carried a faint, burnt scent that wasn't overpowering but persistent.

"Is it true that you are led by Jacob Valance?" the small man asked.

Ayan's eye reflexively looked to where he stood in the distance, getting ready to move supports under the rear section of the Samson so they could move it into the hangar. His armoured hood and darkened faceplate were up. There was no way of telling who it was, especially since he'd removed all identifying markings from his vacsuit. "I'm the voice of my people, and he's one of them," she answered, deciding that hiding the fact that he was somewhere on or near Tamber was pointless.

"Ah, I was just curious. Anyone who saves that many souls so shortly after an Eden Fleet attack might be able to help here."

"You're not concerned with Regent Galactic's allegations that he's responsible for the Holocaust Virus?" she asked.

Ugo shrugged. "What motivation would he have? Regent Galactic's allegations make little sense, especially when they are the only party to benefit from this disaster. I'm not going to ask you to inform my opinion of the situation. In fact, I'd rather you didn't. From what I heard in Drifton, he's done more good than harm recently."

"I hope that knowledge spreads."

"It may, but not if you keep him hidden from sight too long. The longer he shies from the light of day, the more people will suspect him of having something to hide," said Ugo.

"You have a point." Ayan thought before asking the next question on her mind. If there was any doubt in their guest's mind that Jake was somewhere in their encampment, she would be dismissing it. She watched as a group of crewmen walked under one of their ships with hand lights, visually inspecting the outer hull for damage. Her companion was patient, and looked around the landing site in silence. "What do you think would happen if he came out into the open?" she finally asked.

"You might have a few more visitors. The Carthans would most likely want to speak to him, but not about Regent Galactic's allegations," he said.

"What about bounty hunters, or under cover Confederate agents?"

"That's the problem with being new here, you haven't gotten the whole picture yet. Before long there will be just as many warrants out for Confederate agents, known patriots, well known criminals, and the price for prisoners of war will be written into law by the Carthan government. From what I hear, it would be easier to capture a Regent Galactic Officer and hand him over to the Carthans for a reward than it would be to hunt down Valance and transport him across enemy lines. His value as a bounty will wane as other opportunities come up," he said.

"He'll always be at some risk," observed Ayan.

"Not if he's the first hero of this new war. I have seen the footage of him urging people to sign privateering agreements. He is a fantastic speaker, and his reputation as a bounty hunter gives him great credibility with the right people. To see that go to waste at a time like this would be a shame. We need warriors now more than ever, and he's the kind that can bring fighters together, give them the right focus."

"I'm sure the Carthans can find their own poster boy. He's content to work in the shadows, that's how he survived so long as a bounty hunter, by moving on before most people even knew what he was up to," she said.

"Funny that you mention poster boys. They're only hiring human mercenaries. Out here the purists have the power, and as I understand it, Valance doesn't discriminate." Ugo made a mild gesture towards Alaka, who was casually carrying a crate of supplies that must have weighed half a ton. He folded his hands into his sleeves and continued. "But I don't think the Carthans are worth as much attention as you might think. As the new masters of this star, and the ones who will most likely draw the first line in the sand, they have greater concerns."

"So you're trying to tell me that Jacob could attract the other races. I think you give his name too much credit," said Ayan.

"Oh? Didn't he save an entire cargo ship filled with nafalli and issyrians not long ago? I have met three of them, they are here, and they are going to offer their services very, very soon. They don't come because they expect him to protect them like some shield. No, they will enter your camp seeking him out like a battle standard."

"You're just trying to convince me to arrange a meeting," Ayan retorted with a smirk.

"To what end? I believe that you would be much more convincing than I could ever be if I show you why Valance coming out into the open could work to your advantage, to everyone's advantage. He's probably listening in on our conversation right now," Ugo replied simply. His tone was mildly dismissive, but light. "I do have a few more questions about you and your people before I bring up the central matter behind my visit."

"Ask away," invited Ayan.

"Is it true that Triton is a stolen Earth ship?"

"There are no easy questions with you, are there?" Ayan retorted with a chuckle.

He nodded and smiled back. "People come to me for help and information. If I have the answers they keep coming, and those that have something to trade keep trading."

"Triton was stolen by Lucious Wheeler, then captured by Jacob Valance, as far as I know. The Aucharians recognized his claim on the ship as a war time capture."

"Fair enough. Your turn, what else would you like to know?" he asked her.

"Do the Carthans have allies? What kind of chance do they stand in this war?"

"Carthan territory spans across sixty solar systems, most of them are only days or weeks away, and yes, they have many allies in the core worlds. Over the next few weeks I'd be surprised if you didn't see representatives from several worlds located near the Eden solar system on the Stellarnet announcing their support. As it stands they have hundreds of military capital ships here, and I think Tamber is taking a deep breath before the soldiers from those ships start visiting."

"Visiting?" she asked.

"For leave, of course. There are over a million pilots, soldiers, and officers up there, and what's more inviting than a busy port and hundreds of kilometres of sparkling quartz beaches? This," Ugo raised his arms in a grand gesture, "is Port Rush on a quiet week. The Confederation just finished moving out."

Ayan looked skyward at the never ceasing traffic above and shook her head. "Well, that's a thought."

"If there's anything you should take away from this meeting, it's the knowledge that this moon is about to become a hub of activity, and not only because of the soldiers. The call has gone out for freelancers across the galaxy. Criminals have the opportunity to get full pardons, to become war heroes, and crusaders with too much money and too little sense will buy the best fighting tools to engage in this war so they can say they were there. Someone like Valance, and someone like you, can take advantage of that, make them all your allies and show them how it's done. I think that is why Patrizia Salustri has taken an interest in you, because she'd rather stand beside you than find herself in your shadow," said Ugo.

"Do you know much about her?" asked Ayan.

"I hear she's ruthless when faced with an enemy, generous with friends, and I can tell you first hand that she doesn't believe in charity. I only ever asked her once for help with my little mission in Drifton. Several of her crew like to stop in, though. If you want to pick up some inside information about her operation, you'll do well to sit several of your more discrete people in a pub corner while they're in attendance."

"Thank you for the tip, I appreciate it. I'm wondering, do you know much about how the rest of the galaxy is getting on? I haven't had a lot of time to catch up on news since the Holocaust Virus."

Ugo nodded and spoke more solemnly. "You can see the pulse of the universe in her people. They're lost, angry, and feel that there's nowhere to go, no help coming. Tamber is a fair example of how most old colonies are faring. The collective consciousness of man misses his cold minded partner, artificial intelligence. Chaos has gripped people by the throat, its hopelessness, helplessness. Several fringe banks crashed for good, a few core world ones, and the value of the common credit is down tremendously. Even the Carthans are looking to the Commerce Board to mint a bullion coin of their own. That's why I'm here, why Drifton exists, so I can offer a place for people who don't have anything left. A place where they can heal and find hope again."

"What about the city? I saw a lot of activity there," she said.

"The landlords with power and people took over as soon as law left. The Carthans stay in Greydock, where they have enough room to make themselves at home, especially since anyone with a Confederate passport took advantage of free transportation out of the system as soon as it became available," said Ugo.

"I could imagine. I'm still having difficulty believing that there's no law outside of Greydock."

"There are a couple of cities controlled by privately owned security agencies in the southern hemisphere, but the people who pay them are in control. New tyrants are making their own kind of law. That's happening on a lot of worlds, from what I've heard. You must have seen it in your travels since the Holocaust Virus started appearing."

"We've been too busy running from one disaster to the next," said Ayan.

"Well, every highly automated city from here to New Earth at the centre of the core systems has been set back to the early colony days. People invested so much trust and depended on artificial intelligences to manage things that society has been torn apart. I hate to be the bearer of bad news, but this port and others like them are bright spots in the galaxy now. We're starting over. This world barely survived the Holocaust Virus and we saw it coming. You'll notice I only keep the most basic ident comm." He pulled an old black cross on a silver chain out from under his robes. "Very basic, an AI would suffocate if it tried to move in."

Ayan's heart sank. She remembered Pandem vividly, what the Holocaust Virus did there and how rare it was to find survivors. The thought that there were many worlds like it was terrifying. "Then it's true. We're living through the fourth fall."

"That depends on who you ask. Those who signed with the Order of Eden believe it is nothing more than a cleansing, some kind of natural culling. For us it's a terrible turn away from progress. For them it's a garden of opportunity."

"If I hadn't seen Pandem myself, I wouldn't believe it," said Ayan.

The colour drained from Ugo's face. "You've been to Pandem?" he asked, his voice hushed and alarmed.

Ayan nodded solemnly. "I was there shortly after the Holocaust Virus struck. A few of us barely escaped."

"So few survived. I've never met anyone who was there during the destruction. The last transmissions from that world..." He shook his head as if to clear it of the memory. "I can't imagine what you saw while you were there."

"If that's what most heavily populated worlds are like now, then I'm not surprised we found trouble on our next stop."

"Well, many core worlds managed to clear most of the artificial intelligences before they were infected, but that also disabled transportation, whole sectors of the economy, communications, and most of the infrastructure. Transportation is unsafe, with Eden Fleet mounting random attacks along well known routes, and there are parts of this holocaust no one understands yet," he said.

"Like why it coincided with the return of the Eden Fleet," said Ayan.

"Exactly. I wouldn't tell too many people you survived Pandem, though. They call it New Eden now. Millions of initiates are working to rebuild, millions more are making the pilgrimage there. If there's a dark heart to everything that's happened in the last few months, that's where it lies. Some believe that Pandem is where it all started, that Valance really had nothing to do with it. If word gets around that you were there, his first in command, then I can't say what people might start thinking," Ugo told her.

"Thank you for the warning. I can't picture how they can call Pandem New Eden, though. It was a ruin, even as I was leaving."

"Not according to the propaganda I've seen. The Child Prophet has brought countless numbers into the fold, telling them that fear will come to an end on Pandem."

"Considering the terms, I've been tempted to send him a hundred thousand credits myself. The guarantee that you won't be killed by a rogue machine is pretty valuable," said Ayan.

"It's already gone past that. I've encountered dozens of true believers who stop here to trade for provisions. They believe a new age is dawning, and the Child Prophet is at its centre. I think it is all rubbish, but then I've had faith in my own higher power all my life."

"What does Earth think of all this?"

"I haven't been able to make contact since the virus first struck," he said sadly.

"I hope they're not facing the same problems we are."

"Doubtful. The types of artificial intelligences they use have different seed code, and wouldn't be at risk of infection. We also don't trust our artificial intelligences to administer over critical infrastructure." Ugo sighed and smiled wearily at Ayan. "But none of that matters here, now. I suppose I should get to the important questions. Will you be staying long and what do you need? I hear you've already done some purchasing with Ruby Sima."

"You really do hear everything," she said.

"Her first mate, Lombardo, is a regular at the Slim Chance."

"What's the Slim Chance?"

"Ah, it's the pub and greatest source of information. Talking and trading are really the only things to do if you're not a gambler, doser, or drinker."

"I think I get the picture," she said, regardless of the fact that she'd never been inside a place that accommodated all those things in combination. Her imagination was filled with visions of darkened tap rooms and drug dens she'd seen in holomovies. "We saw Ruby Sima's listings on the Mackey exchange and we struck a bargain."

"What was the asking price for this sliver of land?" he asked.

The question was surprising; somehow it was unexpected coming from the Samaritan.

He didn't let the silence grow stale. "No need to answer, I suppose it involves your fire power. I imagine you're going to assist her in a number of future captures."

"I was able to strike a deal we're all content with," she offered as an answer.

"Well, watch Patrizia, she's not wealthy because she makes good investments in the stock market. People like that will turn on you if it suits them."

"Are you sure there's nothing specific you can tell me about her? Maybe about her officers?"

"Well, she's even wealthier than she looks, and has been here for years. Most people come here because it's the first relatively safe place they've found. She stays here because she operates from a position of strength. Any more information will cost you," he said.

"It sounds like you have more to offer than we do."

"Information-wise? Probably, but Drifton is always running short on everything but residents."

"Well, we haven't finished an inventory yet, but I know we'll need parts for repairs, a heavy lifter or two so we can get under one of our ships, and extra shelters if we have to stay here for any length of time," said Ayan.

"You expect to be moving on?"

"I hope we get the option." Ayan was momentarily distracted by the descent of one of their Uriel starfighters. The blue light of its thruster pods shifted to bright yellow as they switched to repulser mode and the ship made its final descent. The struts between the engine pods had expanded into wings, giving the fighter the look of a long, double winged firefly without a tail. It set down between two other fighters, leaving just enough room for someone to walk along side. Jake, accompanied by two other similarly armoured crewmen were already on their way to greet Minh and his co-pilot. Ayan was suddenly very conscious that Ugo Dallego was watching her. "What can we offer you?" she asked.

"I see you have a lot of armed personnel. I would like to hire a few on occasion for security, and any extra food or other survival supplies you might have would be welcome. We're also low on mass power cells, so if you have a spare it could help us grow Drifton vertically. With space at a premium, and all the land around the town occupied, the only way to build is up, and there's plenty of scrap metal to get it done but we're at capacity for power."

"I'll see what I can do, but like I said, we haven't completed an inventory."

"All right. I can offer real money for security details, starting in a couple of days," he said.

"Expecting dignitaries?"

Ugo chuckled softly. "There are many residents who can afford protection. If I arrange it, they'll trust the source."

"For a fee," said Ayan.

"I'll take a finder's fee that will go towards the improvement of the Drifton Mission. The rest of the funds will go to you."

"I'll need to know what or who our people are protecting. I make educated decisions."

"How much would protection without question cost?" he asked.

"You mean protect someone without knowing the details? I don't know that there's an amount your customers could afford."

"You'd be surprised. These are desperate times."

"We'll cross that bridge when we come to it then," she said.

"Until then, why don't I give you a day or two to perform an inventory and determine what your protection is worth. Meanwhile, I'll quietly find out if anyone is in need of your services."

"Emphasis on quietly. I don't want to ruffle any feathers with anyone who's already in the business."

"They already have more business than they can handle. They'll welcome the help," said Ugo.

"So, I'll be in touch with you when we have a list of things we can trade, aside from protective services."

"Here's my ident. Be careful with Patrizia above all others." They had walked to the edge of their encampment. A young boy in a ragged green long shirt and large shoes that had been taped to his feet waited on a small antigravity sled that showed numerous dents and divots from any number of misadventures. Ugo sat on the back of it and nodded to the sandy haired youngster, who revved up the machine and plopped a broad faced impact helmet on.

"Thank you for the warning, I'll keep my eyes open. See you sometime in the next couple of days," said Ayan.

"It has been a pleasure meeting you, Ayan. Don't let the wonders of man distract you from the marvel of His stars," replied Uno Dallego with a skyward glance. He pounded on the flat bed of the small antigrav truck and it accelerated away at an alarming speed.

CHAPTER 39
THE LIBERATION ARMY

They couldn't have picked a worse time to burst into the main section of medical. Ashley had finally gotten Zoe back to sleep after her meal of dumplings and papaya salad. They bustled in like thugs, giving Larry more than enough time to reach into a duffel bag and toss Ashley a wide barrelled, threatening looking sidearm. She nearly recoiled; Stephanie had tried to teach her to shoot months before, only to fail miserably.

"Take it, it's better than a stun weapon, non-lethal, and completely point and shoot. Oh, and it looks like hell in your hand."

She picked up the weapon, a single barrelled handgun with a rotary cartridge loaded with four of the biggest slugs she'd ever seen. "I hate guns," she whispered back.

"If you shoot someone with that, they'll be completely immobilized and unharmed. Hell, even if you shot Zoe she'd be fine and she might stay still for more than three minutes," he said.

Ashley put the weapon down in front of her and brought up Agameg's ident number. "Aggie, I think your people are here. Are you already on comms with them?" She waited nervously, watching the blip near the rear of the command deck on the holographic display of the Triton, hoping he wasn't in a dead spot. "Seriously, why would wireless be offline there?" she asked no one in particular.

The boot steps drew nearer, and she moved the gun to her lap. It was surprisingly light, more like a ceramic toy. Ashley tried to open comm channels to Oz, Jason, and several other people who she'd heard on the command channel since she arrived in the conference room.

Larry brought up an analysis screen and checked the channels. "Looks like all channels are being jammed." He pointed to the static wave that spiked randomly across the small portraits of everyone she was trying to communicate with.

"Hand's up!" demanded the first soldier as he rolled into the door, pointing his rifle at Ashley.

She threw her hands in the air and scowled at him. "I'm in uniform, you jack off!" She was just as insulted as she was terrified. It looked like he and his weapon had seen more combat than she could imagine.

"How do I know you're not from the Command Carrier in a stolen uniform?" he asked, genuine suspicion written all over his face. Two more ragged soldiers stepped into the doorway.

She glanced at Larry, who was no help. He looked rattled to the core, hands up in the air, mouth and eyes wide. His performance was impressive, but it also rendered him absolutely useless.

"I'm piloting the ship. Didn't anyone tell you I was up here, making our escape possible?" Ashley demanded.

"No, someone's been jamming us for hours," said the soldier.

"Funny, as soon as you arrived, my signals got, well, jammed."

Zoe stirred, waking up thanks to the racket. The lead invader's gun was pointed at her the moment she made a peep.

Ashley didn't think; she found a kind of bravery and speed she didn't think she had as she jerked the gun from her lap and levelled the broad barrel at the lead man. "If you don't put your gun down right now and start acting like someone with half a brain, I'm going to blast all three of you to pieces," she said.

"Explosive slug thrower," one of his cohorts whispered, wide eyed. He was already slowly lowering his rifle.

The lead man looked towards her slowly and held eye contact.

Ashley could feel herself sweating. The only thing keeping her angry was where the man was pointing his rifle. The barrel finally lowered enough so Zoe, who was sitting up, startled to tears, was safe. The terrified huffing breaths of the child were almost enough to put her over the edge.

"How do I know-" one of the soldiers started.

Ashley was as surprised as anyone else when the gun in her hand went off. In the blink of an eye the three men were suspended in thousands of thin blue strands. It was some kind of restraint material that looked as malleable as a spider's web, but held them firmly in place. It struck all three of them so hard they were frozen in mid air. After a moment of stunned silence, she dropped the gun and rushed to Zoe, whose blue eyes were as round as saucers.

Larry picked the gun up and held it on the doorway, though it seemed more like an instinctive reaction than a useful act.

"What is this?" asked the lead fighter, trying to struggle but unable to move more than his lips. "Why does my face feel numb?"

Zoe's arms were around Ashley's neck like a thin vice, her face pressed against her cheek. The child was quivering. "What's your name?" she asked him.

"They call me Corky," he said.

"Okay, Corky. You're going to be stuck there for a while, and you're going to listen. I'm the Master at the Helm, the highest ranking pilot on this ship, and I've been watching that display for a very long time, making sure we get to a safe solar system where Captain Valance will put this ship in order. I understand you've been fighting for a long time, and you're probably twitchy, but I'm not the enemy." Her tone was soft for Zoe's sake, but her expression was fierce. She'd never been so angry in all her life. The sounds of more approaching boot steps drifted towards her. "That's what you're going to tell all your friends so I can keep us five by five in this wormhole."

"I hear ya, lady," said one of the new crewmen behind Corky.

"All right, just get us down. I don't know what my people will do if they see us all tied up. I'm also feeling a little dizzy."

Larry pulled a tab from the hilt of the gun and tossed it into the mess of strands. They started dissolving as a chalky gas escaped from the chip. As soon as the door was clear, Ashley pressed the close button. "They're gone, Baby, don't worry," she cooed to Zoe.

"I really didn't think you'd fire," Larry chuckled.

"Neither did I, it just went off," she admitted.

"I guess Stephanie didn't get to the part where you're not supposed to hold the trigger like it's part of the grip."

"Nope, I got to the 'picking the gun up, realizing how dangerous it was then putting it back down' stage. I have to admit, I like that gun just fine, though. Earth design?"

"No, it's a much older style of grenade pistol that was used to get past primitive weapon detection systems. I didn't realize the stunner was off. Good thing though, because if it were on, they would have all been unconscious the moment you shot them. I'll be turning it on for you, just so you know."

"Wait, that's a grenade pistol?"

"Yup. I only gave you crowd suppression rounds. Completely harmless but perfectly inconvenient."

"Okay, here," she said, offering the weapon to Larry. "If this thing can kill people, then I don't want it."

"Keep it, really. I didn't make any lethal shells and you're the only one with ammo for that thing on the entire ship."

"You're sure? I'm not a killer," she said.

"I don't want to turn you into one. If you're really that worried, just look at the display whenever load it. It'll tell you what kind of rounds you have and whether the stunner is engaged."

"Okay, now I just have to learn how to shoot, I guess," she resigned hesitantly. She turned it over in her hand and saw the display at the top of the grip. Beside it was a red switch that said SAFETY OFF. She carefully flipped it on and watched it turn green as it said SAFETY ON.

"I'll give you a few lessons when we get the chance, the practice rounds are just paint loads," said Larry.

"That actually sounds like fun," Ashley said as she leaned over the gurney in an attempt to move Zoe back to her blanket. Her tightening grip was accompanied by a whimper. "Now I'll never get her to sleep."

"Why don't you lie down for a while? I can take the first shift at the controls, especially now that we've got protection right outside."

"I don't think I could sleep either, not after that."

"Just sit up, the gurney reclines. Look away from the console for a while, give your eyes a break," he urged.

"I'm not going to argue there," she sighed as she eased onto the gurney. With a push of a button the upper half raised to recline. It felt really good to lie down, and Zoe seemed to calm down a little, reassured that Ashley wouldn't be leaving. "Now what do we do?"

"I was thinking I'd go out and talk to them for you. That's if you'd like me to, Lieutenant Commander."

"Oh please, don't call me by rank. I'll watch the autopilot from here while you go make nice. Think you could get someone running between the command deck and here so we can start talking to Oz again?" she asked.

"Just what I was thinking, but I suspect that jamming signal is coming from something those people are carrying. They probably don't even know it."

"Oh. Well, while you're figuring it out, make sure you apologize to the guys I just shot. Tell them it was a mistake."

"Not on your life. You were absolutely in the right, and you showed them you mean business," he said.

"You sure?"

"Definitely."

"'Kay, go. I'll keep watch in here."

CHAPTER 40
JAKE AND MINH

The uncharacteristically serious expressions on the faces of Minh and his co-pilot were enough to prompt Jake to lead the pair away from their fighter. The nearest enclosed space was the rear emergency cargo door of the Samson, and he led the way there without a word. With a tap on his comm unit, he directed the pair of soldiers shadowing him to start walking a patrol through the middle of their landing space.

"Welcome back, Commander. What's the word?" asked one of the fighter pilots as they passed.

"I'll be back in a minute, Finger," Minh-Chu replied quietly.

Jake swung the heavy hatch closed behind them and pulled the pressure lever to make sure it was sealed. The lower cargo hold had been modified to accommodate the plasma cutters, breach airlock, and motors for the maxjack. The heavy components were just up a set of stairs and isolated by a flimsy mesh cage, just enough to keep cargo from sliding into the machinery.

Jake checked his tactical screen for any sign that there was anyone loitering in the hold and retracted his armoured hood when he was sure they were alone. "Welcome back, I was getting worried," he admitted.

"You worry? What happened to the steadfast captain who was here when I left?" Minh smirked.

"An illusion for the masses. What's the situation?"

"It's bad, but it could be worse." Minh brought up a hologram of the Triton and cleared his throat.

Jake's legs turned to jelly at the sight of it and he sat on the stairs. The markings on the exterior of the ship indicating damage were too numerous to count at a glance, but what caught his eye more was the name at the top of the casualty list. "Oz is dead?"

"No, ignore that thing, it's wrong," Minh said as he deactivated the list with a gesture, leaving just the exterior display of the Triton. "He flat lined long enough for what's left of the ship surveillance systems to assume he wasn't coming back, but his emergency meds got him back on his feet."

"I think his words were 'I'm plenty alive,'" added Slick.

"That sounds like him." Jake sighed in relief.

"We did lose a lot of people, but things were turning around just as I arrived. From where I was sitting, it looked like they booby trapped the bridge, sealed off main engineering, the Botanical Gallery, and part of medical. I even got a chance to talk to Ashley and someone she rescued." At the mention an image of Ashley and Zoe appeared beside the Triton.

"That looks like medical, and she's using a flight console."

"Yup, she's got brains to go with her looks," said Minh.

"What caused all this damage?" Jake asked, pointing to the port side torpedo launchers and the torn edges of the hull.

"Oz hard wired most of the torpedo launchers around the port and starboard side hard mooring points to launch at some point. When they managed to get control of the bridge, thanks to some fancy espionage work by Agameg Price, Oz threatened to activate them if they didn't surrender."

"They didn't take him seriously," Jake groaned, running a hand down his face.

"Actually, they did. Instead of surrendering, they tried to decouple the destroyers that were docked to either side of the ship. There must have been some welding holding things together, because they didn't make it in time."

"It might be worth mentioning that we got a lot of this intel through the wormhole we had just started accelerating into. Our concept of how fast a lot of this happened might be a little off," Slick added.

"Right. Still, you should have seen the other guys. Oz tore those two destroyers apart," Minh said.

"The recording is in your report?" asked Jake.

"Of course."

"So, what's their current situation?"

"They're on their way here with one of the destroyers riding piggyback. Jason and Frost were directing a boarding action on the destroyer moored to the dorsal side of the Triton when I left."

"A boarding action? If it weren't Frost, I wouldn't believe it. They're nuts." Jake said.

"Well, I think it might work. When they get here we'll have a pretty good jump start on privateering," said the wing commander.

"That's if the whole thing doesn't destabilize in the wormhole and shred into little pieces."

"Who's side are you on?" Minh asked Slick.

Jake shook his head. "Ashley's our best, and all we can do is hope, and prepare. I think she can do it, and she's probably got some kind of safe guard in place in case things do destabilise. For once I feel good about getting ready for the best case scenario. Whatever credit we can get for that capture will be going towards repairing the Triton and setting up something here, though. No one's getting a bonus out of this."

Minh cocked his head, glanced at Slick then back to Jake, who was bringing up Minh's report on his own comm unit. "Setting up something here?" he asked.

"Both versions of the virus have already been through here, and a new government is establishing themselves. There are going to be opportunities here, and it might be safer than anywhere else in range. The attack on the Triton has shown me that we need a home port, somewhere we can take liberty, make a name for ourselves, and build alliances," said Jake.

"Shore leave," Minh said wistfully. "I saw beaches when we took off. I wonder if they teach surfing."

"If the waves are big enough, there's got to be surfing," Slick agreed.

Jake couldn't help but smile at the antics of the pair. It helped him keep his mood from darkening as he looked at the list of damage. He could tell whole sections of it were out of date, someone had taken whole sections of the ship off line, most likely to slow the boarding actions against the Triton crew. "If we can find the materials to repair the ship and sell the destroyer off as a capture, then we might actually be able to get the Triton fit in a couple of months. That's if this report is accurate."

"It's based on scans taken down the back trail of a wormhole. I don't think you should make any estimates based on it. Two months seems way too little from what I saw," said Minh.

"Well, there are a lot of people here looking for work. Our work force will only be limited by what we can earn. We might be able to get away with paying a few hundred with food and a bunk at first."

Minh thought for a moment, leaning against the hull. "Then what?"

"What do you mean?"

"That's not all there is to it, is there?" asked Minh in a hushed, darkened tone.

Jake didn't have to ask what his friend meant. Instead he looked up from his comm unit and sat back.

"You want in on this war," said Minh quietly.

"No, maybe I would have when we were on the First Light, but we have families aboard the Triton now, people who would be nothing more than refugees caught in the middle. Besides, I'm sure you and everyone else from Freeground didn't come all the way out here to go to war."

"But if it weren't for the civilians you'd get right in the middle," insisted the wing commander.

"I'd find a way to fight in my own way, sure, but given the choice I'd rather get Triton back together, find a safe home port, and start a life. We're going to privateer for the cause and for the cash, but we have to be smart about it. I'm not going to put our people at risk unless we've got a good chance at coming out ahead," said Jake.

"That's not how wars are won, Jake. We both know it," Minh said.

"It's not our war. We just got caught in the middle."

"Are you forgetting Pandem? I still have nightmares. There's no way I can let some imperialist corp get away with what I saw while I was down there. I can't see how that can pass with you either, especially since they're trying to blame you for creating the virus," said Minh.

"See, that's the kind of thinking that'll get us killed. I've been running this situation through my head ever since we set down here, and the stakes are too high for us to get too deeply invested in this war. There are civilians at the heart of the Triton, people who didn't do anything to deserve the danger they're in. I didn't ask to be responsible for them, but I am, and the only thing that feels right to me is getting those people back, finding a safe place for them, and making sure that they stay out of harm's way. We'll make our mark in this war as privateers, no doubt, but we're not going to put civilians in harm's way again," said the captain.

"I get your point, I've felt like there's been a brick in my stomach ever since we left the Triton behind, but we can't turn down opportunities to make a real difference if they come along," said Minh.

"You know how we can make a difference? We can make sure these civilians can start making a home for themselves, and when this war is over we might have a place to go. Somewhere we can live where we don't have to carry a sidearm. I'm tired, Minh. Watching my daughter slip away in front of me was enough to remind me of what most people have at stake here. Alice almost died for nothing, if the Triton wasn't already on her way here with the Botanical Gallery intact, I don't know what I'd do."

Minh took a deep breath and let it out slowly.

"He's right," Slick said quietly.

Minh studied the deck at his feet for several moments before nodding. "Yup. How did we get here, Jake? I remember I was the wise advisor just a few years ago, and you were the angry one."

"Oh, I'm still angry, no doubt. We just can't afford to be now."

"Anger is seldom without an argument but seldom with a good one," Minh said with a sigh.

"Now I know that's not an old Oriental expression," Jake replied.

"He's been expanding his repertoire," Slick explained. "That's one of the gems."

"Lord Halifax, I had a lot of time to myself," Minh shrugged.

"So, what do we tell people? We're going to get mobbed the moment this hatch opens," Slick asked.

"Triton is coming. She survived a siege, took some serious damage, but there are a lot of survivors and they managed to make a huge capture. Only confirm survivors you're sure of and make sure that they know we have a lot of work ahead of us."

"That's not the most positive message," said Slick.

"But it's an honest one," Minh said in an approving tone. "I'd rather have people who shy from work walk away now than have them get in the way later."

"Oh, and we'll have our first privateering run soon. We're probably going to end up doing a little work for our new landlady, who happens to be a crime lord, or crime lady, I guess you'd call her."

"That sounds like an interesting story."

"You'll have to get Ayan to tell you about it." Jake got to his feet and started up the fore stairway. "But wait until morning. Get some sleep tonight, I think tomorrow's going to be interesting."

"Where are you off to?" asked Minh.

"I'm going to do the rounds and make sure all the ships are locked down tight. Don't want any of our deserters trying to make off with anything, even if it's only half way flyable. Before you guys find a place to get some rack time, go tell Laura that Jason's alive."

"Aye, aye, Captain," Minh replied with the first earnest grin Jake could remember seeing from his friend since he arrived in the sector.

CHAPTER 41
THE ILLUSION OF CONTROL

Ashley woke to the feeling of Zoe climbing onto her chest, planting her hands on her cheeks and pushing up. To her surprise the toddler said clearly and insistently, "Ake up." Ashley gasped with half exaggerated surprise and tickled the little one into submission. She writhed and giggled wildly. "When did you start talking?" Ashley growled playfully.

"She's getting more comfortable with you," said a young woman sitting beside Larry. She was in a standard grey vacsuit, looked too thin, but could be pretty, especially with the riot of brown curls atop her head.

"How long have I been out?" asked Ashley. There were many other questions on her mind, but that was a good place to start.

"Almost eight hours. I woke you up as soon as Zoe started getting restless," Larry answered. He had half the bridge displays hovering over the conference table, but he was focusing on the virtual navigational station.

Zoe was catching her breath, propped up on her hands atop Ashley's chest. "Hungry?" Ashley asked.

The toddler nodded emphatically.

Ashley sat up slowly and put Zoe down. "Go sit at the table, I'll get us somethin', 'kay?" To her surprise Zoe listened, running over to the chair beside the pilot station and climbing up. "So you put me out last night and stimmed me up this morning." It was a statement and an accusation.

"I'm afraid so. It might not feel like it, but you're still recovering. You need as much rest as you can get over the next week," Larry replied, not looking up from what he was doing. The young woman beside him watched his every action as he worked the controls but kept her hands to herself.

Ashley started for the duffel bags and was intercepted by the spry, skinny girl. "Have a seat, I'll get you and Zoe what you need," she said.

Ashley took her place at the pilot station, glanced at the status screen long enough to verify the auto pilot was doing it's job, then back at the young woman. She filled Zoe's cup with synthetic orange juice from a liquid ration bag and handed it to her. "I'm Nerine, sort of the self appointed runner between you guys and everyone else trying to fight for the ship."

"I'm Ashley, just trying to keep this boat afloat," she replied, taking the sip cup from Nerine and handing it over to Zoe, who bounced in her chair in anticipation.

"I know. Larry here has been telling me and David how you guys have been getting us from A to B so the captain and the rest can get things under control. We didn't know you were here, otherwise we wouldn't have let that hollow head lead the way when we first came in."

"Hope there are no hard feelings about the itchy trigger finger thing," Ashley said sheepishly.

"Oh, they had it coming. If you hadn't done something about it, David would have," said Nerine.

Ashley was glad for the change in topic. She didn't want to dwell on the fact that Larry had drugged her to sleep. She had no idea how to approach it, but knew it couldn't happen again. "So, who's David?"

Nerine's barely veiled smile told Ashley more than the younger woman could express. "He's sorta taken charge since Agameg had to split. I can introduce you."

"If he's between here and the bathroom, it'll be a quick introduction." She turned to Larry then. "Can you watch things while I-"

"Sure, we're less than an hour away from emergence, though."

"I can see that," Ashley replied off-handedly as she got to her feet. "C'mon sweetie, time for morning potty." She offered her hand to Zoe. She took it and dropped off the chair, her mouth not leaving her spill proof sip cup. "That must be some orange juice."

The youngster nodded and smiled around the drink.

"It's a breakfast drink, I've pretty much been living on the stuff," Nerine whispered. She had a gun belt loaded with shells in her hands.

It took Ashley a moment to realize the shells were the right size for the gun she'd unintentionally used the day before, and that the weapon itself hung in a black holster. "I guess that's mine," Ashley muttered. If it weren't for Larry, whose eyes she could feel on her, she would have made sure the weapon was safely packed back into the duffel it came out of. If it weren't for him, she would have never fired it in the first place. Guns were something other people had to worry about, dangerous objects that were only made for one thing.

Nerine misjudged her hesitation, glancing to Zoe. "Doesn't look like you'll be getting your hand back, let me help." Before Ashley could object or vocalize how awkward she felt about it, Nerine slipped the belt around her waist and clipped it closed.

There were cartridges locked into loops around the entire strip, and the bullets were as thick as her thumb. It didn't matter that they might all be suppressive rounds, and Ashley hoped they were, it just looked ominous. Like the kind of thing Oz, Stephanie, or even Captain Valance would wear on a mission.

"Oh, I can get that," Ashley said as Nerine moved to clip the thigh strap that held the holster proper to her leg.

"Never mind, I've got it," Nerine said, the clicking of the strap punctuating her words. "Used to dress the captain on my old ship sometimes, and compared to him I don't mind at all. You smell a lot better."

It was the most awkward thing Ashley had ever heard anyone say, and she couldn't help but fix the girl with a surprised look as she blushed for reasons that were unclear even to her. "Um, thanks."

Nerine just went about her business, opening the conference room door and leading the way. Ashley followed behind with Zoe in tow. She wasn't ready for the sight that awaited her. For the first time since she'd been aboard, the large infirmary was full. There was barely room to move. They had managed to open the large emergency bulkhead and made good use of the extra space.

In every corner, on every gurney or bed, and around the nurse's station were slaves who had turned to soldiering. It was a quiet, resting crowd of people in basic vacsuits or stolen armour. The hundreds fell silent and most of them stared at her. Zoe wrapped herself behind her leg and Ashley found herself envying the youngster, wishing she had someone to hide behind.

"Apologize," spat someone in a whisper.

The man who had led the group into the conference room the night before stepped forward and regarded her mournfully. "I'm sorry for putting you in danger yesterday." It was a practiced apology, someone had told him what to say and how to say it.

It was good enough for Ashley, who felt like the eyes on her were pressing down. They expected her to be some kind of commander, a leader. "It's all right," Ashley said quietly. "Thank you," she added, not knowing why.

The need to get herself together, to have a minute in front of a mirror before doing anything else was more urgent than ever. "I have something to take care of. I'll be right back." She crouched down and picked up Zoe, who buried her face in her hair.

Former slaves quietly parted as she made her way to the medical bay's public bathroom.

Ashley took care of her and Zoe's immediate needs, and wished she had time to take a shower. Instead, she let the vacsuits run a quick cleaning cycle. She activated Zoe's without thinking, and the youngster was so surprised at the air scrubbers in her suit that her juice cup went flying across the room, Zoe leapt from where she was sitting on the counter and started running around shrieking. She was out of her vacsuit faster than Ashley could have imagined.

Ashley picked her up and stroked her head soothingly. Zoe looked at her with big, terrified eyes as she fought to catch her breath. "It's okay, I'm sorry. It was just the scrubbers in the suit. I was a little surprised when I first tried 'em too," Ashley soothed. "Though nowhere near that surprised. Then again, I knew what an auto cleaner was."

"Everything okay in there?" asked Nerine through the door.

"Just finishing up!" Ashley called back. She stepped towards the little vacsuit on the floor and changed direction as Zoe cringed. Instead she picked up the discarded juice cup and rinsed off the mouth piece before handing it to the toddler, who took it happily.

When Zoe was busily drinking the rest of her orange breakfast drink, Ashley stooped down to pick up the vacsuit. It was eyed warily. "Let's put this back on, 'kay?" Ashley asked gently.

Zoe shook her head as vigorously as she could while her mouth was on the juice cup.

"I won't turn on the auto scrubber again, promise. It won't do anything funny."

"No!" Zoe shouted, tossing her cup in protest. It bounced off a closed bathroom stall and spun across the floor.

Ashley looked at her with stunned shock for a moment before chuckling and shaking her head. "Guess that settles it for now." She tucked the vacsuit into her belt. "Good thing nafalli are never really naked." She stooped down and picked up Zoe's cup. Before handing it back to the girl's eager hands she warned, "Don't throw it again, 'kay?"

Zoe stared at the cup, not acknowledging the conditions of its return.

"If this hits the floor again, you're gonna be on your own to pick it up," Ashley reinforced as she handed the cup back.

Ashley leaned against the counter and looked around the room as she waited for Zoe to calm down before she walked back into the main medical bay. She didn't know what to say to the people waiting outside. She knew they expected something from her, maybe not direct leadership but, something. "What would Captain do?" she asked herself aloud.

She tried to picture him, to remember how he spoke to her, how he treated the crew. He'd taught her so much: how to pilot a ship, how to be a part of a bridge team, even how to find her way through most port towns. There was more, a lot more, but he'd never directly started teaching her how to take charge of people. Her comm vibrated and she breathed a sigh of relief as she saw it was Oz. "How's it going down there, Ashley?"

"I'm surrounded by liberated slaves, Zoe's had her first hissy fit, and I look like I haven't showered in days. On the brighter side, we're thirty one minutes out from our destination and deceleration has gone perfectly. Oh, and it looks like comms are working down here again, otherwise we wouldn't be talking."

She could hear him chuckle on his end. "Turns out the shielding around the charge chambers on a lot of the rifles manufactured on Triton burned through. Your co-pilot came up with a pretty simple solution."

"He's been a real gem. Took care of things while I caught some sleep, not that there was much to do but watch the auto pilot run my program," she said.

"I'm glad things are going smoothly down there. Everyone here is pretty anxious to get to a safe port. The fighting is over, the captain surrendered, but there's nothing left of the destroyer's reactors," said Oz.

"Too bad, that's a big ship. Is Agameg around? I could use his help," Ashley asked.

"He's busy checking on the Botanical Gallery. I could send him up if it's urgent."

"I guess it's not urgent. I'll get on comms if I need him. Glad he's nearby, though."

"It must be shoulder to shoulder down there, Agameg said there were a lot of volunteers."

"You said it! There are so many I almost couldn't get to the bathroom. What do I tell 'em? Now that things have calmed down, what should they do?"

"Just tell them the good news. Soon we'll be in port and anyone who wants to stay can join the crew and help clean up. Then we're probably taking a privateer contract."

"What do they do?" she asked again.

"Send them towards the Botanical Gallery in case Agameg needs help. There's more space for them there, anyway," said Oz.

"All right, thanks."

"Oh, and Ashley?"

"Yeah?"

"We couldn't have done it without you." Oz didn't give her a chance to reply before his signal closed.

Ashley took a deep breath and let it out slowly. Zoe put her hand over her pursed lips playfully when she was half finished. In response, she blew the last of her breath against the little hand, wheezing exaggeratedly and making a face. The toddler smiled around her cup, which seemed to have gone dry.

"Let's go talk to some volunteers," Ashley said to her charge.

It took a while for the group of liberated slaves to calm down after Ashley announced that the enemy captain had officially surrendered and the fighting had stopped. Zoe was a little frightened and confused when they burst out into cheers but it didn't take her long to realize that Ashley was smiling, so everything must have been all right. Before long she was looking around at the revellers with an uneasy smile, as though she were trying to understand why they were so happy.

When the group did calm down, Ashley told them that there was room for them in the Botanical Gallery, and within minutes half of them were gone, retracing their steps towards the centre of the ship.

"Ashley, this is David," introduced Nerine from her left.

She turned to face the square-jawed man. He looked only a little older than herself until she looked into his eyes. They looked like they'd seen too much, and spoke of the man's true age. There were holes across the chest of his vacsuit, all perfectly round burn marks. The bare skin underneath looked new, like Stephanie's mended wounds after they first took the Triton. He held a Triton security rifle across his chest, only it looked like it had been through a full on war. The muzzle had melted back several millimetres, and sealant tape covered several parts of the weapon on the main body. His smile was open and disarming. "Good to meet you, Commander."

"Thank you, David," she offered. Ashley didn't know what to say to him at first, but then it came to her. "We couldn't have done it without you and your people," she stated in earnest.

His smile faded, revealing the weariness it disguised.

Nerine's arm went across his shoulders. All eyes were on them, but Ashley forgot everyone else at something she couldn't help but recognize. It was something she'd seen on the Samson, right before one of the boarding team members, Amanda, left the ship at port and never returned. She'd nearly been killed when her weapon failed on a boarding action with Stephanie. When Ashley saw Amanda after that encounter in the mess hall, it was like a light inside her had gone out. The normally pleasant woman she'd come to know was gone. When she asked Stephanie about it after Amanda had left the ship for good, she wasn't ready for the answer. "That's what getting scared to death looks like, Ash. People aren't the same after that, especially if they weren't ready for it in the first place."

Ashley knelt down and whispered what she was sure she'd want to hear if she were in David's place, "You'll never be a slave again and you don't need to hold a rifle to join this crew."

A tear rolled down his cheek as a different kind of smile began to emerge. "Thank you," he whispered.

Zoe offered him her cup, thrusting it at him eagerly. He laughed and put his hand up. "No, I think you should keep that." The gun across his knees caught his eye then, and he carefully handed it over to someone standing nearby.

Zoe insisted, turning the cup and waving it in front of his face. "Well thank you, I'll give it back when I'm done," he said, finally taking it.

The conference room door opened. "Ashley, the wormhole is beginning to degrade, I need you," said Larry.

"Can we do anything to help?" Nerine asked.

Ashley looked to Zoe, whose big blue eyes looked back at her. "Would you like to play with Nerine and David for a while?"

Nerine stepped forward and took Zoe's hand. "Hi Zoe, let's let the Commander go to work for a while, okay?"

David stood up behind her, cleared his eyes and smiled at the toddler, who beamed at him.

Ashley tried to hand Zoe over to Nerine, an act that was met with desperate resistance as she gripped hair and whined. "Okay, we'll try that in the conference room. Let's go."

Without hesitation she led the way into the conference room and slowly put Zoe down. David and Nerine were right behind her, and before the little one knew what as going on, the pair were kneeling down in front of her, asking what she wanted to do.

"What're they doing in here?" Larry asked as though they weren't within earshot.

"They're going to take care of Zoe while we bring the ship into port," Ashley replied as she looked at the profile of the wormhole they were travelling through. "Someone's started an emitter on the other ship, it's forcing the wormhole to degrade."

"How far into the deceleration phase are we?" David asked as he watched Nerine pick Zoe up by the hands and gently swing her from side to side.

"Right at the end, I always plan trips so there's room to spare," said Ashley.

"Smart, most pilots only plan a drift time of five minutes at the end of a wormhole."

"You're a pilot?"

"Nope, a mechanic. I've been on plenty of ships, though."

"Well, whoever wanted us to come out of this wormhole early is about to get their way. I'm not going to wait for the wormhole to go off balance. If we come out the wrong way or breach the compression wall, we could get torn apart. Larry, how much longer will it take us to get to Carthan space if we emerge right now?"

"We'll be a few minutes away at half power."

"Good enough." Ashley opened a comm channel. "Oz, we're emerging from the wormhole in a few seconds. There shouldn't be any bumps, but pass the word."

"Problem?"

"No biggie, we're almost home."

"All right."

Ashley worked the controls and rechecked the wormhole emitters every few seconds. She knew how the wormhole systems were supposed to work, but normally had a field specialist who managed that system backing her up.

"We could just compensate, there's enough power in the system," Larry offered.

"There could be damage we're not seeing, a burnout waiting to happen. I'm just happy the emitters work at all."

"All right, I'll focus the emitters so we have a better exit point."

288

Before Ashley's eyes the integrity of the wormhole dropped near collapse then recovered. The entire ship shook, and the holographic diagram of the Triton flashed red for several seconds, alerting her to an impending structural failure along the dorsal section of the ship. "Okay, set for dispersion, we're getting out now," she said.

Neither of them spoke as they worked at the controls, and in seconds the energy of the wormhole surrounding them peeled away like a blossoming flower. Ashley watched the diagram of the Triton nervously as stress warnings spread across the upper hull like angry red spider webs. To her relief, most of them faded away, leaving damage notifications mostly around the upper mooring. She breathed a sigh of relief as she brought up the navnet display. The local network connected right away and began to fill the holographic system with markers.

"Nice work. I've never seen someone disperse a wormhole before," David remarked.

"Triton has a lot of power, and her emitter system has backups built in. I'm just lucky they were working properly, otherwise we would have come out tumbling or I could have blown the whole array."

Ashley's eye was drawn to the smaller diagram of the Enforcer's exterior, where escape pods were jettisoning by the dozen. "Oz, do you see this? It looks like the rats are leaving the ship."

"Looks like I owe Jason a fifty. He said the Enforcer crew were probably using life support power to disrupt the wormhole so they could try and escape. There's nothing we can do, don't worry about it," he said.

"All right, just wonderin'. Navnet's loading up nicely, it looks like we're going to be okay."

Seven Carthan carriers, each of them three and a half kilometres long and two across came up on navnet, and behind them were more gunships and mid sized cruisers than she could count. The port instructions came up in large red letters that said HOLD POSITION. A battle scarred command ship loomed in the distance, featuring three thick parallel hulls that were set in increasing length from top to bottom. The slanted main body of the ship, set behind the secondary sections of hull, was a flat oval. The Triton's computer immediately began marking its systems, numerous docking bays and measuring her total pressurized volume, raw tonnage, and overall firepower. It was a sleek hulled beast of a vessel, measuring six kilometres at her most broad point, three kilometres tall, and twelve point three kilometres long measuring from the greatest section of secondary hull to the rearmost of the oval primary hull. The thousands of lit portholes seemed as numerous as the stars, and as it began to propel itself the space around it distorted, as though fields with incredible energy were curving around the vessel. Navnet finally finished loading its registry information, and Ashley would never forget the name; The Oracle.

Behind it was what Ashley would later describe as several battle groups, and a non-orbital ship yard that was so large it looked closer than the Oracle itself. The boundaries set on that segment of the holodisplay couldn't contain it. "Oz, tell me you're seeing some of this," she muttered.

"We're looking at it here. I haven't seen anything like it since Freeground. That ship, the Oracle, there's something familiar about it."

"It's Expansion Age. It must have been adrift for over two hundred years," Larry added.

"Well, it looks like someone dusted it off. The entire Carthan fleet has made itself at home, too. I'm guessing this is nowhere near the rendezvous coordinates," Oz assumed.

"You're right, we came out early and we're off by about half a million kilometres. We're on the wrong side of Kambis. The moon where we're supposed to rendezvous with the rest of the crew is still on the night side," said Ashley.

"It could have been a lot worse. We could have come out of the wormhole on the extreme angle of its curve," Larry said as he watched armed shuttles, gunships, and cruisers begin moving towards the Triton.

The communications system lit up with a priority message and Ashley stared at the virtual panel on the table. "Something's up. Oz, do you see this emergency channel?"

"Yup, link me up."

"All right, mind if I listen in? They're not issuing instructions through navnet and I need to know what's going on," she said.

"No problem."

Ashley linked the incoming communication with Oz's communicator and sat back.

"Welcome to Carthan space and the Rega Gain solar system. By treaty I must give you or any passengers that may be United Core World Confederation military the opportunity to retreat peacefully."

"This is Commander Ozark McPatrick of the Free Ship Triton. We'd like to request safe harbour, rescue services, and I'm declaring the ship moored to our dorsal side as a war time capture. I hope you take prisoners, because I'd like to remand the entire crew of the Enforcer 1109 into your custody. Do whatever you want to 'em, and if there's a reward, we're interested."

"We're dispatching security and rescue ships right now. We were expecting you. My orders are to safely conduct the crew of the Triton and any passengers to the Tamber moon."

"We're safe aboard the Triton. In fact we have repair crews aboard who can begin work right away," said Oz.

"My orders stand, Commander. Please ready your crew and passengers for transport. You have ten minutes."

"Stand by while I consult my command team," Oz said with a note of finality before ending the communication.

Ashley tried not to look dismayed. David and Nerine did a good enough job at looking shocked for everyone. They look so tired, she kept thinking. Zoe had quieted down a little, but was still content to swing from her hands, her feet reaching up to touch the seat of the nearest chair. "What do we do, Oz?" Ashley asked quietly.

"I'm going to talk to Jason before making a decision. Be ready to move."

Oz watched from the flight control deck beneath the main bridge as one of the large armed Carthan troop transports docked with the emergency port. They had just finished clean up, and several crew members were performing repairs on the consoles. "Another ambush, is it Tuesday already?" Oz said quietly.

"No, this sounds political," Jason replied over their encrypted connection. "I knew this was a possibility, especially in a military port. If Jake's been declared a war criminal…"

"Then this ship is a legitimate capture, even if he's on the same side as the Carthans. Minh didn't say anything about any of the other ships getting taken. Wouldn't they be captured under the same terms?"

"They weren't taken from a Sol System military base. They can seize this ship under rights given by a whole different law book," explained Jason.

"So, what you're saying is we don't have a legal leg to stand on," said Oz.

"Not at the moment. How are our military options looking?"

"We don't have any. We're in range of enough firepower to slag half a moon, and I can see at least one long range interdiction array from where I'm standing."

"We've got the Enforcer all to ,ourselves though. We just have to claim it under the right privateering licence. Minh's dispatch said our licence was under Ayan. The Enforcer needs major electrical work, they burned out the controls and her operating software has been wiped. Oh, and her reactors would have to be completely rebuilt," said Jason.

"What you're saying is we've got an oversized pressurized box," Oz said.

"Exactly. It's an intact box, though, without much structural damage."

"Life support?"

"Emergency systems have a couple of days left in them, but I don't know much beyond that. I'm bringing Frost into this conversation," said Jason.

"We turning tail?" Frost said as soon as he knew he could be heard.

Agameg came into the lower bridge and surveyed the room with a sweeping glance. Technicians who were quietly listening in on the conversation were turning away from their work. People who were removing refuse stopped where they were and put their loads down quietly. The issyrian's eyes narrowed to slits and fixed on Oz, who wished he would be giving everyone better news. "No, we're leaving Triton temporarily while we get things sorted out."

"Sounds like you're letting a bunch of bureaucrats tell us we can't stand on the deck of our own ship. I'm speaking for everyone when I say-"

"Can it, Frost," Oz said firmly.

"Now you wait just-"

"Look out a window, shut your hole, and use your brain for one second. This is a fight you can't win with a gun," said Oz.

"What if Captain Valance is on his way here right now? What if he's got something no one's thought of? He's done it more than once," said Frost.

"If he's not on comms, then he probably doesn't know we're here. Besides, it looks like the warrant they have out for him is why we're being ordered to abandon ship. What we need are solutions, so tell me how the systems aboard the Enforcer look, please?" Oz asked forcefully.

"On the Enforcer? They're fine if you're looking for scrap, but I wouldn't even try to turn the main electrical board on, and we detonated a high powered EMP right in the middle of their reactor room. Where's Chief Grady?"

"The Botanical Gallery. He's been controlling Triton's main power systems from there."

"Well, that explains a bit."

"Would you move people onto the Enforcer?" asked Jason.

"I wouldn't move my Aunt Elaine aboard, and she's a crotchety bitch. What we didn't tear up disabling this boat was ripped apart by her crew before they abandoned her," Frost said.

"So much for plan B. Jason, get something ready to transmit to Carthan authorities so we can lay a claim on the Enforcer."

"Already done, and I have a rough appeal for possession of the Triton ready to go. It's all on your comm."

"All right, I'm sending a notification to all sections to get ready to evacuate."

"You could lose the crew over this, Oz," Frost warned.

"Not if I have you and all the other commands backing me." Agameg nodded his acceptance as Oz said the words. He had taken command of the liberated slaves, and it was all Oz could do to hope that they would all follow the cunning issyrian. "I need you to be in line with this," Oz appealed to Frost.

"Aye, on one condition. We come back. We bled for her, we earned her."

Oz hadn't known Frost long, but he was absolutely certain that committing to that promise would define his purpose until he delivered. "You have my word."

"All right, my people will fall in line."

"Oh, and Frost, make sure everyone knows: if it isn't nailed down, we take it with us. Now extract your people from the Enforcer, get anyone who can crawl in a loader suit set up in one and start loading everything you can find into containers. Start with guns and ammo."

"Oz, shouldn't we start with survival gear?" Jason asked.

"Everyone else can work on survival gear. Guns will trade faster than anything else we take with us."

"Good point. I'll pass the word to the commands. You start bargaining for more time with the Carthans."

CHAPTER 42
DEPARTURE

It took everything Ashley had to keep the tears at bay as Larry showed her how to activate the Triton's evacuation systems. Throughout the ship, directions to the main hangar and operational docking points would appear on the floors. No one could get most of those automated assistance systems working while they were aboard the ship, and the fact that she was just learning about them as they were about to leave was almost too much to take. Zoe was back in her arms again; she knew something was going on, and silently looked from one person to the next.

If it weren't for her, Ashley knew she'd be in pieces. David and Nerine had already gone to inform everyone of what was going on. She could hear them packing everything they could find in the medical bay onto rolling chairs, gurneys, and into the few crates they had at hand.

"I'm not staying this time," Larry whispered to Ashley as he finished his tutorial. Wherever the ship had emergency power there would be arrows and written instructions guiding everyone to docking ports or hangar decks. Carthan transports were already linking with the ship, and the first people they took were the captured Regent Galactic contracted soldiers.

"I thought this ship was your assignment?"

"She is, but I can learn a lot more by going to ground with your people."

"Spying on us is more important than staying with the Triton?"

"It's hard to explain, Ashley. Citadel's instructions to someone like me, so far away from the council, are layered. There's a whole list of priorities to consider. I don't know if you'd understand."

Ashley looked at Larry as though seeing him for the first time. His condescending tone was insulting, yes, but she couldn't help but be almost certain in her suspicions. He was lying to her. Anything he had told her, his promises, they could all be as substantial as smoke.

"Well, all the emergency systems are doing what they're supposed to," he said with a nod.

She had never been more nervous in her life as she watched him shut down the conference room table. He didn't even look like he noticed her staring at him. "What's so important about us?" she asked quietly. Zoe buried her nose in her hair and squeezed her neck. The toddler could tell something was going on.

"Ashley, I told you, there's no time," Larry said irritably as he turned towards her.

Just as she'd seen in numerous gunslinger movies, she jerked her gun from its holster and tried to pull the trigger.

"What the hell are you doing?" Larry shouted, rushing her over the table.

Ashley pressed her thumb against the safety and pulled the trigger again. Larry was caught right at the front of the disabling tangle of surging material. The rear half of the conference room was nothing but stretched strands of the stuff, and Larry hung unconscious in the middle.

Zoe looked at the mess, at first astonished, then, to Ashley's surprise, she giggled.

"Fine, don't tell me," Ashley said, cringing at the sound of her own voice. The tears she held back rolled over her cheeks as she reactivated the safety and shoved the weapon back into its holster. Guilt at what she had done was strangely absent as she wiped her face and composed herself. She picked up the last duffel bag and strode to the door. It opened automatically at her approach. A pair of liberated slaves looked over her shoulder wide eyed and she said; "Don't ask," in a far more dire tone than intended.

Without hesitation she dropped her duffel bag, turned on her heel and hit the close and lock icons on the door panel. "Bye," said Zoe in a sweet sing song squeak as the conference room doors closed.

***

Oz had won an hour for the crew to gather their things and clear out of the Triton. He passed the word using Crewcast and then cleared out the few things he had in his quarters. He checked Jake's quarters, his ready room, picking up a few things there and packed as many important looking articles from Ayan's smaller quarters. He then made his way out of the command section. All their possessions amounted to two duffel bags and a medium backpack, all of which rested at his feet with travel tags he barely remembered spraying on with his command and control unit. He'd done it so many times during his Freeground Military career that it was reflex.

The main hangar was filled with crew members getting ready to leave. Most of them helped load survival gear, personal items, and anything else they could manage to cram into a storage unit. Some of the crates were short enough to sit on, while the largest were three meters tall. Transports had started latching on to the rear airlocks, and at first the pilots were surprised to see more crates and bags than people. After seeing the irritated, lost, and weary faces of their passengers, they abandoned any efforts at informing them that personnel were their priority. "This is a rescue mission," one was overheard saying.

"This is an eviction," shouted an incensed crew member. That drew attention, and few of the dozens of Triton crew who turned their heads cared about who said it. They regarded the pilot, who quickly realized that he could be in real trouble if he said or did the wrong thing. Wisely, he quietly returned to the airlock, and took refuge in his cockpit. After all, most of the remaining Triton crew were armed and fresh from a fight they universally felt should have won them the ship. All of it happened as Oz supervised from the sidelines. He, like most of the crew, was in shock. They had narrowly won the day, but an entirely different set of circumstances from a completely different entity were forcing them to surrender. As he checked to see if Ayan or Jacob were in communications range again, he asked himself what he'd do if he were in command of a law abiding fleet and ran across a crew running a stolen ship. He wouldn't dare say the answer aloud, but it nested in his consciousness like an infected sore. The law says this ship should have been turned in as soon as it ran into any large law enforcement or military organization. If it came into the Freeground Docks, it would have been cleared of crew and reported to Sol Defence. If they didn't pick it up after three years, it would either get absorbed by the military, decommissioned, or stripped of arms and put up for auction. He shook his head and watched as one of the airlocks closed and the transport detached, filled with cargo and crew. He was told they'd be holding position near the Triton while everyone finished loading. Then where will we go?

The constant, slight changes in air pressure resulted in a stirring that felt like a swirling wind. It felt strange across the stubble forming on the top of

Oz's head. The smell of ozone, a sure sign of a heavy fire fight, was carried through the air. Surprisingly, most of the other evidence of the violence that had taken place in the main hangar had been removed. The three ruined fighters, damaged equipment and dead crewmen had all been cleared away. The scorch marks on the deck and bulkheads were superficial. Most of them could be wiped away thanks to the resistant surfaces.

Assistant Deck Chief Paula directed the maelstrom with the assistance of the remaining deck crew. Oz tried to picture everything on its way out onto transports on the ground. He could see that the short Deck Chief had a method. She was setting all the packed crates into a certain order, and made sure a couple of her people would stay with each transport to carry her instructions out when they arrived. It was his officer training that kept him from getting involved with the minutia, but it was difficult not to when the alternative was supervision, which sometimes allowed for enough time to think about the long range implications of what was going on.

The arrival of Frost and the gunnery crew on the main hangar was a welcome surprise. They came down over the aft side of the ship carrying bulk containers. Oz watched as they came up one of the secondary elevators leading to the servicing hangar. There were over thirty loading suits left, and Frost wore the taller, armed encounter suit. The machine was pitted and scarred by projectile and heat weaponry, the cost of Frost unrelentingly leading the charge on the Enforcer. It carried heavy cargo containers in both arms, and limped, just like Frost did thanks to his prosthetic leg.

His people had done their part in collecting everything they could carry. Oz's scanning systems informed him that Frost alone carried over four and a half tons of cargo. The rest carried half as much or more each in cargo and ammunition cases. A crowd of lesser armoured crew from the upper decks elevated into the main hangar next; they carried even more equipment between them, and all of it was from engineering stores. Parts, smaller fabrication machines, portable power units, and other semi-portable systems were carried off to the side in haste.

"Feels wrong looting our own ship, lad," Frost said to Oz over a private channel.

"I know. I'll do everything I can so we're loading all this back up before you can climb out of that suit."

"Aye."

"How are things going on the upper decks?" asked Oz.

"Commander Everin's gang are almost finished getting all the footlockers registered to living crew together, they should be down the shaft in a minute. Then they're heading back up to clear weapons lockers and survival gear out of storage. He plans on working until the last minute. There's not going to be much to look at when he's finished. He should be down here soon. Said his people don't need much help on the ransack."

"What about the rest of the crew?"

"They're takin' armfuls from Everin's people, when they get here things are gonna get stacked right quick. Need anyone to head into the ship and pick up some of the heavier gear? We're all finished taking what we could from the upper decks," said Frost.

"Paula's got operations here covered. Head into the manufacturing section and see if you can get one of the medium materializers or mass converters ready for transport."

"That's going to be murder to get out without pulling a few hundred bolts."

"Cut the deck out from under it if you have to. Consider it a timed challenge. You have twenty minutes, tops."

"Aye, we're on it. Makes me wish Chief Vercelli were here, he'd have some idea how that's done."

"I'm just glad we still have Paula," said Oz.

"She's a bit of a screecher, but I haven't seen much better, fine replacement," Frost acknowledged.

"Oh, while you're in the manufacturing bay, have any extra hands you see take finished work and stuff it into containers, we're taking everything we can."

"Aye, I'll watch for guns and ammunition first."

"Good thinking, Chief. Get to it."

"Aye, Commander."

The main freight elevator arrived with the third or fourth load of people from the lower decks, Engineering, and the Botanical Gallery. Everyone was laden with bags, personal items wrapped up in blankets, footlockers, and bags of all different shapes and sizes. Just watching them join the growing mass of civilians and crew members was enough to emotionally exhaust him. Few people paid attention to Oz, standing about twenty meters away from the growing crowd. He served for such a short time on Triton that few, if any, of the crew members had a chance to get used to him. Before the defence of the ship began, all of the respect he enjoyed was borrowed, on loan to him from Captain Valance. Since then he'd managed to gain the respect or the security and gunnery staff.

If Frost didn't have a bond with his people before, it was evident that he'd developed one since they started fighting. To watch them, loaders, mechanics, and gunners, move from one task to the next like one coordinated unit was to see plain evidence of how they had come together. Chief Grady had united his technical teams, and led them in maintaining the security and functionality of the Triton's critical systems. In situations where Oz was forced to use man power and firepower, Liam Grady found ways to use doors, energy fields, and impassable traps. Trying to penetrate into the core of the engineering section of the ship became so dangerous that the enemy had no choice but to turn their attention to the bridge. Agameg Price, not a chief, but a versatile lieutenant commander, had gained the trust and allegiance of all the slave volunteers. Oz would have to find out where the shape shifter learned advanced ship combat tactics and how to keep so many people motivated under potentially confusing and terrifying circumstances.

"Is it all right if we begin grouping the civilians up so we can move them to the transports, Commander McPatrick?" asked one of the security staff from behind.

Oz thought for a moment. There was no contact from Jacob, Ayan, or anyone who had gotten free of the Triton early on. "Start organizing people into familial groups if you can. Don't let them board the transports."

"Familial groups?"

"Don't split up families."

"I know, but at most I think there are a few married civvies, not many whole families."

"If people look like they want to stick together, make sure they stay together," said Oz.

"Aye, aye, Sir."

The Triton soldiers he was seeing were a far cry from what they were before the fighting began. Those who survived had seen ship board combat that made everything any of them had ever experienced pale in comparison. The fighting was beyond Oz's experience as well. Not even Pandem was as relentless, or as painful. The memory of his particle rifle rattling against his shoulder was so vivid that it was like a phantom sensation, real the instant he conjured it. The feeling of being shot, and the emergency medical technology kicking in at the same time as the emergency stasis drugs was at the top of his mind as well. He understood Jacob Valance more clearly than ever before. The man had died at least twice, and it must have been a mind blowing, life changing thing each time. The pain was only a notification that something had happened. When the pain stopped, the real changing experience began, and for Oz it was the fading of light from the outer edges, until all that was left were memories, concerns, and parting thoughts. His sisters, nieces, nephews, and the people he was failing filled his thoughts. Oz had heard some soldiers who passed the brink say it was about letting go, falling free from the world, but for him it was like trying to keep his head above water in a black sea, putting every ounce of effort into taking another breath, grasping at the fleeting light and finally fighting the terrible numbness.

His rational mind knew his heart had stopped beating, his wounds were too great for the medical system built into his ribcage using technology developed by Doctor Anderson and Freeground Special Projects, to heal while he was moving. Medication was being administered, and though what he was feeling may have felt like dying, but it was actually deep stasis. It didn't make a damn of a difference emotionally. The lights were going out and he was being pulled out of the fight. When he watched the enemy commander raise his pistol and point it at his forehead, he was sure he had seen his last fire fight.

"Sir, the Clever Dream is incoming," announced one of the Triton security officers nearby.

Oz looked to the rear of the hangar and could see two armed transports docking, but that's all. "Where are they?" he asked.

"Just caught a glimpse of them sliding into the landing bay below. They should be coming up the elevator soon."

"Someone's jamming their signal."

"What should we do, Sir?" asked the officer.

Oz's eye caught sight of the fellow; he was several meters away helping to organize the civilians and the first of the liberated slaves. His armour showed signs of repair, and his rifle the scratches, dents, and burn through spots on the casing that told him he was looking at one of the security officers who had been right in the middle of the fighting. He could tell from the shrapnel pattern across his shoulder that it was Tim Vernon, one of the last surviving bridge security officers. "We make sure they're safe and clear of any interference once they're on deck," said Oz.

"Yes, Sir."

There wasn't much chance of random interference. The Carthans hadn't put any armed personnel on the deck yet, and they hadn't made any demands other than the general evacuation of the ship. Jason was right, this was political. Oz only hoped that they were doing the right thing by abandoning the best ship they had.

Ashley emerged with the next group on the cargo elevator. Zoe's head swivelled to and fro, her eyes taking everything in from where she sat in the young woman's arms. With an excited cry that Oz could hear from where he was standing, Zoe nearly leapt out of Ashley's arms, finding her way to the deck suddenly, roughly. To his relief, the youngster didn't hurt herself in her haste, and she ran between the legs of startled survivors.

In scant seconds she made it across the growing crowd of civilians to a woman with long dark hair who knelt down to catch the eager child. Zoe collided with the woman so soundly that she was forced from kneeling to sitting. It was the sight of a glad reunion.

That was until he looked back to Ashley, whose vacant arms were slowly lowering. In the corner of his eye, Oz could see the black hull of the Clever Dream rising on one of the main elevation pads, but his attention on Ashley was unwavering. He was watching her slowly fall to pieces as she hesitantly turned away.

A few worried looks followed her as she took hasty steps to an unmarked Uriel fighter that never made it to the loading rack. Oz caught up to her behind it. At first there was no recognition in her eyes when she looked at him. As soon as she realized who he was, she made an attempt to speak that fell apart before she could make a sound.

He took her shaking hands in one of his and wiped tears away with the other. "It's going to be all right."

"S-sorry, I should be happy. Crewcast said she was an orphan," said Ashley.

He guessed she meant Zoe, who was in the arms of another adoptive mother in a loose hem dress over Ashley's shoulder. "Children don't forget us easily. She'll know you whenever she sees you. Take it from someone with nieces and nephews who grow up while he's away for months at a time."

Ashley's shuddering sigh was an attempt at relief, a failed one. He tilted her chin up so he could look her full in the face. "It's going to be all right," he repeated.

Her dark brown eyes averted his, rolling away and finally closing. "Everything's been changing for so long, I wish it would just stop. I don't know what I'm doing anymore, where I'm supposed to be," she wheezed.

Before his eyes Ashley was only getting worse. Her despair was becoming panic, and she was starting to hyperventilate. He'd seen someone fall apart before, when he was delivering the news that someone's son, their child, had died under his command. It didn't matter how old the serviceman was, it was still a mother's child, or a father's son. Ashley was mourning something else, but it was just as damaging. Relentless uncertainty damaged people, it was something he knew, and he'd watched his mother suffer through it while his father as well as both grandparents served the Freeground military. His mother was committed for several weeks after his grandmother didn't return from a tour. That was the beginning of Oz's teenage years, when his grandfather retired from his term of service, and when he went to live with him.

It was a sequence of events that changed him forever, and for a long time it seemed like he was on unsteady ground. He reacted by rebelling, but the young woman in front of him was taking it differently. She was taking it exactly the same way his mother did. He pulled her into his arms and held her tightly.

"Ashley?" asked Liam Grady as he came around the rear of the Uriel fighter.

Oz was rarely so relieved to see anyone. Neither was Ashley, who gently extracted herself from Oz and practically fell into Liam Grady. He was wearing his robes over a thick, armoured vacsuit, and they closed around her like a blanket. "It's all right. We'll be off soon and onto solid ground," he reassured her. "I hear the moon we're heading for boasts a few beaches."

Oz made eye contact with him and mouthed, "what about engineering?"

Chief Grady silently replied, "all set."

The woman Zoe had been so desperate to reunite herself with came around the rear of the fighter with the toddler in her arms. As soon as the blonde youngster saw Ashley she reached for her, and Ashley did her best to wipe her tears and straighten herself up at a moment's notice.

"I'm Vivian, and I see you met Zoe," presented the newcomer. "Thank you for taking care of her, I was frantic when I realized she ran back to the infirmary. The Botanical Gallery was closed off when we realized."

Zoe patted Ashley's face and smiled. "She's very special," Ashley sniffed. "Kept me company while I piloted the ship."

"I adopted three from Pandem. Zoe's the youngest, but she still runs circles around the others. They're only human, after all."

The scene was deeply touching, but more importantly, it was bringing the emotional storm Ashley was suffering through under control. Oz was more than relieved. They didn't have enough pilots to get the last of their fighters off the deck as it was, losing her would mean one less pair of wings, and it would demoralize many survivors. Ashley was well liked, and people would share in whatever sadness she presented.

"What's going to happen to us?" asked Vivian quietly.

"We're headed to a land base that our command crew have established," Jason said as he came into view. "They're going to make room for everyone, and we're taking equipment and supplies with us."

"Why are we leaving?" she asked.

"Triton is going to be inspected and serviced so we can register her with the Carthans," he replied smoothly. There was no hesitation or change in his mannerisms as Jason delivered the outright lie. "We could be off ship for a few days, or it could be a couple of months. We took a lot of damage. But on the brighter side we'll have a lot of time on a terraformed moon."

"Thank God. I might get a good night's sleep," said Vivian.

"Sorry to break things up, but if you could group up with a few people you know over there, and help take charge of the kids we can start organizing things so we can get settled down there as soon as possible," said Oz.

He watched Ashley as she planted a great big kiss on the top of Zoe's head before waving and grinning at her. "See you soon, Zoe!"

The youngster squeaked, "Bye!" as she was carried off towards the growing crowd of civilians. A young boy and girl watched wide eyed as they waited for Vivian to re-join them.

"I'll be okay," Ashley whispered to Chief Grady. "Sorry I cracked up."

"Don't worry, I have three sisters. Freak outs like that used to happen weekly," Oz reassured with a big toothy grin. "I have battle scars."

"Ohmigosh," she snorted.

She was a creature of emotional extremes. It might have been one of the reasons why he liked her, since two of his sisters were the same. As much as he wanted to spend time getting to know her a little better, the sight of the

Clever Dream's main debarkation ramp lowering reminded him that they were in the middle of a crisis. "First round's on you when we manage to find a port tavern," he said as he walked past her.

"Can't wait to deliver on that," she replied.

Jason was right on his heels. "This is like watching a star liner crash in slow motion. There's enough firepower to vaporize the ship four times over pointed at us, and those armed transports haven't even opened their inner airlock doors yet so we don't know what kind of force they're about to put on our deck," Jason whispered irritably. "Any ideas cross your mind?"

Oz stopped a few meters away from the bottom of the Clever Dream's debarkation ramp and watched Ayan, who was dressed in a vacsuit with no extra armour. She wasn't even carrying a sidearm, but her stoic expression and forceful march was enough to inform everyone who saw her that she was there with a purpose. Fourteen Triton troops in the heaviest armour available followed her in a double column.

"Someone was listening during the psych portion of Officer Candidate Training," Jason muttered.

"Your wife is waiting for you inside," Ayan told Jason. "She's missed you."

"It's mutual. I'm going to copy the data from the destroyer into the Clever Dream's computer just in case. I'll be watching from there." Jason nodded and headed inside.

"I hope things are going better down there," said Oz.

Ayan gave him a warning glance that told him everything he needed to know about the conditions of their destination. It was so quick, and so close that only someone watching a close up on a surveillance feed would have caught it. "I'm just glad to see you safe and sound. Had some trouble staying that way though," she plucked at one of the thinner parts of his vacsuit, where it had patched itself after he caught a round in the stomach.

"It's been a hard ride." Oz couldn't help but notice that one of the guards in the middle of the group had a Spectral Dynamics Violator handgun in his holster, the favoured weapon of Jacob Valance. Other than that, there was no way to tell him apart.

"Have you met the locals?" Ayan asked.

"I think we're about to. You probably know more about this government than I do at this point, I think I'll follow your lead." He gestured towards the broad airlocks at the rear of the hangar. They were finally all open, and several military crew people were emerging. They wore grey and light blue uniforms, of an older style, but it was plain to see that they had a protective lining built in that would serve just as well as any basic vacsuit.

"Then fall in, Commander," Ayan said with a crooked smile.

He fell in with the rest of the security detail beside Jacob, who gestured for him to pass into the middle of the detail. He was surrounded by guards.

At first the glances and stares that greeted Ayan were tinged with smiles, but there must have been something in Ayan's expression that conveyed the seriousness of her purpose. Oz only wished he could see it. "Who is the commanding officer here?" she asked clearly and calmly. She had the attitude of someone who didn't have to yell, didn't have to demand, but expected that all her questions would be answered.

"I'm Fleet Warden Kimberly Harrison," a woman with short cropped blonde hair said. She was thin and tall. "And you are?"

"Ayan, Commander of the Triton, Clever Dream, and owner of a privateering fleet currently surrounding this ship. Why have you demanded that my people abandon ship?"

"Ownership of the Triton is being contested by a former Captain. He claims that it was pirated a short time ago. Do you have a warrant or order to repossess that could counter the claim?"

"Produce the accuser and I may consider your charge valid," Ayan retorted casually.

The Fleet Warden turned towards the airlock behind her and nodded. One of her men shouted, "Captain, you've been requested."

Oz watched the dark, plush interior of the armed transport over Ayan's shoulder. He could hear someone walking slowly down the aisle towards the airlock opening. First came the Freeground style, dark military boots. It was said that Freeground combat boots were made so well that when a pair of structural engineers were struck full on by a solar flash, they were identified by the serial numbers on their soles. The hem of a dark imitation trench runner's long coat followed. It was made in the style of the type old Earth infantry once wore during an almost forgotten war. It was made to deflect most projectiles of the day, and to serve as a blanket during long nights in the post nuclear war trenches.

Oz's stomach tightened in a knot, and he made a conscious decision that was counter to his greatest desire. A silent step placed him at the side of the man who was carrying a Violator handgun. He recognized Lucious Wheeler at the sight of his jaw line and, just like he'd seen in footage of Jacob Valance's bounty hunting days, Oz made sure his hand was pressing down on the hilt of the other man's sidearm before Jake could draw.

He beat him by a split second, and when Jake's blackened visor, adorned with the blood red skull mark of the Triton boarding team, looked at him, his heart jumped. In that moment he was grateful he couldn't see Jacob Valance's bare face.

Ayan was more composed, and cleared her throat loudly. She couldn't keep her eyebrows clear of a scowl, but the rest of her face was surprisingly passive. "Secure arms," she said flatly.

"You wouldn't want to kill a Carthan asset, now would you?" Lucious Wheeler said as he stopped at the inner door of the airlock. "Ayan, I see you've made some changes. Too bad you've lost your figure. Any chance I'll get to meet your better half? I see his First Officer here, he can't be far off."

Flushing involuntarily from the barb, Ayan ignored Wheeler entirely. "Fleet Warden, this man is not to be trusted. He was an ally of Vindyne, a subsidiary of Regent Galactic. He's also not the original Lucious Wheeler, who was killed aboard. If the original Lucious Wheeler were here, I'd advise that you arrest him, because he stole this ship from the Sol Defence fleet. He has no claim to this ship, whereas the Aucharian government recognized the Triton as a war time capture and registered it under Jacob Valance. He then made myself and Terry Ozark McPatrick commanders under him. In his absence, legal ownership in the nearest sector falls to us."

"I'm afraid that's not something that will be decided here, Commander Rice."

"They know all about all my associations, darlin'. I've traded my way to their side, and Triton's a part of that sweet deal, so it's time to hand over the command codes," sneered Wheeler.

"Making this personal won't help anyone Wheeler," chastised Fleet Warden Harrison. "I'm afraid he's right, however. I'm here to take possession, and I'll need the command codes."

Ayan looked her straight in the eye. "Never," she said so quietly that Oz had to strain to hear her. "You can remove us from this ship, but you'll never get the command codes. You'll also be rushing hundreds of people from their homes aboard this ship, people who are armed, and will be painfully aware that the Carthan government traded their home in a dirty deal with the enemy. We don't have room for them all on the ground, and they'll rally. They'll gather around someone who doesn't hesitate when it comes to fighting a corrupt government."

"You mean Jonas Valent," Wheeler interjected.

"I've never met a man by that name on this ship," she enunciated coldly.

"You're not getting this ship for free, either." Her attention focused on the Fleet Warden, whose eyes had narrowed, and jaw had set. "If you're forcing us to abandon Triton, it's going to cost you dearly. That is, unless you're willing to do the intelligent thing and turn this stray out. Whatever information he's offering you is tainted, I'm certain of it."

"The Defence Minister himself brokered this deal, Commander… Ayan. Your people are going to have to leave within the time allotted or we will use force."

The pair locked eyes for a long moment. Oz watched them closely, keeping Wheeler, whose smile was fading slowly, in his peripheral. Jake had relaxed, and Oz let go of the man's sidearm, trusting that his long time friend would let Ayan handle the situation.

"We'll leave peacefully, consider it a gift. I'll expect you to offer us a fair trade for Triton's value."

"Without command codes."

"With consideration to the hardship you are forcing on her crew, the civilians we were protecting, and our passengers. You'll compensate us or we'll take whatever I decide is fair value for this ship using other methods."

"Was that a threat? I can have your licences and permits revoked," said Harrison.

"You won't," Ayan said conversationally. "If you cancel all your beaurocratic strings, we'll have no reason to do anything your way. Besides, you need people like us to fight this war our way, because if you're employing people like Wheeler, you're going to lose."

"They don't owe you anything for this ship. It was never yours. Now give me the command codes," Wheeler growled.

Ayan didn't so much as acknowledge him. Instead she calmly stated, "I expect you to transmit your compensation proposal for the full value of this vessel by the time we land on Tamber."

"What about renegotiating the terms of your privateering licence? I'm sure we can make some adjustments for you," replied the Fleet Warden.

"What? These people are nothing! You can't be considering accommodation!" Wheeler objected.

Oz watched as Ayan proved to him and everyone else there that she had passed from being an intelligent young woman to a great lady. "I expect to be vastly impressed. You had better include land grants, and don't leave out the signing bonus."

"I'm telling you these people are just squatters and mercenaries. I bet you Valent is right behind her. If you order them to show you their faces you can capture him and present him for trial yourselves," Wheeler ranted.

Instead of letting her temper get the better of her she smiled, held her head high, and turned back towards the Clever Dream. Her squad of guardsmen began to turn to follow her until Oz watched Jake raise his hand slowly. Instead of stopping him Oz followed his lead. Jake's fist formed into a finger pointed at Wheeler. The thirteen other guardsmen and women followed suit, and for a long moment they all pointed at Lucious Wheeler.

"There! As if you need more evidence!" Lucious shouted.

Other crewmen and women who saw the gesture followed suit, their eyes cold. The hate was so thick in the air Oz found himself breathing more heavily, wondering if he could get a kill shot off and run for cover before the Fleet Warden's people could return fire. Wheeler backed away until he was out of sight.

Jacob Valance led the group as they turned and followed Ayan back to the Clever Dream.

"What are our options, Jason?" Jake asked as he reached the inner leisure compartment of the Clever Dream. The false portholes brightly displayed the active hangar. The Fleet Warden and her people retreated. They were replaced by several squads of Carthan soldiers, who marched to the far end of the hangar and remained there in formation. It was a form of showing a presence, and after a few minutes no one so much as looked at them. Civilian refugees and the former slaves that were too weary to help were gathered to one side of the docking bay near the only working cargo elevator. Everywhere else you looked, people were loading equipment and supplies into crates, piling cases and bags, or working to get things into position. Paula had managed to direct what was left of her deck crew to hand crank two Uriel fighters down from the racks along the side of the hangar, leaving two more hanging near the ceiling. She and a few of her more practised deck hands were desperately trying to keep things organized.

Ayan, Jason, Laura, and Minh-Chu were all gathered around the table at the centre of the lavish entertainment compartment inside the Clever Dream. The holographic display system was hard at work showing different profiles, criminal charge listings, and legal reference material. Oz was hot on Jake's heels, though the rest of the guards had remained on the lower deck of the Clever Dream, ready to mount a defence or help load supplies.

"Legally, this is a huge mess. I've already filed a claim on the Triton in Ayan's name, but they'll reject it. She didn't have her privateering licence at the time of capture and I fulfilled my due diligence, which in this case is finding out if Sol Defence has reported the Triton stolen or issued an order for its recapture," started Jason.

"What about piracy charges?" asked Jake.

"Oh, they've got you there. If they arrested you on piracy you'd either spend months defending yourself in court and get acquitted or you'd be convicted and executed," Jason answered.

"Surprise, surprise. All right, how much power does Ayan have?"

"A lot less than I pretended to," she sighed.

"Pretty amazing negotiation, by the way. Where did that land grant idea come from?" Oz asked as he stopped to stand next to her. He squeezed her shoulders affectionately. "Who'd have thought our little Sunspot would grow into someone with such a commanding presence?"

"Better late than never. I've been working on getting things set up on Tamber since I knew there would be damage to the Triton. I didn't expect this, though. I don't think anyone did. I'm just glad we have something to our names without her."

"Wheeler! I can't believe he's here, or something that looks and acts like him is here," Jacob said, shaking his head.

"God, I've never wanted to throttle someone so badly," Ayan added.

"Couldn't tell. You kept your cool better than anyone," said Jake.

"Thank you. I still think bringing you was too much of a risk. You were right before, you should be in hiding," she told Jacob.

"Him? Hide? Fat chance," Minh scoffed. "I'm just surprised he's taking this so well."

"I made sure I calmed down before I came to this table."

"I saw that pointing antic before I made it to the loading ramp. You could have cost us the little traction I had with that commander," Ayan told him levelly.

"Fleet Warden. It's similar to Admiral in rank. She's right on both counts, though. As much as I want to toss Wheeler out of the nearest airlock, I took a serious risk with that move. There are still prices on the Samson crew's heads, so we'll at least have to hide them while we appeal for the bounties to be cancelled," said Jake.

"That shouldn't be much of a problem, especially since the Carthans didn't try to arrest you here. It'll take time though," Jason mused. "I'm going to set up fake idents for you and your old crew so they can move around a bit. They might be able to show their faces with new names and a DNA mask built into their vacsuits, but you're screwed unless you go get facial reconstruction, which might not work because you have a healing problem."

"Never thought that would be a problem, but you're right. You'll make at least a dozen new best friends out of the Samson crew, though."

"It should be an easy job, especially if there are a lot of new people coming into the Rega Gain system," said Jason.

"You don't know the half of it," Ayan added.

"Good." Focusing on the fine details of the situation helped. All Jake wanted to do was storm off the Clever Dream and open fire on the Carthan soldiers, the Warden, and make sure Wheeler died last. If it was him in a framework body, then he could experiment. Ever since he found out that he was a human of synthetic origin himself, he wondered what it would take to kill him. Wheeler provided the perfect test subject. He shook it off and took a deep breath before continuing. Ayan's hand crept around his waist. "What about the fighters? Do you think we'll have to surrender them to the Carthans?" Minh asked.

"Just having them could have exposed the pilots and Ayan to grand theft charges. If they wanted to arrest anyone, they would have," Jason replied.

"They gave me registration papers instead," Ayan added.

"Well, then the Carthans are on our side, but quietly. They want to please Wheeler because they actually think he has something important. If it weren't for him, I'm pretty sure we'd be fine. Better than. As it is, I'm hoping filing a complaint will tie the Triton up in the docks instead of letting Wheeler have her outright. The Carthans are stepping lightly. I suspect, no, I'm sure that's why they're not sending a huge boarding effort aboard to control our retreat and minimize looting."

"That, and two thirds of the people here are ready to raise their rifles. We've already proven that we can defend the ship deck by deck," Oz stated as a matter of fact. "It's the external firepower that we can't deal with. How long are they giving us?"

"The clock is running. We have forty two minutes left to clear the Triton of all personnel," Jake said. His voice was tight, it was impossible to hide how he felt completely. "Is there any way we can lock down the Triton?"

"I thought you had the command codes?" Oz asked.

"We have a command code chip," Jake said, pulling a small golden rectangular necklace out from under the collar of his armour. "It gives someone control over the Triton's higher functions, but there's no way to know what the codes actually are. Anyone can slip this chip into a command console and take control of the ship, unless someone who actually knows the encrypted passwords comes along and overrides it."

"So someone from Sol Defence could just come on in and take control without that."

"Yup," Jason confirmed. "As far as I can tell the command pass is alphanumeric, anywhere between eight and one thousand twenty four characters and encoded to someone's DNA. I doubt anyone has had this ship running at full efficiency since she was stolen. Even Lewis has tried to hack in - didn't get past the first layer of the computer's central processor security. It's almost as bad as the Carthan's network."

"I've tried several times, and beyond grading the security quality of the various departments, I have no information to offer," said the AI.

"Don't try to break in again, Lewis. Ever," Jake told the artificial intelligence, looking up at the middle of the room.

"I was not detected."

"That doesn't matter. If their defence systems get a whiff of you, just enough to realize an intelligent AI is crawling around, you'll bring the entire Carthan military down on us," Ayan explained. "They've outlawed Artificial Intelligences completely."

"You've also made the Holocaust Virus a part of your core program," Jason added.

"So I can cure other artificial intelligences and protect myself," Lewis countered.

"That's commendable, but if the Carthans see that code-" said Jake.

"They'll assume I was the initial carrier of the virus, and they would be partially correct. I did carry the virus to Pandem, after all," said Lewis.

The room fell silent. Jake suspected he was the initial carrier, the time line was a match, but he didn't want to know for certain. "Just don't initiate contact with any military network, or any other system unless we order it, and don't tell anyone else you delivered the virus to Pandem. We understand, you weren't in control of yourself and you've corrected your programming. Others won't."

"Understood, Sir."

Jacob sighed, trying to put the lecture he wanted to give Lewis aside and went on. "So, could the Carthans get control of Triton as is?"

"I doubt they ever will. Chief Grady's implanted a series of packets that will kill the organic circuitry, and he's got the reactors hard wired on a feedback loop," Oz added.

"How do they activate?" Ayan asked, surprised.

"As soon as someone tries to bring Triton's main systems online, it all goes into motion. The reactors start overloading, and the command systems will begin to fail. He made sure it would take a close visual inspection to tell if there's anything wrong."

"All right, so, when someone tries to start her up, the reactors and main control systems will burn out. How long would it take to repair?" Jake asked. The thought of destroying the primary systems of the greatest ship he'd ever seen made him feel ill.

"The reactors would have to be rebuilt from scratch, same with the primary computer systems. The core is isolated though, so that's a mercy," explained Oz.

"So in dry dock it would take six months?" Jake asked.

"If they have a specialist who understands how the bioelectric systems work and can manage to grow replacement materials then it could take three with their facilities. Without a specialist they'd have to replace the computer systems ship wide."

"Chances are they can get a specialist."

"I'd say so," confirmed Oz.

"Then let's take things a step further," Jake said darkly. All eyes were drawn to him. "Send a message to Sol Defence. Tell them we found their ship and the man who stole her."

"You're joking," Laura burst.

Oz, Minh, and Ayan started smiling. "That's going to make things very interesting for the Carthans," she said quietly.

It was obvious that Jason's mind was busy at work. "I'm going to send a compressed version of the command logs since you captured her from Wheeler, Jake. The best way to avoid blowback from this is to make sure they know everything about us and what we've been doing with the Triton since you took possession."

"I think Sol Defence will approve," said Liam Grady from the entrance. "You won't have their endorsement, but they won't press charges against you for taking command of one of their ships. Especially since you weren't responsible for her initial theft and you've rescued thousands of refugees, freed half as many slaves. We're going to lose her, though, and for good if my guess is right."

Silence fell over the room for a long moment. "It was a dream," Minh said finally. "A new day brings new opportunities."

www.ingramcontent.com/pod-product-compliance
Lightning Source LLC
Chambersburg PA
CBHW071105250626
47159CB00002B/605